HER SAVAGE DREAMS CAME TRUE

"We're outcasts, you and I," the handsome half-breed said. "We've both lived in two worlds as different as night and day. We chose the world where we were accepted for what was in here . . ." He took her hand and placed it over his heart.

Sky Dreamer tried to decipher his words, but the touch of his skin beneath her fingers made her gasp with passion.

"We'll fight," she whispered. Her long black hair surrounded his face and chest as she clung to him in the darkness.

A longing ache began to work its way through his loins as he ran his hands over her tumbling tresses. He wasted no more time with words. Just as he had done in those passionate dreams that claimed her every night while she still lived in the white man's world, he lowered her trembling body to the ground beneath the magical silver pine tree and covered her with his tall frame.

No muffled cry escaped her lips before the handsome Apache warrior commanded her total surrender.

SAVAGE DREAMS

VERONICA BLAKE

ZEBRA BOOKS
KENSINGTON PUBLISHING CORP.

ZEBRA BOOKS

are published by

Kensington Publishing Corp.
475 Park Avenue South
New York, NY 10016

First printing: February, 1989

Printed in the United States of America

In doing research for this novel, I gained a deep compassion for the American Indian. Therefore, it is with great respect that I dedicate this book to the Apaches . . . and also to the savage who stalks the deepest recesses of my mind's secret passages.

I would like to extend a special word of gratitude to Heather—with love!

Chapter One

"Are we still out in the middle of nowhere?" Susan said as she leaned forward and glanced out the stagecoach window. She pushed her wide bonnet off her forehead, causing a soft flurry of thick blond hair to tumble over her blue eyes. Wrinkling her upturned nose, she continued her disapproval of the Western frontier. "It must have been a moment of insanity when I told Charles I would come out here to Arizona for our wedding. I shall never learn how to cope in this uncivilized hellhole!" She fell back against the hard seat and added in an exasperated Southern drawl, "Why, I'll grow old before my time in this wretched heat."

From the opposite side of the coach, Regina Atwood nodded dutifully, but did not offer a reply. She had been listening to her father's fiancée's nonstop complaints for the past several weeks. Nothing would please her more than for Susan Wilkins to decide that she could not live in this "hellhole," and for her to return to Georgia. With a sigh of resignation, Regina pulled a cotton handkerchief from a side pocket in her dress and began to twist it angrily between her slender fingers. Once again, she reminded herself that her father's happiness was all that really mattered, and after fourteen years of being a widower, he was entitled to mary whomever he desired. But why did it have to be Susan Wilkins?

Attempting to avoid another useless round of bickering with her soon-to-be stepmother, Regina turned her attention toward the small window in the door of the stage-coach. A shiver of excitement raced through her as her gaze focused on the vast acreage of golden sand and the tall saguaro cactus, whose towering forms dotted the landscape like silent sentries. Off in the distance, the midday sun enhanced the deep hues of the distant bluish-purple mountains, which rose dramatically from behind the brown and gold mesas like ancient castles. She blinked with wonder at the majestic sight, while she thought of her reasons for returning to this land once again.

Over sixteen years ago, Regina had been born some-where among the rugged foothills of the Chiricahua Mountains, deep in the Indian territory of Apacheria. But owing to the untimely death of her mother when Regina was only two years old, she had been sent to live with her paternal grandparents in Savannah, Georgia. Her father had told her very little about his Arizona bride, so Regina knew virtually nothing about the woman who had been her mother. To return to her birthland to live with her father and to learn more about the first two years of her life—years she had spent here, with both of her parents—were Regina's greatest desires. Not even Susan Wilkins was going to ruin it for her!

With a sincere effort, Regina tried to ignore the twinge of jealousy she felt at the thought of sharing her father's attention with this woman, when all she really wanted was to have him all to herself for a little while. His career as an officer in the U.S. Cavalry had kept him in Arizona for the past fourteen years, and Regina had come to cherish every moment she spent with him. Lately, though, she had almost come to regret his latest visit to her in Savannah. It was there that he had met Susan Wilkins, and surprised everyone—especially his own daughter—when he had be-come engaged to the young woman before returning to his regiment at Fort Bowie in the Arizona territory. To watch her dear, sweet father marry a woman like Susan was almost beyond Regina's comprehension. Not only was Susan Wilkins barely three years older than she was, but

10

Regina was certain that her father's fiancée was also the vainest and most mealymouthed woman in all of Georgia.

"Why," Susan huffed indignantly, oblivious to the girl's attempt to ignore her. "It's no wonder you've been having such horrible nightmares about those disgusting savages who live in this awful place. Even a strong-willed woman could go stark raving mad out here, let alone a girl with your weak disposition."

A renewed bout of fury washed over Regina; she ground her teeth and fought to remain in control. She was rapidly reaching the last of the courtesy she could extend to this woman. Knowing that any retort to Susan's snide remark about her personality would result in even more hard feelings between the two women, Regina decided to retreat into a faked slumber. Reclining back against the uncomfortable seat, though, she could not resist the urge to irritate Susan just a little bit more. Donning the most helpless look she could assume, Regina dabbed daintily at her upper lip with one corner of her white hanky as her eyes leveled their lavender gaze on her companion.

"Oh Susan, you are so right! I shall have to depend on you for every little thing out here in this uncivilized place. I'm just so fortunate to be getting a new stepmother who will be willing to take such good care of me."

With a loud, contented sigh, Regina closed her eyes again and pretended to drift into a peaceful sleep. It was hard to resist the urge to glance at Susan, however, since Regina could feel the woman's hateful glare. She was confident that her comment had struck a raw nerve. She knew that the last thing Susan wanted was a stepdaughter to look after once she was reunited with her fiancé. She had made no secret of her goal to become an officer's wife, and Regina had no doubt that she would play the prestigious role of a captain's wife to the very limit once she had obtained that status.

Regina found herself fighting to stay awake as the stagecoach continued to bounce over the uneven desert ground. She did not wish to spend the remainder of the trip listening to Susan's expressions of discontent and carefully aimed insults, but to allow herself to fall asleep might mean enduring another one of her amorous dreams.

Just the thought of the disturbing images caused her whole body to become drenched in perspiration. The suffocating air inside the stagecoach was almost unbearable, but an involuntary shudder shot through her body in spite of the scorching heat. Embarrassment made her cheeks flame in shades of deep crimson as she began to recall every minute detail of her recurring dreams ... passion-laden dreams, which she did not understand, nor did it seem that she could escape from them once she had given into the weariness that had plagued her throughout the long journey from Georgia to Arizona. With an unsteady hand, she pushed back a stray tendril of ebony hair that clung to her damp brow, while her mind attempted to wipe away the lingering visions from her most recent dream. She desperately hoped Susan was not still observing her, because there was no way to stop the ecstasy that flooded her whole being whenever she entered into this strange paradise. Why would she continue to conjure up the same visions each time she fell asleep, and why would the Indian warrior who dominated her sleep grow bolder and more demanding each time his imaginary touch dared to trespass across her body?

Afraid even to glance in Susan's direction, Regina forced her eyes to remain closed. Did the beautiful mountain meadow she pictured in her dreams, with its shadowy forests of tall trees and deep grasses ablaze with rainbow-colored wildflowers, truly exist? Or did that magical place dwell only in the elusive mists of slumber, when reality is laced ever so briefly with the fleeting breath of reverie?

Her violet eyes flew open with alarm and her troubled gaze immediately settled on Susan, but Susan was dozing, so her thoughts returned to her land of fantasy almost instantly. She assured herself that the secluded meadow was a nonexistent place, a place that her mind had invented. Because, if her dreams were more than that, it would mean that the raven-haired savage who stalked her mind's most secret passages must also be real!

A new rush of heat soared through Regina's already fevered body as she considered this remote possibility. She squeezed her eyes shut again, but the vision of the Indian only grew more intense. Even as she fought to elude his presence, she could see him walking among the knee-high grass, reaching out to her through the hazy light of this peaceful clearing. His skin was dark, akin to the rich earth and all that it encircled. From the concho band that surrounded his head, his long raven hair flowed like gossamer threads past his broad shoulders, framing the strong features of his bronzed face like a curtain of bluish-black satin. Though he was clad in nothing more than a leather breechcloth, the warrior appeared almost spiritual—too perfect to be anything other than a mere illusion.

In this fantastical place, Regina's mortal being was also transformed into all the glory of her unrestrained womanhood. The tight chignon, which she had always despised, no longer bound her thick hair at the base of her head. Instead, her jetblack tresses fell long and lush past her shoulders in reckless disarray and fanned out across the soft material of her clothes. The heavy corsets and encumbering petticoats of the Southern fashion were no longer a part of Regina's attire. A dress made of smooth animal hides, and adorned with long fringe, clothed her slender form in this mystical existence.

Within the small compartment of the stagecoach, a smile drifted across Regina's trembling lips and draped her young face with a look of rapture, a look that did not even begin to hint at the enchantment her wandering mind was envisioning. Lost to the new and exciting emotions she was discovering in her private domain, Regina's limp body slumped back against the wooden seat, unaware of the jarring motion created by the bouncing coach. A very small portion of her senses fought to awaken her from her sensuous hallucinations, but her innocent and curious heart battled for the right to remain—if only for a little longer.

Regina wished she could remain in this land of myth forever, though she knew that the man and the place were too wondrous to be real. Still, when the hands of the handsome hostile pulled her quaking body into his strong embrace, she could not help thinking that these feelings of passion could not have been conceived in a mere dream. Since the very beginning of her strange visions, Regina had never left her secluded mountain meadow without allowing her eyes to ascend and meet with the magnetic gaze of the man who shared in her secret perceptions. The fiery promises his eyes contained within their dark pools of charcoal gray served only to fuel the strong feeling of affinity she had felt ever since this savage man had evolved from her musing. She sensed that each and every dream would continue to carry them farther, until their dreamland could no longer control their hungering souls.

Regina bolted awake again and struggled to clear her mind of these confusing images. Once more, she glanced anxiously at the woman across the aisle, and exhaled a relieved sigh. Thank goodness she had not disturbed Susan with another one of her explicit visions. Although Regina desperately wished she could talk to someone about the details of her dreams, she knew better than to hope that her soon-to-be stepmother would lend her a sympathetic ear. Shortly after the two women had begun their journey to Arizona, Regina made the mistake of mentioning to Susan that she had been having a series of disturbing dreams. Regina's lack of sleep had become just one more barb for Susan's sharp tongue. Perhaps when they reached their destination, Regina would be able to talk to her father. However, she found herself blushing with embarrassment again, just thinking about the Indian who had seduced her into wanton depths of desire with no more than his make-believe specter. Could she discuss these lustful musings with her own father?

A questioning look crossed Regina's face, drawing her

black eyebrows into a curious arch. She leaned forward and observed her sleeping companion with close scrutiny. What did a woman like Susan dream about? Regina wondered. The wide brim of Susan's pale blue bonnet nearly hid her features from view, but the downward curve of her mouth was apparent even as she slept. The frown had been a permanent fixture throughout the whole journey. Putting up with Susan's disdainful attitude was beginning to take its toll on Regina. With a little luck, though, they should reach Fort Bowie before nightfall. Regina was certain if she had to be confined in this dusty coach one more day with that woman — well, she could only hope that she would not be held responsible for her actions!

Regina still clutched her white hanky. As she attempted to fan herself with the small square piece of material, she continued to watch the other woman. Blue was definitely Susan's color, Regina noticed with aggravation. The light blue material of her dress and matching hat were striking companions for Susan's wavy golden tresses and big blue eyes. Regina was sure that Susan's beauty had played an important factor in attracting her father in the beginning, but why hadn't he been able to see past her outward appearance?

The fact that the two woman had come to dislike one another intensely during the past few months was something Regina was determined to hide from her father once they reached Fort Bowie. She had made a promise to herself when he had first told her of his engagement to Susan Wilkins, and Regina intended to keep her vow. She would not cause any distress for her father by telling him what she really thought about his fiancée — difficult as it was at times to contain her true feelings. Besides, as much as she hated to admit it, Regina had come to the conclusion that her father must care for Susan to some extent. Charles Atwood had never been an impulsive man, so there had to be a good reason for his sudden proposal to this arrogant woman. Although, for the life of her, Regina could not imagine what that reason might be.

With a gesture of annoyance, she shoved her handkerchief back down into the pocket of her muslin dress. Oh, why had she chosen to wear this drab outfit? Next to Susan's pretty pastel gown and hat, Regina's tailored gray-and-black dress and short-cropped jacket made her look as though she were headed back to boarding school. A feeling of dismay joined Regina's self-pitying mood when she began to compare Susan's voluptuous figure with her own slender, modestly developed form. Regina ran her fingers over her heavy mane of black hair and glanced at the cascade of Susan's soft blond curls. Becoming angry at the jealous thoughts that were going through her mind, Regina silently reprimanded herself for fretting over such unimportant matters. If beauty meant being as shallow as Susan Wilkins, then Regina was glad to be skinny and to have hair that was too straight and thick for any amount of hairpins to hold.

Actually, with the exception of Susan, the trip from Georgia had gone very well. Her father had dispatched a troop of soldiers from Fort Bowie to accompany the stage through Apache Pass, the most dangerous stretch of land in Apacheria. Since meeting up with the battalion at Lordsburg, New Mexico, Regina had put to rest nearly all her fears of being ambushed while traveling to her father's outpost. The threat of an Indian attack was terrifying, and always present in this untamed territory, but the closer the group came to Fort Bowie, the more confident Regina was that they would not meet any Indians along the way. The only savage she had encountered during this trip was the one whose magic touch burned her mind and body whenever she dared to dream.

Insignificant in the beginning, the repeated dreams had been only muted visions of strange-looking houses with thatched roofs, and dark-skinned people, whose sad expressions seemed to cry out to her through a tangled web of unconsciousness. The closer Regina came to reaching her journey's end, however, the more involved the dream became. The sea of faces that had captivated her original dreams had slowly faded away, and now they were dominated by one face — the face of a man with eyes the shade of a stormy gray dawn. As they came nearer to Fort Bowie, the dreams reached a point where Regina was almost afraid to fall asleep for fear of how far her lascivious musings would lead her. At other times, she almost willed herself to fall asleep, just so she could glimpse her imaginary lover once again. These overwhelming emotions frightened her most of all. She was undoubtedly the woman who stalked her own slumber. Yet Regina could not imagine why she would be dressed in the garments of an Indian maiden, or why the images of an Indian village would be so distinct in her mind. And just who was the mysterious and dangerously handsome savage who had consumed her body with dream-induced longings which she could not shake off — even when she was wide awake?

It was a good day to kill the hated White-Eyes, regardless of what Grandfather said. Nachae reined his brown-and-white stallion at the edge of the high cliff, and let his piercing gaze descend until his eyes were focused on the coach that was traveling through the valley below. Maybe Grandfather was just getting too old for war, Nachae surmised. Why else would the old shaman be so opposed to the warrior's decision to attack the Butterfield Stage today? Nachae's jaw set hard in a stubborn gesture as he tried not to think of his grandfather's vision again, but he couldn't erase the vivid pictures his grandfather had planted in his mind for the past decade . . . images of a woman who would claim his heart with a love so powerful that it could never be denied. But Nachae's determined mind would not permit itself to dwell on the old man's prophesy, nor would Nachae ever allow it to come true!

The warrior was not proud of his decision to disobey the elder man. Until today, he had always complied with his grandfather's wishes. But as strongly as Eskinzan was convinced it was a bad omen to attack the stagecoach, just as determined was Nachae to go to war on this day. If his grandfather was correct about the woman who was riding on the stage, then this might be the only opportunity Nachae would ever have to change his grandfather's prediction. And Nachae would not rest until he knew that the woman from the shaman's vision was dead.

The tall Apache brave raised his solemn face up to the sky, closed his eyes, and let the sun cloak his countenance with its intense heat. He could feel the jagged edge of his heavy hair tickle the middle of his bronzed back when he tilted his head up. A strange, almost terrifying tremor bolted through his body. For a moment he wondered if perhaps his grandfather had been correct about this attack today. Maybe it was not right to tamper with fate. Just as quickly, Nachae pushed the thought out of his mind. If it was the plan of Usen—the Apache God—that Nachae would soon meet with his destiny, then the warrior would do so without resistance. The realization that he was about to go against his grandfather's commands, and defy Apache customs, caused beads of sweat to form across his upper lip. As the drops of perspiration mixed with his war paint and began to run down his face, he could taste the sulfur in the vermilion that he had meticulously rubbed into his skin to color it a brilliant shade of red.

As always, just before he rode into a battle, Nachae thought briefly of the life he had once lived in the white man's world, and of how different his life would be now if he had chosen the other road. Like every time before, he also recalled the agonizing memories of his youth, then reminded himself that there was no other way of life for him now—or ever! The powerful muscles in his arm contracted as he slowly raised his hand into the air and shook his feathered lance. Though the Apaches usually did not grant their enemies any sort of warning before an attack, Nachae could not stop the tortured sound that erupted from deep within his soul. Exposing the strong corded muscles in his neck, he tossed his head back again and issued forth a chilling war cry. The sound seared the

18

copper-colored walls of the deep canyon, shattering the permeating stillness.

For a moment the bloodcurdling howl seemed to float along with the wind at the top of the steep ravine. Then, as though it was a heavy black cloak, the sound struck the floor of the canyon, and surrounded the stagecoach with an invisible blanket of doom.

Chapter Two

"Please let me still be asleep," Regina whispered when the eerie sound penetrated her drifting mind. But even before she opened her eyes, she knew her worst nightmares could not compare to the tragedy which was about to take place. On several occasions she had listened to her father's accounts of the brutal wars between the soldiers and the Indians that occurred in this desolate part of the country. To hear about the fierce battles was exciting, while sitting in the comfortable parlor of her grandparents home in Georgia, but the clashes he had spoken of had sounded so unreal. Even when the cavalry unit had met the Butterfield Stage in Lordsburg yesterday, Regina had thought her father was being overly protective.

Outside the carriage she could hear the frantic voices of the soldiers as they hastily prepared to face the surprise attackers. She had felt so safe with her father's men escorting them to the fort! At the stagecoach station where they had spent the previous night, she had overheard several of the soldiers joking about the deadly tactics they would use to slay the enemy if they should happen to encounter any savages on their way to Fort Bowie. The men's lighthearted attitude had put to rest the last of her fears about the possibility of an attack. Now she realized that those same men were every bit as horrified as she was of meeting up with an Indian war party.

Regina was invaded by a terror so engulfing that it stole her breath away, and turned the blood that raced through her veins to fragments of ice. The pained image of her father crying when he learned that he would never see her again, never see Susan, drifted through her spinning mind. Hot tears welled up in her eyes, then slipped through her closed lids and burned fiery trails down the sides of her cheeks. This was so unfair! She had waited all these years to be reunited with him, and she was so close to reaching her destination.

The first sight that greeted Regina's eyes when she forced them open was the petrified face of her traveling companion. Regina had never seen such a look of fear. When her gaze locked with Susan's, an odd thought passed through Regina's mind: Now they would finally have something in common. Today they would die together.

Regina's arms felt detached from her body when she attempted to lift them from her lap. The violent shaking of her hands was visible as she reached her arms out to Susan. When the other woman's hands clasped hers, Regina could feel the tremors that vibrated through Susan's form. The two women gazed out at the scene unfolding outside the coach window. What had been a picture of serenity just moments before was now a drama of unbelievable horror.

The Indians began to fire their rifles as they charged from the top of the high bluffs, swarming down the canyon walls like a cascade of descending destruction. They were nearly to the bottom of the ravine before the cavalrymen had a chance to return gunfire. The Apache attack was so unexpected that not even the scouts who had ridden through the canyon ahead of the stagecoach suspected that a war party was nearby.

The young lieutenant who was in charge of the regiment yelled at the stagecoach driver to make a run for the canyon exit. It did not appear to him that the opening was already blocked off by the hostiles. The gallant soldier then whirled his horse around to face the ambushers in a head-on confrontation. He had hopes of holding the

Apaches within the canyon walls long enough for the stagecoach to escape, but as he raised his rifle to his shoulder, he realized that he had failed. His men were outnumbered two to one, and there was nowhere in the narrow gully for the soldiers to take cover. Captain Atwood's daughter and fiancée would not reach Fort Bowie today. If the two beautiful young women were fortunate, they would be killed by a flying bullet or flaming arrow before the coach was overtaken by the savages. The lieutenant could not imagine a horror greater than that which decent white women were forced to suffer when they were taken captive by warriors after a raid.

Through a maze of swirling dust, Regina and Susan watched in terror as the coach bounced across the shimmering gold sand at a neck-breaking speed. They fought to hold on to one another, but it was a useless effort. Regina knew they were helpless as long as they were at the mercy of this wildly careening vehicle. However, her spinning mind would not think clearly enough to devise any course of action. She began to pray that the stagecoach driver was skilled enough to bring the coach under control before they all found themselves smashed against the canyon wall. All at once, she realized that they were going to die anyway. Perhaps death from the crashing of the coach would be more merciful than the methods the savages would use upon them if they were taken as hostages.

Somewhere outside the coach a shrill cry pierced the air. It wasn't until their driver toppled past the window that Regina and Susan realized where the scream had come from. A blurred glimpse of the horror on the driver's face when his descending body passed the window reaffirmed the women's hopeless predicament. They were imprisoned in a runaway coach — without a driver. The soldiers who had been sent to protect them were too busy fighting for their own lives to come to their rescue.

Susan began to scream and claw at the door in a vain effort to free herself from the speeding coach. There was nothing either of them could do to stop the stagecoach, but in the wake of Susan's hysteria, Regina's determination to survive began to surface. Judging from the wild lurching of the coach, Regina was sure the front hitch was about to break away from the chaise. Once the team of horses were separated from the carriage, it would be only a matter of seconds before the stagecoach would collide into one of the stone walls of the canyon. Regina called to Susan to get down onto the floor of the coach. Perhaps they would be able to survive the impact of the crash if they huddled together on the bottom of the small compartment.

But Susan was beyond hearing Regina. She was in a state of panic, and all that mattered to her at this moment was escape. Regina grabbed for the door just as Susan managed to pull the latch free. The wind whipped the door open.

The stagecoach tipped to the right, almost heaving itself over into the deep sand. The vehicle then swung back onto all four wheels, but the sharp tilting motion was enough to toss both of the women through the narrow doorway. The team of panicked horses continued to flee across the desert ground for several hundred yards before the front hitch snapped in two, freeing the horses and sending the coach crashing aimlessly into a huge stone boulder at the base of the embankment.

Nachae, confident that his comrades would finish off the last of the soldiers without his assistance, was following the coach toward the canyon exit. His desire to kill the woman who rode inside—the woman who threatened his very existence with her presence—drove him onward with a savage obsession. But each time the hoofs of his huge war pony thudded down against the ground, drawing him closer to his most feared enemy, he felt an overwhelming urge to flee from this site and never look back again.

The stagecoach driver was quickly dispatched by Nachae's well-placed bullet. The warrior tugged on the reins, causing his horse to slide to a halt as the coach rounded the final bend of the canyon and collided with the barrier of stone. Nachae was unprepared for the rush of emotions that flooded through him when he saw the two passengers flung against the dirt and rocks. His body felt paralyzed for a moment as a strange sensation of sadness overcame him. Was he experiencing this remorse, he wondered, because he would not be the one to end the woman's life if the fall from the stagecoach killed her? Or was it something else—something that was not yet in his comprehension to explain?

The sound of a woman moaning brought his mind back to reality. He swung his muscled leg over his horse's back and dropped to the ground. As his moccasined feet moved cautiously toward the woman who was lying beside a mesquite bush, he pulled his bone-handled knife out of the sheath that hung from his belt. His heart threatened to explode within his chest, and his feet felt as if they were burdened with heavy clay. He had waited so long for this day. Why would he be so reluctant to gaze upon her face?

When Nachae had first returned to live among his father's people, his grandfather had told him of a vision he had repeatedly experienced, concerning Nachae's destiny. Ten years had passed since that day . . . ten long years of trying to escape from the hatred he had been forced to endure during his youth because of his mixed bloodline. Grandfather envisioned a woman who would show Nachae how to love and whom he would love in return. But Nachae would never permit himself to love anyone, especially a white woman. After today he would be free of his grandfather's prophesy—forever!

His knees felt weak as he knelt down beside the woman. Grandfather had been correct about her beauty, he observed as he stared down at her still form. The knife in his hand began to quiver slightly when he reached out toward her slender throat. Just as the tip of his blade touched the soft skin below her chin, her eyes flew open. Her scream startled Nachae into withdrawing his knife. Another horrified scream escaped from the woman as the warrior sprang to his feet.

Nachae stared at the hysterical woman at his feet. This could not be the one from his grandfather's vision. Eskinzan had told him that he would know the woman at first glance. Her eyes would be an unusual shade of lavender, the color of the desert sky at sunset. The woman whose face he looked down upon now had eyes as blue as the midday sky. Was Grandfather mistaken?

From the opposite side of the bush came another weak groan. Nachae remembered the second woman he had seen thrown from the doorway of the coach. He began to back away from the screaming woman, but her constant wailing was more than his tormented mind could handle. He stepped toward her again and raised his hand up into the air. He had only planned to threaten her into silence, but he did not have to waste his efforts. Susan fainted the instant she saw the towering Indian advancing in her direction.

Nachae was positive now that she was not the one he sought. Grandfather's visions were always accurate. He walked around the mesquite bush. The lower half of the other woman's body protruded from beneath the jagged branches, but her face was hidden from his view. Nachae began to sweat so profusely that he was forced to wipe away the rivulets of perspiration that ran down his face when they threatened to blind him as they rolled past his eyes. What had come over him? he thought angrily. He should be feeling more triumphant than he had ever felt in his life. Once he had accomplished this deed, he could hang the woman's scalp on his coup stick and show Grandfather that a man could control his own destiny!

But Nachae did not expect the flurry of tenderness that washed over him when he pulled the woman's limp body from beneath the bush. He knelt down beside her and placed one of his hands under the long silken strands of ebony hair which had been released from the chignon at the back of her head and now fanned out across the dry desert ground. If it was possible for a man to hold his

25

destiny in his hands, then Nachae was sure that, at this instant, his fate rested within his shaking palm.

He reminded himself of the reasons why his preservation depended on this woman's death. If he allowed Grandfather's prophesy to materialize, more people would suffer as he had for the past twenty-five years. He could not allow it! He would not permit himself to fall in love— nor would he ever father a child whose innocent soul would be permanently branded by a society determined to annihilate anyone different from themselves.

"Half-breed!" Nachae spit out in a bitter tone. The mere mention of the name brought back the awful recollections of life among his mother's people in New Mexico. "Half-breed" . . . spoken like the taste of poison on the tips of white men's tongues. He placed his knife against the base of the young woman's exposed neck. She was more beautiful than he had ever imagined. The knife nearly slipped from his fingers. Why? he asked himself. Where was the scorn and the anger he so desperately wanted to feel at this victorious moment?

The woman's lips parted as though she was attempting to speak. Nachae watched in fascination as the curve of her enticing mouth took on the soft outline of a trembling heart. He leaned closer until he could feel the heat of her breath against his face as she fought to regain consciousness. Nachae clutched the knife tighter in his hand. She must die! his anguished mind repeated.

Once again, he held the sharp edge of the blade against her throat. Her thick black eyelashes fluttered like the gentle wings of a butterfly before they slid apart and revealed the sultry gaze of her violet eyes. She stared up at the face that hovered above her, but she was still too shaken by the fall from the stagecoach to focus clearly.

Nachae's hand froze; he was not aware of the knife when it fell from his numb fingers. Those eyes . . . they were the ones that haunted his dreams and filled his waking hours with despair. Grandfather's vision had been precise. She had eyes the very shade of the fading desert sky—just before the sun fell behind the silent mountain peaks. But Eskinzan's prediction had lacked one very important detail. Until this moment, Nachae did not know that when she gazed upon him for the first time, his heart would be lifted from his body and placed at her feet.

Regina felt the strong hand supporting her head. Her first thought was that her father had come to her rescue. A faint smile began to touch the corners of her lips. But when her eyes were able to make out the face of the man who held her head within one of his large palms, the tender look upon her face turned to one of horror.

Before going into battle, it was Nachae's habit to paint himself in a gaudy depiction of his mixed heritage. On one half of his face, he rubbed a bright red pigment which he obtained from vermilion; on the other half, he smeared blue micaceous stone that made his skin glitter in a ghostly shade of white.

Regina's first instinct was to scream, but the cry lodged in her closed-up throat. Her mouth opened and closed without a sound, while her eyes bulged from their sockets with fright. There was no escape from this horrendous creature, and the only way her mind could cope with her fear was to lapse back into the false security of unconsciousness.

Nachae saw her body grow limp again as her head lolled back against the cradle of his hand. He drew in a ragged breath as he tried in vain to think coherently. If he did not kill this woman, or take her as his hostage, one of the other braves would claim her as his own. But to follow through with his original plan was impossible now. The shock and confusion he felt over finding the woman whose entity dominated his every breath was too great for him to understand. He would kill her . . . but not today. First he had to fight against the alien feelings of compassion he was experiencing. He had to free his mind of her beautiful image, and expel from his body the strange yearnings that had possessed him the instant he touched her.

27

He could hear the war cries dying down from around the bend of the canyon wall. Soon the other warriors would join him to rejoice in their victory. Nachae glanced nervously around the area until he spotted an alcove at the base of the stone wall. Moving quickly, he picked up the woman and carried her to the opening. After he had placed her beneath the rock ledge, he immediately began to cover the front of the hole with branches from the mesquite bush. He did not have time to reconsider his rash actions, because only seconds after he was finished concealing the woman's body, the rest of the war party came to survey the wreckage of the stagecoach.

Nachae fought to control the quaking of his limbs as he pretended to partake in the excitement. Not one Apache life had been lost during this attack. But fortune had not shone on the soldiers today. Every one of the men who had ridden with the doomed coach had been slain without mercy. Since it was the Apaches' belief that a man would pass into the afterlife in the same form as he left his mortal body, the Indians did not hesitate to mutilate the dead men so that they would also be deformed in their spiritual life.

Nachae did not share in his companions' enthusiasm as they torched the remains of the stagecoach and watched it burn to the ground. He felt completely drained of energy and motivation. He wanted only to get far away from this canyon and from the woman who had hurled his whole being into turmoil. The other men noticed his impatience as he hastily tossed the unconscious yellow-haired woman over the back of his stallion. The warriors looked up to Nachae; he had proven himself to be fearless and powerful in battle. They had also learned to avoid him when one of his dark moods overcame him. At times, his feelings of unrest would engulf him in the midst of combat. He could be his own worst enemy, or that of any other man who dared to cross his path when he was in this frame of mind.

Nachae swung his leg over the back of his horse behind the limp body of the woman, then looked down at his white hostage with disgust. To take her back to the Apache rancheria with him was a troublesome burden. He should have given her to one of the other braves, but none of his actions was in character today. On this fateful day, he had discovered that there was a power greater than he had ever known could exist. The Great Spirit had taken control of Nachae's destiny and placed it beyond his grasp.

Chapter Three

Regina tried to move, and wondered if death was supposed to be so painful. She had always believed that when someone died, he would no longer feel any pain or sorrow. If this was true, she was definitely alive. There was not one inch of her battered body that did not hurt — even inhaling the musty air caused her chest to ache. A throbbing spot at the back of her head made her aware of another injury, and when she carefully touched the swollen lump, she nearly cried out from the pain that flared up throughout her body and neck.

Her glazed eyes fought to see through the darkness, but it wasn't until she raised her arm up into the air to explore her surroundings that she realized she was in some sort of cave or dugout. Fear engulfed her like a shroud, yet the deafening silence that surrounded her made her even more anxious to know what was happening outside this black hole. Using extreme caution, she began to feel around the small area until her hands touched upon the prickly branches of the mesquite bush. Had someone hidden her in this cave, then placed the branches over the opening to save her from the Indians? She tried to recall what had happened after she and Susan were thrown from the stagecoach, but her mind would not cooperate. The last thing she could remember was grabbing for the door when Susan pulled the latch open.

Susan! Oh God, where was Susan? Regina turned over on her side, trying to ignore the pain in her bruised body, while she began to dig her way through the branches. By the time she had cleared away enough of the barricade so that she could crawl out of the hole, the sleeves of her jacket were in shreds, and her exposed arms were covered with long bloody scratches and cuts. She recalled the childish thoughts which had been going through her mind earlier, when she was comparing her choice of dress to Susan's attire. How silly she had been to worry about something so trivial. And how foolish they had all been to think that an Indian attack was so unlikely.

As she slithered out from the darkness under the rock ledge, the late afternoon sun caught her unawares. She threw her bleeding hands over her face until her eyes could adjust to the glare. When she lowered her hands, she spotted the smoldering carcass of the Butterfield Stagecoach. An icy chill trailed down her spine when she noticed the long feathered lance stuck into the ground beside the wreckage. The spear was tilted in an ominous slant and the crop of feathers which adorned the stick hung to the side like an unmoving mass of black-and-white doom. Had it been left there by those horrible savages as a reminder that they had won their vile assault upon the unsuspecting travelers?

With a determined attempt, she tried to stand on her wobbly legs. However, it was several minutes before her head stopped spinning enough for her to walk. Her fear was almost strangling as she began moving toward the coach with slow, agonizing steps. She was convinced she would spot Susan's body somewhere among the remains of the coach, and she wasn't sure if her terrified mind could handle what else she was likely to find. From stories told to her by her father, and also since listening to the soldiers talk during the past couple of days, Regina was not ignorant of what Indians did to their enemies. She also remembered her father telling her how the Indians had learned the practice of mutilating their victims from the white men who had first invaded their lands.

Upon reaching the boulder which had ended the stagecoach's wild retreat, Regina paused to rest. She felt so dizzy from the bump on the back of her head that everything before her eyes was spinning in rapid circles. She fought against the weakness which threatened to overcome her as she glanced nervously at the ground surrounding the coach. Not a sign of life could be seen anywhere in the narrow canyon, and the unnatural stillness in the air made Regina feel as though there were not another soul left in the whole world. When her dizziness cleared enough for her to walk again, she began to move toward the bend in the canyon wall, toward the direction where the ambush had occurred — and where she might find some soldiers who had survived the attack. She had taken only a few shaky steps when she spotted an object lying on the ground a few yards from the stagecoach.

Falling to her knees, Regina slowly extended her arm and picked up the tattered remains of Susan's pale blue bonnet. As she hugged it to her bosom, a desperate loneliness filled her heart. She knew she would not find Susan among the ruins of the coach. Now she understood why it was so deathly quiet — the soldiers and the stagecoach driver were all dead. And Susan . . . oh Susan!

Visions of Susan undergoing unmentionable tortures at the hands of the hostiles who had ambushed the stagecoach began to color Regina's thoughts with explicit horror. The confusion she had been feeling a few minutes ago returned, even stronger this time. She tried to force her whirling senses to focus on the events that had taken place after her fall from the carriage, but it was useless. Her thoughts became filled with distorted images of the recent attack, but nothing came to mind that would help her to remember what had happened afterward. Did one of the soldiers hide her under the narrow ledge? Why wasn't the same thing done for Susan? Regina began to experience a terrible sense of guilt for all the unnecessary bickering she had done with her father's fiancée during the past few months. She thought of the heartbreak her poor father would suffer once he learned of Susan's disappearance. Regina wondered how she was ever going to tell him about what had happened to the woman he was supposed to marry in just a few days. She clutched the bonnet tighter against her breast, and surrendered to the tears that flowed from her eyes.

Exhaustion rapidly took advantage of Regina's already weakened condition. The uncontrollable tears which shook her slender form were the final insult to her battered body. Reality began to fade from her mind, and when another bout of dizziness overcame her, she was helpless to remain alert. She tried to ignore the faint feeling, but she was not strong enough to prevent the blackness that engulfed her as she toppled forward into the hot desert sand. Nor was she able to escape the images her mind began to conceive—images of a tranquil mountain meadow. . . .

Regina's heavy lids closed with sweet expectation, and her pulse quickened with desire when she felt herself being drawn in by the magnetic embrace of the handsome savage. The moment her awareness had wavered, he had come to her without hesitation. It seemed that each time she entered this mystical land, his advances grew bolder and her yearnings became stronger.

The tall grass that cushioned the meadow floor brushed against her bare legs beneath the ragged edge of her fringed dress, and she could feel the hard muscles of the Indian's body pressing against her slender form through the soft material of the garment. She couldn't help noticing the way the man's heart was beating in his muscled chest when their bodies meshed together in this intimate manner, and soon, her heart was pounding in unison. Her breath caught in her throat for a moment, stolen away by the indescribable longings his nearness inspired. In the midst of this wondrous passion, a strange sensation of fear passed through Regina. Her arms moved out in a rush of panic and encircled the powerful body of her dream warrior, almost as though she were afraid that he would disappear from her grasp.

The man pulled away slightly and gazed down at her.

His dark features were so handsome — almost regal — with his high cheekbones and straight nose, that Regina was taken aback by his visage. The look on his dark face became masked with perplexity when he felt her gripping embrace; his mind appeared to be fighting some secret battle within itself.

The tall Indian bent over and claimed her parted lips with his own. Their mouths conformed to one another, hesitant at first, then growing more and more demanding until just this mere kiss had ignited a chain of fire throughout their whole beings. When they parted, the glistening sparkle in his dark gray eyes lit his narrowed gaze with unspoken words of passion. Regina trembled when she saw the enraptured look upon his face, yet his dark gray eyes still carried a distant look of fear and turmoil. She sensed it was inevitable that they would yield to the fervor in their bodies, and already she was prepared to submit. But the affinity which had first beckoned them to this quiet mountain meadow must also conquer the lingering reluctance within his heart.

It became Regina's only goal to ease away the deep hurt that she could see in his gaze. She wanted to surround him with so much love that he would never allow her to leave him again. She slid her fingers through the long strands of his raven hair, drawing his head down to her while her lips began to flutter lightly along the corded muscles of his strong neck. The man's hands began to move lower over the material of her garment, tenderly caressing the soft curves that beckoned to him beneath her buckskin dress. A tremor shot through Regina with the descent of his gentle embrace. His touch was like a lightning storm, and the cravings he caused to flare up in her were comparable only to a cloudburst of torrid rain.

A growing sensation of uncontrollable desire worked its way through Regina's quaking body, leaving her lost to this new world of wanton fantasy. She wanted — needed — to have this savage stranger touch her virginal flesh as no man had ever dared to do in reality. As his hand continued to mold his exploring fingers over the swell of her bosom, past her slender waist, and over the gentle slope of her hip, each minute pore of her being experienced a new awakening. Unexpectedly, her breasts became alert, their tiny kernels straining against the material of her dress as a sweet, torturous ache swelled up through her limbs. An instinctive wish to arouse the same vast feelings of pleasure in this man made her curious hand move lower along his bare back and down to the barrier of his meager loincloth. She felt him quiver beneath her fingertips when her hand slipped just a slight bit lower and stopped to rest on the taut rise of his muscled buttocks. Was it possible that such a powerful man could be as tremendously affected by her timid retaliation as she was from his bold actions? she wondered. Could it be that this time there would be no stopping or turning back from this sensuous journey, which constantly led these two dream lovers farther into this land of yearnings where it seemed their passion was limitless?

Regina felt herself being lowered into the blades of knee-high grass, though she was not certain if she was moving on her own accord or if the man was easing her down to the ground. Her senses were hopelessly lost somewhere within the maze of her body's increasing appetites. She felt his massive weight press her into the downy bed of deep vegetation as his body fitted itself against her waiting form in an intimate entanglement of limbs and torsos. In her reverie, they had never been this close before, and now, Regina wondered if her dreams planned to take them beyond the boundaries of her moral conscience. . . . Why didn't she care if her total surrender should turn out to be the ultimate destination of this musing?

Regina's trembling increased when she felt the Indian's hand sliding over her thigh. His hand moved upward, bringing with its tender touch the edge of her soft dress. Each pore of her skin that his fingers brushed became alive with a rush of anxious excitement. In a moment of surprised revelation, she was made aware of the fact that she was wearing nothing beneath the fringed dress, but in this dreamland, even that abnormality seemed appropriate. As if her whole body had a will of its own, Regina felt herself crane upward in a welcoming arch as her hands continued their private quest over his smooth bronze skin. His body was solid and hard, yet it seemed the perfect companion for her soft, silky flesh.

The brief loincloth the savage wore did little to hide his reasoning behind this delicious assault on Regina's innocent being, and the feel of his swollen manhood pressing against her bare thigh caused her to fill with a frantic indecision for an instant. But a hesitation in his actions made Regina's desire to remain here with him, and to continue with this beautiful conjunction, even stronger. The ache in her loins was unbearable; even in her inexperience, she knew this man was her only hope for relief. Her arms imprisoned his brawny form, tightening to an almost brutal embrace . . . she could no longer halt the deep calling in her body.

Somewhere—far, far away—Regina heard voices. Someone was calling her name; someone was trying to keep them apart. She tried to pretend that she could not hear the sounds, yet the tensing up in the man's body signaled that he had heard them too. His mouth came down upon her lips again as though she were his last hope for salvation. Using every ounce of her energy, she pressed against him and returned his kiss with an urgency that could not be denied. This time, she told herself, she would not permit him to leave her alone to face life outside this beautiful reverie. Without this man who had captivated her soul with the realms of her dreamland, returning to reality seemed too frightening to comprehend. But even as she repeated that vow with renewed vigor, she could sense that he was slipping away.

Since she knew that it was a foolish desire to remain with her imaginary lover forever, Regina wanted only to savor the memory of his touch for a moment longer; she needed to gaze upon his handsome face one more time before they were forced to part. When she pulled away from him, however, the image that met her gaze was no longer the stately countenance of the Indian brave who had consumed her most wanton dreams. The face that loomed above her now was a hideous image, half red and half white, and the sooty gray eyes that stared down at her from within the chiseled mask were filled with unspeakable contempt. Regina felt a scream well up in her dry throat. She tried to cry out for help to the source of the voices she had just heard, but all that escaped from her terrified body was a pain-racked gasp. . . .

"Regina? Please wake up, Regina, please?"

Regina's eyes flew open. She expected to see the horrible face from her most recent dream. Instead, the worried face of her father looked down upon her.

A relieved smile overcame Charles Atwood's tired face. "Thank God! You sure gave me a scare."

Nothing had ever sounded so good to her ears as her father's voice. A weak grin touched her parched lips, but her voice eluded her. He was really here—and he had saved her from the demon who had turned her beautiful dream into a devastating nightmare.

Charles's hand gently stroked her face. "Don't try to talk. There will be plenty of time for that when we're safely back at the fort."

"But Su—" Regina began in a hoarse whisper.

"Save your strength—we'll talk later." Charles called out to the soldiers who were standing behind him. Regina did not have a chance to explain to him what had happened, because at her father's orders, she was being lifted into the back of a wagon. Outside the wagon she heard the men discussing the morbid fate of the men they had discovered around the bend of the canyon walls. Dead—they were all dead! She was thankful now that she had not succeeded in her quest to find the soldiers.

She listened to the calm voice of her father as he ordered his cavalry unit to load the remains of the dead men in the buckboard and transport them back to Fort Bowie for a proper military burial. His voice sounded so controlled. Regina wondered how he could concentrate on his duties at a time like this.

Her heart was breaking apart. Regina was certain that her father's brave exterior was just a way to avoid thinking about the awful events that had occurred. Surely, he did not need her to tell him what had become of his fiancée. Regina understood her father well enough to know that he coped with grief by pretending it did not exist. She had observed that trait in him every time she had tried to talk to him about her mother. A sudden rush of tears tumbled from the corners of her violet eyes. It didn't seem possible that the excitement she had been feeling about their new life in Arizona could turn into unbearable sorrow in such a short span of time. She thought of the brave young soldiers who had lost their lives today, and another flood of guilt ripped through her heart. Although she knew it was ridiculous, a tiny voice deep inside of her kept telling her that—in some unknown way—she was responsible for the Indian attack.

"You're safe now, Regina. Although you certainly have a valid reason to cry." Charles tried to force himself to sound normal when he climbed into the back of the wagon. But Regina did not miss the small quiver in his voice when he spoke.

"I'm so sorry, Father," she said through her tears.

"This is hardly your fault," he answered in a quiet voice, then he leaned over and kissed her softly on the forehead. Regina was struck by the thought of how much he had aged since the last time he had been in Georgia—less than a year ago. She had always felt that her father was the handsomest man she knew, and he was especially dashing in his navy blue cavalry uniform and white hat. Though his good looks were undimmed, the lines of worry and the heavy responsibility of his position were evident upon his lean face.

"I'm the one to blame," he said with anger flashing across his drawn features. His hands coiled into two tight fists at the sides of his heavy army trousers. "I never should have allowed you and Susan to come to Arizona when there was so much trouble brewing."

Regina could not permit him to blame himself. Since the overwhelming feelings of guilt was still with her, she would prefer to shoulder that burden all on her own. But her father did not give her a chance to disagree with him. He hit his thigh with one of his doubled-fists. "I have been working so hard, Regina—so hard!" He drew in a ragged breath and slumped down next to the makeshift cot where she had been placed by the two soldiers who had carried her into the wagon.

"All these years, I've been trying to make some sort of improvement out here in this godforsaken country, and for what?" He stared out through the open flap of the canvas with a faraway look in his eyes that appeared to reach beyond the boundaries of the Arizona desert. "Each time I gain just a small amount of the Apaches' trust, this damn army destroys everything I worked months—no, years—to achieve."

Regina knew she had to convince him that what had happened today was not his fault, but for now, she remained silent. This was her first observance of her father in this mode of his professional life. Whenever he had visited her in Savannah, he had rarely divulged details about his duties as an officer in the U.S. Cavalry.

"You know, Regina," he continued, "I enlisted in the army right after your mother's death. I took you to live with my parents in Georgia, then immediately returned to this uncivilized country. I know it sounds absurd, but I thought I could keep your mother's memory alive if I stayed out here in Arizona. And I had this crazy notion that I could make a difference." A bitter laugh emitted from the captain's throat. "Well, I was crazy all right; crazy to think one man could stop the destruction of a whole nation of people."

Regina was growing more confused with each passing second, yet she was also becoming very intrigued. He had never offered any information about his reasons for joining the cavalry before now. Many times in the past, Regina had sensed that his devotion to his career might also have something to do with her mother. But she had never summoned up enough courage to ask him if her suspicions were correct. She hoped he was finally ready to talk about the past life he had lived with her mother.

"What are you talking about . . . the destruction of what nation? And what does that have to do with my mother?"

Charles sighed and placed his arm around her head in a loving gesture. "Oh, don't pay any attention to me. I shouldn't be rattling on about something that is not in my power to control. Besides, just knowing that my little girl is alive is all that concerns me now."

Regina did not want to avoid the issue again, but before she could question her father more closely, they were interrupted.

"Sir?" A young private poked his head through the opening in the back of the canvas wagon. "Should we take this back to the fort with us — you know — for evidence?" The private held up the long feathered lance that Regina had seen stuck in the ground beside the burned stagecoach. Even held within the soldier's grip, the eerie object caused Regina to shiver with terror.

"No, that's not necessary," the captain answered briskly. "I know who led this raid today." He shook his head in a defeated gesture and murmured, "I just wish I knew why. The latest peace negotiations were going so well." A deep frown ceased his tired face as he added, "What could have set them off again?"

The private's expression turned cold, his eyes narrowed with the hatred which was apparent in his expression. "It was that troublemakin' breed who attacked the stage, wasn't it? That Chiricahua buck who paints himself up like a court jester with red-and-white war paint. Isn't that right, sir?"

Charles's face became hardened with fury. "That's enough, soldier!"

The private saluted curtly, then backed away from the wagon. But the soldier's brief exchange with her father had not gone unheeded by Regina. Was it really possible that the man whose demonic face she had seen in her dreams was not just a figment of her wild imagination? Regina's musing began to take on a whole new meaning with the realization that the Indian truly existed somewhere in this cruel land.

Her mind filled with questions. What had the soldier meant when he'd called the warrior a "breed"? Why would the sound of that word cause her whole body to grow cold and clammy with a sense of foreboding? When Regina's worried gaze moved up toward her father's troubled face, she decided now was not the time to burden him with questions. Still, there was one question she could not avoid.

"What will happen to Susan?"

Charles's arm grew limp around her head, and his shoulders sagged beneath the gold stripes which hung from his dark uniform. "Susan?" he repeated in a quiet tone of voice. "Well, I suppose all we can do for Susan right now is to say a few prayers." His back began to straighten up as he added in a strong voice, "But just as soon as I know that you're going to be all right, there's a hell-sight more I intend to do!"

Regina saw the stubborn tilt of his chin, and she knew that he planned to go into the Indian nation in search of his fiancée—regardless of the tremendous risks. She wished there was something she could say, or do, to ease the pain she could see written across his exhausted face. However, the thoughts which were racing through her mind at this time would only add to his burden. How could she make him understand that what had happened today was beyond his—or anyone's—power to prevent? He was bound to think she had lost her mind if she told him that the dreams she had been having were closely connected with the ambush on the stagecoach today. She would never be able to convince him that there had been a drastic mistake—that she was the one who was supposed to be taken hostage, not Susan Wilkins. Nor could she explain to her father why she had to conduct a dangerous search of her own. She could not even explain this demented compulsion to herself.

Somewhere in this untamed land was the man who had come to her through the hazy chambers of her dreamland. It did not matter that he was a savage: a killer, a breed, or even that he was the man who was responsible for Susan's abduction. In the visionary passages of Regina's mind, she had glimpsed the real man behind the mask of deadly red and white paint. No matter how long it took, or whatever she must do to discover the reason, Regina had to know why such a man could command her heart's total surrender.

Chapter Four

The band of Apaches moved steadily across the burning sand. They chose the route that would take them past the most accessible waterholes, more for their horses than for themselves. The Indians knew exactly which desert vegetation contained enough water to prevent them from perishing when they were unable to reach a waterhole.

They spoke very little as they traveled. There would be time for talk and celebration once they reached the village. Several men sported navy blue coats, which they had taken from the bodies of the dead soldiers; others led horses that carried the brand of the U.S. Cavalry upon their flanks, and almost all the warriors were armed with newly acquired army repeating rifles. The darkening sky did not slow their relentless stride. Renewed energy pulsed through their bodies from their recent victory, making them tireless as they moved onward. Fresh scalps dangled from their long feathered coup sticks — the grotesque rewards of their successful raid on the Butterfield Stagecoach. During the daylight hours, columns of flies had swarmed around the bloody masses. Now in the silence of the night, the drying scalps swayed hideously in the glow of the moonlight like faceless specters.

Eagle, Nachae's big brown-and-white painted pony, led the cavalcade through the last swells of the dry desert. As surefooted as the man who had trained him, the big stallion moved easily along the craggy ridges leading into the range of mountains that sheltered the Apache village during the summer months. Eagle did not fail his master when he was called upon to perform deeds of endurance or swiftness of foot. It was for these reasons that the big horse was such a rarity among the Apache herds since the Apaches usually did not regard their horses as an essential commodity. It was the warrior's nature to move just as quickly on foot, and twice as silently as they could upon a horse. In fact, they would just as soon make a meal out of the animals as ride them, though they preferred to eat mules above all other types of meat. Army mules, since they had to be stolen from the despised soldiers, were a particular delicacy.

"Shik'isn, why are you so angry?" Juno asked of his closest friend as he rode his Appaloosa pony up beside Nachae's horse.

Nachae glanced fondly at the man who had just called him by the Apache name for brother. Though they were not kin by blood, Juno was as close to a brother as Nachae had ever known. Nachae was usually able to talk to the other man about most things that troubled him, but he found that he could not explain the strange emotions he was experiencing since his encounter with the woman from his grandfather's vision—not even to Juno.

Nachae could not push the dark-haired woman's image from his mind. He kept remembering the way her thick lashes slanted around her misty-shaded violet eyes and how the soft curve of her full lips reminded him of a trembling heart. His hands could still feel the silken touch of her long raven hair within their calloused grasp. He wished that he had listened to his grandfather, that he had not led an attack against the stagecoach today. Ever since he had first learned of his grandfather's visions—over ten years ago—Nachae had been certain that the woman's death would be the only way he could be at peace with himself. Now he realized that his plan to kill her had been the most foolish notion his mind had ever concocted. How could he have thought that the woman's death would end his own agony? To actually see her—and to hold her for such a brief time—had only made him realize that it

44

was not her destruction that determined his future. Without the woman from his grandfather's prophesy, it was his own fate that was put to the test.

"Did we not make our *shik'isn* proud today?" Juno asked with a broad grin. He held the palm of his hand against his bare chest as he beamed with pride.

Nachae nodded his head. "My brothers were very brave to go against Eskinzan's wishes for me today. I will be forever in your debt." Their speech was a mixture of the Apache language and Spanish.

"And," Juno added with a sly grin, "it is time that you had a woman to take care of your wickiup." He motioned toward the limp form of the woman who was flung over Nachae's horse.

Nachae grunted in reply to his friend's comment, then added in a foul tone, "She is a gift for your wife." His eyes narrowed with a mask of silent defiance.

A knowing smirk inched into Juno's expression. He knew his friend like the back of his own hand, and he also knew Nachae's reasons for the ambush on the stagecoach. But since Nachae had not been able to kill the woman as he had planned, Juno saw no reason for him to take over his friend's responsibility.

"My wife does not need her," Juno said with a nonchalant toss of his dark head.

Nachae's tall form stiffened, though he remained silent. Juno had just dared to insult him by refusing the gift he proposed to give to his wife. For that, Nachae could challenge him to fight. Nachae's lips drew into a tight line. This woman—whoever she was—wasn't worth losing his closest friend, he decided as he returned his thoughts to his unwanted hostage.

What insanity had possessed him to bring this white woman with him? She was useless, and he did not need a woman to care for his wickiup. Grandfather's youngest wife, Waddling Woman, kept him fed and tended to his wickiup. Nachae did not even care to use the white woman's body for his own personal pleasure, even though that was usually the only purpose a female captive was worthy of providing. Several times during the ride back to the village, he wondered if he should kill her rather than be burdened with her. His conscience, however, would not allow him to commit such a deed. To kill soldiers and the White-Eyes who intentionally infringed upon Apache lands did not cause Nachae any distress, but killing innocent women and children was something he did not have the stomach to do. He only wished the white men felt the same compassion toward the Indians when they raided an Apache village.

Nachae's skin crawled with the memories of the dead or dying children whose small forms were stuck on the long knives that the soldiers carried, or the tiny pieces of their hacked-up bodies strung about in the smoldering ashes of a burning village. His mind would never erase the images of the women who had first been raped, then had various parts of their bodies carved off while they were still alive and screaming, so the soldiers could make tobacco pouches or some equally obscene object to show for their conquests. Less than a year before, Nachae's own father, Alderay, and his father's wife, the gentle and quiet Breeze of the Forest, had been among the casualties of the soldiers' murderous wrath.

When they were close to the Apache rancheria, Nachae stopped Eagle and dismounted. The other men sat straight and silent upon their horses, waiting for their comrade to prepare his captive for her entrance into their village. Nachae pulled the woman from his saddle and casually dropped her to the ground. A muffled cry escaped her lips as her eyes slowly opened. She peered through the darkness, unsure of her surroundings. As she struggled to push her pain-racked body up to a sitting position, she spotted the ghostly glow of Nachae's red-and-white face hovering overhead. Her mouth flapped open, but no sound came forth—shock and terror had rendered her speechless.

To show sympathy toward his white hostage would belittle Nachae in the eyes of other men, so he tried not to look at her face while he tied a rope around her neck and swung back onto his horse. He yanked on the rope, causing Susan to scream out in pain as she was pulled to her feet by the pressure around her throat. Her fingers clawed at the rope, while her pale face became distorted with an increasing look of horror. She began to cry, loudly and in choking gasps. Through the tears, her big blue eyes looked pleadingly up at her captive for release, but the tall warrior remained cold and aloof.

Nachae began to grow angered by her tears. She would gain his respect only if she showed strength, and it seemed to him that she was not strong enough to fight for her own life. He dug his heels into Eagle's sides, causing the horse to move forward. He willed his ears to be deaf to her screams, nor did his eyes waver from the trail as he led his horse — and the wailing woman — through the deep grasses, toward the towering silver fir trees that surrounded the Chiricahua summer camp.

The rising of the shadowy moon above the treetops signaled that the time was nearing midnight when they rode into the sleeping encampment. The barking of the mangy dogs who hung around camp to scavenge for discarded food announced the men's arrival, and within minutes the quiet village was alive with activity. Women rushed out in various stages of undress to greet the returning warriors, their faces flushed and anxious. Each time their men rode from the village, there was an unspoken fear among the women. To kill and not be killed, to raid and not be caught, was the Apache creed. Too many times, though, the warriors returned to their villages in less numbers than they had departed. Not one woman would have a reason to grieve on this joyous night, however.

Drowsy-eyed children poked their dark tousled heads out from the doorways of their wickiups to listen to the warriors' description of their victory over the soldiers. Their young eyes grew wide with excitement when the men showed off the scalps they had taken from the loathsome soldiers. The old men, with their solemn, time-worn faces, eyed the young bucks with tentative gazes.

For hundreds of years, the Apaches had engaged in fierce battles with their hated Mexican enemies; now the white men had become their most vicious foe. The older men knew their nomadic way of life was nearing its end. The encroachment of the white settlers and the miners who were moving into their lands were forcing the Apaches onto disease-infested reservations in lands where they were not accustomed to living. The great Chiricahua chief, Cochise, had managed to maintain a semblance of peace among the white men and his own people for the past decade, but Cochise had died the previous year, and now the younger and more rebellious warriors had grown tired of the white man's weak promises and constant betrayals.

Every day, the Apache lands grew less expansive, and their people diminished in alarming numbers. The elders remembered a time when no one except their own kind had wished to live in the rugged Chiricahua Mountains or among the rocky bluffs of the adjoining Dragoon Mountain peaks. Once, the vast deserts of Sonora had belonged entirely to the various Apache tribes. They had roamed these regions, which were deemed undesirable by most people, because this was the land where they had chosen to live. Their race of people were bred to survive in these harsh elements. For this land, La Grande Apacheria, they would fight until the last drop of Apache blood was spilt.

Eskinzan watched his grandson approach with great curiosity. The old shaman had not expected Nachae to take any hostages from the stagecoach. When he had left the village that morning, the warrior had been so obsessed with the idea of killing the woman who rode in the coach that Eskinzan wondered if Nachae had brought her back here because he was planning some sadistic ritual for her death. To purposely inflict pain on anyone other than the people who threatened the Apache way of life was not his grandson's typical behavior. However, where the woman from the old shaman's vision was concerned, Nachae was completely irrational.

Nachae led Eagle through the throng of women and

children who were gathering in the center of the village. He did not halt his horse until he reached the waiting figure of his aging grandfather. From the back of his stallion, the warrior's troubled gray eyes peered down at the old man for a few minutes before he spoke.

"I have failed, Grandfather."

The shaman pulled his tattered blanket tighter around his bony shoulders, and met his grandson's gaze with a knowing look that bespoke ancient wisdom. His long silver hair reflected the gleam from the moonlight when he slowly nodded his head.

The expression on Nachae's tired face filled with wonderment. "You knew, didn't you?"

"Yes," Eskinzan replied. He had always believed his vision was too powerful to be erased from the course of Nachae's life, but his headstrong grandson had been determined to prove otherwise. Eskinzan felt his grandson's turmoil, and he wished he could help the young man to overcome the bitterness in his heart, but the woman whom he had seen in his vision was the only one who could help Nachae — if he would ever permit her into his life.

Eskinzan's old eyes looked toward the woman with an even greater interest. Since his grandson no longer planned to kill her, just what did he intend to do with her? The old man's mind filled with joyous pictures of the great-grandchildren that Nachae's union with this woman would soon produce.

"This is not the woman from your vision," Nachae stated bluntly when he noticed his grandfather's expression.

Eskinzan's silvery eyebrows raised with surprise. He stepped closer to the white woman and peered into her swollen red eyes. How could this be true? Eskinzan had been certain that the woman he had repeatedly seen in his visions would be a passenger on the stagecoach today. The old Apache's head dropped down in shame. It was seldom that one of his predictions was so mistaken.

"The woman you spoke of was on the stagecoach,

Grandfather. This woman was traveling with her."

"Is she—the other one—dead?"

Nachae slid down to the ground and drew in a heavy breath. He began to shake his head slowly. His powerful form slumped against his horse as though the weight he carried on his shoulders was too great a burden. "I could not go through with my plan to kill her."

Eskinzan exhaled with relief, then drew his brows together in a questioning arch. He started to ask Nachae where she was, and why he had brought this woman in her place. But the younger man began to speak before he had a chance to voice his questions.

"I am very sorry that I went against your wishes today."

The sagging skin around Eskinzan's eyes crinkled into deep lines as he smiled up at his tall grandson. He had been angry, first at himself for telling Nachae that the woman from his vision would be traveling on the Butterfield Stage that day. He thought Nachae would avoid seeing the woman at all costs. Instead, his hotheaded young grandson had formulated the crazy notion that he would attack the stagecoach and kill the woman. Eskinzan had been hurt when Nachae had insisted on going through with the ambush, even after the shaman had warned against it. Now the old man realized that what had happened today was only the first step of Nachae's long journey toward fulfilling the prophesy. Nachae relaxed slightly when he noticed the relieved smile on his grandfather's aging face.

"I have much to think about, Grandfather. I must learn to understand the strange feelings that I have discovered within myself today." His eyes glanced at the blond woman who was standing beside Eagle. She was still sobbing and appeared to be completely oblivious to her surroundings.

"Why I brought this woman back to the village is unknown to me." He drew his muscled frame up to its full height and looked down at his grandfather as he asked in a serious tone, "Do you think I should kill her?"

Eskinzan shrugged his drooping shoulders. He was confident that it was not his grandson's nature to destroy another human being without a good cause. But Eskinzan still felt the need to warn the younger man against any rash actions.

"It is your decision. But if this woman dies by your hand, her death will lie heavy upon your heart." Eskinzan reached out his gnarled hand and touched Nachae's arm in a show of affection, then turned and walked back into his wickiup without offering any further explanation. He was afraid to tell Nachae that his happiness with the other woman would somehow be overshadowed by this woman's fate. Eskinzan, himself, was not sure why. But he sensed that the woman Nachae had brought to the village tonight was closely connected with the woman in his vision.

Nachae looked at his hostage with increasing exasperation. Did this woman play a part in his grandfather's vision, too? he wondered. Her hands were covering her face as she continued to sob uncontrollably, without any regard to the crowd of Indians who were gathering around to watch her with extreme fascination.

Nachae's foul expression deepened when he spotted the look of humor upon his friend's face. Juno tried to hide his smirk from the scowling man, but he was not able to do so. Nachae stepped toward him and asked in an indignant tone, "Does my brother laugh at me because he thinks he can handle this weeping woman better than I can?"

Juno found it hard to keep a straight face, but he quickly lowered his eyes. He had already angered his friend over this white woman once today, and Juno knew that to do so again was extremely dangerous.

"Forgive me, *shik'isn*," Juno said in a more serious tone before backing away from the crowd of curious spectators. Normally Nachae was a willing partner for Juno's harmless gibes; tonight, though, it was obvious Nachae was retreating into one of his dark sulking moods. Juno, as his closest friend, knew it was best to leave him alone when he was in this frame of mind.

Nachae gave his head a slight nod in acceptance of

Juno's apology and returned his attention to the woman. She had dropped to the ground and her knees were pulled up against her chest, while her body was drawn into a tight ball. With little success, she was trying to shield herself from a group of children who were pulling at her long blond hair. Several young girls were ripping strips of the blue material from her dress to use as ribbons for their own hair. Nachae chased the children away from the cowering captive. His unfriendly tone of voice soon had the rest of the inquisitive Indians who were gathered around the yellow-haired woman scurrying off to join in the celebration for the returning warriors.

From the center of the village, Nachae could hear the beat of the drums and the singing that accompanied the gathering of the clan. That night, and for the next few days, the villagers would rejoice in the victory the warriors had won. Mescal, the Apaches' homemade whiskey, would be consumed in large quantities, as would the white man's whiskey that was stolen from the soldiers after the attack. Whiskey was an affliction that was hard for the Apaches to deny. Nachae did not feel so victorious though, and even the thought of drinking the treasured brew did not improve his mood. He was more confused than ever, and his turmoil served only to fuel his anger.

He grabbed hold of the leash he had tied around his captive's neck and pulled her to her feet. She did not resist, although her legs seemed too weak to support her weight as she stumbled against him. Nachae wished she would show some fighting spirit. He was growing more and more sickened with her constant crying and passiveness. An unexpected pang of remorse gripped his heart when he realized that it was not her fault she happened to be riding in the fated stagecoach today. He grew furious with himself for allowing such a sensitive thought to enter his mind. He reminded himself that the Butterfield Stage had carved its route right through the heart of Apacheria, and every time a coach traveled along its trail, they trespassed on Apache lands. For a moment — when he had felt guilty for abducting the woman — he had been thinking like a white man, and that was dangerous to his salvation—and to his sanity.

With his thoughts deeply involved in his problems, Nachae nearly collided with the woman who appeared in his pathway. He sighed; Llamarada was the last person he wanted to see that night. Her name, which meant "sudden flame" in the Apache tongue, seemed a worthy title at this moment, he noticed, in spite of his attempt to ignore her. Within her round face, her black eyes burned with a rage that resembled the devil's fire, and her pouting lips were drawn into a pinched frown. With an exaggerated gesture, she tossed her head toward the woman who was slumped against Nachae's side, making her thick braided hair cascade over one shoulder. When she returned her attention to Nachae, he could not help noting the look of malice in her dark face.

"So," she spat out as she clamped her hands down upon her rounded hips, "you prefer to share your robes with a white woman instead of me?"

A grunt, actually more of a snarl, was Nachae's reply. He had made the blunder of returning several of Llamarada's very forward advances in the past—a mistake he was beginning to regret. He was just a man, though, and to the male eye, Llamarada was a pleasing sight to behold, even if her personality was as fiery as her name implied.

"You did not answer me," she said, trying to sound calmer, though her face was a mask of rage.

To grant her a reply would be a wasted effort, Nachae decided as he stalked past her with his hostage and entered his dark wickiup. He did not intend to face a confrontation with Llamarada tonight, or ever. Their brief but passionate relationship had been over for the past few months as far as Nachae was concerned. Right now, he just wanted this day to end, too. Tomorrow he planned to ask Grandfather's wife, Waddling Woman, to look after his captive so that he could ride northward into the White Mountain range. He knew of a quiet and peaceful place near the summit where he could be alone. Beneath the vast expanse of the Apache sky, he would lie in the meadow where the grass grew high and lush. The tall pine trees would shelter him from the rest of the world, while he pondered his displaced existence.

"Nachae!" Llamarada demanded. She did not care that it was not the custom of her tribe to address someone by his proper name without permission or proper cause. "You will regret this," she said in a whisper. Her expression hardened into a chilling stare as the buffalo robe that covered the entrance to Nachae's wickiup dropped shut in her face. Her flashing black eyes continued to watch the closed flap for several more seconds before she swung around to leave.

"You were meant to be mine," she mumbled while she slowly walked into the dark forest that bordered the rancheria. "And if I can't have you, then no woman will!"

Chapter Five

Under the cover of darkness, the solemn soldiers of C Company trudged back toward Fort Bowie. Among the dead men whose mutilated corpses rode in the buckboard were friends — fellow soldiers and, in some cases, relatives of the men who transported the grim cargo through the fading desert dusk. Although he knew he was being foolish, Captain Atwood reprimanded himself time and time again during the returning trip to the fort because of his failure to foresee the ambush. He told himself that he should have sent a larger battalion of men to Lordsburg to accompany the stagecoach, or he should have gone himself, or . . .

It was useless to go over it again, his tortured mind echoed. Since the death of Cochise, the young Chiricahua bucks were upredictable and angry. The more forceful of the remaining warriors who had not been coaxed onto the reservations no longer listened to the older chiefs when they talked of peace. They were outraged with the treaties which continually whittled away their hunting grounds and the wide-open spaces where their wandering souls had traversed since the first days of their ancestors.

Charles Atwood was angry, too. His commanding officers in Washington continued to lie to him every time he pleaded with them to leave the Apaches alone and to allow them to live in peace. From their big oak desks and fancy padded chairs, the generals would promise him that the Indians could remain in their beloved mountains.

Then, those same men would turn around and order him to attack a whole village. If he balked at the order, his bloodthirsty lieutenant would gladly lead the charge.

Captain Atwood glanced through the canvas flap as his eyes sought out the man who was second in command at Fort Bowie. As always, Randy Decker rode at the head of the detachment. The lieutenant's white hat was tilted slightly to the right side of his head in a cocky manner, and his posture was straight and proper in his saddle. Charles Atwood sighed and gazed back down at his daughter. Her eyes were closed, although he knew she was not asleep because of the pained expression on her young face. It had been a mistake to permit her to come back to Arizona. He should have resigned from the army and returned to Georgia to live with his family where it was safe. Now, not only had he placed his daughter in the gravest danger, but he had also lost his fiancée to a fate worse than death.

With a defeated sigh, Charles leaned back against the wooden interior of the wagon. He knew where his fiancée was, and with whom. A shiver ran down the length of his spine when he tried to envision Susan's lovely young body within the clutches of the Apache buck who had led the ambush against the stagecoach today. The man who was rapidly becoming a major figure in the recent outbreak of destructive raids, which were occurring across the New Mexico and Arizona territories, was undoubtedly the same warrior who had chosen the Butterfield Stage as his latest target for vengeance. Half Mexican and half Apache, Nachae was the grandson of Eskinzan, the most powerful medicine man of the Chiricahua Apaches. A young warrior could earn himself the respected position of warlord by the number of brave deeds he accomplished; this being determined by the coups he counted, the size of his herd of stolen horses, and his daring feats of bravery during a battle. Nachae was proving himself to be unequaled in these areas of savagery.

Captain Atwood had met Nachae only once, during a visit to Cochise's stronghold near Apache Pass shortly before the death of the chief. The captain had sensed immediately that the army would never corral a man such as Nachae on a reservation, or anyplace else he did not want to reside. The warrior, Nachae, was the most dangerous kind of man — he cared nothing about his own life, and very little for anyone outside of the small band of Apaches whom he had chosen to claim as his family. Since the slaughter of the warrior's father and several other members of his Apache family the previous year while Charles had been visiting Regina in Georgia, Nachae's hatred and revenge had known no limits. The captain cringed with disgust and sorrow at the idea of Susan being with Nachae and his band of renegades. He almost wished that his young fiancée were dead, rather than still alive to suffer the fate that became most white women.

Regina did not have a hard time staying awake during the uncomfortable ride to the fort. The bouncing of the wagon made the bump on the back of her head scream with pain. Even if she could have dozed off, though, she would not have allowed it. She was too afraid of having another dream that would summon up the hate-riddled face of the painted warrior again. She was just as fearful of having one more of her passionate reveries; the next time she lapsed into her land of fantasy, there was no telling where the dream would end. She longed to tell her father about the dreams, and about the Indian whom the private had mentioned, but how did one tell her own father about such intimate things?

Their arrival at Fort Bowie was met with little fanfare. Regina had no way of knowing that there had been a grand gala planned for this evening to welcome the captain's daughter and fiancée to the fort. Now, however, a grim silence settled around the occupants of the post when the regiment rode through the parade grounds in the center of the outpost. This was not the first time the family of an officer or enlisted man had met with a tragic fate while traveling to the desolate fort.

Fort Bowie was an intimidating stone fortress built on

the slope of a barren hillside. With the exception of the few clumps of greasewood that protruded from the base of the high walls that surrounded the fort, there did not seem to be another living thing in the whole area. Erected in 1862, the fort served as headquarters for the troops who controlled the dangerous route of the Butterfield Overland Stagecoach. The route of the stage line led to all points west of Tuscon and everything east of Apache Pass.

"Miss Atwood?" Regina jumped at the sound of the man's voice. "Lieutenant Decker at your service." The officer tipped the brim of his snow white hat with his gauntleted hand. His smile revealed a row of perfectly straight teeth. A closer observation would reveal a glint in his brown eyes that did not match the smoothness of his voice, nor the broad grin that consumed his expression, but in the waning light Regina was not aware of these minor discrepancies.

She glanced around with a feeling of uneasiness. Her father had already climbed down from the wagon and was busy issuing orders to his men. She looked back at the lieutenant and managed a small grin. "I can walk," she offered. But the lieutenant shook his head vigorously.

"No, ma'am. Captain Atwood gave me strict orders that I was to carry you to his quarters." He smiled again and stole a sly glance in the captain's direction as he added, "And I never disobey an order."

Defeat edged its way into Regina's aching limbs. Besides, it was hard to argue with a man who had such a beguiling smile. A slight nod of her head was all the lieutenant took the time to acknowledge before he carefully lifted her from the wagon and pressed her lithe form against his chest. She was surprised at the feeling of security she experienced in Lieutenant Decker's arms, and for the first time since she had heard the bone-chilling cry that signaled the onslaught of the attack, she began to feel at ease. Since her father had entrusted her care to the officer for the time being, Regina gave into the exhaustion that overcame her and rested her head upon the lieutenant's broad shoulder as he carried her into a nearby building.

Her father's living quarters were a welcome sight after her initial glimpse of Fort Bowie. The stucco walls of the parlor were adorned with colorful paintings, and the stuffed cushions of the chairs and sofa were all finished in coordinating materials of dark floral brocade. Several vases of wildflowers sat on small tables around the room. The officer's house was exactly as she had always imagined it would be, and she immediately felt as though she had finally come home.

Lieutenant Decker carefully lowered her down onto the sofa. "A doctor will be here shortly to see to your injuries, but if there's anything that I—"

"No, Lieutenant, thank you anyway," Regina cut in before he could finish. With a quick glance upward, she was surprised to note the forlorn look on his face. Feeling guilty, she quickly added, "You've already been so kind, I just couldn't impose on you any further."

"It was my pleasure, Miss Atwood." He lightly touched the brim of his hat with his gloved hand as he began to back out of the door.

Once he was gone, Regina glanced around at her surroundings again. While she was growing up at her grandparents' home in Georgia, not one day had passed that she didn't yearn to be here in Arizona with her father. If only her arrival could have been under happier circumstances. She tried to ignore the throbbing pain in the back of her head because it served only as a reminder of the past few hours. She began to think of how wonderful a hot bath and a soft mattress would be at this time . . . then she thought of Susan, and decided that just being here was more than enough.

Regina watched as her father entered the room quietly and removed his wide-brimmed hat and the navy blue cape which matched his perfectly tailored uniform. Slowly, he pulled the gauntlet gloves from his hands, releasing one finger at a time. He then tucked the white gloves into the wide black belt that encircled his trim waist. He was not yet forty years of age, but Regina noticed that on this night he walked like a man twice as old. He sat down on the edge of the sofa and picked up her hand while he gazed lovingly at her face.

"You know, Regina," he began after several moments of silence, "in spite of all that has happened, I always want you to remember one very important factor." A poignant smile touched his lips as he added, "For the past fourteen years, I have lived for the day when we would be together again."

Regina blinked back the tears that suddenly sprang into her eyes. To know he felt the same way she did about their reunion made that day's awful events a little easier to cope with. She sat up and wrapped her arms around his neck and hugged him until a small laugh escaped his lips.

"I don't think anybody who can hug that hard can be hurt too badly."

"I'm not all that hurt," Regina admitted. "A small bump on my head maybe, and a few scratches here and there."

Charles smiled fondly and pushed her back against the soft cushions of the sofa. "That's bad enough. I have sent for the doctor to see to those cuts." He motioned toward her arms. "Then I want you to put the events of this terrible day out of your mind, and try to get some rest." With an affirmative nod, he started to rise up. A startled expression came into his weary face when Regina clasped the sleeve of his jacket.

"Please—talk to me first?"

The captain hesitated. He knew he should talk to her about Susan's abduction, but he wasn't sure if he was up to discussing the other woman's fate yet. Regina's escape was a mystery to all the soldiers. Even though she had explained about the fall from the coach and her conclusion that one of the soldiers had hidden her beneath the rock ledge, there were still some questions Charles knew he should ask her about Susan. Perhaps she might even remember something which would lend a clue as to why the Apaches had attacked the stagecoach. At that moment, however, the captain felt too tired to delve into all the reasons for the gross injustices that abounded in this untamed country.

"Please?" Regina repeated.

Charles glanced toward the doorway, wondering what was taking the doctor so long. His mind was trying to avoid the thoughts of what Susan Wilkins was probably going through at this exact moment, if her life had been spared, and the last thing he wanted to do was to voice those horrors out loud to his daughter. He drew in a long breath and sat back down. "All right, for a few minutes."

Regina could see the guarded look in his eyes, and noticed how it was also conveyed in his tense voice. Why was he so reluctant to talk to her? Was there something in his past that he had avoided telling her all these years? Soon, she planned to ask him about her mother again, but now she had other thoughts on her troubled mind.

"Tell me about the Indian whom the private was speaking of earlier."

Charles was caught off guard. He was expecting to be bombarded with questions about what had happened to Susan after she had been taken hostage. Without lying to Regina, there was no delicate way to talk about the tortures a white woman usually suffered at the hands of a warrior once she was taken captive. His mind had been searching for the most sensitive way to avoid telling Regina more than what was absolutely necessary about Susan's disastrous outcome, so the last thing he was prepared to hear from her was an inquiry about the warrior called Nachae. "Th-the Indian?" he stammered.

"The one the soldier called 'breed," Regina said with a tone of urgency. "There is something about him. I have such a strong feeling that I am going to meet him soon . . . that I . . . I must meet him." She clung to her father's arm in desperation, knowing that she would have to tell him everything before he could even begin to understand about the strong affinity she had for this savage man whom she had only met in her slumber. "I've been having these dreams—"

"Dreams?" Charles cut in abruptly. A dreaded sensation

61

began to seep throughout his whole being. Regina's mother had had dreams—vivid dreams that were always accurate premonitions of forthcoming events. "Tell me about your dreams," he said, his voice unusually strained. He fervently hoped that the Apache warrior, Nachae, was not a predominant figure in his daughter's dreams.

Regina could not miss the look of panic in his expression, and it caused her to be gripped with a renewed bout of fear, too. How could she ever tell her own father how she dreamed of a savage Indian warrior making passionate love to her?

"In my last dream I saw an Indian who paints his face half red and half white, but in most of my dreams he is not wearing any war paint. He is making—" Regina paused. Her body grew flushed with the memories of those explicit dreams. Her lips burned with the feel of his kisses, and without warning, she began to yearn for the reality of his touch. She glanced over at her father and with an enormous rush of embarrassment, saw that he was watching her with a look of despair.

Charles felt an icy tremor shoot through his body. What sorts of thoughts could be going through his daughter's mind that could cause her lips to tremble so? Was it the dreams of the Apache brave that aroused such a look of rapture upon her young face? Charles gazed down at his little girl and saw a woman looking back up at him. When had she grown up? he wondered. When had she become so beautiful? With the exception of the color of her exquisite eyes, she was the exact image of her lovely mother.

He knew for certain now that it had been a terrible mistake to bring her back to Apacheria, yet his heart ached with the thought of sending her away again. He loved her so much, but was it too late, he wondered, to change the course of events which had already been activated in her innocent mind?

"Regina," he said firmly before he had a chance to change his mind. "I think it would be very dangerous for you to stay here. Tomorrow, I will make arrangements for you to return to Savannah."

"But Father—"

The captain stood up and turned away. He could not bear her look of disappointment. The last thing he wanted was to be separated from her once more. But if Nachae was somehow involved in his daughter's future, it could be fatal to allow her to stay.

"My mind is made up, Regina. I must go into the Indian nation after Susan. But first, I have to know that you will be safe. I do not feel that you will be out of danger as long as you're in Arizona."

"But I don't want to leave here, or you." Regina began to grow angry with her father. Why had his attitude changed so suddenly? "I should be here for Susan when she returns," she added with the hope that her father would agree that his fiancée would need someone to help her get over her horrifying ordeal once she was recovered from the Apaches.

"Susan will probably not even be ali—" He stopped himself from saying the last word. He would never forgive himself for what happened to his intended bride, especially since he had proposed to Miss Wilkins with such ulterior motives. His mind began to recall the lovely young woman whom he had promised to take as his wife. Susan Wilkins was a flirt, and she used her beauty to her advantage with every opportunity. Even though Susan's quest to be an officer's wife and to someday live in Washington, D.C., had not eluded Charles, he had still fallen into her carefully laid trap. He had allowed himself to be flattered by her obvious interest in him. Besides, he had wanted a female companion for his daughter when she joined him here at Fort Bowie. Unlike the few older women who lived at the fort with their husbands, Susan was young and enthusiastic, and it was Charles's hope that the two young women would become close friends by the time they reached the post.

In a flurry of irrational thinking, he had asked Susan to marry him and she had accepted without a moment's hesitation; now she was his responsibility. But since he had returned to Arizona and had taken the time to think about marriage to a woman as flighty as Susan Wilkins, he sometimes found himself wondering if there was some truth to the saying "There's no fool like an old fool!"

Regina observed her father in silence. He had just admitted that Susan would probably not survive her captivity. Yet Regina had no doubt that he would risk his own life to go in search of Susan. Surely he would not ask her to retreat back to Georgia when everything she had ever sought was here in Arizona?

Regina quickly smoothed down the unruly strands of her heavy black hair that had once again escaped from the confines of the loose bun at the back of her head. With a nervous glance at the visitor who stood on the front stoop of her father's house, she opened the door wide enough for the lieutenant to enter.

"I hope I'm not disturbing you," he said, "but I've just been so anxious to see how you are feeling." His sweeping gaze took in the pink blush that deepened as he gave her a head-to-toe inspection.

In an unconscious gesture, she lowered her eyes to the floor, then tilted her head to the side and glanced up shyly at the officer. The thick ebony lashes that surrounded her violet eyes fluttered and the lieutenant felt his knees grow weak. When he had carried her into this room the night before, he had been aware of her beauty, even though her face had been covered with grime and her long hair had been tangled and dusty. Now, however, Randy Decker found himself staring boldly at her youthful beauty as he tried to gather his wits before she decided he was a complete idiot.

"I was about to have a cup of tea. Would you care to join me?" Her invitation was offered out of politeness, since she would have preferred not to be the object of the lieutenant's scrutiny. Men always looked at her in that manner, though, for the life of her, Regina could not understand why. When she looked into the mirror, she saw a young woman with hair that was much too thick and dark to complement the apricot hue of her complexion. Though everyone always noticed her eyes, as far as Regina was concerned, even violet eyes did not compensate for her lack of voluptuous curves. However, raised as a proper Southern lady, Regina had learned to tolerate the amorous suitors who had bombarded her grandparents' home once she had reached a marriageable age. At times, Regina found the silly and overly polite conversations that men and women were forced to endure for the sake of being sociable extremely trite and boring, and right now she was not looking forward to playing this game with Lieutenant Decker.

The lieutenant stumbled over to the sofa and sat down beside Regina. He perched his hat squarely in the middle of his lap, then seemed unsure of where to place his hands. He folded them finally and laid them on top of his hat—oblivious to the fact that he had just crushed the carefully shaped crown of the headgear.

"Do you prefer sugar in your tea, Lieutenant?" Regina asked, while trying not to stare at his flattened hat.

He cleared his throat loudly and nodded his head. "Yes, please." Shifting awkwardly in his seat, he added, "No one would ever guess what a horrifying experience you had yesterday. Why, if you'll excuse my forwardness, Miss Atwood, I would like to say that you are just about the most beautiful woman this old Southern boy has ever gazed upon."

"Lieutenant! Are you from the South?" she asked with a tone of excitement, ignoring his exaggerated compliment when she noticed that his accent was nearly identical to her own.

He took the teacup and saucer from her extended hand. "Yes, ma'am. I hail from Atlanta, Georgia."

"We were practically neighbors. Did you ever spend any time in Savannah?"

Randy nodded his head of dark blond hair and chuckled. "Some of my fondest memories are of Savannah and its lovely ladies." A sly smile curled his lips

65

with innuendo.

Regina shook her head with amazement. "Isn't it a coincidence that you're from Georgia."

"Not so much," the lieutenant said. "My uncle, who is a general in Washington, is also a good friend of your father's. They were stationed together out here in the West, and also during the War Between the States. My uncle felt it would do me good to serve under the command of a fellow statesman, and that's why I happen to be here in Arizona. And I would like to add"—he leaned toward Regina, a wide smile crossing his face—"that it is an honor to be in Captain Atwood's unit."

Regina felt a rush of color stain her cheeks once again. Through the fringe of her thick lashes, she chanced a quick glance at the lieutenant. He was extremely dashing, she told herself, and he certainly knew how to win her affections by complimenting her father. Maybe this socializing wasn't so bad after all.

"I should let you rest now," the lieutenant said, and rose to his feet. He bowed from his waist in a gallant manner and picked up her hand. As he raised her hand to his lips and lightly kissed it, their eyes met for a second. Regina blushed and turned away.

She pulled her hand free and stood up abruptly. Without thinking, she dropped her gaze to the floor in the shy manner she resorted to whenever she was unsure of how to act. She wished he would quit staring at her so intensely. Thank goodness he was not able to see the wanton images that had just invaded her thoughts. The way the lieutenant's lips had brushed against her hand had reminded her of the passionate Indian who had kissed her in her dreams.

"Good day, Lieutenant," she said when she felt another flush burn its way across her cheeks. With a hasty step, she led the lieutenant toward the door while making a useless attempt to clear away the vision of her dream warrior. Would the lustful memories from her dreams overcome her every time she was in the presence of a man? she wondered.

"May I call again?" Randy Decker asked, aware of her sudden unrest. He was confident in her reply; he had not missed the sultry look on her face a moment ago.

Regina nodded her head, but did not speak because of the image that had stolen her breath away. What sort of power did the Indian warrior possess that could arouse something so strong in her . . . something she had not even known existed until he had drifted into her dreams?

Randy Decker left the room and paused on the small veranda that adjoined the front of the captain's living quarters. He was quite pleased with himself. Regina Atwood would be a real asset to his blossoming career, especially since her father was such a good friend of his uncle. He pushed back a dark ash-blond curl that had dropped down onto his forehead, and glanced out over the expanse of Fort Bowie. How he despised this ugly desert and the ugly savages who inhabited it. He longed to be back in the South—to lie in the shade of a magnolia tree and to sip on a sweet mint julep. Those days were gone, though. The War Between the States had put an end to the South's genteel lifestyle forever.

But the Civil War had ended eleven years ago, and Lieutenant Decker was tired of fighting Indians. He was twenty-nine years old now, and he was ready to move up in his chosen profession, and away from the dirty outposts where he had been stationed for the past several years. First, however, he must prove to his uncle that he had settled down enough to deserve a promotion. He closed his eyes and envisioned himself wearing a plumed chapeau upon his head, and heavy golden epaulets across the expanse of his broad shoulders. Randy decided that he would cut a striking figure as a major general, and a beautiful, well-bred woman like Regina Atwood at his arm would definitely be a deserving accessory. His uncle would surely approve.

The lieutenant opened his eyes, and the image of his bright future was stripped from his mind when he recalled a portion of the conversation he had just had with Regina Atwood. Yes, he did have many memories of Savannah and the numerous . . . associations . . . he had been involved in there, but none he cared to dwell on.

He stepped down from the veranda and headed toward the supply store. He was in need of a new hat, but it was such a small price to pay. A smirk curled his lips upward when he thought of his performance earlier. Women liked it when men acted nervous and shy, and he was positive that Regina Atwood was quite taken with his charms.

Several small Navajo children, whose families lived peacefully on the outskirts of the fort, were playing on the steps of the store. Lieutenant Decker glanced around to make sure no one was watching, then he kicked the nearest child and sent the little girl sprawling out into the dirt.

"Go play someplace else, you little heathens!" he spat. He stomped up the remainder of the steps as the rest of the children scrambled from the porch to escape the wrath of his heavy boots. Damn Indians, he thought with regenerated contempt. They should all be destroyed before any more of them could breed and produce more little savages. Even worse was the idea of interbreeding. Why—the very thought made the lieutenant shake with rage. As far as Lieutenant Decker was concerned, there was only one thing lower than an Indian—and that was a good-for-nothing half-breed!

Chapter Six

The blackness of the desert night seemed to swallow up the small flames of the campfire, but Regina was grateful just to have the added comfort of the blaze. Since it was a certainty that the Apaches knew the regiment's exact location, there was no need for a dry camp. But not wanting to venture out too far into the Indian-infested area for firewood, the fires the soldiers had built were no more than a few handfuls of mesquite twigs. Ever since they had left Fort Bowie the previous morning, the cavalry unit had seen smoke signals rising from the hilltops to the north of the stagecoach route. Swift Eye, a Navajo scout for the army, had begun studying the white funnels from the time they had first appeared in the cloudless blue sky.

"A strong, steady stream of smoke without any pauses means only one thing," Swift Eye said with a tone of authority. "Apache warriors are gathering to form a war party somewhere in the surrounding foothills."

Regina pulled the long blue army cape tightly around her body. Lieutenant Decker had given her his wrap earlier this evening for added warmth against the cool night air. She had been in such an upset state ever since they had left the fort that she had even forgotten to thank him for the cloak. With a weary sigh, Regina decided she should apologize to the lieutenant for treating him with such indifference. Ever since her arrival at Fort Bowie, he had gone out of his way to be polite and considerate toward her. Not one day had passed when he didn't stop by just to ask how she was feeling, and he was always such a gentleman whenever he came to call. He had even volunteered to escort her all the way back to Georgia if her father would permit him to do so.

Regina stared into the darkness that lurked beyond the confines of the camp. She saw nothing, but was thinking a thousand thoughts at once. Tomorrow her father was going to meet them here at the San Simon River, and she was not looking forward to the rendezvous. The captain had sent a messenger back to the fort to inform them that he had not been able to find any clues to Susan's whereabouts. His message also included orders for Regina to be escorted to this area, where his battalion would join them. From here, they would take her into Lordsburg, New Mexico, where she would catch the southward-bound stagecoach on the Butterfield line.

The last thing Regina wanted was to go back to Savannah, but did she have any other choice? The handsome face of the Apache warrior, who still claimed her every dream, bolted through her mind again. Nachae, "the breed," that was the name she had heard the soldiers at the fort call the Indian who had led the attack against the stagecoach the previous week . . . the same man whose image left her weak and breathless each time she remembered his elusive touch.

"Nachae," she said in a whisper, letting the lyrical sound of his name roll from her tongue. A shiver raced through her body. She had heard that he was half Mexican and half Apache, but years ago he had denounced his Mexican family and cultivated the Apache way of life. He was, according to the soldiers, the devil's assistant and twice as evil. With the exception of her father, it appeared that there was not one other man in C Company who did not want to claim the breed's death by their own hand. Yet the threat of an attack by his band of renegades had sent the whole regiment into a complete panic ever since Swift Eye's prediction the day before.

One of the ponies whinnied, and Regina's head jerked around to the source of the sound. Her eyes searched through the opaque moonlight, but it was too dark to spot her little brown mare grazing among the herd. She could not even see the half-dozen soldiers who were somewhere among the black shadows keeping guard in case of an attack.

Feeling lost and alone, she crawled beneath the cover of her heavy blanket. The black sky was sprinkled with millions of stars. When she was growing up in Georgia, she used to sit out on the huge white-columned porch at her grandparents' home and gaze up at the stars for hours at a time. Back then, she had really believed that if she made a wish upon a star, it would come true. To remain in Arizona, she would do just about anything, even ask the distant stars for their assistance. Unfortunately, her only real hope was to convince her father not to send her back to Georgia when he arrived the next day. That would not be an easy task, especially since he had not found any evidence that Susan was still alive. He would be more determined than ever to ensure Regina's safety by seeing to it that she returned to the protection of her grandparents' home in Georgia.

The first timid rays of the morning sun did not find Regina in a good mood. She had spent a restless night rehearsing the numerous reasons she would give her father as to why she should stay in Arizona. Wasn't the fourteen years they had lived apart reason enough? But what if he still insisted on sending her back? The insane idea of running away had even crossed her mind several times during the long night. Of course, she was smart enough to know that she had no chance of surviving the Arizona wilderness on her own, yet she also knew that she was not leaving here . . . not until she had learned more about her mother, and why she could not escape from the Apache brave who beckoned her to come to him, even though they had never met.

"Will you join me for breakfast?"

Regina twirled around at the sound of the lieutenant's voice and tried to cleanse her mind of the foolish thoughts of her dream warrior. She focused her unsteady gaze upon

71

Lieutenant Decker's freshly shaven face and took note of how his damp hair was combed in neat waves across the top of his head.

"First, may I have some privacy down at the river?" she asked as she bent over and picked up the saddlebags which contained the things she needed to make herself presentable. The lieutenant's immaculate appearance made her feel like a ragamuffin, although at this moment, she would rather that the lieutenant noticed her wrinkled clothes and disheveled hair instead of the way her breath was coming in short labored gusts or the heated flush in her cheeks. Just the fleeting thought a minute ago of the Apache warrior who haunted her dreams was enough to steal her senses away, and these strange feelings kept growing stronger with each passing day.

Lieutenant Decker's face took on a serious look as he glanced around the surrounding landscape. "I don't think it would be wise to go to the river alone, not with the hostiles so close. I'll escort you to the river and will avert my eyes so that you may have some privacy."

Regina's lack of sleep, compounded with her ever-growing annoyance over this unwanted trip, made her aggravated with the lieutenant's reply. "I do not wish an escort," she said in a more severe tone than she had planned. "I am perfectly capable of attending to my personal grooming without your assistance."

"I didn't mean to imply—"

Immediately, Regina reprimanded herself for taking out her frustrations on the lieutenant. He was, after all, only thinking of her welfare. She turned her sheepish gaze in his direction, then graced him with a bashful smile.

"Forgive me, Lieutenant. I didn't mean to be so rude. I realize that it is only your job to protect me."

Randy Decker stepped up to her in one long stride. He stopped before her, standing straight and tall, almost as if he was preparing for an important inspection. "Oh, Miss Atwood, I hardly think of protecting you as a part of my job. I mean—I want to protect you because—" He looked away for a second as though he could not find the right words to convey his feelings. When he glanced back at her, his brown eyes were shining brightly. "Well, because you have become so very important to me in the short time we've known one another. I hope we will become much, much more than just friends." A timid smile touched the corners of his lips as he waited for her reply.

Regina did not grant him an answer. She was too stunned by the sudden admission of his intentions. Although he had been attentive to her during her brief stay at the fort, she had no idea that he was already thinking along such intimate lines. She threw her hands up into the air and turned away from his anxious stare, presenting him with her flawless profile.

The lieutenant was not slow to notice how her appearance had not been affected by the hardships of their perilous journey, nor did her obvious feelings of turmoil distract his approval of her classic beauty. Quite the contrary, her lack of enthusiasm over his admission of devotion only fueled his desire to possess the captain's young daughter for his own selfish purposes.

"I don't mean to rush you. But I do plan to sweep you off your feet by the time we reach Georgia, Miss Atwood." His slow Southern drawl held a suggestive hint when he reached down and picked up her fingers, then engaged his lips in a lingering kiss on the back of her hand.

Regina turned to stare at him with her darkening violet gaze. Her voice was lost somewhere in the back of her throat as her limp hand dropped at her side when he released it. She drew in another heavy breath and raised her eyes to meet his bold gaze. After a quick glance at his face, Regina looked down at the ground again. Lieutenant Decker was almost too charming for his own good, she decided.

"Don't go out of earshot," he said, tilting his head to the side. "And"—he placed the white hat which had been resting under his arm upon his neatly combed hair, then tipped the brim with his fingertips—"just call out to me if you are in need of anything at all. I will be waiting for you

73

behind those bushes over there." He motioned toward the thicket of heavy brush at the river's edge. With a sharp and precise motion, he twirled on his heels and walked away. He could feel her eyes watching him while he crossed the campsite. The calculating smile upon his face increased as he thought of how she would be putty in his hands by the time they reached Lordsburg—let alone Savannah, Georgia!

For two days, he had followed her . . . and watched her. It had been difficult to remain out of the soldiers' scopes. But Nachae excelled at elusiveness, and he was unequaled when it came to being cunning. He rode Eagle part of the time and at other times he would stalk the group on foot, always out of sight. After seeing the warrior's smoke signals, many of his comrades had joined him the previous night, eager to partake in another attack on the despised White-Eyes.

Even from a distance, it was evident to Nachae that the woman he was following was not happy. She remained separated from the troop of men, sitting sidesaddle atop her little mare with an air of formality, and also with an aloofness that suggested how upset she was about this journey. To Nachae, she seemed too melancholy for one so young. A part of him longed to swoop down and take her into his arms—away from anything that might harm her or cause her any unhappiness. Yet another part of him still feared her immensely, and the threats that her existence might mean to his life.

Hidden in the thick bushes that surrounded the river, Nachae watched as the lieutenant kissed the woman's hand. He strained to hear their words, but he was out of earshot. His stomach twisted with rage while he watched the touching scenario, even though it did not appear that the woman was returning the officer's advances. Since jealousy was not an emotion the warrior had ever dealt with, he vented his fury on the lieutenant. Officer Decker had earned himself the title of "baby killer" among the

Apaches with his habit of attacking unsuspecting villages filled with women and children. When the time was right, Nachae intended to put an end to the lieutenant's murderous trail by the same brutal manner in which he had killed many defenseless Apaches, including Nachae's own family. But that was not the quest which had brought Nachae back down from the mountains on this day.

His soul-searching trip to the summit of the White Mountains had only increased his desire to see the beautiful young woman with the unforgettable violet eyes again. He hoped that if he saw her just once more, his obsession with her would begin to fade. But the instant he had spotted her leaving the fort with the soldiers, his confusion had grown to enormous proportions. He kept telling himself that if she was going back to wherever she had come from, then he would be rid of her, and his grandfather's prophesy would never come to pass. So why was he following her? And why did he feel such a burning in his heart each time the vision of her sweet young face passed through his mind?

Crouching lower in the bushes beside the muddy riverbed, he watched her approach the water. Nachae thought it was strange that the lieutenant would allow her to come down here without the protection of any of the soldiers, especially since he had seen them studying his smoke signals. His hate for the lieutenant reached a new limit. A wicked smirk curled Nachae's lips as he added one more item to his personal list of reasons of why he intended to make Lieutenant Decker suffer a long and painful death.

His ears caught the sound of her voice, and the breath stopped short in his chest as he craned his neck through the brush to get a clearer view of her.

"You are such a foolish girl, Regina Atwood," she said aloud, thinking about her insane notion of running off by herself in this rugged country. She flung the saddlebags over a low-hanging branch and proceeded down to the water's edge. Instinctively, she glanced around before starting to unfasten the tiny row of buttons which ran down the front of her white blouse.

Nachae quickly drew himself back into the cover of the pyracantha brush. He continued to hold his breath as he waited to see if she had become suspicious of his presence. Secure that she was alone, the woman diverted her attention back to the business of her disrobing. Once more, Nachae leaned forward, just in time to watch as she slipped her blouse from her shoulders and hung it on the branches of a nearby mesquite bush. Clad only in a thin white chemise and her brown riding skirt, she began to step carefully down the small incline that led to the edge of the slow rolling river. She bent over and swished her hand around in the water for a second, then scooped up a handful of the cool liquid and splashed it on her face. As she rose up, she threw her head back and drew her hands over her face and neck to rub the water into her skin. As was almost always the case lately, her mind was filled with the alluring images of the savage who was her constant partner in her thoughts each day, and always during her long nights. The thin sheen of moisture upon her smooth skin made her flushed complexion glisten with a sensual glow of blossoming womanhood that was evident in the way her lips curved slightly at the corners with the visions of some secret desire—one which was known only to her young mind.

Her eyes were closed when she turned around. Nachae still had not taken a breath, although he was not aware of it—he was too engrossed in watching her every move. It almost seemed as though she knew she was being watched, and because of this, she was performing some sort of seductive ritual for her captive audience. Nachae's eyes devoured her like a starving animal. He traced the lines of her face—the aristocratic arch of her cheekbones, her full lips which curved in the delicate shape that reminded him of a heart . . . lips made for a man to kiss, he told himself. He was close enough to see the thick black lashes which feathered across the tops of her cheeks, and the rise and fall of her small yet firm bosom beneath the revealing chemise she wore. As she let the morning sun dry her wet skin with its gentle warmth, he envisioned his large hands encircling her slender waist, and his hard body molding up against the silken touch of her bare skin.

He swallowed, and almost choked when he was forced to take a breath. He froze to the spot, waiting to see if she had heard him. With a casual stance, she grabbed up her blouse and began to slip it over her silky undergarments. Nachae relaxed, confident that she did not sense anyone was watching her as she pulled out the hairpins at the back of her head. After she had released the abundance of hair and permitted the heavy mass to cascade down her back, she opened up the saddlebags she had carried to the river and removed a rosewood-handled mirror and comb. Holding the mirror up in front of her face, she began to comb the long mass of ebony hair. The bright morning sun reflected the almost obscure tendrils of dark auburn that intermingled with the shiny black strands as she ran the comb through the heavy veil.

The wispy tips of her raven hair draped across the edge of her skirt's waistband, so it was necessary for her to fling her head back in order to reach the ends of her hair with the comb. When she straightened her head back up and looked into her oval mirror, her hand stopped in midair while the comb dropped through her fingers and fell to the ground. Her mouth opened to emit the scream that was surfacing from the back of her throat, but his large hand clamped over her mouth before she could make a sound. She continued to hold the mirror in front of her face, too terrified to do otherwise. Her eyes widened, fear making their purpled hue even more dramatic as she continued to stare into the mirror. Through the wavering glass, their gazes held for barely a moment, yet to each of them, the meeting of their eyes seemed to last an eternity.

Regina recognized him immediately, and it was the realization of finally confronting him that filled her with a strange sense of satisfaction and relief. Her mind had already memorized every contour of his face, and she had known the exact shade of those stormy gray eyes from her consistent dreams. She should have been more scared than she had ever been in her life, but the burst of fear which

77

had consumed her an instant ago began to subside and her mouth relaxed within the tight grip of his hand as she slowly began to lower the mirror.

Against his better judgment, Nachae released his tight hold on her mouth. It was an unspoken Apache law never to trust an enemy. For the past ten years — in his mind — this woman had been his worst foe.

As if she was being drawn by an invisible magnetic pull, Regina turned around until they were face to face — close enough to hear one another's breathing, and for Nachae to see the tense lines of confusion and something stronger which was written into the conflicting expression upon her face. It was the look in her violet eyes that set Nachae's blood on fire. Her wide gaze stared at him as if she had always known him . . . almost as if she had been waiting for him to come for her. He had not even bothered to wear his war paint today, so he told himself there was no way she could know he was the same man who had spared her life during the attack on the Butterfield Stagecoach last week. Then a startling thought crossed Nachae's mind: Was it possible that somehow she had known about his existence before they had even met — just as he had been aware of hers for all these years?

He did not have time to waste on speculation. Besides, it was not possible that this white woman could have known about his grandfather's vision. Nachae cleared his head of the outlandish thoughts and glanced around with anxiety. At any instant, the lieutenant was bound to come searching for her, and if Nachae's comrades had not acted by that time, Nachae's plan would never come to pass. Thinking of the Pinda-Lixk-O-Ye, the White-Eyes, whom Nachae despised so fiercely, threw his mind into a rage. The look of violence and contempt was portrayed in his stony expression when he focused his dark eyes on the woman.

Regina saw the murderous look in his gray eyes. The scream which had only been a threat moments before sprang from her mouth. But her cry was lost to the war whoops that rose up from all sides of the encampment at almost the same instant. In the Apache way, the warriors had crept up on the cavalry unit without so much as the sound of a twig breaking beneath their moccasined feet. Within the time span of several seconds, Regina began to relive the horror of the ambush on the stagecoach. The soldiers who had died during the last attack had been buried only a short time ago, and now it was happening all over again. Her mind went into a panicked spin and her only thought was to escape.

She charged against the tall form of the Apache brave, catching him completely off guard. He staggered sideways, which gave her the fleet second she needed to make her attempt to get away. Her legs ran faster than they had ever moved, through the prickly branches of the shaggy brush that grew thick beside the riverbank and up the small incline which led to the campsite. Her skirt and blouse caught on the sharp edges of the bushes, leaving little pieces of the material and bloody traces of her torn flesh speared upon their spiny points.

Nachae had not been prepared for her attack and for an instant lost his footing in the entanglement of the low-growing pyracantha, but once he had regained his balance, his swift feet overtook her fleeing form as she tried to climb up the slope of the riverbank. He grabbed one of her tall boots by the ankle as he came up behind her, causing them both to roll back down to the bottom of the incline. In the tumble through the rocks and brush, Nachae's tight grip slipped from Regina's boot, but he had her pinned beneath him almost the instant they landed at the base of the slope. She began to kick at his legs and claw at his face with every ounce of strength she possessed until he effortlessly managed to grab her flailing arms and imprison them above her head with one of his own large hands.

Nachae, though irritated that this slender young woman could give him even the slightest amount of trouble, was beginning to admire her courage. He could have easily killed her with one blow of his hand or one slice of his knife, still it was apparent to him that she would prefer to

79

die bravely if he should decide to end her life. Even though she was powerless beneath the weight of his body, she refused to give him the satisfaction of admitting defeat. However, with his strong legs straddling her lean form there was little she could do except try to push him away, and that was merely a waste of her energy. Above them, the roars of the rifles and the screams of the men filled the air. But here, beside the murky banks of the San Simon River, Nachae was waging the worst battle he had ever fought, and it was within himself. As an instinctive impulse, he drew his knife and pushed it against the woman's throat with little thought as to what he would do next.

Regina felt the sharp tip of his weapon pressing into her skin, and she ceased to fight. Her horrified gaze was drawn up to his face as the memory of the last time his menacing form had hovered above her began to flash through her mind in distorted recollections. After she had been thrown from the stagecoach and had regained consciousness, he was the man who had knelt beside her . . . holding her in his arms. Although his face had been painted in the hideous red-and-white mask, she had seen the same look of turmoil in his dark gray eyes even then. She somehow knew that he was also the same man who had placed her under the rock ledge and spared her from the same fate that Susan had suffered. So why had he emerged from her dreams to save her life once before, if only to come back and kill her with such savagery now?

Tears began to fill the rims of her eyes as she thought of how easy it would be to give into the emotional downfall that threatened to claim her weakening senses. But ever since she had first returned to this land of her birth, she had sensed she was being drawn back here for some reason that she had yet to discover. This Apache warrior was involved in her destiny, whether either one of them wanted him to be or not. If she had traveled all this way just so that he could put an end to her life, then she wanted it to be finished—once and for all! But if she had returned to Arizona to meet with a greater destiny, then she was not going to allow this man to rob her of her fate.

Their eyes met, and Regina's expression hardened into tight lines of determination. She would not give him the satisfaction of making her cry.

Nachae was startled by her look of cold defiance. He had never encountered a white woman who did not beg and cry for her life, or make promises which she had no intention of keeping just so her life would be spared for a short time longer. This woman would make a good Apache woman, he thought with an unexpected touch of admiration. He continued to stare at her, suddenly wishing that his life could be different . . . that somehow it would be possible to fulfill his grandfather's prophesy. Yet he knew that this wish could never come true.

He jumped to his feet, angry and full of contempt for his meaningless existence. Then he yanked the woman to her feet, hating her because she existed too. She stood rigid before him, not backing down from him, nor did she attempt to escape again. In the time that they stood beside the river, amid the sounds of death and mayhem which raged around them, Nachae finally understood one thing in this vast entanglement of his life: If at this very moment, a bullet or arrow should crest the ridge above their heads and aim itself in her direction, he would gladly become a shield for her protection.

Chapter Seven

The warrior was relentless in his quest to get away from the soldiers with his hostage. Knowing exactly what Eagle's capabilities were in the desert heat, Nachae alternated the stallion's gait between a fast gallop and an easy trot. Every so often, he dismounted and trotted beside the animal to relieve the added weight of his body from the animal's back. During these times, Regina hung on to the horse's long blond mane in an attempt to stay upright on his back. When the Indian rode behind her, she dozed fitfully against his broad chest or she would try to concentrate on the surrounding countryside. She knew she had little hope of escaping from him and finding her way back to the fort, but studying the landscape helped keep her sanity intact. Repeatedly, her mind kept hearing the screams coming from the men who were being slain at the campsite. Though she did not want to remember, she would always see the dead soldiers lying in pools of their own blood. An animalistic curiosity had drawn her eyes to the site of the battle as she and the warrior had ridden away. She had noticed the odd way their faces looked, then nearly vomited when she realized she was looking at the bloody pulps of their scalped heads. Many times, Randy Decker's handsome image flashed before her eyes, and she wondered if he was one of the men whose faces were no longer recognizable because of the horrible method by which they had died.

She had always sided with her father in his beliefs that the Indians had a reason to fight for their lands and for their way of life. Now, however, she was beginning to understand why most of the soldiers at Fort Bowie hated the Apaches so much. She had observed the Indians' murderous ways twice, and had already come to the conclusion that the unspeakable crimes the Apaches committed against white men made the Indians less than human. From this day forward, she would never allow herself to forget the cruelty an Apache was capable of inflicting upon his enemy. She constantly reminded herself that she, too, was an enemy. And at this moment, she at the mercy of one such inhuman savage.

Regina's stomach cramped from hunger, and her tongue felt swollen and heavy in her mouth. Several times throughout the day he offered her water, which she readily accepted. But they did not take any extra time to eat, or to try to talk to one another. Regina was in such misery that talking would have been too much of an effort anyway. Her whole body ached from straddling the horse's back and her legs kept cramping with tight knots that nearly caused her to pass out from the pain. Although she had ridden frequently at her grandparents' home in Georgia, she had rarely sat on anything other than a sidesaddle. All that covered this horse's back was a woolen blanket. Fear of what the Indian had in store for her, though, overpowered all her vast discomforts, and she was relieved that they had not made any prolonged stops throughout the long hot day.

The brief episode at the riverbank, when he had held his knife to her throat, was enough to scare Regina into believing he was capable of killing her if he wanted to. Therefore, she was not about to complain or give him any new reason to carry out the obvious thoughts of murder she had seen written across his dark features earlier.

By nightfall, Regina had given up her intent study of the countryside and the direction in which they were traveling. They had not followed any sort of a trail, and now with the density of the woods they were entering, she decided it was futile to worry about where he was taking her. Apparently, he had a definite destination in mind; not once did he pause to contemplate their route, even as the moon rose and the forest became dark and foreboding beneath its glow.

Regina's exhausted body swayed from side to side, almost to the point where she was about to fall from the horse, when the animal finally came to a halt. The sudden stop startled her into alertness. The light from the moon was nearly obscured by the tall trees that surrounded them, yet her eyes strained to see through the shadowy light. Her frantic gaze followed the Indian as he moved to Eagle's side. Even in the darkness of the night she could see that his face was stony and emotionless when he looked up at her. A renewed sense of dread entered her worn-out being. Had he brought her all this way just so he could finish what he had started this morning? When he reached up to take her down from the horse's back, she flinched away from him with fear. His eyes narrowed as he grabbed on to her arm and pulled her down, using no gentleness in his actions.

Too weak from the long hours spent in the saddle to support herself, Regina's legs buckled under her weight. She sank to the ground and tried to keep from passing out from the pain that shot through her limbs like sharp daggers. After taking several deep breaths, she looked back up, expecting to see the angry face of the Indian glaring down at her. She was surprised to see him leading the stallion away, completely ignoring her.

For a long time, his attention was devoted entirely to the welfare of his horse. Pulling the blanket from the animal's back, Nachae began to wash the horse down with water from his flask, then he rubbed the sweating animal's hide with handfuls of the long grass which grew abundantly in the area. When he was finished with that task, he let the animal drink water from his cupped hands before turning him loose to graze on the lush vegetation.

Content that his horse was no worse for wear after the

grueling day of nonstop riding, Nachae turned around and eyed the woman. She had not moved since he had dumped her from Eagle's back. He had, however, felt her eyes on him the whole time he was tending to his mount. At a loss as to what he should do with her now that he had brought her up here to his special place, Nachae looked through the shadows of the moonlit forest and returned her intent stare. Twice, he had held his knife to her throat—twice, it had been within his power to change his grandfather's prophesy. Yet in each attempt, he had failed. And both times, he had felt such an overpowering connection to this young woman that he now realized it was impossible to deny the feelings which had grown so strong.

He began to walk toward her while Regina shrank back into the deep grass with an engulfing terror. He was exactly as she had pictured him in her vivid dreams. The only garment he wore was the breechcloth that hung from his narrow waist. The moonbeams which filtered through the tops of the towering trees glistened across his dark skin and danced upon his rippling muscles as he walked. Regina retreated from his advancing form while also trying to flee from the wanton cravings that rose within her. Her hands slipped against the thin layer of dampness that coated the thick grass from the cool night air, but she quickly pushed herself back up. A muffled cry escaped her when she realized that his bare legs were straddling her body as his tall frame hovered above her. The lids squeezed shut over her eyes, too afraid to ascend and meet with the steely stare of his deadly gaze. While she waited for him to make his next move, her tired mind immediately conjured up the image of his crude knife slicing across her throat.

Nachae bent over and grabbed her by the arms, then roughly pulled her to her feet. Her unsteady legs buckled again and she staggered forward against his chest. He heard her give a startled gasp, but she quickly straightened up until she was as rigid as his own stiff stance. His eyes searched her downcast face, expecting to see the tears that she had not shed earlier. Much to his surprise, she was not crying. It amazed him that she had not cried at all throughout the long day. Nor had she ever pleaded with him for her release, or complained about the nonstop riding they had done. An increasing respect bolted through Nachae for the woman's courage and strength. What made her so different from most other white women?

Regina could no longer avoid looking at the man when she was standing so close to him. Her eyes slowly raised up as her head tilted backward. He was closely observing her although his unfriendly expression had not relaxed. Why did it seem that he hated her so? She swallowed back the alarming fright that was rising up in her throat, but did not look away. His silent and deadly bearing scared her senseless, yet she was totally captivated by his mere existence. It took all her self-control and determination not to give him the satisfaction of knowing what an unnerving effect he had on her.

She tossed her head back, flinging the long mass of her tangled black hair over one shoulder. Even in the faded light, Nachae could not miss the vibrant shade of her violet eyes when they flashed with defiance. He almost smiled at her bravery, but not quite—he was too aggravated with all the strange sensations that her nearness aroused in him. He even began to grow angry with his grandfather; the old shaman had not told him that the woman from his vision would be so strong and willful. But then, there were a lot of things about the woman that Grandfather had forgotten to mention.

Nachae grunted and released his grip on her arms, then twirled around and stalked to where Eagle was grazing. His soul had never known such tumult. Just once, he wished his life could be simple—once, he would like to know what it felt like to have a sense of peace within his aching heart. He had never been a part of the El Flores Rancho when he had lived with his mother in New Mexico, and although the Apaches were the only people he had ever felt he belonged with, there were times when he

86

wondered if he belonged anywhere. His father, Alderay, had been a great war chief. But Nachae constantly felt the need to prove to the Chiricahua that he was a true Teneh Chockonen—an Apache—in his heart as well as in his blood. When he ran away from his mother's home at the age of fifteen and searched out his Apache relatives living among the rugged Chiricahua mountains of Arizona, he had taken the Netdahe oath as his own rule to live by from that day forth. At one time the Netdahe oath meant "Death to all intruders." Now it simply meant "Kill all white men!"

His eyes traveled back in the direction of the woman, and met her unwavering stare. She was a white woman, and she was a threat to his way of life—to his whole identity. Wasn't that a good enough reason to end her life? A weary sigh escaped his throat as he began to gather dead twigs from beneath the nearby trees for a fire, while trying not to glance in her direction again. Defeat was not easy for him to admit, but once again his grandfather had been correct. Nachae had to accept the fact that he could never destroy this woman. His thoughts were churning with new ways to avoid his grandfather's predictions when she came up beside him and started to help him pick up bark and sticks to use for the fire. He avoided acknowledging her assistance.

Regina timidly piled her armload of firewood next to his stack while he started a small blaze in the circle of rocks that he had just placed at his feet. She did not wish to anger him any more than he seemed to be already, yet her own survival was relevant too. Perhaps if he saw that she was not going to fight him again, then he would not find it necessary to kill her—or so she fervently hoped.

He worked over the fire longer than necessary, placing one twig at a time into the flames until the entire woodpile was ablaze. As she watched him, a startling revelation struck her—he appeared to be as much at a loss at what to do with her as she was with him. His anger, her confusion—it all boiled down to the final realization that neither of them could explain why their fates were so tightly entwined.

He rose to his feet and stalked to where his possessions were piled. After digging through the buckskin pouch that hung over his horse's sides, he pulled out a small bundle containing several round cornmeal cakes. He held one out to Regina, but she shook her head and turned away. Exhaustion was rapidly claiming what little energy she had left. She wished she could lie down in the soft grass and fall into a deep sleep—a sleep that would not be disturbed by his uninvited specter for once. But did she dare sleep when the man from her sensuous reverie was really here . . . close enough to fulfill her wanton musings? Were all those dreams some sort of premonition of an impending ritual—one that was about to take place that night?

The very idea of this savage man actually performing all the intimate actions that had occurred in her dreams threw Regina into a panic. She had to escape from him before it was too late. She had to force herself to flee from the desperate compulsion that made her yearn for his touch, even now in the wake of dangerous reality. Without warning, Regina charged past him, into the grove of tall pine trees—running without knowing where she was running to, aware only that she was running away from her own treacherous feelings of desire.

Behind her, she heard the sounds of his moccasins padding against the ground, closing the distance between them. She pushed herself to the extent of her strength in her effort to get away from him. But in the dense trees it was pitch black, and her feet stumbled over the tangled brush and rocks that lay on the forest ground. With a thud that stole the breath from her lungs, Regina crashed to the ground.

Nachae did not have time to stop himself when she fell. He collided with her sprawling form and smashed down on top of her. A muffled cry of pain and fear flew from her mouth, while a deafening horror overcame her whole being. He remained on top of her, which served only to increase her fear. Surely he would be enraged enough to end her life after this stupid episode. Long moments passed without any sort of movement from him until Regina could no longer stand the uncertainty. Raising her face up from the dirt, she drew in a deep breath and began to vent her own anger.

"Damn you!" she gasped with the first words that either of them had spoken throughout the long grueling day. "Damn your savage hide! What is it you want from me?" She spit the dirt from her mouth and continued, her tone of voice growing furious in spite of her precarious situation. "Every night you have come to me in my dreams, and haunted my waking hours with the intrusion of your unwelcome image. I can't think straight. And it's impossible to sleep for fear of how far my next dream will take us. I don't understand why this is happening to me. Why can't you just tell me what it is you want from me!"

Nachae's heart skipped a beat. What was she talking about? What dreams? Would his heart ever resume a normal pace again? To the Apaches, the interpretation of a dream was the forerunner of an event that their god, Usen, had predestined. Whether it be a circumstance of evil or good, there was no power strong enough to change the course of an occurrence conceived during a dream. He rolled away from her and fell back against the hard ground. How was it possible that this white woman had dreamt of him before they had ever met? Only someone as spiritual as Grandfather could have those kinds of powers. Nachae had lived in the white man's world long enough to know that they did not possess magic that strong. Who was this strange and beautiful woman whom Grandfather had envisioned for the past ten years, and how did she inherit the power which was bestowed only upon an Apache shaman?

Regina rose up on her elbows, oblivious to the pain that raced through her body from the fall, and also from the heavy weight of the man landing on top of her. Expecting to see his knife poised in a deathlike grip again, she was taken aback by his strange behavior. In the waning light of the moon in the deep forest, she could barely make out his unmoving form, so it was impossible to read the expression upon his face. Had he understood what she had just said, or was his silence just a prelude to his next plan of action? Regina did not care to wait around to see. She pushed herself up onto her knees; still, he did not move. Very cautiously, she rose up to her feet and began to back away from him.

Without any warning, he sprang to his feet. His movement was so swift that a surprised scream escaped Regina as she prepared to face her final fate—one more time. No mortal man had ever seemed so tall, or so fierce. She began to wish that he would be merciful and put an end to this agony once and for all. If he intended to kill or rape her, then why did he insist on prolonging the pain? Was this a method of torture that the Apaches used to make their victims so frightened that they would gladly welcome the outcome?

The warrior took a hesitant step forward, which matched the mask of indecision upon his brooding face. Almost instantly, he swung around and began to walk away. Regina's gaze followed him until the dark woods swallowed him up in their black embrace. A shudder, which made her whole body quake, seared through her limbs until she could no longer bear just to stand there and peer into the emptiness where he had disappeared. She told herself that she should be relieved he was gone and that she was free to get away from him. Instead, she was overcome with the oddest type of fear she had ever known. Not even the horror of the ambush on the stagecoach, or the attack at the camp that morning, could equal this strange new feeling.

Without any forethought she began to run, back toward the man whom she had wanted so desperately to escape from only minutes before. There was no explaining her impulse, no understanding this madness which drove her through the ghostly clutches of the tall trees . . . and led her back to him. She tripped and caught herself before she tumbled to the ground again, then she continued to stumble forward until she could see the beckoning orange flames from the campfire through the black trees.

Nachae was hunkered down by the fire, staring into the demonic shapes of the flickering blaze. He stood up slowly when she emerged from the curtain of blackened trees. An expression of surprise was evident upon his troubled face as she charged into the circle of the campfire glow. He had expected her to run in the opposite direction—as far away from him as her feet would carry her. Instead, something had drawn her back to him. The fire reflected the wild look of fear in her eyes, and her lips seemed to tremble with a silent plea. In agony, he turned away from her again. He did not want to gaze upon her face, nor did he wish to acknowledge the growing emotions of tenderness that she was causing to surface within him.

Regina's turmoil was every bit as great as Nachae's. Whatever had pulled them together was beyond their control to stop—no matter how much they each resisted. This greater power had brought her back to him, even when she had thought that the only thing she wanted was to get away. She sank down beside the fire, suddenly too tired to ponder the derangement in her life for one second longer. The dampness from the deep grass penetrated through her clothes and cooled her flushed body. Such a deep slumber claimed her tired mind that no dreams—disturbing or passionate—were permitted to venture through her unconsciousness on this quiet summer's eve.

Nachae, however, did not sleep at all. That night, it seemed as though he might never sleep again as he studied the form of his young captive. Where was all the animosity he had felt toward her throughout the years when he had refused to admit to her existence? The very thoughts that he had always denied were now raging through his mind, and they adamantly refused to disperse when he tried to force them away. Why couldn't he be just a normal man? Not a white man or a red man—but just a man who truly belonged somewhere! If he could live his life like a normal man, this would be the woman he would chose for his mate, in spite of their vast differences.

Already, she had shown him how much courage she possessed, and her youthful beauty was the kind that drew a man's soul into a fiery ball of uncontrollable yearnings. He reminded himself of the consequences of such a union, and his thoughts drifted back to El Flores Rancho.

How could he have sons and daughters to carry on the lineage? Another half-breed would be born into this prejudiced and heartless world to suffer as he had throughout most of his life. When he was a little boy, he used to wonder why his mother never hugged him or showed him any sort of affection. She saw to his needs and nothing more. To Rita Flores, he was a burden she did not need or want. He would watch the other children with their parents and wish he had a caring family to return some of the love that he harbored in his young heart. Then one day, after a gathering at the church, an older boy had called him a name—a name that little Antonio Flores had never heard before, and when he asked his mother what a half-breed was, he could still see the icy curtain that fell across her face.

Antonio was barely five years old, but her words were as clear to him now as they had been on that Sunday afternoon when she had told him what it meant to be the bastard son of an Apache buck. His young ears had not fully understood why she harbored such hatred for the man who had taken her captive and forced her to bear an unwanted child. He only understood that he was at El Flores Rancho because she had escaped from the Apache village before he was born, or else she would have left him with his father's people. And as Antonio began to grow older, he also came to realize that his only hope of survival was to return to the man who had sired him, in the hopes that he would be accepted among the Apaches with more compassion than he had received from the Mexicans. Leaving behind his hateful and cynical mother had not been difficult for Antonia Ugarte Flores, and burying his life at El Flores Rancho had left him with a feeling of complete freedom.

At the tender age of thirteen, he had set out in search

of his Apache relatives, encountering more of the same contempt against his mixed heritage everywhere he traveled, until he was certain that he would never have a true home anywhere in this cruel land. Two years later, when he finally discovered his father, the boy was once again an outcast. He had to convince his father's people that he had given up his Mexican heritage and was willing to live his life as a true Teneh Chockonen. Antonio Flores died in the ashes of his bitter youth, and in his place was born the Apache warrior, Nachae. Even after he had proved himself again and again, Nachae was still afraid that one day he would no longer be a wanted member of the Chiricahua because of his Mexican bloodline. He strove to become the most dedicated warrior in the tribe, and he isolated his heart from any emotions that might interfere with his goals. His grandfather's vision of this woman's love and the children they would produce as a result of that love was the most terrifying distraction in his life. If it should come true, more innocent children—his children—would suffer a life of prejudice and loneliness.

Nachae was not blind to the plight of the Apache people. Life as his Indian ancestors had known it was gone forever. Now, their choices were two—a proud death as a brave and loyal Teneh Chockonen, or a slow death of imprisonment. He would never live in the filth of the white man's reservations, so all that remained for him was to fight until there were no more wars to fight. What, then, would he be able to leave for his own children, except the same type of displaced life he had lived?

He reclined back into the deep grass and gazed up at the moon . . . an Apache moon . . . full and crimson. Mexicans referred to it as a Blood Moon, made red by the spilt blood of Apache victims. To the Apaches, the moon was always a source of beauty and mystery. It ruled over the reproduction of the Apache race and all the animals of Usen's great earth, and it was also in charge of the changes in the weather. Nachae stared at this great source of life until it became a distorted blur above his head, and he was lost to the weariness in his body. His last thought before he joined the woman in a deep slumber was that tomorrow, he would settle the anguish in his heart and mind—once and for all!

Chapter Eight

A sense of awe overcame Regina when she opened her heavy eyelids and glanced around her. Although it took her drowsy mind a minute to recall the events of the day before, she immediately recognized the place where she had awoken: the secluded opening among the tall trees . . . lush and green . . . a place where forbidden lovers meet. This was the exact location of her amorous dreams.

She forced her aching muscles to support herself as she slowly rose to her feet and surveyed this paradise. It seemed unreal that such a beautiful place truly existed, but then, the dangerously handsome savage was not a mere fantasy either. There was only one thing left from her dreams that had not materialized yet. Her body grew weak with the thought, but even more worrisome was that she no longer felt the need to fear her dreams. The previous evening when she had made the choice to stop avoiding something which seemed so inevitable, she had also been overcome with a feeling of tranquility.

Regina scanned the dense woodlands that encircled the meadow once she realized that she was alone. There was no sign of the Indian, not even his horse was anywhere to be seen, and the fire he had built last night was nothing more than a pile of cold ashes. Regina began to run in a frantic circle through the deep grass, ignoring the acute pain in her muscles from the hard riding they had done the day before. How could he just leave her like this? Every tree, every gap in the thick forest, looked identical.

She swung around and exhaled sharply. How long had he been there—watching her? At the edge of the tall firs, he sat atop his large painted stallion like a bronzed statue. Her relief at seeing him stole away her senses as she ran across the expanse of the clearing.

Nachae watched her moving toward him, thinking that her lithe body moved like a perfectly coordinated jaguar. The long strands of ebony hair floated in the breeze about her shoulders, and the flush on her lovely young face lit up the forest like a bright sunrise. His breath caught in his throat, and he was certain his eyes had never gazed upon anything so beautiful. During the night he had crept away with the intention of never returning to her, but now he knew that his choice to come back had been the right one, no matter what the consequences. He only hoped he would be strong enough to follow through with his new vow, now that his eyes had gazed upon her gentle loveliness once again.

Regina stopped abruptly when she reached his side. She was breathless, aglow with the exhilaration of his appearance. "Thank goodness, you came back," she gushed. "I thought you had left me here all by myself. But I knew"—she paused and cast her eyes downward in a shy manner—"you would just have to come back here, to me, and to our meadow—I mean—this place." Her sparkling violet eyes traveled over the meadow and then back up to his face.

Nachae remained unmoving, his face straight and without emotion. It was not in his nature to show his feelings to others. But at this moment, his insides were exploding. It seemed impossible, yet somehow she had already known about him, and this meadow—his secret meadow—but how could that be possible? He had discovered this meadow nearly ten harvests ago, right after Grandfather had first told him about his prophecy for Nachae's future with the violet-eyed woman. Many times through the years, he had come up here to contemplate his life, and not once had he encountered another living person. This place had been his escape during his worst times of trial and despair, and his haven whenever he just needed to gaze upon the beauty of Usen's fantastic creation. He had brought this woman up here after he had taken her from the soldiers yesterday, because he knew it was the only place where he could ever hope to sort out all the new complications she had brought into his life. Now he realized that bringing her to his secret mountaintop had only added to his perplexity. It appeared that she felt the same mystical aura about this meadow as he always had—and she referred to it as "our place."

He had a sudden urge to ask her what she had meant by her remarks, yet fear kept him from doing so. What if she confirmed his growing suspicions? How could he ever hope to corral the feelings he refused to admit to if there was a greater plan than the one he could control with his mortal actions? Another rush of panic overcame him, and caused his blood to grow hot within his veins. He kicked Eagle in the sides and moved forward, back into the center of the clearing. He attempted to erase the turbulent thoughts from his mind as he dropped his long legs down to the ground. From the leather pouch that was suspended by a long strap across his broad chest, he produced a dead squirrel for their breakfast.

Regina quickly searched the ground for dry kindling, then approached him with a handful of wood for the fire. When she placed the twigs and bark at his side, he acknowledged her gesture by glancing up toward the sky—the Apache sign for "thank you." Although Regina knew absolutely nothing about Apache mannerisms, she sensed that he was grateful for her small contribution. A timid smile lit up her face with a rosy glow and danced through her violet eyes, while Nachae's heart turned over in his breast.

He continued to work on the fire until it was ablaze and the small squirrel was roasting over a rude twig spit, filling the glen with its appetizing aroma. Regina's mouth watered as she waited for her share of the animal, but she sat patiently at the Indian's side and tried not to act greedy. She studied him out of the side of her eye while he tended to their meal. The powerful muscles contracted in his back as he turned the spit over, and a light sheen of perspiration coated his smooth skin. She knew she should be scared to death of him, but all she could think of was the magnificence of his beautiful body. And the way he made her feel inside was twice as unnerving. She wished he could talk to her, but she guessed that he did not understand English since he had never showed any real response to anything she had said to him. She did not know any Apache or Spanish so there did not seem to be much hope of communicating with him by conversation.

She blushed a deep shade of red when he shook a piece of the meat before her face. She had been so engrossed with her observation of his masculine form that she had not noticed when he had cut a portion of the meat off the spit for her to eat. With shaking hands, she reached out and took the food from his extended fingers. She had never eaten squirrel meat before, but she was too hungry to care what he was offering to her as long as it was edible. She knew he had caught her scrutinizing observation of his barely clad body and the color in her already reddened cheeks deepened when she chanced another glance in his direction through the thick fringe of her raven lashes.

"Thank you," she mumbled. Then she remembered his gesture when she had brought him the firewood earlier. She glanced up toward the sky and quickly lowered her eyes back to the ground.

Nachae suppressed the impromptu smile that threatened to claim his mouth. Her curiosity with his body was evident, and disturbing as it was, he was quite pleased with her obvious approval. But he was especially touched by her imitation of the Apache gesture for expressing her gratitude. A sense of pride filled him as he thought of how he would teach her all the Apache ways once they reached the village. He was especially anxious to talk to Grandfather about the dreams she had spoken of, and to learn if they held a significant meaning in the entanglement of their lives.

He sat down opposite her, watching her devouring the meager breakfast he had prepared, and tried to deny the intense attraction he felt for this young woman. Maybe he could not avoid his fate in meeting her, and it might not be possible to keep her out of his life from now on, but there was one promise Nachae had made to himself after his long night of indecision: He would never allow himself to make love to her—never!

Regina sighed and glanced at the empty spit with a look of disappointment. She had not eaten at all the day before and she was still famished. Not wanting to appear ungrateful, however, she tried not to let on about her hunger, but her deprived look was picked up by Nachae at once. He looked down at the greasy piece of meat he still held in his hand. For some reason, he no longer felt hungry.

"Oh, I—I couldn't," she stammered with a negative shake of her head when he offered his chunk of meat to her. He pushed it toward her and gave his head a firm nod. Regina swallowed hard, hoping he was not growing angry with her again. "Well, all right. Thank—" She stopped and raised her eyes up to the sky again.

An unexpected smile came to rest upon his lips when their eyes met for just an instant. How long had it been since he had found a simple joy in life for no particular reason? He couldn't even recall the last time.

Regina had no idea what had aroused the tender look upon his usually stern countenance, but she was relieved to know he was not upset with her. Without thinking, she leaned forward and began to talk to him as if he could understand every word she spoke to him. "Oh Nachae, you should smile more often. You've got a wonderful smile. I've never seen you smile before, not even in my dreams."

His spine stiffened, and the smile faded from his face. Once again, she talked of having dreams that involved him, but what did these dreams mean? And she had just spoken his Apache name as if she had known him forever. How did she know who he was—and since she did seem to know him, why was she not afraid of him? The mere

99

mention of his name was usually enough to inspire terror in the heartiest of men. This young woman's lack of fear aggravated the fierce warrior even more than her talk of dreams. Nachae decided that he must talk to Grandfather as soon as possible. But until the old shaman could explain all these mysteries to him, Nachae realized that he would have to work extremely hard at keeping his emotions under a tight rein. That would not be an easy task. Already, this woman had walked across his well-guarded heart, and in doing so, she had exposed his very soul.

He motioned for her to eat the rest of her meal with a brisk wave of his arm. Regina fell silent, cursing inwardly at herself for making him angry with her once again. Maybe it was an Apache custom not to talk during a meal, but how was she to know what he wanted her to do? She choked down the meat, although she did not really feel hungry anymore. From now on, she told herself, she would not speak unless he told her to do so.

While she finished the last of the squirrel meat, Nachae kicked dirt over the hot coals of the fire. It was imperative that they return to the village as soon as possible so that he could talk to his grandfather about the dreams she continually mentioned. With haste, he gathered up his few belongings and shoved them in the leather bags that he carried across his horse's back. Regina stood by, feeling helpless yet afraid to do anything that would anger him again.

He pointed at his horse with a sharp gesture. Immediately, she began to move toward the large animal. With a dark glare upon his face, Nachae followed her. He did not hesitate once they reached the stallion, and Regina could tell that he had suddenly grown impatient to leave this meadow. Placing his large hands around her waist, he lifted her onto the animal then swung up behind her. Even in his anxious state, though, he paused as they both glanced around at the little clearing before he pulled on the reins and swung his horse around. Regina didn't know where he was taking her, or what he planned to do with her, but knew she would be back here—someday. She glanced up at the man and saw a strange expression upon his broodingly handsome face. Did he sense it too?

As the horse began to move through the trees, Regina sat straight and tense on the animal's back. How could this man affect her so? There was not one inch of her skin that did not tingle, her heart was pounding like a sledge-hammer, and her blood had turned to smoldering fire . . . just because his nearly naked body was rubbing against her backside as they rode together on his horse. She tried to remind herself that she was in the company of the man who was responsible for the death of many soldiers and innocent white people, and also for the captivity of her father's fiancée.

However, it was hard to think of him as a savage killer when he was treating her with such kindness. They had not gone far when he reached around her and lifted up one of her arms. He pushed aside the torn shreds of her white blouse and observed the injuries on her tender skin. The long scratches and cuts she had obtained during her useless escape attempt had begun to fester and now were swollen with infection. Nachae halted his horse and dismounted, then dug in his buckskin bag until he located another small pouch. From this bag, he took out a handful of crushed leaves. Regina watched in complete fascination as he chewed on the leaves, then rubbed the moist vegetation over her arms. She had no idea what type of leaves he was using, or what medicinal purpose they served, but they took the stinging sensation out of her cuts within seconds after he was finished doctoring her arms. Once again she bashfully glanced up toward the sky. He nodded his head and his solemn expression visibly softened for a moment before he mounted the horse and headed them back down the mountain.

They traveled at a steady pace, but compared to the harsh riding they had done the day before, this journey seemed almost leisurely. Regina, having decided that it was a wasted effort to worry about where he was taking her, spent her time taking in the beauty of the land which they traveled across. Several times during the day, Nachae pointed toward the majestic mesas or motioned for her to observe a fleeing antelope or jack rabbit. But not once did he make any attempt to speak to her. Regina longed to converse with him about the wondrous sights he was showing her if only to hear the sound of his voice, but she decided it would be best if she remained silent. He usually became angry whenever she did try to talk to him.

They left the dense forest behind them by midday, moving into gently rolling foothills that were adorned with crooked little trees that reminded Regina of crippled old men. By evening they had entered the desert region, which was a far cry from the lush green mountain where they had been earlier that day. The golden mesas, with their colorful array of tall cactus and desert foliage, were every bit as awe-inspiring to Regina as the dangerous man whose arms held her in their tight embrace. This land was a part of him, and now she was under its hypnotizing spell too. She realized that she had returned to her birthland to find her destiny . . . she had found Nachae.

As the sun began to rest its final rays upon the craggy peaks of the westerly hilltops, the blue sky became a pallet of wispy shades of pink and purple. The pale gold sand grew shaded and eerie, lending itself to the impending nightfall with a hushed silence that closed over the land like a giant seal of secrecy.

Nachae halted Eagle beside the rocky slope of a hillside, which was dotted with an occasional clump of sage, and dismounted. When he lifted Regina down beside him, he began to motion toward the sunset with an exaggerated sweep of his arm, then he pointed excitedly at her eyes. For an instant, words hovered on his tongue, but he stopped himself from speaking. Allowing her to believe that he could not talk in her tongue was easier than telling her otherwise. He was not yet ready to engage in a conversation about their strange affinity.

A timid smile curved Regina's lips. Confusion drew her black brows together and caused her lips to pucker slightly as she continued to stare at the distant horizon. "I'm not sure what you're trying to tell me."

Nachae hesitated briefly before he pointed at the sky again and back at her eyes. What was it about her lips that constantly reminded him of a softly outlined heart? Ignoring the slow ache that traced through his limbs, he peered down at her as he held his outstretched hand up toward the faraway hilltops and drew his arm through the air. Regina concentrated on the area he was gesturing at for a few moments longer before she realized that the comparison he was trying to point out to her was in the colors in the setting sun.

"My eyes," she said enthusiastically as she motioned with her own hand toward the purpled sunset and then back to her own eyes. "You're trying to tell me that my eyes are the same shade as the sunset?" A small smile teased Nachae's lips as gave his head a firm nod.

"That's lovely," Regina said in a voice filled with tenderness. For the first time in her life, she began to feel a special pride in the unusual shade of her violet gaze. She turned to stare up at the fading pink and violet hues of the desert sky. How could a man who would observe something so beautiful be the brutal killer that he was accused of being? Perhaps he had not done all the terrible deeds that the soldiers at Fort Bowie had placed upon him, she thought with a fleeting hope.

The evening passed quickly by the time they had eaten a light supper of corncakes, along with a strong concoction of black tea that Nachae had brewed over their small fire. Regina was exhausted, and after he had tended to her wounded arms once more, she eagerly accepted the thin woolen blanket he spread out upon the ground. Without any qualms about spending another night in the presence of her savage captor, she casually stretched her weary body out upon the meager bed, and was sound asleep in no time.

Nachae reclined back against the base of the rocky incline where they were camped, and once again observed her while she slept. This young woman's attitude toward him—and his abduction of her—was a complete mystery to him. It was more than obvious that she held no real fear toward him, and it was impossible for Nachae to treat her with any sort of hostility—even though she was supposed to be his enemy. He had to fight himself to remain aloof.

He leaned over until he was within touching distance of her sleeping form. Gently, so as not to awaken her, he ran his fingertips along the outline of her soft cheek. A shiver ran up the length of his arm and did not stop until it had raced throughout his whole body. He did not know her white name, but it did not matter. Tonight he had chosen his own name for her.

"From this day forward," he whispered to her inattentive ears, "you shall be called Sky Dreamer, of the Chiricahua Apaches."

Traveling together—with her riding in his arms—seemed the most natural thing in the world. She felt relaxed in his presence as she reclined back comfortably against his bare chest. It was all Nachae could do to keep his mind off the thoughts that tugged unmercifully at his mind. But he had made his vow: He would protect her and teach her the ways of his people, yet he would never allow himself to make love to her. He would be like her big brother—and nothing more! However, in just two days' time, that decision was already proving to be the greatest test he had ever put himself through. For at least the tenth time since they had started riding this morning, his yearning mind was repeating his vow of restraint when they rode up a cedar-infested incline.

A thick black spiral of smoke, which emitted a putrid stench, immediately filled their nostrils. A feeling of death hung heavy in the air even before they crested the ridge. At once, Nachae knew he had made a gross mistake by allowing her to see the ruins of the smoldering farmhouse. He could tell from the look on her face that her fear and hatred for his people had just returned with renewed intensity.

He pulled on Eagle's reins and attempted to turn away

from the scene, but Regina slid beneath his arms without warning and fell from the horse's back. Regaining her balance after she thudded against the ground, she began to stumble forward until she reached the edge of the embankment. She clasped a hand over her mouth and fought to hold down the bile she felt rising up in her dry throat when she looked down at the sight before her.

Among the blackened ashes of the farmhouse were the unmistakable charred remains of two people. Beside the ghostly black frame of what had once been a barn was sprawled the naked body of an elderly man. He was riddled with arrows like a chartered map with feathered pins to designate grotesque locations. Buzzards circled above the scalped head of the corpse, their eyes puffy and their claws extended, waiting—calculating—their anticipated descent to the dead flesh below.

Nachae dropped from Eagle's back and stood beside Regina. He wished he could have spared her this added horror. She had already been through so much pain in the past week's time. Yet he knew that her life with the Teneh Chockenen would never be easy once they reached the Apache rancheria. She would be faced with this type of deadly reality every day of her life. He glanced down at the ruins of the white settlement and sighed heavily. The attack on this family was not nearly as devastating as some of the raids that the soldiers had led against whole villages of Apaches. But how could he ever explain such injustices to this woman at this time? Nachae knew it would be impossible to make her understand the evil that ruled over this untamed land—this was something she must witness for herself.

Without any thought to his actions, Nachae gently reached out and placed his arm around her trembling shoulders. His touch sent shards of ice shooting through Regina's body. The past several days she had been so blinded by his imitation of kindness toward her that she had permitted herself to forget—and forgive—the type of heathens his people were capable of producing. But the sight of the dead farmers and the smoldering ashes of what had once been their home brought back the remembrance of the pain her father had suffered when he had discovered that his fiancée had been taken captive by this savage's band of renegades. She recalled the face of every dead soldier she had looked upon since her arrival in this unfeeling place, and she began to despise this man—and everything he represented—with renewed vigor.

She reached up and pushed his arm from her shoulder. "Don't you ever lay your filthy hands on me again," she spat impulsively.

Nachae's eyes drew into two narrowed slits; he had seen the same look on other members of her race a number of times before. Still, he had hoped that she would be immune to such prejudices. It made no difference to a Pinda-Lixk-O-Ye what tribe was responsible for an attack on another white man. They inevitably blamed the whole Indian race. By a glance, Nachae could tell that his band of Chiricahua Apaches had not conducted this raid. The arrows that protruded from the dead man were from the Western Apache—northern neighbors of Nachae's band. But to this woman, that was of no importance, and he knew from past experiences with her people that it would do little good to tell her otherwise.

Regina was too mad, too sick, to notice the dangerous look upon his face as she began to run away from him. Before she had gone no more than a few feet, he lunged toward her and grabbed her arm. His fingers pressed into her injured skin when he pulled her up to him. She gasped with pain, but her face was covered with a mask of contempt when she raised her chin up and met his cold look.

"I said don't you ever touch me, you—you—half-breed!"

Nachae felt the sharp words sear through his heart as bluntly as if she had plunged a knife into him. Fury blinded him with black contempt, making his grip on her arm grow tighter. At this instant, he was closer to fulfilling his original plan to kill her than he had ever been in any of his previous attempts.

The pain from his crushing hold on her arm made Regina unable to speak. Tears sprang to her eyes, but she refused to let them fall. She glared up into his darkening gray eyes for a period of time that seemed endless, until he finally began to ease up on his deathlike hold.

"I'm sorry I called you by that name," she choked out in breathless gasps. "But most of all, I'm sorry that I was beginning to trust you enough to think that your kind was capable of any sort of compassion and tenderness." She realized that he didn't understand a word she had just said to him, but she had to speak her mind, or risk losing her sanity. When he replied in a voice that was filled with as much animosity as her own, she nearly fainted from the shock.

"And do you also feel sorry for the helpless Indian women and children who are slaughtered by the soldiers while they sleep in their homes? And what of the old ones—the ones who cannot even attempt to outrun the long knives of the White-Eyes? Tell me, white woman"—he spat out the title with a bitter taste upon his tongue—"will you ever grieve for my people when your kind has wiped every last Apache from the face of this earth?" He held her by her arms and shook her until she cried out in agony.

His perfect English had stunned her, but his words had reached down into her soul. Her father's voice drifted through her mind: ". . . the selfish annihilation of a whole race." Had her father tried to tell her the same horrible truth that Nachae had just forced her to hear? It was not possible that her father, or any of his men, could be so cruel as to attack unsuspecting women and children while they slept.

"You're lying!" she said with defiance.

Nachae released his grip from her arms and turned away. Every nightmare he had ever witnessed of mangled and mutilated women and children ran through his mind suddenly: his grandmother, who had been Eskinzan's first wife, his father's wife, Breeze of the Forest, and too many more. He recalled the unrecognizable body of his proud father, hanging limp upon a smoldering stake. And he thought of the man who had tricked his father into believing that his family would be safe in the protected area outside Fort Bowie, then had ambushed the slumbering Indians in the middle of the night.

There were so many things that could have prevented that massacre last year . . . but Captain Atwood had gone away to see his family in the South, leaving his command to Lieutenant Decker. Even Eskinzan had not been able to foresee the tragic ambush because he had been called away to tend to a sick child in the hill country. Nor had Nachae been present to witness the assassination of his relatives. Nachae had been in Mexico with a raiding party when the lieutenant's invitation to parley at the fort had been delivered to his family, and he had returned later, only to discover that everyone except his grandfather had perished in the carnage. A hundred times or more, Nachae had plotted the death of the man responsible for the murders, and he lived for the day when he would take his revenge.

He turned back around and looked down at the terrified face of the young white woman. There was no way for him to prove to her that he was not lying about her people's treatment of the Apaches. He wished it wasn't so, but he knew that someday she would see what her own kind were capable of doing to anyone who did not conform to their precise laws. When that day came, he would forgive her for the things she had just said in her anger and ignorance—and with every fiber of his being, he would help her to accept the hellish truth.

Chapter Nine

The Apache rancheria, like the mountain meadow, was exactly as Regina had pictured it in her dreams. Even the faces of the Indians with their dark piercing eyes looked familiar to her. It was almost as though she had been here before, but of course, she reminded herself, it was only in her dreams that she had glimpsed this alien region.

In the late afternoon, when they entered the village, the women were still busy tending to their chores: never-ending drudgery for the Indian women, who carried the whole work load of preserving and cooking the food, tanning hides, sewing clothes, and caring for their children. Even when the village was relocated for the change of seasons, it was the women who disassembled the wickiups, transported all their families' belongings, and rebuilt their homes at the new living site. A man's work was to provide meat and protection for his family.

Nachae's arrival with another white captive was received with great interest — especially among the unmarried women in the village. Eskinzan's grandson, though temperamental and brooding at times, was the most sought-after warrior in the tribe. Not only was he an excellent provider, but it was rumored that he would soon be a powerful warlord among the Chiricahua tribe. His physical appearance, too, was an asset that could not be overlooked. With his long thick hair, which was so black it took on a bluish sheen, and his striking gray eyes that contrasted with his ebony lashes and smoothly tanned skin, he stood out among the other Apache braves. His mixed bloodline gave him his towering structure, and many years of conditioning for his rugged life-style had made his body lean and muscular.

Nachae led Eagle directly to his grandfather's wickiup, where Waddling Woman was concentrating on stirring a large pot of simmering vegetables. When the approaching horse caught her attention, she looked up from her cooking. A large, toothless grin converted her round face into a jigsaw puzzle of pudgy creases. *"Ciye,"* she cried out, dropping her long-handled spoon in the pot and rushing forward. She had affectionately referred to him as her son ever since the rest of his Apache family had been killed the previous year.

Nachae smiled down at the little woman. Her fifty years made her the youngest and most spirited of Eskinzan's two wives, and Nachae loved her unabashedly. Her long braids, still coal black without a trace of gray, fell over her hefty shoulders as her head slanted in a curious tilt so that her eyes could study the woman who shared Nachae's horse.

"This is the woman from Grandfather's vision," Nachae said in reply to Waddling Woman's questioning look. Before the older woman could speak, her husband came out of the wickiup.

Eskinzan walked as straight and proud as a man half his age. Only his silver hair and aging face hinted at his seventy-eight years. His black eyes sparkled when his gaze moved back and forth between the young woman and his grandson. Nachae did not have to tell him that the woman had already found her place in his grandson's heart— Eskinzan could tell by the look on the younger man's face. It was plain to see Nachae's turmoil was far from over, but the old shaman sensed that his headstrong grandson had finally accepted the fact that he was not capable of killing this woman, even though his whole life would change drastically because of her presence.

"This is the one, Grandfather," Nachae said quietly. "Her eyes are the same as the desert sky at sunset, just as you said they would be. And she has dreams that foretell of things which she has not yet seen or experienced. Because of these unusual traits, I have decided to call her Sky Dreamer."

Eskinzan's shock was apparent on his weathered face as his gaze returned to the young woman. She had not moved, and her face was solemn and white with a fear that she was unsuccessfully trying to conceal.

"Nadzeels?" he asked as he stepped toward Nachae's horse to peer up at her with a closer observation. Regina stared down at him and swallowed back the lump of terror that she felt rising in her throat. She had a feeling that this old man was someone who was very important among his people, and she wondered if her fate would be determined by him.

His gnarled hand motioned toward his wickiup. "Come, my grandson, tell me more about her *nadzeels*—these dreams you speak of." He turned and began to walk toward his wickiup, while continuing to voice his surprise. "In my visions I did not see this—I wonder why." At the doorway of the thatched house, he paused and turned to stare at Regina again. He shook his head and shrugged, then disappeared behind the animal hide which hung over the opening.

Nachae quickly dismounted, then lifted Regina down to the ground. His eyes traveled over Regina's upturned face as a small, almost invisible smile curved his full lips. Ever since her outburst at the farmhouse earlier that day, they had traveled the rest of the way to the village in complete silence. He was certain that the worst of her feelings toward his people had mellowed a great deal after she had taken the time to think about her rash words. Hoping this to be the case, and that she would not attempt to do something foolish, he gave his head a reassuring nod and turned away from her. To Waddling Woman he dispatched a rush of orders before following his grandfather into the wickiup.

Regina stood rooted to the spot, staring after him, too terrified to move. His comforting look did not dispel her

111

anxiety at being in the Apache village. She hadn't understood one word that was exchanged during the brief conversation between the warrior and the elderly couple, but it was evident they were talking about her. Had Nachae rushed off to discuss with the old man what they were planning to do with her now that he had brought her back to his village? she wondered with growing apprehension.

The short heavyset woman began to tug on the torn sleeve of Regina's blouse, while muttering something in the Apache tongue. Regina shook her head to indicate her lack of understanding, and the Indian woman added hand gestures to her words to convey her meaning.

Regina continued to shake her head as the woman motioned for her to follow her. A crowd of curious women and children had gathered to gawk at the newcomer and Regina found herself being probed by their inquiring eyes. As Waddling Woman led her through the onlookers, several children crudely pinched her arms and legs while Waddling Woman shouted and waved her arms in anger to shoo them away. The group reluctantly separated to allow the two women to pass, although Regina was still forced to endure the groping fingers of everyone who reached out to touch her hair and face as if she was some sort of oddity.

While they made their way through the crowd, Regina moved closer and closer to the fat little Apache woman. It seemed that this woman was her only protection against the rest of the women, and even the children, who did not seem overly happy to have a stranger in their midst.

Regina followed the older woman to the edge of the village, where they stopped at another wickiup, one that was much smaller than the one where Nachae had remained with the old man. The pounding of her heart intensified when Regina realized that this thatched house must belong to Nachae. She did not have time to ponder over the reason she was being brought here, though, because they had no sooner reached the house when a woman's very unfriendly voice called out to them.

Waddling Woman swung around to the familiar sound

and rolled her eyes upward in aggravation. *"Ugashe!* Go away before my *ciye* sees you making a fool of yourself again," she said to the other woman.

Llamarada was undaunted by the old woman's insult. Black diamonds flashed from her gaze as she glanced at Regina with a cruel scrape of her eyes. "How dare he bring another Pinda-Lixk-O-Ye here to belittle me." She waved her arms through the air in a display of rage. "To move one white woman into his wickiup was disgraceful enough, and now . . . this!" A haughty toss of her head swung her thick braids through the air as she motioned toward Regina with a wide swipe of her arm.

Regina's spine stiffened. She did not need to understand their strange language to know that this woman was a definite threat to her well-being. The Indian woman's brisk actions, along with the hate-filled look upon her pretty dark face, were all the evidence Regina needed to know that she had encountered her first real foe in the Apache village. Was this Nachae's woman? Regina wondered with a surge of jealousy in accompaniment.

"My God!"

Regina's heart rose to her throat as she twirled around to look for the woman whose voice had just rung out from the door of the wickiup. "Susan," Regina gasped. Her father's fiancée was almost unrecognizable with her blue dress in tattered rags upon her hunched-over body. Her once beautiful blond wavy hair hung in dark and oily tangles around her pale face. Regina rushed forward without hesitation and threw her arms around the other woman's neck. Susan clung to her in a deathlike grip, crying and babbling in Regina's ear. Susan's words, however, were lost to the roar of the commotion that surrounded them.

The sight of the two white women, whom Nachae had chosen to take into his wickiup over her, made Llamarada more furious than ever before. Her short fiery temper exploded, and only Waddling Woman's interference stopped her from lunging at them. Regina's attention was diverted away from Susan when she heard the older Indian screaming at the fiery-eyed woman.

113

Grabbing Regina's arm, Susan tried to pull Regina away as she said breathlessly, "Come into the hut, Regina. That young one is mean. She beats me and trips me every time the old one is not looking. Hurry, Regina!" Susan's voice was hysterical as she began to tug viciously on Regina's arm in an effort to get her to retreat into the wickiup.

Susan's words and the obvious terror she felt toward the hateful Indian woman caused Regina's own anger to flare up. She had never been particularly fond of Susan, but she did not relish the idea of knowing that her father's intended wife was being mistreated either. Using more impulse than bravery, she effortlessly pushed Susan's trembling form aside and took a step forward.

A smirk claimed Llamarada's face when she noticed Regina move away from the doorway of the wickiup. This dark-haired one was not as weak as the woman with golden hair, Llamarada thought, as she shoved Waddling Woman out of her way with one forceful gesture. She could not wait to put the newcomer in her place and, at the same time, prove to Nachae how much stronger she was than either one of his sniveling white women. It mattered little to Llamarada that Nachae would be outraged if he knew she had disobeyed his adopted grandmother—she would worry about that later.

Regina's knees buckled for an instant as the Indian woman walked her way. Her stomach suddenly developed a knot that threatened to double her over with fear. She had never fought another person in her entire life, and to her horror, she realized that she was going to have to fight this crazed woman or be reduced to a groveling coward as Susan had during her captivity in the Apache camp. Though neither choice seemed very appealing, the latter was definitely not in Regina's nature. She would fight if she must. But much to her own aggravation, she wondered if she was going to battle for her own dignity or was Nachae the reason behind this driving force to have control over the other woman? For her own honor, Regina would gladly fight. However, if winning Nachae's admiration was also part of the reward, she would not stop until the victory was hers.

"Regina, what in God's name are you doing?" Susan cried. Slinking farther into the shelter of the wickiup, she added, "That heathen will kill you."

Regina trembled visibly, yet she did not back down. Her violet eyes drilled into the dark eyes of the Indian woman without wavering. For a reason which was unknown to Regina, this woman was trying to frighten her into the same frame of mind that Susan had retreated into, and Regina was determined not to allow it to happen. Behind her, Regina could hear Susan screaming, begging her to run into the hut, but she forced herself to concentrate on the movements of the Apache woman. She was not even aware of Waddling Woman's frantic retreat to go for help.

Instinctively, Regina began to pace in a circle in the same manner as the other woman was doing. With each stalking step they took, the women closed the short distance between them until they were no more than a few feet apart. A pounding in Regina's ears blocked out the shouts and taunts of the crowd who had gathered to watch the scuffle. Was Nachae somewhere among the crowd, too? She wanted to turn and see a look of reassurance on his dark handsome face, but there was not time. She was alone as she met this new challenge, even Susan had disappeared into the safety of the wickiup.

Llamarada made a wild lunge at Regina, hitting her full force in the abdomen and knocking her back onto the ground. A round of cheers rang out from the crowd. To best a White-Eyes in any sort of contest was pure enjoyment to the Apaches. Regina gasped as she tried to catch her breath from the hard fall, but the other woman was upon her again before Regina knew what was happening. She thudded back against the unyielding earth once more, feeling the last of the air rushing from her lungs. Certain that she was about to be killed by this mad woman, Regina felt all hope drain from her aching body when the Indian woman leaped upon her still form and issued a victorious cry as she pulled her knife from the sheath which hung from her belt.

Regina saw the flash of the shiny blade in front of her face and for an instant was too stunned to think. When her mind began to function again, she realized again that this woman had every intent to kill her. The feel of Nachae's knife against her throat reclaimed her mind, and a resurgence of energy rushed into her limp body. She had not been ready to die then, and she was not going to accept defeat this time either. Her whole body bolted upward, while she used every ounce of power in her arms to push the woman away from her.

Llamarada had been basking in her triumph and was not prepared for the white woman's sudden retaliation. She was certain the battle was over and that she was the winner. With a startled cry, she flipped over onto her back as Regina sprang to her feet. Both of the women's gazes were drawn to the bone-handled knife which had been flung into the dirt during the scuffle and was now lying beside Llamarada's head. In unison, they lunged toward the weapon, knowing the possession of that knife meant the difference between life and death.

Regina's nails dug into the dirt as her hand touched the smooth tan handle. She felt the other woman's hand clamp down on hers in an attempt to regain the knife, but Regina clasped her fingers tighter around the handle. The women rolled over, their bodies smashing into one another as they continued to tumble across the ground, struggling for control of the weapon. They came to a stop at the feet of the crowd, who watched and cheered them on as the spectators scooted back to give the two women more room to fight. The chanting of the crowd grew louder with the intensity of the fight, while they shouted Llamarada's name, urging her to kill the hated enemy who did not belong there.

Llamarada was on top when they finally stopped rolling, yet Regina still did not surrender the weapon to her. Her ears were deaf to the shouts of the people around them — only her strong will to survive was left in her weakening body. Her fingers trembled around the handle of the knife, while the Indian woman continued to try to

116

pry it from her hands. Regina's head rolled back and her eyes fluttered upward. One image among the sea of dark, jeering faces caught her attention. Why didn't he help her? she thought in despair when her wavering vision spotted the tall warrior standing at the edge of the crowd. Was this his plan all along—to bring her here to his village so that this crazy woman could finish the job that he could not do?

Nachae watched the two women fight with the greatest distress he had ever experienced. If he were to stop them now, Llamarada would never be satisfied until she had taken her revenge on the white woman. Until then, Sky Dreamer would never be safe from the other woman's wrath. He had to allow them to fight without interfering, but he also knew that if Llamarada killed the white woman, he would not hesitate to sever Llamarada's life either. His heart twisted in his chest as he stared at his Sky Dreamer's pleading face when he noticed her looking up at him, but he could do nothing to help her. He silently began to pray to Usen that she would be granted the strength to fight off the evil attack from Llamarada, even though he feared his prayers were useless. It was doubtful that the slender young white woman would be any match for the well-conditioned Llamarada—still he did not allow that to stop him from saying another desperate prayer.

Regina tore her eyes away from his face. He was not going to help her, but that realization served only to refuel her desire to win. She would show him that she did not need his help, and she would prove to this savage female that she was not so easy to kill. Like a cornered animal who suddenly makes one last desperate attempt to survive, Regina jerked her arm forward and used every muscle in her body to propel the other woman's weight from her body.

Llamarada screamed from shock as she flew backward and lost her grip on the knife. The full cotton skirt the Indian woman was wearing foiled her attempt to regain her footing when she accidentally stepped on the hem. She tripped and landed face first in the dirt. Regina, still wearing her split brown riding skirt, moved with determined ease and used Llamarada's clumsiness to her own advantage. With frantic speed she charged at the Indian and flung herself upon Llamarada's sprawling form. Loose dirt rose up from the dry ground like a bellow from hell when Regina's weight crashed down against the other woman. She was blinded by the cloud of dust for a moment, but she did not let it falter her renewed instinct to survive.

Her eyes burned and she could feel the grains of sand coating her tongue and threatening to choke her as she grabbed one of the long braids that hung over the Indian woman's shoulders. She yanked the woman's head back with one hand, and with her other hand, she positioned the knife against Llamarada's exposed neck.

There was not time to contemplate the animalistic sensations which were pulsating through her blood until Susan's ghastly wail snapped Regina from her savage trance. When she realized how close she was to executing this woman who was at her mercy, Regina's hand began to shake so violently that the knife pierced Llamarada's tender skin. A trickle of blood ran down the side of the woman's neck and disappeared into the loose brown earth beneath her unmoving form.

Susan's screams pounded in Regina's ears until she was certain her mind was about to snap. A quivering gasp flew from Regina when she looked at the blood that was trailing down the side of the Indian woman's neck. Regina knew that she could have easily killed this woman in her mindless rage—an instant ago, she had envisioned the knife slicing into the woman's flesh. A sick feeling engulfed her whole being as she slowly released her grip on the woman and rose to her feet. Her legs still straddled Llamarada's body as she stared in horror at the tip of the bloodstained knife in her hand. She threw the weapon to the ground as if it had suddenly begun to burn the flesh from her hand. The knife fell into the dirt beside Llamarada's stiff body, while an eerie hush fell over the crowd of onlookers. Even Susan, whose shrieking had drowned out almost all the other shouts, was now deathly quiet.

Regina's gaze sought out the face of Nachae among the crowd. But even before she had located him, he was standing beside her. He bent over and retrieved the knife from the ground and held the weapon out toward Regina. Her confused eyes moved from his emotionless face and back down to the knife that rested in his extended hand. She focused her gaze on the thin red line of blood that had already dried upon the blade from the heat of the afternoon sun. Her thoughts grew more muddled as she wondered what he expected her to do now.

He shook the knife at her then pointed down at Llamarada, who still had not moved from her facedown position on the ground. Regina's eyes followed his hand, unable to decipher his command. Giving into her confusion, Regina stepped over the woman's body and began to back away. Nachae reached out and grabbed her, pulling her back to Llamarada's side.

"You must kill her," he demanded in English, emphasizing his words with a sharp wave of the knife in front of his own throat.

Regina gasped in disbelief. "I—I can't!" Nachae shoved the knife at her, but she cringed away from him and shook her head wildly from side to side.

"If you do not kill her, she will be forced to live in shame. She will never be able to hold her head up proudly in our village again." His sooty gray eyes narrowed as he leaned closer to Regina and added, "It is your duty to allow her to die an honorable death."

Regina couldn't believe her ears, yet she had no doubt that had the situation been reversed, the Apache woman would not have hesitated to slice her throat with the knife. . . . But that woman was a savage! Regina reminded herself that she was not like these murderous animals; she would never stoop to their level and take the life of another human being. She jerked free of Nachae's enslaving grip and took another step backward. Her eyes never left the face of the tall warrior as her spinning mind

119

tried to prepare itself for his reaction. Had she fought for her life only to be slain because she had been the victor?

A low murmuring began to circulate through the crowd as the Indians began to walk away. Within minutes, the sounds of the drums and the voices of the villager's guttural singing filled the air once again as their celebration resumed. Nachae's expression unexpectedly softened as his eyes met with Regina's frightened gaze. He acted as if it was difficult to look away from her when he finally tore his eyes from her haunting expression. His long straight hair fell over the side of his solemn face as he turned and looked down at Llamarada. In a casual gesture he dropped the knife down beside her head and stepped toward Regina.

Llamarada's eyes focused on the weapon as she slowly began to rise up onto her knees. Without looking at anyone, she retrieved her knife and stood up.

Regina started to move toward her, to tell her that she would not hold a grudge, but Nachae grabbed her again. The silent look of warning that filtered into his face made Regina grow numb with foreboding. Her mouth felt dry and she almost felt as though she might gag as she cast her uncertain gaze down to the ground.

Llamarada began to lumber away from the spot where she had suffered defeat and shame. Her departure seemed to go unnoticed by everyone in the village. Not one person acknowledged her presence, or spoke to her when she passed. Like a wounded dog, she hung her head and disappeared through the maze of wickiups.

Regina looked back up at Nachae with a desperate plea upon her young face. Why couldn't he explain it all to her? She felt guilty because she had fought for her life and won. All the other mysteries of her recent past began to jumble into her thoughts, making her head pound. She did not understand these strange people or this brutal land, nor could she comprehend why she felt it was so essential that she learn to understand them.

The sound of him speaking in his Apache tongue to Waddling Woman snapped Regina's thoughts back to the present. His speech held an urgent tone, and when he gestured toward Regina, she knew that he was talking about her again. Beyond feeling anything other than numb confusion, Regina dutifully followed the older woman to the wickiup. She glanced back toward Nachae before entering the hut, but he was already walking away.

Only a dim light filtered through the thick brush which covered the frame of the little thatched house. Regina had to pause for a moment to allow her eyes to readjust to the contrast from the bright glare outside as she glanced around at the interior of the barren hut. She spotted Susan standing against one wall and started to move toward her. More than anything else right now, she needed to feel close to Susan. It was apparent that they were the only white women in the village, so Regina felt that it was imperative for the two of them to form a close bond. When she held out her arms, though, Susan's cold voice stopped her from continuing any further.

"Well, that certainly was a touching display." Susan's grimy face became a chilling mask of contempt.

Regina's lips trembled as she fought to hold back the tears which were very close to surfacing in her eyes. "What are you talking about? I was fighting for both of us."

A forced chuckle flew from Susan's mouth. "You fought like one of those heathens out there and—and then—" Her voice grew haughty with a toss of her tangled mane of dirty blond hair. "When that . . . buck came up to you, well, the way you looked at him made it quite obvious that the two of you are on very friendly terms." She emphasized her meaning with a suggestive raise of her mink-colored eyebrows.

"You're wrong," Regina retorted in a tone of disbelief. "He has not touched me. As a matter of fact, he has been extremely kind to me."

"Kind?" Susan's head flung back with a crude laugh. "These savages don't know how to treat someone with kindness. If he acts any differently toward you, I'm sure that it's because you have lifted your dainty little skirts and—"

"How dare you accuse me of stooping to something so low," Regina cut in sharply as she took a step forward. All the reasons she had come to despise her father's fiancée in the past few months came flooding back to her. The look of fury on her face caused Susan to recoil in defense, although it did not halt her scathing voice.

"Are you going to fight me, too?" Susan spat out hatefully while she backed against the wall of the primitive hut. "Why, if I didn't know better, I'd swear you had become one of them." Her icy blue eyes darted over to Waddling Woman with a loathing glance.

Regina's gaze moved toward the short Indian woman, who observed them with a worried frown on her round face. Something twisted in Regina's breast and caused her heart to ache. Why did she feel such compassion for these people when she should feel as contemptuous as Susan felt?

"I'm sorry, Susan. I only fought that woman because I thought it would help our situation."

Susan continued to glare at her, but her cold expression began to fade slightly. She did not have a chance to discuss it any further, however, because Waddling Woman started to wave her arms about and talk rapidly in her native tongue. The older woman completely ignored Susan, while she directed all her attention at Regina. She bent over and pulled a colorful skirt and blouse from a stack of blankets and clothing that stood in one corner, then she held the garments out to Regina.

"Don't take them," Susan ordered. "She tried to make me wear them too, but I refused to touch their filthy rags."

Regina glanced at the clothes and sighed. They appeared to be clean and in much better condition than her own dirty and tattered clothes, but she did not wish to anger Susan again either. With a negative shake of her head, Regina refused the clothes the woman was offering.

Waddling Woman shrugged and replaced them on the pile. Then, still speaking to Regina as if she expected the girl to understand her every word, she began to usher her out of the wickiup. Regina had only enough time to glance over her shoulder at Susan as the Indian woman grabbed her arm and pulled her through the low-hanging flap in the doorway. As they departed from the wickiup, Susan suddenly became alarmed.

"Oh Regina," she gasped as she followed them through the hide-covered opening. "I hope you won't be punished for fighting with that savage." A terrible fear passed through Susan when she realized that she would be left here alone again if Regina should be killed or tortured. Even her fiancé's daughter would be a comfort in this hellish hole, Susan decided as the other two women disappeared from view.

Chapter Ten

Once again, Regina stumbled along behind Waddling Woman with no idea where she was going or what would happen next. She was too worried about the next phase of her introduction to this strange place to notice that no one seemed overly curious about her anymore as she followed the other woman back through the rancheria.

She swallowed her fear when she noticed that the woman had taken her back to the same large wickiup where they had stopped when they had first entered the village. Before she had time to wonder why she had been brought here again, the hide was pushed aside from the entry and Nachae leaned through the doorway. His eyes grated over Regina's trail-worn attire, then flashed angrily toward Waddling Woman. The older woman shrugged and turned her attention to the pot of stew that was simmering over the fire. A deep frown burrowed across Nachae's face as he motioned for Regina to enter the hut. She moved slowly toward him. Visions of the grotesque tortures she had heard at the fort were spinning through her mind when she leaned down and walked into the wickiup. At any second, she almost expected to be tied to a stake and burned alive, or stripped of her clothes and tied to a tree, then riddled with arrows—or worse!

Unlike the small and nearly empty hut where Susan had remained, this big wickiup almost held a welcoming sort of comfort. Soft brown furs covered the dirt floor, and colorful blankets decorated the walls. Several vibrantly painted shields adorned the rest of the space and leaning against one wall were a couple of long feathered lances. A hole in the ceiling of the thatched structure invited the afternoon sunlight into the interior and made the primitive dwelling seem bright and cheery. Even the old man who sat cross-legged in the center of the room did not appear as frightening in here as he had when Regina first saw him standing outside the wickiup.

"This is my grandfather," Nachae said with a proud twinkle in his eye. "He has granted you permission to call him by his name—he is Eskinzan, the most powerful medicine man in our tribe."

Regina's gaze moved timidly toward the old man as she gave her head a slight nod. It was obvious that he was an extremely prominent man in the village, and Regina felt intimidated just being in his presence.

"Come, sit here," he said in English while he motioned to a spot beside him among the furs.

Regina was surprised that he, too, could speak her language, although he did not sound nearly as fluent as Nachae. She lowered herself down next to the old Indian, then glanced at Nachae. The tall warrior did not offer any explanations as he sat down opposite her, nor did his eyes ever leave the elderly man's face.

"My grandson tells me that you have seen him and parts of our land in your dreams." He leaned in her direction and asked in an inquisitive tone, "Will you tell me of these dreams?"

Regina was surprised that the Indian would be interested in her dreams, and she thought it was strange for Nachae even to mention them to his grandfather.

"Well," she said in a quivering voice, "there is—is really not much to tell." Without warning, she felt her cheeks grow hot and flushed. All of a sudden she wished that it was as dark in this hut as it had been in the other wickiup. How could she ever tell Nachae's grandfather about her sensuous dreams, especially when Nachae was sitting right here staring at her? Her eyes moved downward as she fought to keep from glancing in Nachae's direction, but she could not make her disobedient gaze do as she commanded. Much to her annoyance, she was confronted with an unmistakable expression of mirth, which danced in the depths of his glistening gray eyes. She did not recall telling him anything about the nature of her dreams, only that he was a part of them, and he couldn't read her mind—so why was he looking at her in that manner?

Eskinzan glanced at his grandson with a look of aggravation. "Should we talk of this alone?" he asked Regina.

"I do not wish to speak about my dreams," she replied with an upward tilt of her chin. She had no intention of telling either of them what her dreams entailed, particularly since Nachae was acting so smug.

Eskinzan sighed and relaxed his withered frame back against a pile of fur robes. She was stubborn—that was obvious by the expression upon her pretty face. And she had proven herself to be a good fighter when she had taken on the troublemaking Llamarada. These qualities pleased Eskinzan beyond measure. The woman from his visions was proving to be more than he had ever dared to hope. Just in the short time that this woman had come into the Apache territory, she had already made an improvement in his grandson's indifferent attitude, and Eskinzan had a feeling that she had only chipped the tip of the warrior's icy exterior.

The old shaman studied the girl closely for a few minutes, oblivious of her uneasiness as he watched her. He had seen her face many times in his mind, but something had eluded him, even in his visions . . . something that seemed vaguely familiar about her. However, the aging medicine man could not quite put his finger on the missing clue.

"You will tell me about the dreams later," he said with a definite shake of his silver-gray head. "Tell me about your life in the white man's world now."

"My life?" Regina asked, wondering why the details of her life should matter to this old medicine man. She glanced at Nachae and noticed that even he was staring at his grandfather with a questioning look. Taking another trembling breath, she looked back at the old man and shrugged. "I—I am Regina Atwood. My father is Captain Charles At—" she began. The loud gasp from the old man stopped her from continuing. Her own breath halted in her throat with another bout of fear. The elderly shaman sat up and pushed himself toward her until their faces were only inches apart.

"I should have known!" he exclaimed with an excited clap of his rough hands.

"What?" Regina cried out in alarm. Her frantic gaze darted toward Nachae, but he was staring at his grandfather with a bewildered expression that matched her own.

"Grandfather, what is it?" Nachae implored. The shaman rarely showed such exuberant emotion.

Eskinzan's aging face lit up with a wide smile that claimed his whole being. His dark eyes grew luminous as he continued to look at Regina. In her young face, he saw another young woman—one whose beauty was equally precious, a gifted young woman whose dreams were as unique as his own visions. Lucero—which meant Morning Star in the Mexican tongue—the beautiful Apache maiden who had lost her heart to the young trader named Charles Atwood.

The old man's thoughts echoed back in time as he recalled how the white man had first come to their village to trade his colored beads and cloth for buffalo hides. He remembered how Lucero and the young trader had fallen in love almost from their first glance at one another. And his heart still ached when he thought of how the dreaded white man's sickness, smallpox, had stolen her life away.

He shook his head in wonderment as his dark eyes continued to study the girl before him. All those harvests ago, when Charles Atwood had told him that he was taking his baby daughter away after Lucero's death, Eskinzan had asked Charles to allow him to adopt the little girl so that she could grow up among her mother's people. But Charles had said she would be better off with his family, and since the trader was the only white man whom the shaman had ever trusted completely, he agreed. However, it had almost broken the old man's heart to think that the little girl had been taken away from her birth land, and had also given up all of her Apache heritage. Even when Charles Atwood had returned to Apacheria as a soldato—a soldier in the hated white man's army—Eskinzan still found that Charles Atwood was a man of his word. Among the various Indian tribes it was well known that Captain Atwood was one of the few white men who understood the plight of the Apache people, and always did whatever was in his power to help their declining situation.

Through the years, Eskinzan had often thought of the little dark-haired girl whose mother undoubtedly would have been a great Apache shaman had she lived. But each time he thought about her, he reminded himself that she was being raised in a land which was far removed from her mother's people—and her life was that of a white woman. It was rare that he would speak to Charles Atwood about the girl's progress in her new home, because the memory of her mother was still painful for either of them to talk about. So much time had passed since Lucero's daughter had been taken away that long ago Eskinzan had resigned himself to the fact that he would probably never see the girl again.

Now he could not help staring at her in awe. But he also felt very ignorant for not recognizing her in his visions. As an infant, her eyes had already been an unusual shade of blue intermingled with lavender, and in growing older, the purple hue had become more predominant until there was not a trace of blue in her startling violet eyes.

Eskinzan's chuckle broke the silence which had prevailed throughout the hut, and his eyes moved back and forth between Regina and Nachae. How fitting it was that the woman from his vision would be Lucero's daughter. Surely his hardheaded grandson would find some comfort in knowing that the woman he was destined to spend his life with was also a half-breed—half white and half

128

Apache. The old man rocked back against the robes and continued to smile broadly, revealing a mouth that was missing several teeth.

"Lucero's little girl has come home to her Apache family," he said with an excited light in his eyes.

Regina shook her head, growing even more confused. Who, or what, was Lucero? And what did it have to do with her? She looked to Nachae for an answer, but he was just as dumbfounded.

"Lucero?" he repeated. He had heard his grandfather speak of an Apache woman called Lucero. Eskinzan had told him on several occasions that there had been only one other person among the Chiricahua whose powers had ever come close to matching his own, and she was a young woman called Lucero, or Morning Star.

"Grandfather, what does a dead Apache woman have to do with this white woman?"

Eskinzan, still grinning like an excited child, waved his bony arm toward Regina. "She is the daughter of Captain Atwood and Lucero. I should have known!"

Neither Nachae nor Regina could speak for a moment while Eskinzan's words sunk into their stunned minds. They both stared at the old man as he began to speak rapidly in broken English, lapsing at times into his Apache language. Since no one bothered to correct him, he rattled on in fragmented phrases of both tongues. In his animated speech, he told his captive audience of the great love affair between the young trader, Charles Atwood, and the Apache girl, Lucero. It was apparent how much Eskinzan had loved the young woman as he told them of her great ability to dream about the future with exact accuracy, and of his enthusiasm when instructing her in the ways of an Apache shaman once her mystical powers had become evident. He spoke of her marriage to the white trader, and of how the young couple had lived peacefully in the hills above the banks of the San Simon River. He reached over and hugged Regina as he talked about the joyous birth of their daughter, whom Charles Atwood had named Regina. But to the rest of the tribe she was known as One Who Smiles, because she was such a happy infant. He ended his tale with the tragic death of the beautiful medicine woman, telling them of how, afterward, the child was taken away by her father to live among his own race of people in a very distant land.

Regina hung on his every word as she tried frantically to fill in the gaps in his story, which were left because of his lapses into the Apache language. A part of her wanted desperately to dispute him, while another part of her knew that everything he said was the truth. All that he had just told them fit together too perfectly to be a lie. She thought about the many times when she had asked her father to tell her something more about her mother, but somehow he had always managed to avoid the issue. Even her grandparents knew nothing about their deceased daughter-in-law. Regina's father had told everyone virtually the same thing he had divulged to his daughter whenever he was pressed to talk about his dead wife: He had met her at a trading post in Arizona when he had come out West looking for adventure and excitement. His bride's name had been Linda, and she had died of smallpox when Regina was two years old, but then he would always say that he didn't want to talk about her anymore because it was still too upsetting.

A single tear formed in Regina's eye as she thought about the similarities in the old shaman's story and the version her father had told to his family in Georgia. The captain had not really lied to them; he had merely switched a few of the important facts around. He had not met his wife at a trading post, but they had met when he was trading goods with the Apaches. And the name "Linda" was an easy adaptation of the name "Lucero." But why hadn't he been able to tell anyone the truth about his Indian wife? When Eskinzan paused in his verbal trip through the past, Regina seized the opportunity to ask him that very question.

"I know what you're saying is the truth," she said quietly. Her pleading gaze cried out to the old man for an answer when she added, "But why didn't my father want

130

me to know about her?" The hut fell silent for a moment as each of them pondered over the vast array of reasons behind Charles Atwood's decision.

"I can answer that," Nachae finally said. His expression became distant, as though his mind had become clouded by another time and place. The dark look in his gray eyes took on a chilling undertone, which Regina had seen in their troubled depths several times since they had met. She sensed that whatever it was that aroused such turmoil in his soul would involve the future she had envisioned for the two of them.

"Because," he said in a sharp tone, "he chose to spare you from a life that he knew would be filled with hatred if he should allow you to grow up knowing about your true bloodline." He rose stiffly to his feet. In the low confines of the wickiup, it seemed that he was a towering giant. "Why did he ever permit you to return?" he added in a voice filled with anger and emotion.

Regina slowly stood up and faced him. She had to understand what it was that caused so much rage to surface within him, but her mind would not cooperate. All she could do was think about the mother she had never known—the mother whose life was suddenly so intertwined with her own. "But if he loved her, why did he feel it necessary to hide her memory from me?"

A cruel smirk curled Nachae's lips. "Even his love for your mother could not protect you from being branded a half-breed!" The last word sprang from his mouth like a deadly enemy. He stepped back as though he felt the need to escape from his own words. For an instant, his head dropped down to his chest in a gesture of defeat. His long ebony hair shaded his face from view as the reality of this new discovery hit him. A tremendous feeling of sorrow overcame the warrior when he thought of all the pain she would be forced to endure once it was made common knowledge that Captain Atwood's daughter was a "breed." He thought about his own mother and about his cruel upbringing at the El Flores Rancho. Since his first breath he had been conditioned for his displaced existence, but

131

how would Regina Atwood ever prepare herself for the prejudices that would be thrust upon her innocent being from this day forth?

His head slowly rose until his eyes met hers. On her face was a look of horror, one which had been put there by his harsh words. This violet-eyed woman had already broken through the heavy wall that guarded his heart from such strong devotion, and she had done so even before he had learned of her Apache heritage. It would be foolish for him to think that he could save her from all the heartbreak she would encounter in this selfish land where people were judged by the color of their skin, rather than by the person they were inside. But from this day forward and until his last breath, Nachae knew he would kill anyone who ever did anything to harm his beautiful Sky Dreamer!

Chapter Eleven

"This will be a good harvest," Juno said when the two men reined their horses on the rocky slope above the Apache village. It was late August, the month referred to as the Little Harvest. *Shii,* or summer, was nearing its end and after the next full moon—the Big Harvest—they would move their camp once again for the impending winter. Juno was correct about this being a good harvest, even though since the death of their chief, Cochise, the Chiricahua had been forced to move more often than usual in their attempt to elude the soldiers and the imprisonment of the white man's reservations.

In the flat expanse of barren ground below them, the Apache women toiled with their daily chores, unaware of the two men who observed them from the hillside. Juno's raven eyes sought out his own wickiup first. His home stood at the far edge of camp, beside Nachae's smaller thatched hut. A tender smile curved Juno's mouth when he spotted his young wife, Ta-O-Dee, stretching a hide across a stick frame. She was barely seventeen harvests, but she was a good worker and a loving wife. He knew that he would soon have a new buckskin shirt to wear from the hide she was laboring over with such dedication. Beside Ta-O-Dee, their infant son, Ino, waved his chubby little arms through the air as he watched his mother working from his canopied cradleboard. So far, this harvest—the past thirteen months in an Apache year—had been a happy one for the proud warrior.

Juno's gaze then followed his friend's eyes to the opposite end of the camp, toward the wickiup of Eskinzan, where the old shaman was busy teaching Sky Dreamer the ways of an Apache shaman. His heart filled with gladness when he glanced back at the other man. The woman had been there only for a few days and already Nachae's attitude was improving. For the first time in a long while, Juno had heard his friend talk about the future without a trace of bitterness in his voice.

"She learns fast, *shik'isn*," Juno said as they watched Eskinzan and Sky Dreamer mixing a bowl of moxa, the herbs used in a shaman's medicine bag.

"Yes, she does," Nachae replied proudly. "When Grandfather has taught her how to use her healing powers and how to interpret her dreams, I will begin to teach her how to ride an Apache pony. She will also need to know how to protect herself, and how to survive in the desert." He patted his chest and added sternly, "I will teach her all of the things she must know about the Teneh Chockonen." The expression on his face grew unusually excited. A wistful grin toyed with the corners of his lips and put a bright twinkle in his dark gray gaze.

Juno chuckled. "It seems to me that she already knows how to protect herself." He thought of the way Sky Dreamer had put the troublemaking Llamarada in her place on the day of her arrival in the rancheria.

Nachae immediately knew what his friend was referring to, but he did not wish to discuss that episode. The fight between the two women had only reminded him of the few times he had allowed Llamarada to join him out in the woods in the middle of the night, while the rest of the village was asleep. His natural instincts had overpowered his common sense during their secretive rendezvous and he did not particularly wish to relive the memories of those shameless nights. No one had seen the insolent woman anywhere in the rancheria since she had suffered her disgraceful defeat to Sky Dreamer, and that suited Nachae just fine. These days he preferred to concentrate on more appealing prospects.

"Sky Dreamer must learn how to protect herself from her real enemies—the white men." His voice changed, taking on the icy tone it always acquired whenever he talked of the White-Eyes.

Juno shrugged and reminded Nachae, "She is partly white, and although you have chosen to deny it, so are you."

"Not anymore." Nachae kicked Eagle in the sides and loosened his reins. "Come, let's get this fresh meat to the women before it spoils." He motioned toward the pair of scrawny venado—the two deer—which hung from the back of the pack horse.

Juno quickly dug his heels in his horse's sides and caught up to the other warrior. Curiosity was getting the best of him, in spite of Nachae's reluctance to talk about his obvious feelings for the young woman who had become known throughout the village as Sky Dreamer. "Maybe you should keep both white women—marry Sky Dreamer and have a spare one too," Juno suggested with a sly chuckle.

Nachae grunted with aggravation since he knew that Juno was just trying to goad him into another one of their silly teasing matches. Juno was aware of the fact that Eskinzan was already making plans to send the fiancée of Charles Atwood back to Fort Bowie. Captain Atwood was a good man, despite his bloodline or his choice of career as a soldier, and Nachae was not pleased with himself for bringing the officer's soon-to-be bride to the Apache rancheria. However, it was Juno's assumption that he was planning to marry Sky Dreamer that fueled Nachae's anger most of all. How many times must he repeat himself on this issue? Grandfather's unrelenting meddling was bad enough, but did his closest friend have to hound him about the woman, too?

"I am not going to marry Sky Dreamer!"

Another chuckle came from Juno's mouth when Nachae's dark glare issued him a silent warning. Still, it did not discourage his inquisitive probing. "Then why are you so anxious to teach her the ways of the

Teneh Chockonen?"

Nachae's face drew into a fierce frown, but he did not bother to answer. He had repeatedly told himself—and anyone who would care to listen to him during the past couple of days—that his desire to help the young woman adjust to her new life was only because their mixed heritages gave them so much in common with one another. A loud chortle from Juno's direction once again increased the irritation Nachae was feeling toward his comrade's nosiness.

"I will never marry her!" her repeated with a defiant toss of his long ebony hair, then quickly added, "I will only think of her as a sister, and no more!" Nachae shoved his heels into Eagle's side again and the horse bounded forward, leaving the other man behind to wallow in his trail of dust. Juno cleared his throat loudly while he watched his friend ride ahead of him on his big painted stallion. A wide smile overtook his dark-toned face. Tonight, he thought as he followed Nachae down into the rancheria, he would ask Ta-O-Dee to start working on a matching set of beaded necklaces. They would make a gift of them to Nachae and Sky Dreamer on their wedding day.

Nachae had anxiously been awaiting the opportunity to take Sky Dreamer out into the open country surrounding the Apache stronghold so that he could show her the Apacheria, which he had come to love in the past decade that he had spent with the Teneh Chockonen. Although it seemed to him that Grandfather had intentionally prolonged this sojourn. Since she was adjusting so well to her new role in the Apache world, Nachae knew that it was not his place to interfere with his grandfather's teachings. But the short-tempered warrior had nearly lost the small amount of patience he did possess by the time the old man had decided that Sky Dreamer deserved to take a break from her intense studies of the Apache medicines and the use of her undeveloped powers. The return of

Lucero's daughter made Eskinzan's heart leap with joy, but the fact that she had also inherited her mother's powers of a mystical Apache shaman was beyond Eskinzan's greatest expectations.

When the couple reached the area where Nachae planned to teach her how to shoot a bow and arrow, he called out to her to stop. He watched with a satisfied expression as she pulled on her horse's reins and brought the steed to an immediate standstill. They had ridden a long distance from the rancheria and she had done well, considering that she had never ridden bareback by herself before. With the intention of helping her dismount, Nachae jumped from Eagle's back and hurried toward her horse, but she was already sliding to the ground. He clasped onto her waist and gently eased her the rest of the way. His hands rested intimately around her narrow waist, lingering longer than necessary atop the gentle curve of her slender hips. He felt her tremble beneath his touch, which made his own limbs suddenly grow weak and shaky.

When he turned her loose, a bright red blush had claimed her cheeks and her eyes were cast downward. Nachae felt foolish and young when he found that he was feeling exactly the same way. Growing angry for the less than brotherly thoughts that had entered into his mind, he made a determined decision. He would not touch her again!

"Follow me," he said more abruptly than he had intended, then felt slightly guilty when he noticed her jump at the sound of his harsh voice. "Stand here," he ordered, pointing to a barren spot in the golden sand. He walked several more yards to where a tall organpipe cactus stood, then drew his hunting knife from its sheath. With the blade, he carved a large circle in the center of the tough-skinned plant.

Regina held her breath as she watched his actions, her hands toying nervously with the deep folds of her full skirt. Waddling Woman had brought the clothes to Eskinzan's wickiup and offered them to her again. The old shaman had taken Regina into his home the moment he had learned of her Apache connections. She had not seen Susan again since the first day of her arrival in the village, so she had no reason not to accept the clothes the second time Waddling Woman had made the offer. The colorful skirt of red and yellow stripes and loose-fitting shirt of soft buckskin, which slipped over her head, were suited for the type of life she was living now—not to mention that they were much more comfortable than the confining dresses she was accustomed to wearing. The only thing that bothered her was that, even here with the Apaches, it was still not acceptable to let her hair hang loose. Because it was not considered proper for an unmarried woman to wear her hair down, Regina's long thick tresses were bound tightly at the back of her head with a beaded nahleen, a large hairbow, which wrapped the tresses into a tight ponytail that was held close to the head. Tall knee-high suede moccasins, or kabuns, covered her feet and legs to protect her from the prickly cactus and other hazards of the desert ground. Dressed in these garments, Regina was every inch the vision of an Apache woman, right down to the fringed rawhide *hodenten,* the medicine bag Eskinzan had made especially for her, which dangled from her wide leather belt.

As she watched Nachae walking back toward her, Regina's nervousness increased. His handsome face still carried a look of discontent, although she could not understand why. Nobody had forced him to be with her—he was the one who had asked his grandfather if she could join him. Actually, Regina was quite content to spend her days with Grandfather as she learned about the Teneh Chockonen. There was nothing to compare with the tremendous feeling of unity she experienced whenever the aging shaman told her the very same things that he had once said to her mother. Each time the old medicine man complimented her for accomplishing another one of her lessons, Regina could somehow sense her mother's presence. Although she missed her father a great deal, it was this comforting feeling of being close to her mother that kept Regina from becoming too upset about being away from the captain again.

She was greatly relieved to hear that Eskinzan had decided to permit Susan to return to Fort Bowie. The shaman also promised to send a message to her father, letting him know his daughter was safe and living with the family of the Apache medicine man. Regina knew her father would realize immediately that she had learned the truth about her mother, and no doubt it would not be long before he came to the village himself to explain his decisions of the past with her. She was anxious to talk to him and to tell him that she understood why he had chosen not to tell her about her Apache bloodline, but she did not have any desire to return to the fort with him. Every day that passed found her growing more at ease in her new environment, and more at peace with herself.

Only one thing bothered her and it was an annoyance that caused her great distress: Knowing Susan was living in Nachae's wickiup tended to fan the spark of jealousy that smoldered in Regina because of her growing attraction for the tall warrior who had recently materialized from her dreams. If Waddling Woman had not told her that Nachae rode out from the village every night and did not return until early morning, Regina was sure she would have acted on impulse and probably would have made a fool of herself by accusing Nachae of living with her father's fiancée.

"Here," he said sharply, holding out his short bow. Regina's eyes widened with uncertainty at his harsh tone, but she slowly reached out and took the weapon from his hand. From the leather quiver which hung at his back by a thin strap and crossed over his broad chest, he pulled out a short skinny arrow. He then stepped behind her and encircled her quaking body with his arms while he prepared to show her the proper way to hold the bow.

"Like this," he said, taking a firm grip on her hands. He raised her arms up until they were positioned correctly. He could feel the violent shaking in her limbs and wondered why she was so frightened of him all of a sudden. In time, he hoped that she would come to trust him—as she would a brother, or so he constantly told himself.

Regina could not concentrate on anything he was trying to tell her. Even her teeth felt as though they were clanging together loudly from the uncontrollable shivering in her body. He was not doing anything to warrant these devouring thoughts, but his nearness was her undoing. He told her to grip the bow tighter; she felt the heat of his breath upon the back of her hair. He placed the arrow between the curve of the wooden arch and the bow string, and she noticed the way the muscles of his bare thighs were pressing up against her backside through the thin material of her skirt. His strong hands pulled back the bow, and she became aware of the pounding in his chest as their bodies meshed together. Seconds later the arrow thudded into the dirt in front of Regina's feet in a pitiful attempt to fly the short distance to the target he had drawn in the towering cactus.

Both of them stared down, dumbfoundedly, at the ground where the arrow had fallen. Regina was afraid to move. The lustful thoughts pouring through her mind had her paralyzed to the spot. Like a confident artist, her mind began to paint the scene for her passionate dreams, and the pictures that covered the canvas in her mind were even more vivid than they appeared in her dreams. She felt Nachae back away from her, yet the feel of his firm body against her backside still lingered with an intense reminder of the engulfing rush of wanton longings that had overcome her entire being only seconds ago. She was powerless to halt the way her stomach constricted with the desirous cravings, nor could she stop the slow ache that inched its way though her body. Her flesh tingled with the memory of his illusionary touch and her loins throbbed with the vision of his long legs intermingled with her own slender limbs.

Unware of her actions, Regina glanced down at the hard desert ground and thought of the deep mountain grass where they had lain together in her sensual reverie. Every portion of her body, which had known his makebelieve touch, became inflamed, and the feeling of their

140

bodies molding together became so strong that she began to wonder if she had lapsed into another state of unconsciousness. An overwhelming urge to swing around and beg Nachae to turn her dreams into a reality caused her to grow light-headed and shaky. What kind of demons had attacked her unsuspecting senses and made her a mindless creature who could not control her own lascivious needs? She rubbed at her eyes like a confused child while attempting to wipe away the detailed picture of their imaginary lovemaking, but it was an unsuccessful task. Being alone with Nachae, and wanting him to fulfill the loving actions she had perceived in her dreams, had grown too great to ignore. How much longer would it be before this stubborn man realized that he, too, was unable to escape their fate?

Nachae, it seemed, was fighting a strangling fear of his own. Just standing close to her had affected him so strongly that he was unable to think straight. An Apache warrior could not allow such distractions. He realized that being alone with this woman was not a good idea at all if he ever had any hopes of keeping his self-imposed vow.

"We should head back to the village." His voice cracked and the words barely escaped from his mouth.

Regina managed only to nod her head; words eluded her. While an infuriating rush of heat colored her cheeks, she stumbled toward her horse. She was sure that her feet never touched the ground and she feverishly hoped he wouldn't notice the embarrassing blush upon her face. Her only consolation was that he had no way of knowing how immensely she yearned for his touch—or of how completely she already loved him. Without his assistance, she struggled to remount her horse. Her determination helped her accomplish the feat—much to her relief—because she knew that she could not take another encounter with his touch without giving in to her undeniable longings.

Nachae would have to be blind to miss the flashing sparkle contained within her violet eyes, nor could he help noticing her reddened cheeks. He wished he knew what was going through her mind right now, but his thoughts were in enough of a turmoil without adding her apparent confusion to them too. As they made their way back to the village, he forced himself to concentrate on teaching her the important things she would need to know about survival in this brutal land. Grandfather had already taught her how to say many of the Apache words, so Nachae talked to her in both the English tongue and in the Apache and Mexican language of the Teneh Chock-onen. She amazed him with her ability to learn everything so quickly, and her enthusiasm at wanting to absorb all the knowledge of her new surroundings caused him to grow excited too.

By the time they had reached the rancheria, the distracting feelings which had plagued them both during their brief lesson were temporarily forgotten. They chatted easily about horses and desert plantlife and the various things she had learned from Eskinzan during the past few days. They even laughed together when Regina's clumsy attempt to speak in Apache had her mispronouncing her words and asking questions that did not translate as she had planned, such as why he had named his horse Sparrow, when she meant Eagle—Itsa.

Nachae laughed at her misguided inquiry and caused her to blush again. Her innocence and youth were as refreshing to his empty heart as her rare beauty was to his eyes. "I call him Itsa, because he is fleet of foot and he soars like an eagle when he gallops across the desert ground," he replied with a proud tilt of his head. Eagle was his pride and joy, despite the way the other warriors always taunted him about his fondness for his horse. Many times during the men's jesting, they had even threatened to eat Eagle for their dinner whenever the wild game was not available.

Since becoming a man in the Chiricahua tribe, Nachae had grown accustomed to the other men's joking, but this was the first time during his twenty-five harvests that he had felt so at ease with a woman. It seemed impossible that this was the same woman who had caused him so much distress for the past ten years. The stronghold of resistance he had carefully constructed around his heart, while trying to hone his feelings of animosity toward this woman, had crumbled into a useless pile the very instant he had set eyes on her lovely young face.

Although he knew it would never be possible for them to become involved in the way that his grandfather perceived, Nachae knew that the shaman had not been wrong about the profound effect this young woman would have on the way the warrior lived his entire life. Since she had appeared, he had not even thought about leading any raids against the white settlers. The last few days he had thought about nothing except Sky Dreamer—and the way the sunlight reflected the rusty hues which peeked out shyly from the heavy strands of her ebony hair. He marveled at the way her luminous eyes alternated from a pale shade of lavender to a sparkling array of violets with her many emotions and moods. His entire being was dominated by the manner in which her slender hips swayed naturally beneath the soft cloth of her full skirt, and of how her suede shirt draped in a teasing manner over her enticing young bosom. Since Sky Dreamer had entered his life, the battles Nachae was waging now were not half as brutal as the ones he was accustomed to fighting . . . though they might prove to be just as dangerous.

Chapter Twelve

Ta-O-Dee's round face scrunched up excitedly as she turned Sky Dreamer around and admired the dress that she had painstakingly sewn for herself to wear on special occasions. To give the garment to the future wife of her husband's closest friend was an immense honor. Although there had not yet been an announcement of the wedding, Juno had assured her that it was not too far in the future. Ta-O-Dee did not mention her husband's prediction to Sky Dreamer, though, since she hoped her new friend would confide in her about the forthcoming event. Much to Ta-O-Dee's disappointment, Sky Dreamer did not say a word on the subject.

"This is so kind of you," Regina said in English, forgetting to speak in the Apache tongue, which she was working hard to master. She ran her fingers down the front of the soft buckskin dress. The craftmanship of the garment was extraordinary with its long fringed sleeves and hemline. Delicate rows of beads adorned the round neck of the suede dress and formed the shape of a brilliant sunrise across the top in front. Regina realized that the other woman had not understood her because she had accidentally spoken to her in English, and quickly raised her eyes up into the air in a gesture of thank you. Ta-O-Dee's face lit up with a wide smile.

Sky Dreamer searched her mind for the Apache words to convey her gratitude, but at this time, her mind was on a more pressing problem — one she would soon have to face although she did not look forward to the impending meeting with her father's fiancée.

"Do you miss your white family?" Ta-O-Dee inquired when she noticed Sky Dreamer's forlorn look.

Regina knew enough of the Apache language to understand the woman's inquiry. She shook her head in a negative gesture and began to speak in her newly formed language. "No—yes. I miss my father a great deal. I am not unhappy here though. It's just that the other white woman is leaving today, and I have not seen her since the first day I arrived in the village. I must say good-bye to her."

"Will you miss her when she's gone?"

Regina suppressed a rude chuckle. Miss Susan? Hardly! Her father's precarious situation was the only thing that distressed her. What would happen when his uppity fiancée learned that he had once been married to an Apache woman? Already, Regina had been forced to confront the stark reality of her mixed bloodline. It was impossible for her not to worry about the prejudices her father would be confronted with when the identity of his first wife became known. Down South the hatred for the Indians was no less than it was out here in the West. Lately, the Indian wars had even taken priority over the issue concerning the black slaves who had been freed after the War Between the States.

Regina hugged Ta-O-Dee affectionately for her gift, and also for the unabashed friendship that the Indian woman had shown to her in the past few days. She knew Ta-O-Dee's husband, Juno, was Nachae's closest friend in the tribe, but the relationship between the two men had nothing to do with the immediate friendship which had developed between the young women.

"I must go," Regina said when she released Ta-O-Dee. Bending down, she tickled Ino under his chubby chin. The little boy squealed in delight and graced Regina with a wide toothless grin. With a wave of her hand, Regina left Ta-O-Dee and Ino and steeled herself for the confrontation, which she was dreading more with each passing minute. Walking through the village, Regina was amazed at the kindness the women showed toward her since the announcement of her Apache birthright. From every wickiup she passed, Regina was greeted with smiles and waves and words of admiration. Even the children—the same ones who had taunted her on the first day—now grinned bashfully at her from beneath their heavy masses of dark hair. During times like these, it was almost impossible for Regina to think of the Apaches as savages and murderers. Still, she would never again allow herself to forget the destruction and death the warriors were capable of inflicting upon their enemies.

As she approached Nachae's hut, Regina spotted Susan huddled in front of the wickiup beside the doorway. A bowl of uneaten cornmeal was resting in front of her feet. Regina could not tell if Susan was happy at the prospect of leaving or whether she was beyond caring. Her blue eyes stared off into space with a blank expression which was almost hidden beneath the tangles of her long dirty blond hair.

"Susan," Regina called out with a false tone of enthusiasm. The other woman looked up, a questioning look on her face. Dressed in the Indian garments, Regina's appearance was so different from her previous look, she was almost unrecognizable. Susan's eyes traveled over the girl's knee-length dress and buckskin moccasins with a contemptuous glare. Susan still wore the same dress she had been wearing ever since her captivity because she had repeatedly refused to wear any of the clothes that Waddling Woman had offered her. Although she had finally consented to go with Waddling Woman down to the river to bathe, Susan's bedraggled condition was still a far cry from Regina's impeccable grooming.

A hateful smirk curled Susan's lips as she rose up to a standing position. "Well, it's apparent you're being well cared for. I just wonder what you've had to do to receive such grand treatment."

Regina felt as if a knife had been twisted in her stomach. She had not expected Susan to be friendly, but her crude insinuation was still hard to swallow. "I've just come to say good-bye."

Susan's shock was apparent on her face as she gasped, "Surely they're not forcing you to remain in this hovel?" Regina thought she detected a tiny bit of sympathy in Susan's voice. Still, she was certain Susan would be relieved to leave her behind, especially since she had always acted as though the idea of a stepdaughter was a burden she would rather do without. Regina's only worry was that Susan would condemn the love her father had always harbored for his Indian wife, once his past life became public knowledge.

"Well . . ." Regina said with hesitancy edging her words with a trembling note. "It's not that they won't permit me to leave, it's — well . . ."

Immediately, Susan's face contorted into a mask of contempt as she began to draw her own conclusions. "Oh, I see," she spat out. "You don't want to leave, do you?" She sidestepped Regina as though the girl carried a contagious disease. "You want to stay because of that — that savage. Why, just look at you," Susan screamed. "You've already become one of those animals!" Her lips twisted cruelly with the disgust she felt.

"I'm staying because I want to be here," Regina retorted in defense. "It has nothing to do with anyone else."

"There has to be more to it," Susan prodded as she moved closer. "Come on, Regina, if you're really serious about staying here, then I think I deserve a truthful answer."

Regina's head began to spin with indecision. Did she dare tell Susan about her mother or was that bit of information something that should remain a secret until her father was ready to tell his fiancée himself? Susan was standing only a couple of feet away before Regina had enough courage to raise her eyes to meet the woman's inquisitive stare. Maybe she should talk to Susan — maybe she could ask her to be understanding toward her father when word of his past leaked out to the rest of the men at the fort.

"My—my mother . . ." The words snagged in her throat. Would it always be this difficult to admit to her Apache nationality? She squared her shoulders and reminded herself of the great woman her mother had been. "My father's wife was an Apache, and I'm staying because I feel I belong here with my mother's people," she stated with a proud toss of her head.

Susan's mouth flapped open, but no words came forth. Her mind was repeating one thing over and over . . . a half-breed! Charles's daughter was a low-down half-breed. Susan's prudent upbringing clouded her thoughts with rage and revenge. She would never allow Charles to touch her now that she knew he had once been intimate with a savage. Her mind conjured up images of the shame she would be subjected to back in Georgia if word of this ever spread. Oh God! She had been planning to marry a squaw man—that's what they called white men who consorted with Indian wenches. Susan almost wished she could die rather than face the disgrace Charles had cast upon her.

Regina was not able to decipher the other woman's strange expression. Maybe she should have been more tactful with her shocking admission. "Susan," she said regretfully as she extended her arms in a gesture of affection. "I'm sorry. Please let me explain—"

"You're sorry?" Susan interrupted with a wicked laugh. "Well, I'm sorry, too." She backed away from Regina. "Don't come near me . . . you—you dirty . . . half-breed!"

Regina's arms dropped to her sides, her blood turning to shards of ice. Nothing that had ever happened to her before could compare to the way Susan's words had just affected her. Regina could not stop the tears which filled her eyes, then flooded her cheeks. A half-breed! How could a mere word hurt so deeply? With no thought of where she was going, Regina turned on her heel and ran blindly toward the edge of the village. Would every white person from this day forth paste that poisonous label on her?

She didn't notice when Nachae stepped into her path. He grabbed her and prevented her from hitting against him full force. It didn't matter why he had suddenly appeared — all that was important was that he was holding her in his arms. Regina felt too weak to resist when he scooped her up against his bare chest and carried her into the grove of trees that bordered the river. She wrapped her arms around his neck and held on to him as the sobs shook her body.

Nachae gently lowered her trembling form down onto the ground among a dry patch of brown grass. He could feel the dampness seeping into the taut muscles across his chest where her tears were coating his skin. Her pain was his pain, and as he sank down to his knees beside her, he felt closer to her than he had ever felt to anyone. He had followed her this morning because he'd sensed that the white woman's reaction would not be a pleasant one when Sky Dreamer told her why she was not leaving the Apache village. He had known how deep the hurt would seed itself in Sky Dreamer's young heart if she met with the other woman's jaundiced ideas about the Apache people . . . and his assumptions had proved to be correct.

Sky Dreamer had not cried when he took her captive during the attack on the soldiers at the San Simon River, nor had she been reduced to tears when she had been goaded into fighting Llamarada only minutes after entering the Apache village. She had bravely accepted the drastic changes in her life ever since she had learned about her mother, and she was even willing to give up everything she had ever known in the white man's world to follow in her mother's footsteps. None of those things had made her cry until she had been confronted with the cruelty of the white woman's well-chosen word . . . half-breed! Nachae could not count the number of times he had been called by that name, and every time, the loathing tone of voice was the same — no matter who had spoken the cutting words.

Regina was being torn in half. She wanted to run away from her Indian heritage, to pretend that it did not exist.

149

Yet at the same time, she wished she would never have to return to her old life in the white man's world. If it wasn't for her father, she wouldn't care what anyone said or thought, but she did not want him to pay the price for her decision. She knew that the Apache way of life would never be easy, and in the past few days she had thought about how much she was risking by staying with her mother's people. Daily, the Apaches were faced with endless hardships, and still, she was willing to accept their primitive way of living because it had also been her mother's way. There was one other very important factor, though, and it was not something she could ignore. Eskinzan had taught her how to interpret her dreams. He had told her that they were the forerunners of future occurrences. If that was so, then she was destined to be exactly where she was right now — within Nachae's strong embrace . . . forever.

Without warning or thought, Nachae's mouth descended upon Regina's tearstained lips. Neither of them had suspected that a kiss was waiting for its chance to happen, and there was no way to stop the magnetic pull that drew them together. The impromptu kiss was so engulfing that it stole Regina's breath away, yet so brief that it left her wondering if it had really happened.

Nachae jumped to his feet and stared down at her. He had planned never to permit that kiss to happen. But the moment, and the mood, and this woman had overtaken his emotions and made him a man without a mind of his own. If he ever gave in to his feelings for her again, he was sure that he would not be able to stop until it was too late.

Regina did not move when he pulled away; only her eyes raised up to meet his troubled gaze. Her sobbing had dissolved with his unexpected kiss, though she continued to gasp for air each time she took a breath. What was it that he was so afraid of admitting to himself, and why did she feel no sense of fear when she was in his arms? Couldn't he see that they were each an oddity in their two separate worlds, but together they were both complete at last? She wanted to tell him that his reluctant heart could not avoid the inevitable, and that it was useless for him to fight against something neither of them could change, but he never gave her a chance to voice these conclusions.

"Will you be all right?" he asked in a concerned, but reserved, tone.

Regina nodded dutifully, even though she wanted to cry out that she would never be all right again. At least, not until he accepted their fate without any further resistance. When he held out his hand to her, she hesitated. Was there something she could say or do to make him understand that she wanted nothing more than to be near him? Slowly she reached out her hand and permitted him to pull her to her feet. He immediately turned her loose and began to stalk back toward the village.

Regina practically had to run to catch up with him. She tried to concentrate on following him up the narrow path. Fury began to replace the tender emotions she had been feeling such a short time ago as she glared at the back of his stalking form. Forcing herself not to stare at his nearly nude body, she reminded herself of his obstinate attitude.

"Well, I don't want Grandfather's prophesy—or my dreams—to come true, either," she blurted without thinking.

Nachae's footsteps faltered, but he quickly regained his footing. "Good!" he replied sharply. "We're definitely in agreement on that issue."

"Maybe I should go back to Fort Bowie with Susan."

"Nobody's preventing you from leaving."

Regina drew in an angry breath then fell silent. She could leave, just to spite him, but they both knew she wouldn't. She swung around and headed back toward the river. She needed to be alone to sort out her jumbled thoughts. Perhaps it would be better if she returned to the fort—just until that stubborn man realized how deep his feelings ran for her. But what if he never did?

"A lover's quarrel?" Llamarada said snidely as she stepped out from the cover of a thick clump of piñon trees. Regina was too surprised to move for an instant as she eyed the other woman with a leery gaze. She had not seen Llamarada in the rancheria since their knife fight, and it was apparent that being outcast from the tribe was having an effect on the woman's mind. Her long hair was no longer braided and it hung around her face in a mass of tangles. The clothes that hung on her body were soiled and torn. But the demented smile she wore upon her face sent a shiver down Regina's spine.

"Do you have nothing better to do with your time than eavesdrop?" Regina watched her closely, her eyes searching along Llamarada's belt for some sign of a weapon. She did not relish a repeat episode of their first meeting, yet she was afraid that was exactly what the other woman had in mind. Much to her relief, she noticed that Llamarada did not have her knife in its sheath. If the woman decided to attack her again, Regina knew this time their confrontation would have to be a fight to the death for at least one of them. A foreboding sensation overcame her and sapped the little bit of bravado she had left in her trembling being as she realized that even Nachae was probably out of earshot by now. She was left alone to face Llamarada's wrath.

"Thanks to you, Cochino, I have nothing to do at all!"

Regina's overworked mind scrambled to decipher Llamarada's words until she finally figured out that she had just been called a pig. Indignant, Regina quickly turned away. Her time was too valuable for her to stand there and be called childish names by a crazy woman. She had taken only a couple of steps when Llamarada rushed forward and grabbed her by the arm.

"Turn me loose," Regina said through clenched teeth. "Or do you want more of what I gave you the other day?" Her insides began to quiver, but she did not back down from her brave words. She prayed that the woman would not take her up on her threat since it was the thing she feared most of all right now. Fortunately, Regina's words caused Llamarada to release her grip on her arm and move away.

"It does not matter," Llamarada added with a victorious

grin, which only increased the look of insanity upon her grimy face. "Nachae is mine, and he will always be mine!"

"I don't think so," Regina said, turning to leave again. Llamarada's next words sent bolts of flames shooting through Regina's body, and caused her fury to explode within her breast.

"Don't you ever wonder where he goes each night when he leaves the village?" She followed Regina's next couple of steps and continued, "He's with me every night—all night!"

Regina didn't bother to stop and offer a retort to Llamarada's declaration—she couldn't stop. Rage pushed her onward. At the edge of the village, she exhaled the heavy breath that had threatened to strangle her, and slowly turned around. Llamarada was nowhere to be seen. Regina wondered if perhaps she had only imagined her presence—and her despicable admission. How could he? Waddling Woman herself had told Regina that Nachae rode out from the rancheria every night and did not return until the sunrise each morning. Was it because his nights were spent in that horrible woman's arms? Regina could not even bring herself to think about Nachae and Llamarada being together in an intimate manner. Oh—but she would think about what she planned to do about it!

Regina rested among the soft bed of furs and contemplated the past few days. Her fury toward Nachae had been festering ever since her encounter with Llamarada. It was lucky for Nachae that he had not been in the rancheria when Regina had returned, or else he would have suffered the consequences of her anger. It infuriated Regina to an even greater degree that he had left before she had a chance to confront him with her new bit of information. The days she had been forced to hold her temper were taking their toll on her. She refused to ask anyone where he had gone. Since it was common knowledge that the warrior was extremely temperamental, she assumed that he had taken off because of their little quarrel at the riverbank the other day. What bothered her the most, though, was that he might also be with Llamarada. That particular thought made her blood boil.

She snuggled deeper into the furs and sighed with aggravation. A brief kiss on the riverbank was hardly a vow of undying devotion on Nachae's part. Regina knew that she had no valid right to be so upset about Llamarada's involvement with him. The idea that he was free to be with other women did not improve her outlook, however. The past few days it had been next to impossible for her to concentrate on the things that Eskinzan was trying to teach her when all she could think about was the reality of her dreams. When Nachae returned to the village, she was going to have it out with him, once and for all.

She tried to go back to sleep, although the noises from the other two people in the wickiup would not let her do so. She knew how fortunate she was to be living in Eskinzan's wickiup. The shaman's home was larger than most of the other dwellings in the rancheria, since he felt that he needed more room to store his many healing potions and supplies. Though there were several other medicine men in the village, they were not as powerful as Eskinzan. None of the others possessed Sky Dreamer's ability to see forthcoming events through their dreams, so she was already considered to be an important figure in the Chiricahua tribe.

For Regina, however, staying in Eskinzan's wickiup was a mixed blessing. Grandfather's oldest wife, Tarza, snored and coughed nonstop throughout the night, and Waddling Woman was still young enough to arouse the old man's desire every so often. Regina was certain she would die of embarrassment in their moments of intimacy. The only thing she could do during these interludes was to pull her fur blanket over her head and try to ignore the sounds which came from the opposite side of the hut. Sometimes, she wondered if she would ever be able to accept this strange life, which was so very different from anything she had ever known.

With an exhausted sigh, Regina sat up and glanced

around the dark wickiup. Tarza was still asleep, as was Grandfather. The sun had not even begun to shed its rays on the land, but outside the hut Regina could hear Waddling Woman busy putting the morning meal together. From her small pile of belongings, she grabbed up her clothes, choosing the skirt and top that Waddling Woman had given to her. She planned to save the suede dress which Ta-O-Dee had given to her for special occasions. As quietly as possible, she slipped the skirt and baggy shirt on over the same undergarments she had been wearing when she'd arrived. In time she might be able to wear nothing under her dress, like the rest of the Apache women. For now, though, she was still too shy to give in to all of the Indian customs—not wearing her chemise and petticoat was one of them.

She stepped out of the wickiup with her kabuns in her hand. The early morning air held a chill that caused her to shiver as she put on the tall moccasins. She dreaded the thought of going to the river to bathe, yet she knew that she must. The Apaches believed women had to scrub their bodies every day with sand from the riverbed or else they would be covered with thick, repulsive hair.

"Come, stand by the fire and warm yourself," Waddling Woman said with an affectionate smile. She already loved Sky Dreamer, just as she loved her husband's grandson, Nachae.

Regina did not waste any time as she rushed over to stand beside the older woman. The flames lit up the dark dawn and cast a comforting warmth upon the two women who basked in its heat. Around the village other women were beginning their new day, and before too long, the whole camp was glowing with the blazes of the numerous fires. Regina helped Waddling Woman lay out the meager breakfast of dried meat and dried fruits. They ate only one large meal each day, and that was not until evening. Some days Regina felt as if she was going to starve to death before they ate the substantial meal late in the day.

Her grandmother in Georgia would die if she could see how Regina was eating these days, Regina thought as she scooped a handful of fruit into her mouth. Since her grandmother had constantly worried that Regina was too thin for her height, the girl had always been besieged with tantalizing food. Regina had never been a big eater, though, and her grandmother's attempts to fatten her up had always been in vain. Did Nachae think she was too skinny? Regina wondered, then silently scolded herself for caring what he thought about her.

"I haven't seen that man lately," she said, trying to sound nonchalant while giving in to the curiosity that was about to drive her insane.

Waddling Woman knew at once to whom the girl was referring. Eskinzan's plan to keep them apart as much as possible was apparently working. Ever since the shaman had sent his grandson to Sonora to trade hides and pelts for whiskey and other unnecessary addictions which the Apaches had a weakness for, Waddling Woman had noticed that Sky Dreamer spent all her time scanning the village for a glimpse of him.

"Do you mean my *ciye?*" she asked innocently.

"Why do you call him your son, instead of your grandson?" Regina's dark brows drew together in a questioning arch.

Waddling Woman shrugged. "Because I only married his grandfather one harvest ago. Nachae's real grandmother, who was my sister, was killed by the soldatos in an attack on our village during the last harvest. Nachae's father and his father's wife, Breeze of the Forest, also died on that sad day."

Regina felt an eerie feeling wash over her body. A sharp pain shot through her heart when she realized how much Nachae had lost in his life. Was that the source of the grudge he harbored against the soldiers? She refused to believe that her father, or any of his men, had been at fault for such a terrible deed. While she busied herself by throwing more wood on the fire, she tried to convince herself that the incident Waddling Woman had spoken of must have been a gross and tragic miscalculation in judgment on the soliders' part—it just had to be!

"Are you trying to set fire to the whole village?"

Regina's hand froze in midair at the sound of his voice, and the twigs scattered on the ground at her feet. Why did it always seem that he appeared out of nowhere? she wondered with renewed anger. She bent over and gathered up the small branches, then tossed them into the fire before turning around to face him. The reflection of the flames danced across his shadowed face and made little flickering designs on the tan shirt he was wearing with his buckskin leggings. Just the sight of him made Regina's body break out in an uncontrollable sweat. She stopped herself from calling out a greeting. It was not the Apache way, she reminded herself. Besides, she did not want him to get the idea that she was glad to see him.

Waddling Woman did not hesitate to embrace him in a silent form of greeting, yet even as he returned the older woman's welcome, his gray eyes never left Sky Dreamer's face. In the orange flames of the firelight, she looked even more beautiful than he had remembered, and he had been gone only a little while. She had not yet wound her long hair into the tight nah-leen which the young girls wore, and he was sure that the sparkle in her violet eyes could make a blind man see again.

"Was your trip successful?" Waddling Woman asked when she released him. A slight nod of his head was the only reply she received. He was still entranced by the vision of Sky Dreamer.

What sort of trip had he been on? Regina wondered. Had he added new coups to his coup stick with the murders of more defenseless white men? And were more of her father's soldiers among the bloody trail of dead men who had met with his revengeful wrath again? Or had he kept another romantic rendezvous with that woman?

"I will wake your grandfather," Waddling Woman said with an embarrassed glance in his direction. She felt as though she was intruding on something intimate when she noticed the way his eyes were devouring Sky Dreamer.

Nachae snapped out of his trance and glanced down at

the older woman. He raised his arm up into the air, revealing a leather flask. "Yes, wake him—we will celebrate today." His misted gaze moved back to Regina.

"Celebrate what?" she said caustically. "The killing of more of my father's men, or are you celebrating a successful conquest over Llamarada's own personal battleground?"

Nachae staggered the short distance to where Regina stood. His gray eyes narrowed wickedly as he stared down at her. There was an odd scent on his breath, making Regina grow fearful of his strange behavior. When he tilted the flask to his mouth and took a sloppy drink of the clear liquid, she knew at once why he was acting so different. He was drunk . . . stinking drunk! With a look of disgust, she shoved against his brawny chest to push him away. He did not budge, nor did he discontinue his piercing observation of this woman who had possessed him with her ravishing beauty and gentle ways.

A damp mustache of whiskey coated his upper lip and his speech was vaguely slurred by the liquor when he spoke. "You still don't understand why I can't give in to my feelings for you, do you, my beautiful little Sky Dreamer?"

Regina's heart bounded upward in her breast. He had just admitted that he did feel something for her—and he had called her *his* Sky Dreamer. Her mind was thrown into such a spin that she staggered backward as though she were the one who was drunk. Oh, how she loved him! She had loved him since the first moment his image had entered her dreams. And with each passing day, ever since her dreams had begun to turn into reality, her devotion toward him grew. It didn't matter where he had been for the past few days, or with whom. She knew that someday they would be together for all time, because no mortal man could stop the plan of Usen when he had preordained something so powerful.

"But I care too much to let it happen," Nachae added in a determined tone, then swung around and walked away from her without any farther explanation of his confusing words.

Regina watched his tall form move through the smoky veil of the early morning campfires. What was it that he was always hinting at . . . what did she have to come to understand before she could begin to know why he fought against their fate so viciously? And why did she sense that whatever it was, it would be the most difficult thing she would ever have to face in her young life?

Chapter Thirteen

Susan glanced around the officer's quarters at Fort Bowie with a disgusted look in her blue eyes. At this particular time, she hated everything and everybody. She had been forced to travel back to the fort with two Apache bucks and one of the repulsive savages had taken every opportunity to rub his filthy hands all over her body whenever the other one wasn't looking. She assumed they had been ordered to transport her to Fort Bowie without mishap, or else her trip would have been a complete horror. Nonetheless, being at the mercy of those two animals had been more frightening than anything she had encountered in this hellhole so far.

She threw herself back against the pile of pillows which adorned the sofa. The long strands of her wavy blond hair fell in a shimmering disarray across the floral pillow covers. She absently picked up a golden tendril from her bosom and wound it between her slender fingers. How long could she hold Charles off, she wondered. And what should she do with the interesting bit of information she had picked up in the Apache village?

It had been late the preceding night when she'd been dumped outside the walls of the fort by the pair of savages. When the guards saw her approaching the front gate on foot, they had nearly shot her down before they realized that she was a white woman. Needless to say, her arrival at Fort Bowie was not what she had hoped for, but since she had learned that Charles had once been a squaw man, she was no longer impressed with the thought of being his wife anyway.

She drew in a heavy sigh and frowned with disappointment. She really had thought that she wanted to marry Charles Atwood after they had met in Savannah last year. There was not one decent man in Georgia worthy of her attentions, and she had grown quite bored on her parents' plantation. When she had been introduced to Captain Atwood at a friend's party, he seemed to be the escape she desired. As far as Susan was concerned, all the exciting men had left the South after the Civil War and were out West fighting Indians. Charles Atwood was one such man. Not only was he an honored man in his profession, but for a man his age he was extremely good-looking. Besides, Susan had always thought that a man in uniform was irresistible. Her past held several memories of brief involvements with men who wore uniforms—some worth remembering and others she would rather forget. To marry Charles had been an escape from those less than memorable affairs. The idea of living at some godforsaken outpost had been only a minor hindrance, and Susan had been certain she would be able to convince Charles to transfer to Washington, D.C., once they were married.

Learning about his first wife and their half-breed offspring, though, had changed everything. There had always been something about Regina that had made her seem different, but until Susan had learned about her Apache lineage, she had not known what it was exactly about the girl that she could not tolerate. How could she marry Charles now? Just the thought of his being with an Apache squaw made her skin crawl. Yet how could she return to Savannah and admit to everyone that the man she had chosen as her prospective husband was a squaw man? Oh, she couldn't even bring herself to think of the shame!

A soft knock on the door nearly caused Susan's heart to stop beating. "I don't want to see anyone," she called out in an irritated voice. Another knock followed. Susan's anger flared. "I do not—" The door swung open without an invitation. Susan's hands raised up to the sides of her face. At first, she was sure that she was mistaken—this was just too ironic for her to believe. Randy Decker—at Fort Bowie? What else could possibly go wrong?

"Oh my—"

"God!" Susan finished the sentence for him. She slowly rose up from the sofa and faced him with a look of complete disbelief upon her face.

"Randy, what—I mean—how did you find me?" She pulled the front of her silky robe together defensively as though she expected him to attack her.

Lieutenant Decker coughed in a vain gesture to cover up his stunned gasp. He had come here today to welcome the captain's fiancée to the fort—merely a sociable gesture. The last person he'd expected to find was Susan Wilkins!

"Trust me," he retorted in a sarcastic tone when he was able to speak. "You are the last person I would go looking for."

Susan's blue eyes flashed like daggers. "Well, the feeling is mutual—you can rest assured of that." She paused when they were standing only a couple of feet apart. Their gazes drilled into one another while their feelings of intense animosity filled the air with a suffocating silence. Finally, Randy Decker could stand it any longer.

"It's more than apparent that this encounter is merely an unfortunate accident," he said briskly, trying not to meet her eyes. "So now we shall have to decide how we should deal with it, won't we?"

Susan's spine stiffened. "We?" she said viciously. "That's a change, wouldn't you say? Isn't it your normal habit to run and hide whenever you're faced with an important decision?"

Randy's brown eyes narrowed as he lowered them to meet her gaze. He spoke in a controlled tone when he defended himself. "I didn't run away and hide. My uncle, General Decker, transferred me out of Georgia. When my orders came in, I was forced to leave immediately." He raised his chin high in the air as he added in a casual tone,

"And what of the child?"

"How convenient for you that your uncle came to your rescue. And how fortunate for me that it turned out to be a false alarm." Her anger wiped out her sense of modesty, and she released her grip on the front of her robe. The silky garment gaped open, revealing the transparent lace chemise she wore underneath.

The lieutenant blinked and tried not to stare at her exposed bodice. In spite of the way he felt toward her, he still could not deny the fact that she was a desirable creature. It was her obvious assets that had gotten him into that messy situation two years ago, and might have destroyed his career as an officer in the calvary if he had remained in Georgia.

"I can assure you, Miss Wilkins," he replied with a smirk, "that my leaving Georgia so suddenly had nothing to do with you." It was difficult for him to remain in control of his anger. He had allowed his uncle to send him to this dirty outpost because Susan Wilkins had informed him that she was in a delicate condition. Now she was saying there never had been a child. His escape had been for nothing.

"You're such a lair!" For two years she had wanted to claw his eyes out for deserting her. What if it had turned out that she *was* pregnant with his child? He would have left her to face the shame of it all alone. She lunged at him with doubled-up fists, but he caught her wrists before she was able to follow through with her attack. His eyes fought to keep from traveling down to her voluptuous bosom, although it was a losing battle.

"What would Captain Atwood think if he saw you acting like this?" he asked through tightly drawn lips as he shoved her away. He dusted off the front of his jacket and ran his hand over his hair to smooth down any stray strands that might have been messed up in the brief struggle.

Susan's mind froze. Surely Randy wouldn't tell anyone about their past involvement. Oh God! She had nowhere to turn. Maybe marriage to Charles wouldn't be so bad after all. No one in Savannah need ever know about Charles's Apache wife, as long as Regina never came back to the fort. And Susan knew she was capable of doing anything to keep Randy Decker quiet about what had happened between the two of them two years ago.

"All right, Randy, you win. I'll forget about everything that happened if you'll promise never to repeat a word of our involvement to anyone!"

The lieutenant's face drew into a thoughtful expression. He never struck an agreement with anyone unless he gained something from it too. "Well," he said with a winning smile as he pushed his anger to the back of his mind for the time being. "I think we could strike a bargain." He paused and stepped closer to Susan's unmoving form. He ran his finger along the heaving line of soft flesh above her lacy chemise as he added, "But I'll expect something in return."

Susan's complexion paled as she contemplated what he was saying. "I—I couldn't, not here, not with Charles—"

Randy's evil laughter echoed through the room as he interrupted her. "That's not what I want from you," he said. "I want information about the location of the Apache village."

A flash of indignation moved across Susan's face. Just as quickly, though, she realized that if all he wanted were a few directions, then she was undoubtedly getting the easy end of the bargain. "I really don't remember much."

"Anything will do—such as how long it took you to travel from the Apache village to the fort, or perhaps a particular landmark that stood out in your mind?"

She sighed and tried to recall something that would aid the lieutenant's quest. Nothing came to her mind, however. She had been too worried about the actions of the Apache bucks who had been transporting her to the fort to pay attention to anything along the way. "I'm sorry but I just don't remember anything about the countryside. It did take about two days of nonstop riding to get back to Fort Bowie, though."

Randy tried to think. They could have traveled for two

days from any number of directions. He was about to question her further when they were interrupted by the entrance of the captain. Susan gasped and quickly pulled her robe together before Charles noticed that it was hanging wide open for the lieutenant's observation.

The captain felt the uneasiness the moment he entered his quarters. His gaze moved back and forth between his young fiancée and the lieutenant. The looks on both of their faces made it apparent that something was amiss.

"I — I came here to welcome your fiancée back to the civilized world," Randy said in a rush.

With a sheepish smile, Susan moved quickly to Charles's side. "Yes — yes, wasn't that kind of him?"

Charles did not reply for a moment. His mind was overloaded with too many other problems to wonder what was going on between the two guilty-acting people he had just encountered in his parlor. "Yes — very kind," he replied, then turned to Susan and added, "I've come to tell you that I plan to go into the Indian nation to search for Regina." Susan gasped but did not have a chance to answer him.

Taking a long stride forward, Lieutenant Decker asked, "May I have permission to accompany you, sir?"

Captain Atwood frowned at the other man's suggestion and moved a step away. "No, I intend to go alone."

"If you don't mind me saying so, Captain, going along would be suicide and I don't think — "

"You're not here to think, Lieutenant. It's your job to obey my orders, and I have already made my decision."

Randy Decker's face froze with a look of contempt. Yet when he spoke, his voice was calm and obedient. "Yes — sir!" He saluted with an exaggerated gesture and nodded briefly at Susan before turning on his heel and leaving the room.

Charles shook his head in a defeated manner. He did not usually speak so harshly to any of his men, but Lieutenant Decker's overexuberance to slay the Apaches grated on his nerves. If it weren't for the fact that Randy Decker's uncle was an old friend, Charles would have gotten rid of the lieutenant a long time ago.

"Please don't go," Susan pleaded as she clutched his arm again. "Regina is safe—I told you that last night. Please stay with me, so that we can continue with our wedding plans."

Charles rested his hand on her arm and sighed. "You told me that she was safe, but I still don't understand why she wasn't allowed to return with you."

"I know about your first wife," Susan blurted out abruptly. Charles's startled look did not stop her from continuing in a voice that became noticeably haughty. "Regina knows that her mother was an Apache squaw. That's why she stayed at the Indian village. She doesn't want to come back, Charles. Regina has become one of them, and she doesn't belong here anymore."

Charles's face became a mask of torn emotions as he slowly turned away and walked toward the door. Susan's cutting tone of voice made clear her opinion of his daughter. Sending Regina to live in Georgia with his parents had turned out to be a lost cause, just as his gallant gesture of joining up with the cavalry had been a waste. He had never been able to help Lucero's people in their struggle to survive the white man's approach, and now he wasn't able to prevent Regina from being a part of the Apache's dying race.

"I'm leaving this afternoon," he said. He walked toward the door and paused. Without looking at Susan, he added, "When I return we'll discuss whether or not we should continue with the plans for the wedding." With those final words, he left Susan alone with her guilt and agony.

She fell back on the sofa and covered her face with her hands. Once again, her life was headed nowhere. All her dreams of being an officer's wife were being stolen away from her . . . all because of Randy Decker—and that dirty half-breed, Regina Atwood!

As Charles entered the rugged slopes of the Chiricahua

Mountains, he felt as though he were going back in time. But unlike his long-ago trips to the Apache village, he now wore the uniform of a U.S. Calvary officer, and in his hand he carried a white flag of truce in the hope that the Indians would allow him to enter the camp. Two decades ago, he had ridden freely among the scattered camps. Then, he had been dressed in buckskin leggings, which were worn by the traders and explorers who had invaded the Apache lands in search of adventure. Charles Atwood had found adventure, and much more once he had met Lucero.

Today the captain had come to the rancheria alone. He knew the Chiricahua would be wary of a battalion of soldiers, and he did not want to destroy the trust he had earned among the tribe long ago. Also, he did not wish to place the Indian families in danger by allowing any of his men to accompany him to the village. If someone in Washington heard where the Apache village was located, C Company would more than likely be ordered to attack it. When Charles returned to the fort, he planned to tell everyone that he had not been able to find the village, or any signs of his lost daughter.

Before Charles even entered the outskirts of the camp, he was surrounded by a circle of fierce and unfriendly-looking warriors. Without stopping for the crowd of gathering onlookers, he continued to lead his horse through the throng of people toward the large wickiup, which he knew would be Eskinzan's hut. However, as he approached the shaman's dwelling, his horse was halted by a tall warrior who reached out and grabbed his reins.

Charles recognized him at once. Nachae's towering frame always stood out among the other Apache braves, even before one could see the stark contrast of his smoky gray eyes. The two men glared at one another, but neither made a move. Charles hoped that he would not allow his feelings concerning Regina's dreams to interfere with his better judgment. Yet as his eyes spiraled downward, he could not help wondering if Regina's dreams had already become a reality. If they had, Charles knew he would never be able to convince her to leave the Apache rancheria with him.

"Allow him to pass!" Eskinzan shook his head with irritation. It was good that his grandson was not too trusting, but it was plain to see that Captain Atwood had come in peace — as he had always done.

"You are welcome here," he called out to the soldier.

Nachae's look of distrust did not fade, but he released his hold on the captain's horse. As Captain Atwood passed by him, both men sized one another up with a hostile observation. Charles Atwood's frown turned to a smile, however, when his gaze moved to the old shaman. Eskinzan never changed, or so it seemed to Charles. He had looked exactly the same twenty years ago.

Charles dismounted and extended his hand to the shaman. Eskinzan shook hands with him vigorously, then affectionately embraced him. "My old friend," he said, "will you smoke with me?"

"I came to see my daughter," Charles stated as he followed the shaman to his wickiup. "And also, to thank you for returning my fiancée to Fort Bowie."

Eskinzan handed the long feathered peace pipe to the captain. "Will you take your daughter back to the fort, too?"

"If she'll go," Charles replied while he settled down on the fur robes that covered the floor.

"And if she won't?"

Charles answered the man's question with a thoughtful frown. "Then I will return alone." A satisfied smile overcame the shaman's wrinkled face as he took the pipe back from the captain.

"Your daughter will be a great shaman someday," Eskinzan said proudly.

Charles's eyes misted with unshed tears. It was so ironic that Regina had returned to the Apaches after all these years. Already she was walking in her mother's footsteps. There had been a time — many years ago — when Eskinzan had said those exact words about Lucero. Charles realized that it would be a useless effort to attempt to take Regina away. He was lost in thoughts of the past he had shared with her mother, and of the way those distant times were now intertwined with the present, when Regina entered through the low doorway of the wickiup.

She easily could have passed for her mother in her Indian garb. Charles felt an overwhelming sadness mingled with a melancholy happiness. He had loved Lucero more than life itself, and their time together had been so very brief. Since her death, he had only been able to recall those beautiful days through his faded memories. Now as he gazed upon Regina, he remembered every precious second with vivid clarity.

Regina was puzzled by her father's strange expression, but she was so glad to see him that she didn't hesitate to throw herself into his arms. With his arms wrapped tightly around her, she was feeling the same way she had always felt whenever he returned to Georgia for a short visit. She wished they would never have to be separated again, although she knew that it still would not be possible for them to be together. Her only hope was that his thinking would have changed about sending her back to live with her grandparents; she had made up her mind to stay with her mother's people.

"I'm sorry," he said when they finally pulled away from one another. "I should have told you about your mother years ago. It was wrong for me to lie to you, although I only wanted to protect you. Will you ever be able to forgive me?"

She tried not to cry even though her voice held a slight quiver when she spoke. "I forgive you and I understand why you did it. Will you forgive me for staying here instead of returning to Fort Bowie?"

Since first learning that Regina had discovered her Apache bloodline, Charles had known she would remain with her mother's people. But to actually hear her voice her intentions out loud caused him to become filled with a great sense of remorse. His little girl would face so many hardships among the Apaches which she would never confront in the white man's world. Once again, Charles

169

was overcome by the memory of his young wife's death from a disease that her race of people had never even known existed until the advance of the white men into their beloved lands of Apacheria. His eyes traced the soft lines of Regina's beautiful face as she watched him with nervous expectation. He wondered where he would ever summon up enough courage to walk away from here without insisting that she go with him? If only she was still his little girl, then he could demand that she go back to the security of her grandparents' home in Georgia. But she had left the innocence of her youth behind when she stepped foot on the first stagecoach out of Savannah to return to her birthland. Now she was a young woman with wants and needs that extended beyond those a father could grant to his daughter.

If it had been in his power to change the events of the past, Charles would never have allowed her to leave Georgia, but it was useless to worry about his huge error in judgment now. He recalled the dreams Regina had spoken of when she had first arrived at Fort Bowie, and he thought about the proud warrior who had halted his advance through the village earlier. There was no doubt in Charles's mind that Nachae was the greatest factor in his daughter's decision to stay with her mother's people, but the thought of his little girl belonging to Nachae, a man so consumed with bitterness and destruction, only added to the captain's turmoil. He worried that someday Regina would be filled with the same angry resentments which the warrior harbored toward the white men if she stayed here with the Apaches. The words he wanted to say to her became a mass of jumbled apologies and pleas that would not escape from his dry throat. He knew, however, that he loved Regina too much to ask her to deny the pathway which destiny had already prescribed for her heart to follow.

"I'll miss you," he said simply.

A tender smile touched her lips. "I'll never be too far away." She glanced at Eskinzan for reassurance, and received it when the old man gave his head a firm nod.

Charles's eyes also sought comfort when he looked toward the shaman. Eskinzan's promising look did not take away his uneasiness, however. Had Captain Atwood possessed the same foresight as his daughter, he might have noticed the man who had followed him to the Apache rancheria. Charles's mind was too engrossed with his own worries, though, to realize that he had not traveled into the Indian territory alone. Yet as he rode back toward Fort Bowie, and farther away from Regina, he was overcome with such a sense of impending doom that he was certain he would never be at ease again.

Chapter Fourteen

"He hates me," Regina stated with a childish pout.

Ta-O-Dee laughed. "I don't think so."

Regina hoisted the heavy tus, which was called a *tats'aa,* up to her back. A long leather strap, a tumpline, was wound around the neck of the water jar, then positioned across her forehead. This method of carrying the awkward jars enabled the women to keep their hands free to hold firewood or whatever else they needed to carry back to the village.

"He hasn't spoken to me for days."

Ta-O-Dee readjusted the tus around her forehead, then carefully picked up Ino's cradleboard from the ground. The baby cooed happily as his mother strapped him to her waist. While they walked up the narrow trail that led back to the village, his cradleboard swung back and forth from Ta-O-Dee's hip, a motion that made him laugh with glee.

"He told my husband that you accused him of being with that evil woman," Ta-O-Dee said with a shrug of her shoulders as they reached the summit of the incline.

Regina tossed her head back defiantly. "What was I supposed to think when he left so quickly, and without an explanation? I had no way of knowing that Grandfather had sent him to obtain supplies." She lowered her eyes to the ground, suddenly feeling guilty for jumping to conclusions. "Is that why he is so mean to me?"

"No, that is just the excuse he uses so that he won't have to face his real feelings." They had reached Ta-O-

Dee's wickiup. Regina began to help the other woman lift the awkward tus from her back.

"What do you mean?" Regina's heartbeat quickened. "Has—has he said something to you or your husband about me?" Did she dare hope that Nachae's attitude toward her was beginning to change?

"He hasn't said anything to me," Ta-O-Dee replied with a coy smile. She untied Ino's cradleboard from her waist and placed him beside the wickiup.

"What has he told your husband then?" Regina asked in Apache. She was mastering the Indian language with ease and remembered to use the customary way to talk about other people without using their proper names.

The other woman's head tilted to the side as a thoughtful expression overcame her face. She had grown so close to Sky Dreamer in the short time they had become friends, and she hated to see the other woman worrying about something so unnecessary. She motioned for Sky Dreamer to follow her into her wickiup. Once inside, she dug into a large basket and produced two elaborately beaded necklaces. She placed them in her friend's hands and smiled broadly.

Regina stared down in confusion at the necklaces. "They're beautiful, but—"

"They are to be a gift when you marry that stubborn man."

Regina drew her hands together and raised the necklaces closer to her face. They were designed to be worn tightly around the neck. Delicate little strands of beads hung from the wide neckband in vibrant colors of purple, silver, and yellow.

"The purple represents your eyes, the silver is for his; the yellow beads are for the eternal sun which will shine on the two of you as long as you are together."

Regina closed her eyes and drew in a deep breath. Was it really possible that she and Nachae would be together someday? She opened her eyes and stared at Ta-O-Dee with another troubled frown. "But why does he act so hateful toward me?"

"He has a lot of pain in his heart," Ta-O-Dee answered in a quiet tone. "And although he fights within himself to avoid the love that invades his soul, there will come a time when the love will overcome all the bitterness." She wrapped her arm around Sky Dreamer's trembling shoulders. "Be patient. He is a man worth waiting for, no matter how long it takes."

Regina swallowed back the lump in her throat. Ta-O-Dee spoke the truth—she would wait forever for Nachae. She threw her arms around the other woman's neck in a show of friendship. After they pulled apart, their youthful laughter continued to fill the wickiup.

"You are so wise. It is you who should be a shaman—instead of me," Regina said in a serious tone.

"I am honored that you would say something so kind. Except when I dream, I see only those things which have already happened. I do not think this would be something my people would find helpful." They laughed again as Ta-O-Dee took the necklaces from Regina and put them back in the basket.

"Will you come with me to gather *chich' il?*" Ta-O-Dee said as they exited the wickiup. The late summer heat was merciless and the air was still and quiet. She scooped up Ino's cradleboard and secured him on her back, then wiped away the heavy veil of perspiration that coated her forehead.

A thoughtful look drew Regina's dark brows together. She should return to Grandfather's wickiup, in case he wanted her to study with him today. Yet going to look for *chich' il*—acorns—with Ta-O-Dee sounded like much more fun. She nodded her head at Ta-O-Dee and grabbed up another basket. Waddling Woman would appreciate having the nuts to add to her stew tonight, Regina told herself.

As the two young women trudged out to the wooded area where they would find the oak trees, Regina walked behind Ta-O-Dee and made funny faces at Ino. His chubby little arms waved wildly through the air while his gleeful laughter filled their ears.

Regina began to think about how much she had learned since she had arrived at the Apache rancheria. Her life had changed so drastically from the way she had lived when she was in Georgia! Yet in spite of all the hard work and danger, she had never known such a deep contentment. Even the nagging remembrances of the brutal way the Apaches dealt with their enemies had slipped to the back of her mind.

She hadn't realized they had reached the grove of oak trees until Ta-O-Dee stopped in front of her and Regina nearly ran into Ino's cradleboard. Ta-O-Dee taught her how to search the ground for the acorns that had fallen from the trees. Regina went to the opposite side of the grove to fill her basket as Ta-O-Dee untied Ino from her back and placed him beneath the low-hanging branches of a nearby tree. Both women worked quickly, undaunted by the heat that cloaked the parched ground.

As Regina listened to Ino coo and chatter, she thought about Nachae, and wondered if they would ever have a child of their own. She sighed. If their relationship continued at the rate it was going, she would be too old to bear children by the time they reached that point. The sounds of Ino's merriment increased until Regina was compelled to take a short break from gathering nuts so that she could go play with the happy baby.

She walked in an idle pace through the trees, humming a tune she had heard on the drums and flutes which the men of the village played nightly. As she approached the infant, a sixth sense told her that something was wrong. His babyish prattle was too loud, too excited. Regina's pulse quickened, and her feet moved faster until the child was within her sight. He was staring at the ground, his eyes wide with excitement. Several feet in front of him, a diamondback rattler was slithering toward his cradleboard.

Regina stopped herself from crying out. Her mind went blank as she desperately tried to think of a plan. If she attempted to move toward Ino, the snake was likely to attack him. Although the only parts of the child that were exposed in the cradleboard were his face and upper body, they were within easy striking range of the reptile's fangs. A sense of hopelessness overcame Regina as she watched the yellow-and-black snake inch its way closer to the child. Using extremely slow movements she lowered her basket to the ground. Her slight movement caused Ino's attention to shift to her.

The deadly snake coiled into a tight circle the instant the child moved. Regina held her breath, too scared to move or make a sound. The snake was prepared to strike. She slid her knife, which Grandfather had insisted she carry with her at all times, from its sheath. The snake's tail rose into the air like a spear of death, then began to shake rapidly. The rattling noise caused Ino to squeal with delight.

The head of the snake darted forward, but his fangs struck at the base of the heavy wooden cradleboard that supported the child. Regina screamed and jumped toward the snake with her knife positioned tightly in her hand, but she was halted by Ta-O-Dee. The other woman had moved up beside her so silently that Regina had not even noticed her approach, and when Ta-O-Dee grabbed her arm, Regina nearly collapsed with fear.

"You must not kill it," Ta-O-Dee whispered. Her dark eyes were wide with terror and her skin had turned a ghastly shade of white.

Regina tried not to move as she replied, "But I must kill it before it strikes again."

"It is forbidden. An Apache can never kill a snake. You are a shaman, you must use your powers to make it go away."

Ta-O-Dee's statement hit Regina as though a stone wall had just collapsed upon her. Until this instant, she had not realized the responsibility that had been placed upon her by the Indians when they had accepted her into their tribe as a shaman. She knew that as a woman of medicine, she was expected to cure sickness, tend to births and deaths, and lend her supposed wisdom to her people. Eskinzan had even warned her that it was not unusual for a shaman to be killed for failure to cure an ill person. But never had she suspected the depth of these people's faith in a mere mortal. To be in the honored position of a shaman, Regina understood now, was to associate with Usen.

The insistent rattling of the snake snapped her thoughts back to saving Ino; to do so, she would try anything. She stepped forward, still clutching the knife in her hand in a prepared stance for an attack on the reptile. Magic potions and simple words would not make this deadly snake go away, she told herself as a panicked tremor raced through her body.

"You must tell it to take its evil away and crawl back into its hole," Ta-O-Dee whispered again.

Regina tried to think in a rational manner. She wanted to follow Ta-O-Dee's instructions, but she didn't want to risk the child's life with wasted words. She took another step forward, and the snake abruptly swiveled around to face her. Regina stared down into its hideous flat face, her eyes focused on the dark tongue that darted in and out of its mouth. The curled fangs, which held enough poison to snuff out a human life with one clamp of its jaws, flashed at her ominously each time the snake hissed. Fear froze her feet to the spot where she stood. Behind her she could hear Ta-O-Dee still pleading in a hushed whisper for her to say the words that would make the snake go away. Regina sensed that the snake was about to strike at her, and though she was sure it was useless, she decided to console her friend and say the words.

"Go away," Regina's voice came across in a loud tone. Because her body was a quivering mass of terror, the unwavering tone of her voice surprised her. The snake hissed louder, its tail flailing through the air with a pounding rattle.

"Tell it to take its evil back into its hole," Ta-O-Dee instructed.

Regina took a deep breath. "Go back to your black hole and take your evil with you," she repeated.

The ground became silent; even Ino fell quiet. Regina

continued to watch the snake. Its head remained up in the air while its piercing black eyes looked at her, but its tail had ceased to rattle. Ta-O-Dee gasped in awe. It appeared that Sky Dreamer had hypnotized the snake into submission. Regina, however, had no idea what had caused the snake to become subdued. Perhaps just the sound of her voice had drawn its attention away from striking out again.

Becoming braver, Regina called out again. "Go away, you evil thing."

The shiny reptile did not move for a few more minutes. Then, as though it had been pondering her command, it slowly sank down to the ground and slithered away through the brown grass, until the only movement the two woman could see was the slight stirring of the tall blades as the snake departed.

Regina turned around to face Ta-O-Dee. The other woman was staring at her with a look of disbelief and amazement. Her hands flew up to her face as a relieved sob flew from her mouth. "You have saved the life of my son. I will be forever indebted to you," she cried.

Regina raised her shoulders in a confused shrug. She was at a loss as to what she should say or do. The retreat of the snake had surprised her as much as it had the other woman, although it was for a different set of reasons. "I don't know what happened," she answered, then turned to gaze at Ino's smiling face. "But whatever caused that snake to go away, I, too, will be forever grateful."

Still crying with relief, Ta-O-Dee rushed over to her child and picked up his cradleboard. The evidence of the snake's first lunge at the child was embedded in the wood of the carrier. Two deep fang marks were outlined in the frame. Ta-O-Dee hugged the board to her chest but did not bother to strap it on as she hurried back to the village.

Regina ran behind her, not sure of her friend's intent. As the women reached the outskirts of the village, Ta-O-Dee's excited cries bought the attention of everyone who heard them. She continued to speak in rapid syllables about the incident and of the way Sky Dreamer had used her great powers. Regina attempted to understand all of Ta-O-Dee's comments, but the woman was speaking so fast that Regina could not keep up with her. But she was able to decipher enough of Ta-O-Dee's speech to understand that the woman was grossly exaggerating the episode. The snake, which Regina estimated to be less than four feet long, had grown to six or more feet in Ta-O-Dee's account, and according to Ino's mother, the snake had communicated silently with Sky Dreamer before it had hung its head in shame and crawled away to its hole.

A low murmur echoed through the crowd as all eyes focused on Regina. She didn't know if she should try to explain what had really happened or if she should just remain silent.

"Come, my child," Eskinzan said with a proud grin as he walked up beside her. "Tonight, we will celebrate." Shouts and cheers began to rise around them, while Eskinzan leaned over and said into her ear, "Today, you have proved your worth as an Apache shaman. Now I know from where you derive your great powers."

Regina stumbled alongside Eskinzan through the cheering group. "What do you mean?" She was more unsure than ever about what she should do now. How could she permit everyone to believe that she had actually used her powers to save Ino?

"Every shaman who has real powers must obtain them from some living thing; you have been given your gift from the rattlesnake." He gave his gray head a satisfied nod. "This is good."

Regina followed him into his wickiup while she tried to digest his words. The Apaches believed that everything on Usen's earth possessed powers, but she did not see what was so good about receiving a gift from a poisonous reptile. When she told Eskinzan how she felt on the matter, he only laughed, and told her to wear the dress Ta-O-Dee had given to her when she came to the celebration.

Throughout the evening, Regina scanned the crowd in search of Nachae. He was nowhere to be seen. His absence took away the joy from her celebration. She tried to concentrate on the dances and chants that were an imitation of her great accomplishment against the snake, but she only wished she could be alone for a while to think about the events of the day, and of the great responsibility she suddenly felt because of her rank in the Apache village.

When she had an opportunity to escape from the festivities, Regina sought solace along the dark trail that led to the river. She sat down on the sandy bank and stared out upon the smooth sheet of black water. Juno and Ta-O-Dee had gifted her with numerous items of clothing and blankets that she was certain Ta-O-Dee could not spare, yet she knew better than to insult the couple by refusing their presents. Would she constantly be faced with life-and-death decisions which she did not feel capable of handling?

"I've been looking for you."

Regina's startled gasp echoed across the silent water. Her eyes tried to focus through the dim light of the moon upon the face of the tall man who had arrived quietly at her side. Every inch of her body began to tingle with excitement. Her mind would not function and her voice was lost somewhere within her quaking being. He sat down beside her in the dense grass on the riverbank and turned to study her silent form.

"I—I thought you must be gone again because I didn't see you at the celebration," Regina said.

"Did you think I was off killing more innocent whites or was your mind leaning toward the more pleasurable pastimes that I indulge in?"

"Aren't those the two things you're usually doing?"

"When I'm not abducting women."

Regina did not reply. She had felt guilty enough since she had accused him unjustly for his actions during his last absence.

When he realized that she was not going to retaliate, he grunted with aggravation. He was not used to being opposed—especially by a woman. For her back talk she should be beaten, he told himself. If she were his wife, he

180

would definitely consider a punishment for her insolence. He was caught by surprise when that thought passed through his mind. . . . She would never be his wife!

"I made something for you," he said in an angry voice.

"For—for me?" she asked as the trembling in her limbs increased. His arms suddenly went over her head, while he slid something past her ears.

She reached up to touch the object he had just hung around her neck, but in the darkness of the night, her hand clasped onto his hand instead. She heard him gasp softly as he pulled away.

"I am honored that you would make this for me," she said in a hoarse voice as her fingers found the round leather amulet she had been searching for when she accidentally grabbed his hand. He grunted in reply.

A sinking feeling replaced her excitement from a moment ago. Why did he always have to act so mean? "I think I would like to go back to the village so that I can see it more clearly." He remained silent. Regina rose to her feet awkwardly and waited to see if he would follow—he didn't.

With a leaden step and an equally heavy heart, she began to back away. *"A-co-'d,"* she said in barely more than a whisper.

"You're welcome."

He did not make any attempt to move, so Regina began to walk back up the path alone. As always, whenever she had any sort of encounter with that man, her mind was in a turmoil and she felt as if she needed to cry or maybe hit something—or someone. How could he make a gift for her, then be so hateful when he gave it to her? Would she ever understand the strange man who had claimed her heart yet caused her more distress than she had ever known?

The celebration in her honor was still going on, but Regina was too disappointed and furious to partake in the merriment again. She avoided the activity and headed toward the wickiup she shared with Eskinzan and his two wives. In the light of the campfire that burned outside the

181

dwelling, she paused to study the amulet which hung from her neck. The round necklace consisted of a tan circle of leather suspended from a long leather strip that reached past her bosom. In the center of the amulet was carved a coiled snake. The reptile was painted in contrasting shades of yellow and black, but its eyes were a vibrant hue of lavender. Regina raised the necklace up to her face and placed the cool piece of leather against her cheek. It had not been long ago that his hands had worked on this necklace. She wondered if he had done it because he felt obligated to give her something for her encounter with the snake, or if he had made it because he really did care — just a little bit. If his behavior from a short time ago was any hint of his feelings toward her, she did not have much hope for their future.

She sighed in defeat and entered the dark hut. For a change, she was alone. As she lay down among the soft furs, she contemplated her situation and made two decisions: Tomorrow, she was going to find Nachae and tell him of her love for him. And from this day forth, she was going to forgo her white name and think of herself as Sky Dreamer — the name Nachae had carefully chosen for her — Sky Dreamer, a shaman of the Chiricahua Apaches.

With those decisions planted firmly in her mind, her eyes began to grow too heavy to stay open. For once, she did not dream of Nachae as she had done almost nightly since she had left Savannah, Georgia. Instead, her dreamland was filled with the lyrical sounds of faraway music, and with the visions of smoke so thick she couldn't find her way through the deadly haze.

Chapter Fifteen

In some men, there lurks a dark side — a remote coldness of heart which is satisfied only when their hands are stained with the blood of another human. In most of these men, this hidden personality surfaces briefly, then recedes, giving way to a better side. But in men such as Randy Decker, this chilling black trait is the controller; it will not allow the good side to emerge.

The lieutenant leaned forward in his saddle and peered through the hazy light of dawn. The Apaches were sitting ducks. His men had even flushed out the camp lookouts earlier that morning, and had disposed of them without any effort. Randy smiled contentedly to himself. It had been so simple to follow the captain when he had come to the Apache rancheria to look for his daughter. Returning to the fort before Charles Atwood came back from his parley at the Indian camp, and wiring his uncle that the Apache camp had been located, was a cautionary measure. However, Lieutenant Decker did not bother to wait until he received orders from Washington before he led a battalion of men into the area. Since Captain Atwood had no idea that he had been followed, he felt the Chiricahua would be safe when he ordered Lieutenant Decker to conduct a search in the opposite direction from where the village was actually located.

Randy Decker had not been able to get close enough to the rancheria when he was following the captain, so he had no way of knowing if Regina Atwood was still being held captive in this particular village. But he assumed that she must have been traded to another tribe before the captain had been able to catch up to his missing daughter. Why else would the captain return to the fort alone and then order them to search another village in a different site? The lieutenant sighed deeply when he thought about his insubordination. He would undoubtedly be reprimanded for disobeying the captain's orders, but it would be a small price to pay for snuffing out another batch of those damn savages!

Randy's mind conjured up the sweet face of the captain's young daughter, and he released another long sigh. Regina Atwood had been so promising, and now—well, for her sake, she would be better off if she was dead. If she wasn't, then he hoped he would be the one to save her from the savages and earn himself a few more points with his uncle in Washington for rescuing the daughter of his old friend. Of course, the thoughts he had once entertained about seeking the companionship of Miss Atwood were strictly forbidden now that she had been an Apache hostage. What decent white man would want the used goods of some Apache buck?

Lieutenant Decker straightened his spotlessly clean white hat and double-checked his rifle. With his gauntleted hand, he pulled his saber from its sheath. Then, as if he were opening a curtain on a stage in readiness for a grand performance, he raised his long sword into the air and gave the signal to attack.

From the three corners where his men could easily gain access to the village—the fourth being the river—the soldiers charged into the sleeping encampment. As the roar of the ambush filled the quiet morning, the lieutenant cleared his conscience of any wrongdoing with a necessary precaution.

"Spare the women and children—if possible," he said in a voice not quite loud enough for anyone else to hear, except for the few men who were riding close to him. They would vouch that he had, indeed, issued the order to save

184

the women and children should anyone dare to ask.

Sky Dreamer had awoken only moments before the first command rang out. Her disturbing dreams had not permitted her to get more than a few short naps throughout the night. She was in the process of sneaking across the wickiup to wake up Eskinzan so she could ask him what the images of fire and music could mean, when the village was besieged by the soldiers. Sky Dreamer had no idea what was happening outside the wickiup, but Eskinzan, Waddling Woman, and Tarza all jumped up from their beds as though they had rehearsed this scenario a dozen times. When Sky Dreamer saw Eskinzan grab his long feathered lance, she realized that someone was attacking the village.

In a rush of panic she grabbed the buckskin dress that Ta-O-Dee had given to her and hastily pulled it over her head.

Waddling Woman, who was helping Tarza out through the door of the hut, called over her shoulder to Sky Dreamer, "Soldatos!"

Sky Dreamer's heart ceased to beat for a moment. It couldn't be true. Her father's men would never attack a sleeping village filled with women and children. She followed Eskinzan and his two wives out into the cold harsh dawn. The first light of day was barely inching over the distant horizon, illuminating the area with an eerie gray glow. Half-clothed women and children, old men, and even the warriors of the tribe ran in confused pandemonium. Screams from the horrified Indians and shouts from the soldiers echoed from every direction of the rancheria.

Without any destination or plan, Sky Dreamer ran in circles in front of Eskinzan's wickiup. She lost track of Grandfather and the two women. It could have been her imagination, but once she thought she saw the old shaman walking straight through the maze of horses and soldiers. However, the dust was too thick and she soon lost sight of him. She remembered once that he had told her that an Apache shaman possessed powerful medicine that could protect him from bullets and other white men's weapons. She prayed that the old man did not truly believe that superstition; if he did, she feared she would never see him alive again. Her mind would not function; the horror of what was going on around her was too unreal to be happening. She screamed as a soldier whisked past her and nearly missed her head with the butt of the rifle, which he was swinging wildly.

The next instant, she was grabbed from behind by a pair of powerful arms. She kicked and struggled to free herself until the voice finally penetrated.

"Quit fighting me. I'm not your enemy!" Nachae yelled at her. His grip tightened until she was certain he was going to break her ribs. She fell silent, unable to speak from his painful embrace. When he set her feet back on the ground, he did not waste time with explanations. His large hand grasped her forearm as he began to run, dragging her along behind him. She had left the wickiup barefoot, yet she didn't notice the rocks and spiny cactus that dug into her tender flesh. Her lungs hurt from the smoke of the burning wickiups, which the soldiers had ignited with torches.

She saw women, many of them carrying their small children at their breasts, cut down by the soldiers' bullets or bayonets. Their babies were thrown into rejected heaps in the dirt at their sides. Old men and women tried to outrun the soldiers' horses but were trampled to death by the onslaught of deadly hooves. Sky Dreamer's strangled screams were lost to the roar of the gunfire and to the cries of the dying and fleeing Indians. She tried to wrestle free from Nachae's tight grip so that she could help some of the children who were too paralyzed with fear to make a run for safety. Several of them stood rooted to the ground, crying and screaming for their parents with a look of fear that would haunt Sky Dreamer for all time.

The dawn issued in a day of red death as the rays from the early morning sun struck the battleground of what

186

had once been the peaceful Apache rancheria. The sun rose above the distant peaks although it did not seem proper for it to shine on such an evil day. Sky Dreamer's legs felt weak and her stomach kept turning into a tight ball as Nachae dragged her toward the edge of the rancheria. His plan was to get her out of the village and into the trees down by the riverbank. But they were halted before they reached their destination.

"Release that white woman, breed!" Lieutenant Decker's horse reared up on its hind legs as he abruptly pulled on the reins. With his stark white hat and long navy blue cape billowing out behind him, its gold satin lining glistening in the sunlight, he looked like a crusading king upon a fiery steed. The lieutenant couldn't believe his luck at encountering Regina Atwood. Not only was he going to be the one to recapture Captain Atwood's missing daughter, but in doing so, he was also going to kill the worthless half-breed who had always managed to elude him.

Nachae twirled around, and as he did, he shoved Sky Dreamer away from him. She fell into the dirt but sprang to her feet at once. The malice in the officer's voice filled her with doom. The lieutenant had referred to her as a white woman, but all she had heard was the word "breed."

Nachae did not look in her direction as he yelled at her in Apache, "Sky Dreamer—run to the river."

There was nothing she could do to help him, yet she would not leave him either. When she saw Nachae frantically dodging the officer's sword, a terror so great washed through her body that she could not move—even if she had wanted to run for shelter. Nachae's face was filled with so much hatred that his dark features were almost unrecognizable, and the expression on Randy Decker's face was equally malevolent. Sky Dreamer sensed that the war these two men fought today was only the extension of something that had begun a very long time ago.

Nachae hunkered down, moving cautiously around the officer's horse in a stalking movement that made Sky Dreamer even more aware of his deadly and dangerous nature. Lieutenant Decker's calculations were accurate as he twirled his mount in a circle in an effort to snuff out the man who represented what he despised most in the world: someone who did not belong in any society — a half-breed!

His long saber sliced through the air, making a piercing contact with its target. Sky Dreamer screamed when she heard the sound of the metal thud against Nachae's head. Blood spurted from the wound, although it did not stop Nachae from lunging toward the lieutenant's horse. He tried to pull the soldier from the horse's back, but the lieutenant was too quick. His arm came down upon the side of Nachae's head and knocked the Apache back onto the ground. With a powerful pull on the reins of his horse's bridle, the lieutenant made his horse rear up.

Sky Dreamer had no time to think about her actions; all that mattered was that Nachae was about to be crushed by the descending hooves of the lieutenant's horse. She ran forward, taking the soldier's horse by surprise, throwing him off balance. The animal's front legs crashed back to the ground, giving Nachae the instant he needed to roll out of danger. Regina fell backward into the swirling dust.

Lieutenant Decker regained his balance in the saddle and turned his fury-ridden gaze to the woman sprawled on the ground. He noticed the fire in Regina Atwood's violet eyes and thought briefly of how savage she looked in the buckskin dress she was wearing. He was reminded of the horrible suffering she had no doubt been subjected to since her capture. Right now, the poor girl probably did not know who was her foe, or who her savior. Randy tore his eyes from the pitiful creature and directed all his anger at the man whom he blamed for the ruination of Regina Atwood.

"You good-for-noth—" His venomous words were cut off by the sound of a bullet whizzing precariously close to his white hat.

Sky Dreamer's head jerked around to see where the gunfire had come from. Her whole body flooded with relief when she spotted Juno, accompanied by several other young braves, coming to Nachae's aid.

"Ta-O-Dee needs you," he called to Sky Dreamer as he ran toward the lieutenant. Sky Dreamer backed away when the lieutenant's horse reared up again. The officer immediately realized his deadly predicament and made a brave charge through the middle of the oncoming Indians. Sky Dreamer saw an arrow drive itself into his thigh, yet the officer did not pause in his attempt to get away from his attackers. The last Sky Dreamer saw of Randy Decker was his retreat toward the center of the rancheria, where the worst of the battle was still raging. She turned to Nachae and saw him staring at the dust-filled area where the lieutenant had just disappeared. The expression upon the warrior's face was so cold and wrathful that Sky Dreamer cringed inwardly at the thoughts that must be going through his mind. What could compel a man to hate so viciously? Her thoughts snapped back to Juno's last words as she remembered that Ta-O-Dee was in need of help.

Sky Dreamer's mind could not tolerate the horror of what she saw when she began to make her way toward Ta-O-Dee and Juno's wickiup. Dead and dying soldiers, as well as Indians, littered the ground. No mercy had been shown toward the elderly Indians or the youngest members of the tribe. Sky Dreamer threw her hand over her mouth to keep from gagging at the indescribable sights that greeted her eyes. She recognized many of the dead or near-dead soldiers from the short time she had been at the fort, but she no longer felt any sorrow for them. In the past few weeks she had come to know every individual who lived in this village through her work with Eskinzan, and her sympathy was with these people . . . her people.

She could not avoid looking at the mutilated bodies of the dead Apaches. Two women were still fighting a group of six or seven soldiers who had stripped them of their clothes and were forcing them down to the ground. Regina forced herself to look away from the disgusting scene when she noticed the soldiers unbuckling their belts and readying themselves for the brutal rape of the helpless women.

She ran faster toward Ta-O-Dee's hut, trying to block out the hideous sights. She felt certain that the last of her sanity would desert her if she continued to watch the inhuman acts against the Indians. Nachae had tried to warn her about the white man's contempt toward the Apaches, and even her father had attempted to spare her from this madness, but she had not listened to either of them. Now, for as long as she lived, she would never allow herself to forget the violence and death the soldiers had brought upon her mother's people on this black August dawn.

Through the suffocating dust and smoke she spotted Ta-O-Dee running toward her. She clutched her infant son tightly against her breast as she headed toward the meager protection of the riverbed. Something about the way Ino dangled form his mother's arms did not seem natural to Sky Dreamer. Was he sleeping through all of this noise, or was she simply used to seeing him in his cradleboard? She called out to Ta-O-Dee as she approached, but the woman only looked at her with a blank expression. When Ta-O-Dee came closer, Sky Dreamer realized that the young mother was in deep shock.

Sky Dreamer grabbed her friend's arm and began to lead her to the edge of the camp. Her only thought was to get Ta-O-Dee and Ino away from the violence in the camp. Nachae had instructed her to run to the river, so it was this thought that pushed Sky Dreamer onward. Other women and children were also fleeing to the meager sanction of the riverbank. They hurled themselves down the trail that led to the water and into the sparse shelter of the thick grasses and the sharp branches of the mesquite bushes.

Sky Dreamer huddled against Ta-O-Dee with Ino's tiny form pressed between them as they listened to the sounds of the battle that still raged above them. It seemed that the horror would never end, but only minutes later, a bugle began to play a lyrical tune, so out of place among the explosions of gunfire and shrill screams. With the sound of the music, the roaring noise of the guns began to die down until it was almost silent, except for the mournful crackling of the burning wickiups and the groans of the dying soldiers and Indians. Sky Dreamer and Ta-O-Dee did not move, even when the morning became so quiet and still. The silence was as terrifying as the deafening noises had been only moments earlier.

"You are safe," Nachae said in a hoarse voice when he walked down the side of the riverbank. He had been searching for Sky Dreamer among the survivors, and was about to give up hope when he saw her hiding in the deep grass with Juno's wife.

Hesitantly, Sky Dreamer raised her eyes to Nachae's face. She no longer saw the intense hatred that had masked his face a short time ago when he had been fighting with Randy Decker. His expression now was filled with remorse and also with a touch of relief as his eyes searched her face. Now would she understand why the Apaches had to fight the white men?

"Are you hurt?" he asked, ignoring the panic in her eyes when she looked up at the wound above his left ear. She shook her head and glanced at Ta-O-Dee. A distant look covered the other woman's countenance and filled Sky Dreamer with an engulfing sense of dread.

"Let me help you up," Sky Dreamer offered as she pulled away from Ta-O-Dee and started to rise up to a standing position. As she regained her footing, her eyes moved down to the red stain that covered the front of her buckskin dress. A tightening in her chest began to twist her insides into knots of despair when she looked down at Ta-O-Dee with a harrowing stare.

Ta-O-Dee still sat on her knees in the tall wheat-colored grass. Her downcast face was buried in the blanket that she had thrown over Ino as they had made their escape from their wickiup. The woven blanket was soaked with

191

the same red substance that coated Sky Dreamer's dress.

"Dear God," Sky Dreamer whispered in English. Her disbelieving eyes flew to Nachae's face with a desperate hope that she was mistaken, but his expression confirmed what she was already thinking.

Nachae tore his eyes away from the spot of blood on the front of Sky Dreamer's dress, and met her horror-ridden gaze with his own. At first, he had thought she was the one who was injured and that it was her blood that drenched her clothes. A vicious bolt of fury shot through his body as his eyes moved back down to the limp form of his friend's only child.

Sky Dreamer clasped her hands together, feeling help-less and frightened at the reality of this gross mistake. Usen would not be so cruel as to take the life of one so innocent. She focused her sights on the baby once more as she felt her whole being fill with a rage that was more consuming than she had ever thought humanly possible. Never again would she rest with ease until revenge was taken against the men who were responsible for this over-whelming pain—a pain that would be with her for the rest of her life.

Nachae saw the change in her expression, and he under-stood. He had worn that identical look a thousand times, and he also knew the sickness that would eat away at her heart because of all she had witnessed today. He had been a carrier of that illness for most of his life, and he wished he could prevent her from becoming filled with a need for vengeance.

He moved the rest of the way down the embankment and reached out to Ta-O-Dee. She did not resist when he pulled her to her feet, but she clutched Ino's lifeless form tighter to her breast. Nachae felt a lump rising up in the back of his throat and he had to turn away for an instant. He had seen the shredded hole in the baby's blanket and knew that the child had been shot at close range. Most likely, Ino had taken a bullet that had been aimed at his mother. His sorrowful eyes met Ta-O-Dee's wide-eyed stare as he searched for the words that could ease this incredible loss. But such words did not exist.

"*Shik'isn*, you have found my family," Juno's relieved voice called down from the top of the riverbank. He began to walk toward them with anxious steps.

Sky Dreamer could not bear the sight of the lifeless child in Ta-O-Dee's arms any longer. She dropped her head into her hands and turned toward the river. Juno paused when Sky Dreamer's strange actions caught his attention. He looked to his friend for an explanation and knew at once that something was horribly wrong. For ten years he had been silently communicating with Nachae in their moments of sadness and rejoicing. During a raid, this quiet understanding had been developed between the comrades out of necessity. At other times, their secretive looks had contained a private joke or mutual understanding. This time, though, Juno sensed that the look upon the other man's face was that of death.

Nachae held his hand out to his friend in a gesture of support and comfort. Juno's dark eyes glanced at his hand and then moved in the direction of his wife. The blood that saturated the blanket and drenched Ta-O-Dee's hands drew his gaze to his infant son like a magnet. In the instant that followed, he thought of the spring day when his son had been born, and of how he had climbed to the top of the mountain to give thanks to Usen for such a great gift. All the plans, every dream he had envisioned for this child, were all gone.

Juno threw his head back and wailed like a tortured banshee as he fell down into the deep grass. Ta-O-Dee's head turned slowly as she stared down at her husband. Her eyes squeezed shut and she began to breathe in deep uneven gasps. Her arms slid outward until she was able to gaze down at the tiny boy who was wrapped in the bloody blanket. A cry so sorrowful that it raised the hair on the back of Sky Dreamer's neck rang out from Ta-O-Dee. She then drew the infant back against her breast and fell to her knees beside her husband.

193

Sky Dreamer's eyes blurred with a sea of tears and the shaking in the pit of her stomach caused her body to quake like a frail tree in a violent wind storm. She had never known such an engulfing grief and there was nothing that could take the feeling away. Nachae's arm encircled her shoulders and began to pull her along beside him. She staggered behind him, too numb to care where he was taking her. He led her away from the banks of the river, to a quiet place among a clump of yucca trees. When he pushed her down into the shaded area beneath the trees, she did not resist. The sounds of the mayhem were far away now, but she could still hear them . . . she would hear them forever.

"Was my father—" she said in choking gasps, but she could not continue because she was overcome with rasping sobs again. Nachae knelt beside her and picked up her slender fingers in his own large hands. He wanted so badly to spare her this sort of agony. Nachae knew who had been leading the attack on the village today—the same man who always ambushed those who could not protect themselves. Rage colored his gray eyes almost black when he thought of how easily the lieutenant had escaped from them today, then quickly sounded the retreat when the coward had realized that the Indians were killing his men off as fast as they were murdering the Apaches.

"No, your father had nothing to do with this. I am sure he does not even suspect what has happened here today."

"But it was his men!" Another bout of tears flowed from her eyes and coated her cheeks with salty fluid. "And they killed Ino."

Nachae did not speak for a moment. Mere words could not explain such a grave injustice. Ino had never hurt anyone—the infant had barely even had a chance to exist.

"I must go," he said in a voice that contained all the contempt he felt for Lieutenant Decker and the men who had ridden with him today. He rose to his feet, still clutching her hands. Then, in a voice so gentle and different from the tone he had used only a second ago, he added, "I will return to you, and when I do, I will never deny our destiny again."

Sky Dreamer's surprised gaze ascended to his face. His last words had been spoken in a tone that she had never heard him use. Her lips parted to speak, but she could not make a sound come forth. Amid all the death, the hatred, and the sorrow, he had finally accepted their fate. She was not aware of him kneeling back down in the grass. The only thing she knew was that his mouth claimed hers. His body, wet with sweat and tears, crushed against her trembling form. He smelled of smoke and earth, and even vaguely of the dried blood that caked the side of his wounded head. Her mind spun with the thought of his last words, and her stomach reeled with the odors of death. Still, she returned his savage kiss as though she were one of the dying and the feel of his lips was the only hope she had for lasting salvation. And when he pulled away, the taste of her own blood filled her mouth from the brutality of their union.

It was a kiss that was born out of the ashes of destruction. As he rose from the ground and walked away from her without saying another word, Sky Dreamer envisioned her own image walking at his side throughout all eternity.

Only two warriors had been killed during the attack on the village, but many of the elderly men and women had perished. Counting the children and all those who had died from the ambush, the number of dead totaled twenty-nine. Eskinzan's older wife, Tarza, had been one of the unfortunate ones who had been slain, or as the old shaman had explained, Tarza and the others were now the lucky ones. In the world they had crossed into, they could live without the fear of white men attacking them while they slept. The unlucky ones were those who had been left alive to face the uncertainty of the Apaches' grim future.

Ino's burial was almost more than Sky Dreamer's heart

195

could handle. His tiny cradleboard had been draped with charms and feathers to ward off any evil spirit who might try to lure his unknowing spirit away from Usen. The infant was then hung in the branches of an ancient oak tree—in almost the exact spot where Sky Dreamer had saved him from the rattlesnake just days ago.

Ta-O-Dee and the other women who had lost their relatives rubbed mud and ashes on their faces and partook in a ceremony known as black face mourning. They cut their long beautiful hair off in jagged points and disappeared to a private retreat for several days while they grieved. When they returned, everyone gathered up what few belongings they could salvage from the ashes of their wickiups and left behind the remains of what had once been the peaceful rancheria.

Sky Dreamer walked in a daze throughout the whole process. Her emotions ranged from unbearable sorrow to intense anger. She hated all white men—except her father—and even then, there were times when he didn't escape from her mind's wrath. She needed Nachae so badly that she was sure she could not survive from one minute to the next without him. Yet she tried to understand when Eskinzan told her that Nachae was now doing their people more good where he was at this time than if he were here with them now. Every day she prayed to Usen that Nachae was safe and that he would return to her soon, but when they were forced to move the village farther into the rugged canyons of the Chiricahua Mountains, she was certain Nachae would never be able to find them again.

Most of the horses had been killed or had escaped during the attack, so the survivors were forced to travel on foot. The injured were laid on crudely made travois and pulled by the stronger men along the rocky trails. Their journey was slow and allowed far too much time for thinking about the losses they had suffered. The place where they finally stopped and set up their new wickiups seemed desolate and alien compared to the spot beside the river.

As the hot lazy days of summer turned into the gold and orange hues of autumn, memories of the tragedy faded amid the never-ending preparations for the approaching winter. Days became shorter, yet the work loads remained the same. Sky Dreamer threw all her energies into learning more about the customs of her mother's people, and she rarely allowed herself to think about anything that might recall the painful memories of the raid on the village. Not even Llamarada's lurking presence at the outskirts of the new campsite distracted Sky Dreamer's dedication to becoming a true Teneh Chokonen.

Nachae's parting words dwelled in her mind and heart with every single breath she took. And she lived for the day when he would return to her . . . to remain forever!

Chapter Sixteen

Revenge had become almost second nature to Nachae. Each time he learned about the death of an Apache by the hand of a white man, or heard that the despised White-Eyes had stolen away more of their precious lands, he would seek some form of vengeance. At one time, there was not room for anything else in his life. But lately, he had been thinking about Sky Dreamer almost constantly, and of how he now felt the need to put the past behind him and make a fresh start. To do away with the burning hatred that threatened to eat him alive, however, Nachae had to confront the man who had killed his father. Then he must learn to overcame all the painful and bitter memories that still lingered from his youth. Killing a man such as Randy Decker would be an easy task.

The lieutenant had retreated to the safety of the fort immediately following the ambush on the village. Nachae was so obsessed with his quest for revenge that he had even considered attacking the fort to get at Randy Decker. But the Apache warriors were few in number, and to try to infiltrate the fortress would be an act of suicide. Nachae knew that Randy Decker had been wounded in the leg during the battle at the Apache rancheria, and probably would not be leaving the security of the fort until he had recuperated. Although he was almost too angry to wait until the lieutenant was well enough to attack another innocent village, Nachae was still confident that somehow his opportunity to have a showdown with the soldier would arrive before too much time had passed. When that day finally came, Nachae planned to torture Lieutenant Decker in the same manner that the officer had ruthlessly murdered his father, Alderay.

Only a handful of warriors were able to leave with Nachae after the raid on the village. The men who had lost a loved one, such as Juno, would join them later. Their tribe had been left with only a few horses, and the food supplies had been destroyed during the ambush, so it was essential for the survival of their people that the men replace the food and animals as soon as possible. Nachae knew of a place where he could obtain cattle and horses quickly, although it would only cause more resentment between him and his mother than that which already existed. During the past decade Nachae had traveled through his mother's land on many occasions. More than once he had stolen cattle and horses from the vast herds that roamed the huge acreage known as El Flores Rancho. Satisfaction always accompanied his raids upon the ranch. Each time he would make sure to leave a clue behind so his mother would know that the stolen animals were feeding and serving the needs of the Apaches, whom she hated so much.

This time, however, he felt a great sadness as he rode across the wide-open grazing lands of the large acreage. He had not come here merely to cause his mother distress as he usually had whenever he'd raided her herds. He wanted only to take the animals and hurry back to Sky Dreamer and their people. Returning to Sky Dreamer had taken priority over nearly everything else, and Nachae found that he was even more frightened of acknowledging these new feelings than he had been when he was trying to deny them. Yet every time he tried to shake her image from his mind or force the new feelings of devotion from his heart, they only retaliated by growing stronger.

He shook his head and sighed with aggravation. How would he ever be able to live with Grandfather now? The old man loved to gloat whenever one of his predictions came true, and Nachae could no longer deny his feelings for Sky Dreamer. Grandfather had been correct—there was no way to ignore something so strong that it had been preordained since the beginning of time. A frown creased Nachae's dark brow. Sky Dreamer was also a shaman, and Nachae sensed that he would have a difficult time enforcing his own decisions when his woman was able to predict future events with such accuracy. His woman—a feeling of warmth overcame him as that thought passed through his mind. He had never believed that a woman existed whom he would want to claim as his own. Yet Sky Dreamer had invaded him so completely that he was certain she controlled the rising and setting of the sun with her gentle ways. And surely she must silently beckon the moon each night so that it would appear to light the dark Apache sky.

His mind was filled with these loving images when the warriors crested the ridge that banked the house and surrounding buildings of the ranch. They stopped abruptly and looked toward Nachae. It would be dark soon and none of the Indians wanted to chance being seen by any of the hired hands who worked for Rita Flores. Nachae grew furious with himself for allowing his mind to wander from the business at hand. With an irritated wave of his arm, he directed the other braves to stop. There was one man who lived on the grounds and who had never cared that Antonio Flores was a half-breed, and it was this particular man Nachae wanted to see at this time.

Reuben Gonzales had lived with his parents on the El Flores Rancho ever since he'd been a child. His father had worked for Rita Flores, so Reuben and Antonio had become good friends while they were growing up together. Even when the other Mexican children wouldn't play with Antonio because of his Apache bloodline, Reuben had remained his friend. As they grew older, and even after Antonio had run away to join his father's people, the two had still managed to keep in contact with one another. Reuben was now the foreman of El Flores Rancho, and Nachae never came to his mother's ranch without paying Reuben a visit. It was also common knowledge among the

Chiricahua that Reuben Gonzales was the only man on El Flores Rancho who had any compassion toward the Apaches. Even though it was Reuben's job to guard Rita Flores's herds, he usually managed to be in another section of the ranch whenever he suspected the Apaches were in the area.

Since its beginning, El Flores Rancho had belonged to the Flores family. It had been handed down through the succession of generations until only Rita Flores and her son, Antonio Flores, were left to claim the vast acreage. Nachae did not harbor any dreams of inheriting even a small portion of the ranch, however. Nor did he care what happened to the land after his mother was gone. El Flores Rancho had never been his home, just as Rita Flores had never been a mother to him.

Nachae motioned to the other men to wait for him in a grove of cottonwoods while he rode the rest of the way to Reuben's house. Darkness had fallen by the time he reached the ranch house and he had to hide Eagle behind the barn as he traveled the rest of the way on foot. Reuben was overseer to a sizable number of men whom the ranch employed, and even at this late hour, Nachae could see a light in the bunkhouse as he hurried toward the foreman's home. If he was caught sneaking around this property by anyone other than Reuben, Nachae had no doubt he would be shot without hesitation. Since this was not the first time he had arrived at his friend's home in such a manner, Nachae knew exactly how to approach the back entrance without attracting anyone's attention. Once he had reached the back door, he paused to listen for voices, and hearing none, he quickly entered and shut the door behind him.

Reuben was most likely sitting at his desk at this time of the evening, although Nachae checked each one of the rooms as he passed. Using extreme caution, he quietly entered the parlor and moved up behind the figure of the man who was hunched over his desk, intently studying a stack of papers spread out before him.

"What the—" Reuben Gonzales's words were cut off

when the other man's hand closed over his mouth. Reuben fell backward in his chair, causing both men to crash to the floor as Reuben struggled to free himself. Nachae had sneaked up on Reuben in the hopes of stopping the other man from becoming startled and hollering out for help.

"That's a helluva greeting, amigo!" Reuben gasped.

"I didn't want to startle you."

A smile curved Reuben's lips as he studied the other man's trail-worn clothes. "Gracias, but next time, don't try so hard." He emphasized his statement by rubbing his hand across his mouth. Nachae nodded in agreement and gave a nervous glance toward the door.

"Your indiscreet arrival was probably heard all the way into Lordsburg, if that's what you're worrying about."

A concerned look filtered into Nachae's face as he rose to his feet, then extended his hand to help his friend up from the floor. Cautiously, the warrior stalked to the window and peeked out through the drapes. "I've come for horses and cattle."

A small chuckle escaped from Reuben's mouth as he met Nachae's stern look. "So I figured." Reuben nodded his head and gave the doorway an anxious glance. "You shouldn't stay here too long."

Nachae's eyes narrowed with curiosity as he nodded his dark head in agreement. Still, Reuben seemed far more nervous than usual. "Is my mother up to something that I should know about?"

Reuben shrugged then turned away as though he did not want to meet the other man's eyes. "It's not important," Reuben said with a defeated wave of his hand. He dusted off the back of his pants, then walked toward his desk without glancing in Nachae's direction.

"My mother has threatened you, hasn't she?" His sooty eyes grew almost black with anger as he moved up to Reuben.

Reuben nodded slightly and gave his friend a quick sideways glance. "I guess she has grown wise to my deceptions, amigo. If I allow you to steal from her again, she says she will find a new foreman for the El Flores."

Rage colored Nachae's face a dark red. His thoughts were filled with ways to punish his mother for threatening his friend, when it was her unwanted half-breed son she was really seeking to hurt. "I'm going to make her pay for everything she's ever done to me," Nachae said, his voice filled with icy emotion. "But I will not allow her to hurt you!"

Reuben met Nachae's fury-ridden gaze. He dropped his hands to his side with submission, knowing it would be a waste of time to argue with his old friend. Antonio was too headstrong and too filled with anger to talk sensibly where his mother was concerned. But anyone who had to deal with Rita Flores usually came away with the same feelings of resentment toward the woman. Even before her brief captivity with the Apaches, she had been a spoiled, hateful girl. When she was recaptured and returned to El Flores Rancho, pregnant with a half-breed child, her contemptible attitude grew to an obsessive nature. She felt that society would never accept her because she had been forced to bear the child of a savage, so she no longer cared whom she used or hurt in her quest for control. Since she had inherited sole ownership of El Flores Rancho, she had grown powerful and ruthless. Maintaining a monarchy over her own domain was her only consolation, and her half-breed son was a threat to her power. She would do anything to destroy him, and she did not hesitate to ruin anyone who stepped in her way.

"Wait," Reuben called out as he grabbed his gunbelt and ran to catch up with the other man.

"Where do you think you're going?" Nachae said coldly.

"To show you where the herd is bedded down."

Nachae's long strides increased. "I'm going to steal every one of my mother's horses and all the cattle I can round up! If you're with me, she won't hesitate to carry out her threat to fire you."

Reuben's dark eyes glistened and his voice held a hint of excitement. "I know, but I won't get caught."

Nachae paused and glanced over at his friend. Even in the darkness, he could sense Reuben's enthusiasm. "I don't want you involved this time."

"I'm already involved because I know that you're here. While we're riding out to the pasture, we'll work up an infallible plan that will throw the boss lady into a real fit of rage!"

Nachae followed the other man without further resistance. He knew exactly what his mother was capable of doing to the people who got in her way. His mind began to calculate how they would pull off the large raid he was planning to conduct on her herds. Between Reuben and himself and the few warriors who had traveled with him from the Chiricahua camp, there were not nearly enough men to round up all the animals that he needed to obtain from the El Flores Rancho. But their number would increase when Juno and the other braves arrived, so Nachae decided to be patient once again. They would hide in the hills behind Reuben's house until the rest of the Apaches arrived, then they would carry out his carefully planned revenge on the El Flores Rancho. In the meantime, he would seek assistance from some of the bands of desperadoes who rode in the area. For a part of the ransom they would claim from Rita Flores, the Mexican bandits would gladly partake in the raid. The lapse of time between the Apaches' arrival and the attack on the herds would give Reuben ample opportunity to work up an alibi for his own whereabouts.

Nachae told himself that after he left his mother's ranch this time, he would never return. He would make this raid his final vengeance against his mother. In time, he would put his past behind him for good, once he had seen to it that Randy Decker had paid for his murderous crimes against the Apaches. But until then, he planned to return to Sky Dreamer and begin their lives where her dreams had left off.

A slap on the hand from several officials in Washington, and a round of parties in his honor from the good citizens of Tucson, were the only consequences of the lieutenant's massacre of twenty-nine Indians in the Chiricahua Mountains. The officer was quite pleased with himself. Only one thing could have made his victory more perfect — if he had succeeded in killing Nachae. The lieutenant, however, still preferred to call him by the name he was most familiar with — breed.

His thoughts returned to Regina Atwood once again as a thoughtful frown ceased his brow. If she had been in the Chiricahua camp when Charles Atwood went there in search of her, then why hadn't he found her? A million reasons came to the lieutenant's mind, but only one made sense: Perhaps Charles *had* found her at the Apache rancheria, but after seeing the degrading condition she had been reduced to since her captivity, he had decided to leave her with the savages. That must be what happened, Randy told himself. He remembered the wild look in her eyes when she had charged at him during the attack. Why, with the tortures and indignities she had been forced to endure from those animals she was living among, the poor girl had probably lost her mind.

A torrent of cold chills overcame the lieutenant whenever he thought about the close call he'd had with death during the ambush on the Apache village. A bit of luck was all that had helped him escape from the warriors who had come to that breed's aid, but in the end everything had turned out all right. He leaned back in the tattered wicker chair on the front porch of his quarters and smiled to himself. His leg had been badly wounded from the arrow he had caught, but it was not all that painful and the injury lent credibility to his explanation of the hostility he had encountered when he'd approached the village with peaceful intentions. His men knew better than to dispute his claim. On the returning trip after the attack, he had detailed exactly what would become of anyone who denied his story. Since the battle had taken place over a week ago, and to date, none of the men had put his threats to the test, Lieutenant Decker was confident that no one would contradict him.

The best thing to come from the ambush on the Apache

village was the letter of commendation that had arrived from General Decker, praising his nephew's quick perception and unequaled tactics of warfare when dealing with hostiles. A slight smile curled the man's lips, and images of the many Apaches he had slain by his own hand made his brown eyes twinkle with malice. He began to imagine himself at his uncle's side in Washington once again while his mind filled with plans for achieving his goal. Ever since that messy situation back in Savannah, he had been trying to prove to his uncle that he had grown more responsible, and was worthy of a promotion and a transfer out of this hellhole. If his uncle's latest letter was any indication, then perhaps the general was finally beginning to agree. Randy's thoughts of glory quickly turned to aggravation when he spotted Susan Wilkins walking toward him. She had been avoiding him ever since his return, and he definitely did not wish to see her now. He took note of her appearance, though, since it was obvious that she had gone to great lengths to look particularly lovely for this visit.

"Hello, Lieutenant," she said, pointing to the chair beside his. "May I join you?"

"If you must," he replied with a patronizing smile. His gaze lowered, and lingered, on the swell of her bosom above her low-cut blouse.

Susan pulled her long mass of blond hair over her shoulder in an attempt to cover the area that his degrading gaze had settled upon. The blush that crept across her face did not stop until the exposed area of her bosom was also a brilliant shade of crimson.

"I've come to ask for a truce," she said without looking at him. The past couple of weeks had been sheer torture. Returning to Georgia was out of the question, and in spite of what she'd learned about Charles's first wife, Susan had decided to go through with the wedding. First, though, she had to be certain that Randy Decker would not tell her future husband about their past involvement.

The lieutenant sighed, and picked up his cup of tea. "Another truce?" He took a small sip from the cup, then leveled his brown eyes at the woman. His mind recalled the numerous nights of wanton passion they had spent at her parents' plantation back in Georgia. "What sort of truce do you want and"—he leaned forward until their faces were almost touching—"do you have something useful to offer in exchange this time?"

"What do you mean?"

He leaned back again and glanced around at the expanse of the desolate fort, which he could see from his porch. "Well, you certainly weren't much help when I asked you to give me information about the location of the Apache camp." His lips curled into a smile.

Susan felt a rush of anger flood through her body, but she held her tongue in control when she spoke. "So—so what you're saying," she began in a shaky voice, "is that I must give you something valuable in exchange for your silence?"

"That's right," Randy answered nonchalantly. "I do feel you owe me something in exchange for lying to me."

Susan couldn't believe her ears. Tears sprang to her eyes as she jumped up from the chair. "My God, Randy! I really thought I was carrying your child. You owe me for your desertion!"

Randy reclined back in his chair and carefully stretched out his injured leg. A taunting grin touched his lips as his gaze met her teary eyes. "Well, perhaps we are indebted to each other to some degree. I suppose that there could be a way that I could help you and, in return, you could help me."

Susan drew in a heavy breath. Whatever the proposal was, it most likely would be to his benefit. "What do you want?"

The lieutenant rubbed his chin thoughtfully before answering. "Why wasn't Regina Atwood brought back to the fort with you?"

Susan's mind went into a spin. Did Randy know that Regina was part Apache? Her blue eyes searched his smirking face for a clue, but he was too good at playing games for her to read his expression. "I don't know," she replied with a defiant tone. The information she had obtained about Regina Atwood's mother was too valuable to reveal to Randy Decker so easily.

Randy's face hardened as he sighed with annoyance. "That's a real shame, Susan. Your continued ignorance could cost you the prestige you've been chasing after for so long." His dark blond curls became plastered across his forehead as a rash of perspiration coated his face. "You surely know that, as an officer's wife, you must be above reproach. Scandal can be extremely ugly, Miss Wilkins."

Susan wiped away an angry tear. "A scandal would ruin your career too. And besides, Charles told me that your uncle is an old friend of his from Georgia."

"Blood is more relevant than an old friendship, and my uncle is very protective of the family name."

Randy Decker's unspoken meaning was apparent. His uncle had saved him from tarnishing the family name two years ago and his uncle would undoubtedly come to his rescue again if the need should arise.

The idea of confiding in Randy about Regina's Apache bloodline hovered at the edge of Susan's confused mind. But what if she told him everything she knew, and he still wanted more? She had to get away from him to straighten out her thoughts before she revealed something that could destroy her. She sprang from the chair and rushed down the stairs. Once she had reached Charles's quarters and taken refuge inside, she leaned against the door and forced herself to stop crying by telling herself over and over again that Randy Decker was not worth her energy. Someday someone would see the lieutenant for the wicked person he really was. Susan just hoped she would be around when Randy Decker got what he deserved!

Chapter Seventeen

Sky Dreamer sat impatiently on the tree stump and waited for Ta-O-Dee to wrap the nah-leen in her long, thick hair. Before Ino's death, Sky Dreamer had also combed Ta-O-Dee's hair for her, but since cutting her long tresses off as a show of mourning, Ta-O-Dee did not need to have her closely cropped hair attended to. The loss of her son had changed Ta-O-Dee drastically. She no longer giggled and blushed and spoke of her virile husband, nor did she talk about having any more children. Juno had left to join up with Nachae and the other warriors as soon as they had reached the location for their new rancheria, and since his departure, Ta-O-Dee had not even mentioned him. It was heart-wrenching for Sky Dreamer to remember how happy her friend had once been, and to see the emptiness in the young woman's dark eyes now.

Sky Dreamer mourned for Ino, and also for Grandfather's oldest wife, Tarza. She grieved for a loss of a different nature, too. Nachae and the rest of the braves were still gone. She missed him more every day, and sometimes wondered if he would ever return to her as he had promised on that bloody morning after the ambush. Every day she prayed to Usen that he had not been injured or killed, and each night she tried to will her mind to conjure him up in a dream. But since the night that she had dreamt of the music from the soldiers' horns and the smoke from the burning village, her sleep had been empty. She worried that even her lack of dreams held a hidden meaning. What if Nachae never returned because he had found that he did not mean the words he had last spoken to her?

The long weeks since the ambush had been the most trying time of Sky Dreamer's life. The people of the tribe feared that the warriors would not return before winter and they would not have enough provisions to face the colder months ahead. Much of their clothing had been lost, and almost all the food they had gathered to see them through the approaching winter had been burned to ashes. Starting from scratch, the women built new wick-iups and replenished their food supplies with meager amounts of berries and nuts that the birds had not stored away for their winter food supply. When the men returned with meat and clothing, and the weakening tribe was once again strong enough to travel, they would move to a better location for the winter. Until then, the women, the elderly, and even the children toiled to survive, while keeping constant watch for their men.

Sky Dreamer threw herself into her work to take her mind off Nachae. Grandfather allowed her to assist with the birth of a child, and she sang mourning chants over the dead. Hardly a day passed when she wasn't asked to tend to a sick child or one of the elderly who was ailing. The whole tribe had come to respect and trust her, yet she had to force her mind to stay on her duties as a shaman. Her thoughts were constantly consumed with whether or not she would ever see her dream warrior again.

The strenuous labor that Sky Dreamer did each day was beginning to turn her thin girlish figure into the firm and more curvacious body of a woman. Her skin darkened in the sun and wind to a deep golden shade, which enhanced the startling contrast of her violet eyes. Of course, she had no idea of how beautiful she was, or of the way she stood out among the rest of the females in the tribe. Not only was she taller than most of the Apache women, but she also walked with a proud gait that made her striking good looks almost breathtaking as she moved throughout the rancheria on her daily tasks.

"I'm finished," Ta-O-Dee announced as she tied the last knot around the thick mass of hair. "Where are you off to in such a rush?"

Sky Dreamer shrugged as she jumped to her feet. She had no particular place to go, but she hated the time that she must spend grooming her hair. Married women were permitted to wear their hair long and loose if they wished, but if Nachae didn't ask her to marry him, she would never be allowed to wear her hair in that manner.

"Do you need help with your work?" Sky Dreamer asked. There was a time when she had assisted her friend with all her chores, but that was when Ta-O-Dee still had Ino to care for.

Ta-O-Dee shook her head. "I seem to get my work done quickly these days." Her dark gaze grew distant again.

"Then come with me to gather herbs to use in my medicine," Sky Dreamer said with enthusiasm. Ta-O-Dee's face lit up for an instant, but she looked away and shook her head negatively.

"I need help, but I guess I could impose on Waddling Woman." Sky Dreamer faked a look of rejection, which got her the response she hoped for.

Ta-O-Dee smiled. "If you really need my help, I will come. I thought you were just feeling sorry for me."

"Ha," Sky Dreamer said with a grin. "Why should I feel sorry for someone who is as beautiful as you, and who has such a wonderful and handsome husband?" She noticed a slight blush come into the other woman's cheeks, as it used to do whenever they talked about men. "And someone who has such a wonderful friend as myself."

Sky Dreamer's last remark received a genuine laugh from Ta-O-Dee. Sky Dreamer felt gladness soar within her breast. It was the first time in weeks that her friend had really laughed. Maybe everything was going to be all right again — Juno and Ta-O-Dee and the rest of her people would all become strong and healthy once more. And Nachae — well, she still worried that he might decide to flee from their destiny.

Sky Dreamer went back to Grandfather's wickiup to retrieve the fringed bag she used for gathering the many plants she needed for her medicine potions. Eskinzan sat outside the wickiup staring off at the distant horizon. Sky Dreamer was amazed at the old shaman. With all the hardships in his life, and even considering the sorrow he had suffered with the loss of his older wife, he was still as spry as ever.

"I had a vision," he said to her as she approached. Beneath his thick gray eyebrows his dark eyes twinkled with the image that only he could see.

"A good vision, Grandfather?" she asked while she picked up her herb bag. He had proudly adopted her as his granddaughter, even though he had explained that she would become his real granddaughter only when she married Nachae.

His long silver hair fell over his shoulder as he tilted his head to the side. "It's confusing. I saw many, many horses of all colors. They were running about the village wildly."

Sky Dreamer gasped as her eyes met Ta-O-Dee's fearful look. She remembered the dreams of smoke and music she had experienced the night before the attack on the village last summer. Was Grandfather's strange vision of premonition of another attack?

"We must warn the people," Sky Dreamer cried out in alarm. "Maybe we should hide in the mountains."

Eskinzan shook his head. "No, we will not run. I have already talked to the council and they are going to send out scouts to keep watch on the movements of the White-Eyes." His wrinkled face scrunched up. "It could mean something bad, but I have the feeling a very good thing is about to happen."

Sky Dreamer was still skeptical. She would never trust the soldiers again. There were even times when she had blamed her own father for what had happened to her mother's people.

"We're going to go look for herbs." She glanced at Ta-

O-Dee and noticed that the woman's face was pale and drawn. "But perhaps we should stay in the camp today?" she asked as she glanced back at Eskinzan.

The old shaman began to shake his head. "No, you both should go. It is a beautiful day for going into the woods." He glanced up at the clear blue sky and smiled. "It is a new day—a new beginning. The young people of our tribe are the only hope we have to continue our race. Go into the forest and bring back many medicine plants so that we may make much *hoddentin* to make our women fertile, and our children healthy again, and our warriors brave and strong." His old face was shining with excitement when he looked at his young protégée again. He did not see the same hopeful expression on her beautiful face.

Sky Dreamer wished she could feel the medicine man's optimism, but when she looked around at the dwindling members of the tribe, she did not see much hope for a bright future. She leaned down to hug the old man. "We will not be gone long, Grandfather," she said in a voice filled with the sorrow and concern she felt for the fate of the Apaches.

Silence shrouded the two young women when they walked out of the village. The joy Sky Dreamer had felt earlier had evaporated with Eskinzan's words. But they would go gather the plants they needed to make hoddentin anyway. The powder Grandfather had spoken of was blessed by the shaman and used in all the Apache ceremonies. It was sprinkled on women who were about to give birth and on the newborn as soon as they entered the world. Hoddentin was also sprinkled on a dead body before burial.

The tranquility of the autumn morning soon had the two women in a more cheerful frame of mind. Eskinzan's vision had filled them with doom, but they put the images of tragedy in the back of their minds for a while as they searched for the berries and seeds that were needed for the medicine bags. At the creekbed they found cattail pollen, which was the necessary ingredient for the important powder, hoddentin.

The gurgling of the brook drowned out any other sounds as the two women busied themselves with cutting off the thick stalks of the cattails. Sky Dreamer found herself humming and smiling in spite of her uneasiness about Eskinzan's vision. Even Ta-O-Dee looked more content than she had in weeks. It wasn't until they had gathered their bounty and started back toward the village that they spotted the cloud of dust that had risen up in the sky from the direction of the rancheria.

Sky Dreamer grabbed her knife out of her belt in a confused reaction. If her people were under siege again, she did not intend to stand idly by while the hated whites killed them off one by one.

"Are you loco?" Ta-O-Dee screamed in a nearly hysterical voice. She grabbed the other woman's arm and began to tug frantically. "Come, we must hide in the shelter of the thick trees."

Sky Dreamer pulled free of Ta-O-Dee's embrace. She understood why the woman was afraid to go back to the village. Ta-O-Dee had lived only seventeen harvest, but already she had seen all her relatives, many of her friends, and even her only child destroyed by the white men. With a touch of deep affection, Sky Dreamer laid her hand upon her friend's arm.

"I want you to go into the trees and hide, but please forgive me for not coming with you." She turned to leave, but Ta-O-Dee grabbed her again. Her ebony eyes were frantic with indecision and terror.

"I will come with you," she said in a whisper. Her voice quivered, but her expression was definite.

Sky Dreamer knew how much courage it had taken for Ta-O-Dee to decide to return to the village. She smiled and gave Ta-O-Dee's hand a quick squeeze as she said, "Let's go help our people."

Ta-O-Dee's bottom lip trembled, but she did not hesitate to pull her own knife out of its sheath as they began to run back in the direction of the Apache camp. Her mind was overcome with all the horrors she had witnessed during other attacks, and of the loved ones she had lost to the long knives and firearms of their enemies. Still, she ran on, telling herself that she would draw from her friend's source of strength if she could not conjure up her own. She thought about her husband and regret gripped at her heart. They had not even embraced, or spoken of how much they loved one another, when he had left the village almost one moon ago. Their marriage had been extremely strained following Ino's death, and Ta-O-Dee had almost been glad to see him go. Now she realized how much she missed him, and how deep her love for him ran. She said a quick prayer to Usen that Juno was still safe, wherever he was. Would she still be alive to greet him if he did come back?

Sky Dreamer was filled her own morbid thoughts as they got closer to the encampment. Since all the warriors had gone in search of food and supplies, only the women, children, and old people were left to face an attack. There was little hope of fighting off whoever had chosen their weakened village for destruction. As the village came within their sights, however, Sky Dreamer and Ta-O-Dee skidded to a halt at the edge of the piñon and oak trees. They looked at each other in confusion, then returned their startled gazes to the mass of horses and cattle that was being herded through the center of the village.

Sky Dreamer realized that whatever was going on was the same as Eskinzan's vision, but what could it mean? Who had brought all these animals into their hidden rancheria? Her violet gaze scanned the animals as she searched for a clue. Then she saw Nachae sitting atop his stallion, proud and straight as a reed as he rode through the rising dust. Her heart felt as though it had stopped beating for a second when she thought he looked in her direction, but he turned and rode Eagle toward the very back of the large herd without acknowledging her.

"Did you see him?" Ta-O-Dee said in quiet awe as her wide eyes followed Nachae's tall frame. "He has brought all these ponies for our warriors to ride in their battles against the whites, and the meat of the cattle will make our children grow healthy again."

Sky Dreamer felt tears sting the corners of her eyes, and as she watched him riding away, the tiny drops began to roll down her cheeks. The sight of him had always taken her breath away, but was he always as handsome and proud as he looked at this moment?

"Hurry, there's bound to be a big celebration on this wonderful day." Ta-O-Dee began to run toward the wickiups, but before she entered the village, her steps were halted by the advance of another warrior who rode among the herd of cattle and horses. Ta-O-Dee's dark eyes misted with happy tears.

"*Shika' bil nashdeehi,*" she cried out in a choked voice, but her words were lost to the roar of the animals. Juno spotted his wife at nearly the same instant she saw him. The glow in her eyes when she had called out to him was evident even from a distance. He had been fervently hoping that she would miss him as much as he had missed her, and her expression told him that his wishes had not been in vain.

Juno led his horse through the throng of animals toward his waiting wife as she rushed forward. He hoisted her up to his horse and encircled her waist in a loving embrace as she leaned back against his chest with a contented sigh. Tonight, he told himself, he would renew their love—in the memory of their son, Ino.

Sky Dreamer watched them ride into the swirling dust which engulfed the village, then blinked back the tears that still taunted her eyes. She was almost angry at Nachae for not coming directly to her, just as Juno had done to Ta-O-Dee. A flood of panic rushed through her when she remembered her fear that he might have changed his mind about her while he was away. Her uneasiness was quickly replaced by aggravation. If it turned out he had discovered that he did not mean his parting words, then she certainly did not intend to let him think that she had spent the past few weeks pining over him either. She drew in a deep breath and began to stomp through the cloud of dust toward Eskinzan's wickiup.

When she reached her destination, Waddling Woman and Eskinzan were standing in front of their home, watching as the herd of animals was being led into the open field beyond the rancheria. Much to Sky Dreamer's dismay, Nachae stood beside the old couple with his head tilted up in a noble stance. She tried to avoid his eyes, but it was impossible. His gray gaze did not waver from her face while she approached the waiting group. A heated flush crept through her cheeks, making her even more self-conscious as she moved forward with a clumsy step. Why was he looking at her in that manner?

Nachae could not pull his eyes away; he was hypnotized by her unspeakable loveliness. Nachae's whole body shook as she walked toward him, and it took all of his willpower to keep a dignified posture. He had the urge to grab her up into his arms and tell her how he had thought of her every day while he was away, and how he would never deny his love for her again. Instead, he stood straight and aloof, his arms crossed over his chest. Only his sparkling eyes revealed a trace of the thoughts that were devouring his heart.

Eskinzan clapped his hands together like an excited child. "See what my vision meant, my granddaughter?" He embraced Sky Dreamer and drew her closer to Nachae. She stumbled forward with Grandfather, letting her eyes stray back in Nachae's direction. The color in her face deepened when she saw that he was still watching her with a devout intensity. She pulled her reluctant gaze back toward Grandfather. The old shaman's dark eyes were flitting back and forth between his grandson and Sky Dreamer, while a satisfied grin consumed his whole countenance.

Sky Dreamer's mouth drew into a pout. She sensed

something was going on, and that she was the only one who had not yet been informed. Turning toward Eskinzan, she started to voice her irritation, but Grandfather's words rendered her speechless.

"My fine grandson has just gifted me with the finest horses in this herd, in exchange for my blessing over your marriage to him." Eskinzan's face was shining as he told her the news. His vision was finally going to come true. "I have never been so wealthy. Now I have many ponies, and soon, I will have great-grandchildren to carry my blood in their veins. This is a very good day indeed."

Too stunned to speak, Sky Dreamer only stared at the old man. Her eyes grew wider and her mouth opened, then clamped shut. Apparently, her future had already been planned before she had even arrived at the wickiup. Shouldn't the bride be the first one to consent with such an important decision? Eskinzan obviously considered the gift of horses an appropriate exchange for his adopted granddaughter's hand, but Sky Dreamer would have settled for a verbal proposal—one that she could accept personally. A renewed feeling of aggravation pulsed through her.

She turned away from Grandfather and glared at Nachae. "Everyone was sick with worry about you."

"It's good to know I was missed." He remained at a stiff stance, barely moving when he answered her. The way her violet eyes flashed at him made his blood ignite with desire. But his mocking look, combined with his smug voice, infuriated Sky Dreamer.

Her eyes met his emotionless expression. Their gazes locked, drawing her into a silent stare. In his dark eyes she envisioned the images in her beautiful dreams of making love in the mountain meadow. Why was she the one who was suddenly fighting against their destiny? He had returned to marry her, she reminded herself, and his gift of the ponies to Grandfather proved that his decision had not been an impulsive one.

Nachae remained unmoving, waiting for her reply. He

could see the many questions running through the depths of her violet gaze. A slight sense of fear began to seep into his blood. What if she had decided to deny her own dreams, and Grandfather's prophesy? His hands shook with the thought of this notion and he quickly buried them deeper into his arms where they were still crossed over his broad chest. It had never occurred to him that she might change her mind about their fate. He looked away from her; he did not want to see her rejection if that was what she was considering. His face became a mask of stone as his gray eyes narrowed like two slivers of flint.

"I must help build a corral for the ponies," he said in a sharp tone of voice. Then he turned abruptly and began to stalk back toward the herd of animals.

Sky Dreamer wanted to run after him, but her legs refused to move. Had she waited too long to give him an answer to his proposal? Maybe it wasn't too late, her spinning mind prayed as she started to run after him. But Waddling Woman grabbed her and twirled her around before she could catch him.

"Where are you going?" she asked, drawing her pudgy face into a questioning frown.

Sky Dreamer's voice was filled with panic when she replied. "I must go after him and tell him that I do want to marry him!"

Waddling Woman's tense expression faded as she glanced at the grinning shaman. With a twinkle in her ebony eyes, she looked back at the girl. "It is not customary to tell a man that you accept his offer of marriage."

"It — it's not?" Sky Dreamer stammered. "What should I do then?"

The older woman looked at her husband again and gave in to another gleeful smile. She leaned close to the young woman and replied, "You must curry and feed all the horses he has given to Eskinzan, then you will have to arrange to meet him somewhere by accident. Once he has met you, then the courtship has started and you will be married in two weeks."

Sky Dreamer glanced through the dusty camp at the disappearing form of Nachae. Two weeks? That sounded so long. Well, that was the custom, and if she had learned anything during her short time with the Apaches, it was that one never went against the customs of the tribe. With a concerned look at the huge herd of horses that Nachae had brought to the village, she asked, "Grandfather? How many of those horses did he give to you?"

Eskinzan drew in a proud breath and pushed out his chest. "One hundred!" he retorted as he raised his chin high into the air.

Chapter Eighteen

Sleeping was out of the question. Just lying down was enough to cause Sky Dreamer to feel as if she was going insane. Long before the first rays of the morning sun had appeared above the mountain peaks, she was out in the roughly built corral grooming horses. Since she had no idea which of the horses were supposed to belong to Grandfather, and neither did the young Indian boys who were keeping watch over the herd, Sky Dreamer just started at one end of the corral and began to curry and feed every horse in the pen. She was too wrapped up in her tasks to notice when the sun had risen in the sky, or to take note of the crowd at the edge of the corral who had gathered to watch her work.

A muffled laugh, which Sky Dreamer immediately recognized as belonging to her friend, Ta-O-Dee, drew her attention away from the horse she was tediously rubbing down with straw. She hadn't taken time to secure her hair in the nah-leen this morning, and the loose braid she had woven into the heavy mass was hanging over one shoulder. Pushing back the escaped strands that were waving across her face, Sky Dreamer straightened up and glanced in the direction of the sound. She gasped in surprise at the sight that greeted her eyes.

At the edge of the makeshift corral stood nearly everyone from the village. But Sky Dreamer's gaze was drawn to the group who stood in the center of the crowd. Juno and Ta-O-Dee embraced one another as they stared at her, and beside them, Grandfather and Waddling Woman also watched her with excited expressions upon their faces. Everyone else just seemed to disintegrate into thin air when her anxious eyes settled on the tall brave who stood in the center of them all. As always, his arms rested over his muscular chest, and his impassive expression did not give a clue to his true feelings. Sky Dreamer could have swore, though, that she saw a very brief smile cross his lips when their eyes met.

Having no idea how many horses she had cared for since she had begun in the wee hours of the morning, Sky Dreamer looked at Eskinzan and shrugged. As a loud round of cheers rose up from the crowd, she realized that her gesture was acknowledged by the tribe as her acceptance of Nachae's marriage proposal. She immediately lowered her eyes to the ground in a moment of shyness, and also in an attempt to hide the hot rush of color that she felt stain her cheeks. When she looked back up, Nachae was gone. Her worried gaze scanned the crowd, but he was nowhere to be seen. With an irritated and weary sigh, she walked out of the corral. At once, she was surrounded by the well-wishers who had been observing her determination to curry and feed every last horse in the rough enclosure.

"He still might change his mind," Sky Dreamer whispered to Ta-O-Dee as they pushed through the crowd.

Ta-O-Dee shook her head and glanced at her friend. Why must she always look on the dark side of everything that concerned that man? "He would not have asked his grandfather to give his blessing for your marriage if he did not want to make you his wife," Ta-O-Dee reminded her.

"He left in such a hurry." She motioned back toward the corral. "And he looked so mad," she added with a pout.

Ta-O-Dee laughed. "He always looks mad. He wants to make everyone fear him by making them think he is mean. But he is no different from any other warrior. All it takes is a strong woman to tame the beast in them."

"I heard that," Juno said indignantly as he strode up beside the two women. He tried to fake a look of anger, but he was not too successful. When he stared down at his wife, his expression softened and a teasing smile curled his lips. "This woman brings out the animal in me," he retorted.

Sky Dreamer could not hold back her mirth when she noticed how embarrassed her friend was at her husband's suggestive remark. She began to wonder if someday she would share the same type of intimate secrets with Na-chae.

Meeting that stubborn man by accident had sounded so easy in the beginning, but Sky Dreamer quickly learned that simplicity was never the case where Nachae was concerned. He was constantly surrounded by the other warriors, or busy in the corral with the ponies and cattle. Two days had passed and Sky Dreamer was convinced that he was intentionally avoiding a meeting with her. Feeling dejected and irritated, she decide to console herself by visiting the horses in the corral. She had sneaked out to observe the animals several times when no one else was around, and had taken a particular liking to one horse in the herd. The mare was a brown-and-white paint, similar to Eagle in markings but smaller in structure. Sky Dreamer was sure that her interest in the mare was just because the horse reminded her of Nachae's regal mount. But it did appear that the mare grew excited whenever Sky Dreamer entered the corral. The horse immediately made her way to the woman's side and eagerly extended her neck so that Sky Dreamer could scratch the soft velvety area beneath her mane. She was absently rubbing the mare's neck when Nachae's voice nearly caused her to jump out of her skin.

"Running into you here is a surprise," Nachae said, with an emphasis on the word "surprise" as he sauntered up to her.

"I—I—" Sky Dreamer attempted to explain why she was standing there in the middle of the herd again, but her mind went blank as her eyes traveled over his body. He was wearing suede leggings and a white shirt belted by a black sash. His long ebony hair was secured by a brightly colored headband. Forcing her eyes to stop traveling over his well-muscled form, she suddenly realized what he had meant when he implied that their meeting here was unexpected. Since she had not managed to arrange a surprise meeting, he had obviously taken matters into his own hands.

"I—I—well—what do we do now?" She could have kicked herself for acting so ignorant, especially when she saw the wicked grin begin to spread across his face.

A seductive glint entered into his gray gaze and lit his dark complexion with a mischievous glow. "I am tempted to make up my own rules to these courtship customs, but I fear Grandfather would have me tied to a stake if I did not follow the usual procedures."

Sky Dreamer's body turned into a shivering tower. It was so rare for him to drop his fierce exterior and allow his gentler self to emerge. Her eyes were magnetically drawn up to his face. When he was relaxed and carefree, as he was now, the sight of him was dangerous to Sky Dreamer's maidenhood. If he pulled her down into the dirt of the corral and made love to her right there among the stomping hooves of the ponies, she would not have objected in the least.

"I don't care about the customs, and I don't want to wait two whole weeks," she said on impulse as she leaned forward. Her caution was thrown to the wind as she succumbed to the pull of their bodies toward one another. His strong embrace lifted her up until all that touched the ground was the very tips of her rawhide kabuns. Instinctively, she tossed her head back as his lips descended eagerly upon her mouth with a hunger that had been denied far too long. His kiss engulfed her entire being with such an ache that it seemed impossible that anything could ever cure the sweet agony that raced through her limbs. Her arms encircled his neck when she drew herself closer to him. Oh, how she wished that it would never be necessary to separate herself from his tight embrace. Only

224

in her passionate dreams had he kissed her with such ravenous energy.

Reluctantly, he paused as his arms reinforced their possessive hold around her slender waist, then his head turned to seek her soft lips in another kiss even more demanding than the first. Sky Dreamer did not have time to catch her breath, but she could not think of a more deserving way to die than from lack of air while locked in his arms with their lips joined together. A horse whinnied, but it sounded far away, and unimportant. The wondrous pain that his kiss was causing to move through her limbs was all that mattered, and she longed for him to do whatever he could to end this wanton torture. Her sense of morality attempted to invade her thoughts, but it kept being overpowered by the heady scent of mint, which the Apache men rubbed on their bodies so they would smell sweet, and by the enticing taste of his lips as he continued to control her very soul with his touch.

Nachae's suffering was as great as Sky Dreamer's unrest, but in his wisdom, he knew that he could not do what his throbbing groin was urging him to do to this innocent temptress. No other woman had ever driven him to such madness or loss of control. He could easily have carried her into the wooden area beyond the village and made her his woman without anyone ever being the wiser. But he knew that they would both regret an action so rash. He forced himself to move away from her with every ounce of restraint he could muster. He tried to tell her how sorry he was for imposing on her innocence, but he was unable to speak. His raging desire for her had stolen away every sense he had left.

Sky Dreamer also fought to regain her sanity. When Nachae reached out to her again, she began to shake her head no. Her breathing was heavy and did not permit her voice to escape. She knew, however, that she had to move away from him before it was too late. If he touched her again, the Apache customs would be forgotten. She backed away from him, still trying to clear her befuddled mind, her thoughts filled with the ecstasy that her dreams had portrayed of their impending union. It was impossible to dismiss the sensual images from her mind, now that they were so intertwined with reality.

Absently, Nachae began to stumble backward, too. He could read the message hidden in her violet gaze, and he understood, because his mind was also conceiving images of mutual passion and love. And like Sky Dreamer, he was trying to remind himself that the Apaches lived by a strict moral code that must always be obeyed if they did not wish to bring shame down upon themselves and their families.

"I am going to talk to Grandfather," Nachae announced in a tense voice. He turned on his heel and stalked out of the corral without any further explanation.

Sky Dreamer watched him leave, still engulfed in the lingering memories of their overpowering desire for one another. She had no idea what he planned to discuss with Eskinzan, but undoubtedly, it would somehow concern her. The little paint mare nudged her in the back and Sky Dreamer nearly lost her balance. She turned around and draped her arms over the horse's neck.

"Two weeks!" she said into the ear of the mare. "His touch makes a million fires blaze out of control within my body. I will be no more than a pile of ashes blowing in the wind in two weeks."

Something moving through the trees caught Sky Dreamer's attention as she began to walk away from the corral. She told herself that she was only imagining things when she saw nothing unusual in the wooded area after she had stopped to peer into the clump of piñon trees. But that night as she slept, she had a disturbing dream of menacing eyes that watched her every move from the dark shadows.

Eskinzan grinned proudly at Sky Dreamer across the golden glow of the midday sun as she departed from the wickiup of White Painted Woman—the spiritual force of Apache womanhood. For the past four days she had been instructed on the marriage ceremony and the ancient culture of her mother's people. Sky Dreamer listened eagerly to the stories of how White Painted Woman had walked the earth since the beginning of time. In Chiricahua mythology, the woman had conceived a child by Rain and Lightning, and gave birth to a child appropriately called Child of the Water. Both White Painted Woman and her son assisted in puberty ceremonies and marriages. During the rites, their mortal existences were conveyed by various members of the tribe.

Nachae had convinced Eskinzan to do away with the two-week waiting period, and although Sky Dreamer still had not been permitted to see him during her four-day stay in the abode of White Painted Woman, their marriage would take place much sooner than was the normal custom. Since the tribe was eager to return to the Chiricahua Mountains, Nachae reasoned that it would be in everyone's best interest to have the marriage ceremony before they started on their journey.

The old shaman had not wished to disagree with his grandson, especially since he understood the young couple's anxiety. He had felt the same way about Nachae's grandmother many years ago. They, too, had not been able to wait until the two-week courtship period was over. Unfortunately, they had been publicly forced to do just that, and it had resulted in Nachae's father, Alderay, being born two weeks before the nine-month anniversary of their wedding. Eskinzan smiled to himself as he watched Lucero's beautiful young daughter approach his specially built altar. There had been a few times in the past months when he had doubted the credibility of his visions, but at last, destiny had overpowered the heart of his headstrong grandson.

Around the altar, dancers chanted and sang the wedding song. When Sky Dreamer emerged from the wickiup, shouts and cheers began to rise up from the people who had gathered for the ceremony as Eskinzan sprinkled her pathway with hoddentin. Dressed in a long painted war shirt of light tan buckskin that reached to his knees, and

227

wearing fringed leggings to match, Nachae walked out from the throng of onlookers to meet his bride-to-be. His long raven hair was secured by a headband of silver and turquoise that shimmered against his dark tresses like bolts of lightning in a midnight sky. As he watched Sky Dreamer approach him, his head grew light and felt removed from his body. Even if he had tried to imagine how she would look on this day, he never would have been able to conceive such an image of loveliness.

On Eskinzan's insistence, Waddling Woman had feverishly been working on a wedding dress throughout the past several months, and her labors had produced a gown of unequaled beauty. She had traded away nearly all her trinkets and personal belongings to the people of the rancheria for their assistance in obtaining moleskins for this special garment. Many hours had been spent tediously soaking the hides in ashes and water until they were as soft and pliable as velvet. The skins were then bleached in the sun, making them as white and pure as the wispy clouds that floated overhead in the azure sky. Waddling Woman had sewn the hides together with deer sinew, then carefully cut fringe into long strips that hung from the sleeves of the dress and cascaded past Sky Dreamer's slender fingers. On the hem of the dress, she had also cut the same widths of long fringe as those she had fashioned on the sleeves. Starting around the knees, the fringe graduated from short strands on the sides of the hemline to long points that reached past the tops of Sky Dreamer's high white kabuns. The whole outfit, dress and moccasins alike, was adorned with rows of colored beads, delicate shells, and silver conchos, which had been obtained from past raids into Mexico. Waddling Woman had managed to retrieve her sewing supplies from the ruins of her wickiup after the last ambush on the village, and it was these ornaments which she sewed onto Sky Dreamer's wedding gown.

At last, Sky Dreamer's long hair was permitted to flow freely around her shoulders. The thick tresses floated down her back, ending inches past her waist like a shimmering ebony waterfall. A narrow strip of white leather encircled her head and was decorated by a single ivory feather that hung loosely at the side of her head. Long beaded earrings swung from her ears as she walked, and her wrists were weighted with brass bands that reflected the light of the sun with their lustrous finish. The only jewelry she wore around her neck was the round amulet which Nachae had given to her the night after she had saved Ino from the rattlesnake.

Nachae was not sure how his legs were able to support his body as he walked up to her and extended his shaking hand. All the years of bitterness and indecision were wiped from his mind. Even amid the hardships and sorrows of the Apache life they had both chosen to live, he saw a future filled with the happiness that would be produced from their undying love. For the first time in his twenty-five harvests, the prospect of a better life overwhelmed the memories of his brutal past. He silently vowed always to remember what their enemies were capable of doing to his people, but from this day forth, he would also learn how to place those hurtful recollections in a separate part of his heart, so they would not interfere in his new life with his beloved Sky Dreamer.

She stopped when his hand reached out toward her. Her violet eyes stared down at his extended palm. Every breath she had ever taken had led her to this moment, yet she was suddenly so afraid. Outside the Apache rancheria, beyond the cheers and joyous singing of her mother's people, was a cruel and harsh world . . . a world that would never completely accept her or Nachae because they were born of two rival cultures. Until now, her other self had always hovered in the background. If she so chose, Regina Atwood could still emerge and return to her life of genteel grandeur among her father's family in Georgia. But the instant she placed her hand in the hand of this man, she knew there would never be any turning back for either of them. She would give him her heart and soul, then surround him with love from every fiber of her being.

She visibly trembled in the noonday heat. Her shining gaze rose up to his face and she could see the fear that her hesitation had aroused in him. She also saw the love mirrored in his gray eyes as she felt his strength rejuvenate her weakening senses. Alone, she sometimes wondered if she was strong enough to face the adversity the Apaches lived with every single minute of every day. But with Nachae at her side, she knew she would be brave enough to cross the barrier between her past life and a future that would always be uncertain. The endless love she could see reaching out to her from his eyes would lay the groundwork for whatever hardships they must face, and her limitless love for him would be all the security she would ever need. With this thought planted firmly in her mind, Sky Dreamer slowly placed her trembling hand against his palm. As his fingers closed around hers, the last of her doubts flew away like the eagles who soar over the highest mountain peaks.

A smile released the worried look from Nachae's face as his grip on her hand tightened. He gave his head a slight nod, making strands of his long raven hair fall over one of his wide shoulders. With a proud stride, he began to lead her toward the altar where Eskinnzan waited for them. As they neared the shaman, the old man picked up a glistening silver knife, which he used only for occasions as special as this one, and held it high over his head. When they stopped before him, Eskinzan laid down the knife and produced a long wand that held a pointed pine needle at its tip. The long fringe on the arms of his well-worn ceremonial shirt waved in front of Nachae's and Sky Dreamer's faces as he passed the wand back and forth over their bowed heads.

From his medicine bag, he scooped out a handful of hoddentin and sprinkled the fine powder over the couple. Sky Dreamer braced herself for the next part of the ceremony when she saw Eskinzan pick up the wand once more. In a quick movement, the shaman grabbed her right wrist and pierced the tender skin below the brass bracelet she wore. Then he grasped Nachae's left wrist and used the sharp pine needle to make a small cut in the warrior's flesh as well. Two young men who stood to the side of the altar moved forward and wrapped a long white cloth around the couple's wrists, binding them tightly to one another.

Eskinzan sprinkled more hoddentin over their heads as he spoke. "This morning you each awoke as two separate persons. Today your blood has been joined. Tonight two people will go to their dwelling place and tomorrow they will emerge with one life. To the other one, each will be shelter from the wind and rain and cold. Loneliness is a thing of the past, so go now to begin your life together." He paused when his old eyes filled with a glistening sheet of tears. But he did not bother to wipe them away as he added, "May every day be filled with goodness and your stay on this earth, and with one another, be long and fruitful."

His voice trailed off while the rest of the people started to sing. Sky Dreamer was lost to the beauty of Eskinzan's words and to the lyrical tune of the wedding song that echoed around her. She glanced down at her wrist, which was tightly intertwined with Nachae's arm. Her violet eyes ascended until they met his tender gaze. The love that reached out to her from his enraptured expression touched her like a gentle hand caressing her whole essence.

"Shil nzhoo," she whispered, her voice almost lost to the sounds of shouts and singing.

Nachae's eyes traced the outline of her softly trembling lips. "And I love you, my beautiful Sky Dreamer."

She did not need to hear the words to feel as if she had just grown wings and taken flight. Apaches called one another by their proper names only on very rare and special occasions. To see his lips form the name he had chosen made his declaration of love for her even greater. Sky Dreamer closed her eyes and felt a single teardrop roll down her cheek. If it was possible to cherish someone so much that it hurt, then she was about to die from the wondrous pain of this engulfing love.

She opened her eyes when she felt the cloth being untied from their wrists. She was surprised to see that the throng of people had moved forward and were now crowded around them. They tossed gifts at their feet, still singing the songs which reflected the joyous occasion. Sky Dreamer tried to gather the presents in her arms, but there was too many of them. Nachae caught the blankets and trinkets that tumbled from her overloaded arms, then began to pull her away from the group of well-wishers. With eager anticipation, she followed him through the sea of happy faces, laughing and lost to the excitement of the splendrous moment.

He pulled her to the edge of the village, where Eagle and the little painted mare were waiting. Sky Dreamer gasped in awe at the elaborate blankets, trimmed with shimmering conchos and beaded tassels, that hung from the back of both horses. For ten wonderful days she would be alone with Nachae. He had not told her where they were going, but she knew without asking. Last night, she had dreamt of the mountain meadow again.

"I will take your gifts to your husband's wickiup," Ta-O-Dee said shyly when she walked up beside Sky Dreamer.

Sky Dreamer twirled around at the sound of her dear friend's voice. It had been so hectic at the wedding ceremony that the two women had not had a chance to see one another. Sky Dreamer smiled and blinked away another aggravating tear as she held out her bounty to Ta-O-Dee. Juno approached the trio and reached for Nachae's load.

"Be happy, shik'isn," he said. His black eyes silently held his friend's gaze for a moment. Their friendship had spanned ten harvests and continued to grow stronger with every day that passed. Today, Juno felt his friend's joy almost as keenly as if it had been his own. Nachae embraced his friend before moving toward Sky Dreamer to help her onto her horse.

Ta-O-Dee carefully placed the gifts on the ground as she called out excitedly, "Wait, I have a gift for you, too." She reached into the fringed bag which hung from her belt and pulled out two beaded objects. Sky Dreamer looked at the familiar necklaces, then quickly glanced at the other woman.

"I was sure they had been destroyed in the fire during the ambush on the rancheria."

Ta-O-Dee shrugged. "The first ones I made did burn in our wickiup. But Waddling Woman traded me her beads for moleskins, so I made another set." She proudly held out her delicate creations to Sky Dreamer and Nachae.

Nachae glanced up toward the sky in gratitude, but Sky Dreamer hugged her friend and said the seldom-used words in a choked voice, "*A-co-'d,* my sister, from the bottom of my heart."

When the two women separated, they both had to wipe away the tears that flooded down their faces. Ta-O-Dee began to giggle as she helped Sky Dreamer tie the necklace around her neck. She gave a satisfied nod when she stood back and admired her handiwork. These necklaces of purple, silver, and orange beads were even more resplendent than the first set she had made for the couple. But when she had worked on the original pair of necklaces, she had also been busy caring for Ino. Ta-O-Dee did not want to remind herself of sad things on this happy day, so she moved quickly to her husband's side and wrapped her arm around his waist.

Juno's brows raised in a wicked arch, and his look hinted at his lustful thoughts. He glanced at Nachae and said, "See, *shik'isn?* Even after two harvests, my wife still cannot keep her hands away from my body."

Ta-O-Dee blushed several different shades of red, but her face could not suppress the grin that toyed with the corners of her mouth. Indeed, last night Juno had awoken her slumbering appetites, and she would not mind dragging her husband back to their wickiup for a few more hours of passion.

Nachae's head tilted back as his laughter filled the air. He quickly placed Ta-O-Dee's gift around his neck, then lifted his new bride onto her horse's back. Wasting little time, he mounted his own horse and grabbed the reins of

Sky Dreamer's mare. He was anxious enough to reach their destination as it was, and Juno and Ta-O-Dee's obvious insinuations had only increased his desires.

Sky Dreamer waved over her shoulder as they trotted out of the rancheria. When they returned from the mountaintop, this encampment would be deserted and quiet. Their people were traveling back to the Chiricahua lands within a few days' time. Nachae and Sky Dreamer planned to meet them at the new location when they came back from their wedding trip. Sky Dreamer's gaze did not linger on the Apache village, however; she preferred to watch her handsome husband riding his stallion up ahead of her.

She tried to remember what it had been like to be Regina Atwood, but she could not even recall how she used to spend her days before she came to Arizona and learned that she was the daughter of an Apache shaman. At times, she missed her father, but her new life was so full and busy that she had little time to dwell on their separation. She hoped someday soon the captain would come back to visit her, but she never wanted to return to the white man's world again. She had seen what the Apaches were capable of doing to their enemies, and she had also experienced the soldiers' wrath against the Indians. Today, she had made a final choice—she would devout her life to the Chiricahua people, and to the man who led her through the deep evergreens and silver pines . . . to the secret mountain meadow where her dreams would be fulfilled at last.

Chapter Nineteen

Emblazoned by the fiery glow that proceeds the darkness of night, the meadow was alive, and spoke in hushed sounds as the woodland animals who had frolicked in the clearing scurried into the safety of the trees when they spotted the intruders. The Apaches believed that all living things communicate with one another, and at dusk the sounds of the pine branches swaying gently in the mountain breeze sounded like naughty children whispering about their latest escapade. The tallest of the silver pines, with their tops disappearing into the thick clouds of boughs among the fading blue sky, appeared to keep watch over the meadow, guarding it from the rest of the world. Deep grasses in different shades of vibrant green laid a thick rich carpet, broken only by a sprinkling of the last of the season's red and yellow flowers, which lifted their fading petals through the lush vegetation to peek at the great expanse of their universe. The climate in this area seemed almost tropical, and flowers were almost always in bloom to paint the meadow with colors. Sky Dreamer was in love with this meadow, with life, and mostly, with her new husband.

During Sky Dreamer's four-day absence, Nachae had ridden to the mountaintop and built a small wickiup beneath the towering trees. The dwelling stood at the far edge of the meadow and its doorway looked out over the extent of the grassy tract. Now, at sunset, the craggy shadows of the trees hung low across the meadow like long grasping fingers trying to reach out beyond the limitations of their secluded enclosure. Within their opaque clutches, the little wickiup was shaded by the branches of the thick pines.

Sky Dreamer was lost to the mystical beauty of this place, but her attention was quickly diverted when Nachae lifted her from the back of her horse. She waited patiently while he removed the ornamental blankets and tethered the animals beneath the tall trees for the night. When he had finished caring for the horses, his attention was immediately drawn back to his new bride. She was still standing where he had placed her, quietly waiting for him to join her. Just the sight of her made him tremble with excitement and love. With one long stride, he reached her still form then lifted her into his arms. She drew her head down upon his shoulder and submitted to the weakness she felt whenever she was in his powerful embrace. He carried her into the darkening hut and stood her before a pile of soft furs. She felt herself quake with anticipation, and clamped her teeth together to keep them from clattering with nervousness. Her intimate dreams had only led her to the last crucial moment. She had no idea where reality would lead them on this star-studded night.

Nachae, however, was not hesitant in his actions. With a glow in his smoky gaze that could almost light the dim interior of the lodge, he bent over and began to remove her tall moccasins, then reached down and discarded his own knee-high kabuns. Sky Dreamer's visible shaking increased when he bowed down again and started to lift her soft white dress up past her thighs. She held her breath to keep from gasping as his fingers lightly touched her quaking body when he slid the garment over her heated flesh. Her eyes were welded shut when the last of the dress slipped over her head. Even her thick lashes trembled against her cheekbones when she stood in total exposure before his bold gaze. She had recently taken to wearing nothing beneath her loose clothes—now she would have given anything to have her old tattered pantaloons and chemise to cover her naked body.

"To be gifted with so much beauty is rare, little one. But not to share such loveliness with one who loves you as I do would be grossly unfair." Nachae's soft words did not ease her discomfort. Her eyes remained tightly closed as she tried to think of an intelligent reply to his compliment. Was he just standing there gazing at her? A fevered blush began to spread across her shaking body—from the tips of her bare feet to the top of her long silky tresses. She hoped it was dark enough in the wickiup so that he wouldn't notice.

"You are even more ravishing with a pink glow upon your satiny skin," he said with a slight sound of humor in his voice. Sky Dreamer wished the ground beneath her feet would open up and shallow her. A defeated sigh escaped her, yet she still refused to open her eyes. Why hadn't the dreams shown her what to do? She gritted her teeth and clenched her fists tightly at her sides. In her nakedness, she could feel the way her tense breathing was causing her bosom to rise and fall. Did he notice that too? She heard noises—had he become disgusted with her ignorance and left the wickiup?

Fearfully, as though she were about to face her worst enemy, Sky Dreamer forced her eyes to open. Nachae stood before her, every bit as naked as he had rendered her just moments ago. Instinctively, her gaze began to travel over his muscled form. Many times, while he had paraded around the village in his skimpy breechcloth, she had admired his perfectly built body. But now, standing here in the fading light of their wedding day sun, she looked at him in a completely different way that was new and exciting, yet even a bit frightening. Purple sparks flashed through her eyes when she lowered her gaze down past his waist, then quickly tried to avert her eyes before he noticed her curiosity. Another bolt of humiliating fire colored her already flushed complexion when she realized he had not missed her wandering glance.

Nachae grinned, but he did not mock her. Her interest in his body was natural, and so was her embarrassment.

He remained unmoving, wanting to give her some time to adjust to the idea of the impending ritual of their wedding night. Though he knew it was impossible, he wished he could always spare her from the overwhelming fear of never knowing what their next breath could bring. Today, she had made a choice. Her indecision before their wedding ceremony had been apparent to him — he had made the same choice ten harvests ago when he had denounced his white heritage. By picking the Apache way of life, she had chosen a trail that had many treacherous turns. With every breath he took, Nachae was more determined than ever before to make her pathway less dangerous.

He stepped forward until they were only inches apart — close enough to feel one another's heavy breathing. It took all of Nachae's willpower to keep from reaching out to touch her beckoning skin. He was overcome with so much love for this woman that it startled him. In every battle he had ever fought, he had always given of himself completely. And for most of his life, his whole being had been consumed with his determination to remain alone and detached from the entanglements of other persons. But now that he had finally submitted to his deep feelings for this woman, they were more engulfing and powerful than anything he had ever known.

He closed the very short distance between them until the pert rosebuds of her taut breasts were touching his bare chest. Several rebellious strands of her waist-length hair tumbled over her bosom. He reached out and flicked them back over her shoulder, barely brushing against her skin with his fingertips. Sky Dreamer held her breath, too confused to move or breathe. His nearness was maddening; she didn't know if she wanted him to leave her alone with her embarrassment, or hurry up and do something to appease this impassioned agony. Every fiber of her body was aflame, and the ache that kept recurring in her loins whenever he was close to her was once again causing her sweet, unspeakable distress. The worst agony, however, was in the areas where their perspiring bodies were touching. Her breasts felt as though they had just been submerged in hot coals and were melting against his bare chest. If he didn't do something soon, she was positive she would go mad. As if to protect herself from insanity, her arms moved of their own accord and put an end to her plight. Her quaking hands slid into the shining curtain of black hair that hung around his broad shoulders as his arms drew her to him in an enslaving embrace.

He had waited for her to make the first move, and the instant she ran her fingers through his hair, he lost the small bit of control he had still harbored. His lips dove down upon her mouth as though he would perish if he didn't feel her soft lips against his own. Sky Dreamer returned his impatient kiss with an equally desperate desire. His tongue worked its way between her parted lips and between her clenched teeth, then began to intertwine with her shy, withdrawn tongue. She was unsure of how to retaliate against this new intrusion into her mouth, but soon she realized that this was just an extension of the pleasure his expertise would teach her on this night. She imitated his gesture and permitted her own tongue to caress his lips and mingle with his exploring one. But before long, these intoxicating kisses were not enough to sooth their expanding quest.

Nachae's moist lips began to move down the curve of her neck and along her shoulders, making her delirious with the expectation of what was still to come. A moan of ecstasy escaped from somewhere deep within her throat when his hand suddenly appeared upon one of her flushed breasts. His thumb teased the inflamed tip with tantalizing promises until Sky Dreamer wanted to cry out from the fiery sensations his touch aroused within her body. Her hands were still entangled in his thick hair, but her curious fingers began to move down his back, over the abundance of sinew and muscle which rippled beneath her touch as he started to lower her down onto the mattress of soft furs. She sank into the comfort of the deer furs, though at this moment she wouldn't have cared if she were lying on a bed of prickly needles, because all her senses were lost somewhere among the turbulence of her delirious bliss.

Her entire body was alive with awakening desire, yet she was aware only of the strange yearning in her loins. His rigid manhood pressed into her stomach when he positioned his hips between her sleek thighs, but his mouth had conquered her lips once again and restricted her gasps of uncertainty when his intentions became more demanding. He wanted her to crave him as desperately as he did her. The involuntary arch of her body against his own was the clue he had been awaiting.

Sky Dreamer was helpless to stop the possession which had taken control of her body, and her mind no longer had any power over the wanton mania that had taken charge of her senses. She wanted this wondrous torture to end, and she knew it was within his power to save her from this insatiable affliction. His mouth and tongue caressed her swollen lips with enticing devotion, while with slow deliberation, his hands slid down between her legs—to the velvety area hidden below her downy triangle of black hair. A fearful gasp was quickly stolen from her throat with another urgent kiss when she felt his fingers begin to probe the depths of her secret passage. His artful fingers, with their gentle immersion, worked her into such a frenzy of desire that she felt as if her rationality had deserted her, leaving her completely defenseless against this new invasion. When his fingers finally withdrew from her, she was crazy with ravenous greed.

Nachae spread her legs farther apart with a gentle pressure from his knees, while he repositioned himself between her silky limbs. His hands ascended until his fingers became lost in the vast, tangled confusion of her long hair as he drew her head back and kissed her with such zeal that she was not even aware of his entry into her feminine portal until she felt the stabbing sensation of his deep penetration. Her whole body surged upward with the painful spasm, but he soothed the hurt with the gentle movements of his hips, which quickly followed his forced entry.

Waddling Woman and Ta-O-Dee had warned her of the first painful encounter between a man and a woman, yet Sky Dreamer still felt betrayed. His touch had been so tender before the unexpected plunge that it took her an instant to realize he had made the initial contact without warning only to ease her pain, not to increase it. Now, his actions had once again become gentle and loving. With slow fluctuating motions, his body urged her timid form to follow his movements. She obeyed him with only a small amount of coaxing—welcoming his downward lunges and arching upward against his hips with each threat of withdrawal. As her confidence grew, so did the velocity of his performance, until at last it was beyond their power to stop the fierce wave that cascaded over them with an outpouring of boundless rapture.

In silence, they retreated into the soft furs to recuperate and relish this night, and each other for as long as time would permit. Sky Dreamer was still floating among the clouds, too ecstatic to ever want to come back down to earth. Her dreams had deceived her . . . there was nothing to compare with the actuality of this man's touch. How had she ever managed to survive without his love up until now? Beside her, she heard him struggling to regain a normal rhythm of breathing. She made a silent promise always to give herself to him unabashedly, and never again to feel ashamed of their desire for one another.

She had a foolish urge to jump up and run through the meadow—unencumbered and free like the wind that whisked across the tops of the tall trees—while shouting out her love for this man. But their vigorous lovemaking had robbed her of her energy, so she merely succumbed to the welcoming comfort of her husband's strong arms when he pulled her to him in a protective embrace. Soon she fell asleep, feeling more secure and cherished than she had ever thought humanly possible.

Endless nights of unbound passion, and days filled with more of the same, were the course of the quarter moon Nachae and Sky Dreamer spent in their magical mountain meadow. Each new encounter honed their expertise at fulfilling their unquenchable need for one another, until only a glance or a touch bespoke their ceaseless desires. Sky Dreamer's love for her new husband knew no limits. In the rare times when they weren't making love, she cooked the small game he killed for their meals, cleaned the wickiup, and tended to his clothing without complaint.

When they returned to the new rancheria in the Chiricahua Mountains and settled into their life as husband and wife, she would build them a spacious wickiup, and sew his shirts and pants from hides she would tan with her own hands. She was amazed that she was actually looking forward to all the hard work that an Apache wife was faced with daily. Along with her wifely duties, she would also have her responsibilities as a shaman to keep her busy. But to be Nachae's wife, she would gladly do the work of ten Apache women.

Since their arrival, there was not one secret area of their bodies that the other had not yet chartered. Sky Dreamer had grown from an embarrassed young maiden to an uninhibited woman who lavished her womanly gifts upon the man she worshiped. And there was not one inch of the meadow they had not explored either. Sky Dreamer knew there was always a chance that they would never return to the White Mountains again, and she wanted to carry the picture of their mystical mountaintop in her mind for all time.

On their last evening in the clearing, she walked the complete compass of the meadow, and cried for some reason she could not explain. Their wedding trip had been beyond perfection, and though she knew it was time to move on and to begin the rest of their lives, she was consumed with an overweaning sadness.

"It pains me to see you cry," Nachae said as he fell in step beside her. The hour was near dusk, close to the time when they had arrived on their wedding night.

"I never thought it was possible to be so happy."

242

Nachae gave a helpless sigh. His wife was the bravest woman he had ever known, and even the bleakest situation usually could not reduce her to tears. Yet she cried whenever she was happy. Women were complex creatures, he decided.

Her feet halted beside a stately silver pine tree as she turned to look up at her handsome husband. She noticed how the fading sunlight cast a bronzed glow upon his bare chest and highlighted his defined muscles. "This tree is like my love for you," she said. "Each day my love will flourish and grow. It will withstand the harshest elements of Usen's earth, and it will be strong and unyielding for all time. Even when our mortal existences have departed, the deep-seeded roots of our love will grow strong in the rich earth and replenish our love—time and time again." She reached out and clasped Nachae's hands in her own. Her voice grew soft, hardly more than a whisper. "Love me beneath the silver boughs of this tree and plant a seed that will yield the fruit of our eternal love, my husband."

Nachae's hands grew limp in her embrace. He had listened to his grandfather long enough to understand the unspoken meaning behind a shaman's words. The one thing he feared most about surrendering to the love he felt for this woman was the possibility of fathering a child. Yet he knew that if he made love to her beneath this ancient tree on this fateful eve, their union would create a new life within her womb. Her foresight had envisioned it, he sensed it, and destiny had set it in motion. Another child would be born in a world of hatred and devastation. But above all else, he was forced to admit defeat. He would not—could not—deny her request.

He felt like a man who was about to die from a lack of love as he crushed her slender form to his body and pulled her down into the deep green grass. With the inquisitive eyes of the forest watching them, Nachae loved Sky Dreamer with a passionate hunger which could not be equaled. He could never conquer his possessive craving so he made love to her over and over again, until the moon was full and high like a crystal ball that could reflect the future of this magical mating. And when, at last, they fell back into the dewy vegetation and gazed up at the full firmament, Sky Dreamer pointed out to Na-chae the odd shape of the darkened areas in the silvery moon that resembled the unmistakable outline of an unborn child.

Chapter Twenty

Sky Dreamer was expecting to feel sorrowful when the time came for them to leave their private meadow, but she was unprepared for the uneasiness that followed them from the secluded clearing. She chose not to worry Nachae with her feelings of foreboding, because he had already become moody and quiet since the previous night. His attitude bothered her even more than her strange discontent. Though it was a well-known fact that he was prone to dark moods, it concerned her that he would withdraw into one of them during a time when they had been so happy with one another. She reminded herself that he was a man who carried heavy responsibilities upon his shoulders. He was dedicated to his people and their diminishing way of life. Those who still eluded the reservations lived in fear and hiding, never knowing if they would starve to death or be awakened from their slumber by another ambush. The younger and stronger warriors such as Nachae had taken it upon themselves to save their whole race, or die trying.

The couple hardly spoke as they traveled down the mountain, and when they reached the now-deserted Apache campsite, Nachae became even more withdrawn. Sky Dreamer knew it was wise to leave him alone until his mood improved, but she could not help feeling slightly rejected because of his reluctance to confide in her about what had brought about his brooding silence.

The warrior was not proud of his cold attitude. Although he could see how worried Sky Dreamer was, he could not shake off his increasing depression. His love for Sky Dreamer was so powerful that he was obsessed with making her life, and that of their future children, safe and content. Yet he felt helpless to fulfill these simple needs. His own life had never held any real security, so how could he ever hope to provide such a life for his own family?

Nachae quickly gathered up their belongings from the spot beneath a clump of bushes where Waddling Woman had hidden them. Each family had their own burdens to carry whenever the village was relocated and was not able to transport the goods of anyone else. It was decided before the wedding that Grandfather's wife would leave supplies for the couple in the designated hiding spot until they were retrieved by Nachae and Sky Dreamer when they passed through the deserted village. Together, they loaded the supplies on Eagle and the little painted mare, whom Sky Dreamer had named Sparrow. Since it seemed that Nachae was anxious to leave, they did not dally once their things were tied onto the animals.

Throughout the remainder of the day, they moved at a steady pace. By evening, they had left the slopes of the foothills and were rapidly approaching the desert region. Sky Dreamer had hoped their journey back to the Chiricahua Mountains would be a leisurely extension of their wedding trip. Nachae made it clear by his brisk actions that he wished to cover the distance as quickly as possible. Darkness had shrouded the land with heavy shadows by the time they stopped and made camp for the night. Only the light from the shaded red moon highlighted the ominous desert sand. Nachae decided not to make a fire because he felt nervous about the two of them being alone in an area that was inhabited by white men. Since her feelings of uneasiness had continually increased, Sky Dreamer was relieved that he was taking extra precautionary measures.

In silence they sat beneath a twisted juniper tree and

246

ate their meager meal of dried meat and corncakes. Nachae took only a couple of bites, then impatiently tossed his food to the ground. Sky Dreamer's appetite fled the instant her husband grew even more distant than he had been previously. She rose to her feet and started toward the fringed bags that held their food supplies, where she planned to replace her uneaten food. As she walked past Nachae, he reached out and grabbed her arm. She cried out in surprise as she toppled down into his lap. Her food spilled onto the ground, but she was too shocked to worry about the waste.

"I'm sorry," Nachae said as he buried his head into the silky mass of her long hair. "I don't mean to act so cruel toward you." His voice grew urgent and his arms tightened around her waist. "It's just that I love you so much."

Sky Dreamer's arms automatically wrapped around his neck. She had been so worried that he was regretting their marriage that all she could feel at this moment was a huge sense of relief. "Why does our love make you so unhappy?"

A feeble attempt to chuckle made Nachae's voice tremble. "Unhappy? Never!" He snuggled deeper into the thick ebony blanket of her engulfing tresses. "I've never known such happiness, but . . ." His voice trailed off.

"What is the dark cloud that constantly threatens to rain on our happiness, my husband?" She heard him draw in a heavy breath, then fall silent again. Her heart plummeted in her breast with disappointment. How could she ever hope to understand this man whom she loved so much, if he refused to confide in her about his fears and hopes?

Nachae pulled away from her, then traced the outline of her face in the darkness. "We're outcasts, you and I," he said in a quiet voice. "We've both lived in two worlds where it was as different as night and day. Then we reached a crossroads in our lives and we had to make a choice. Naturally we chose the world where we were accepted for what is in here . . ." He released one of his arms from his hold around her waist and hit the area over his heart. "The Apaches cared about us, not the color of our skin or the type of blood that pulsed through our veins."

Sky Dreamer's grip around his neck loosened as she peered through the darkness and tried to decipher his confusing words. "Shouldn't we feel fortunate, then, that we were able to choose to be with the people who do accept us?"

His head moved in a negative gesture. "We chose a way of life, and a race of people, whose days are numbered."

"You're wrong," Sky Dreamer said defensely. She refused to think that someday the Apaches would not roam the rugged slopes of the Chiricahua Mountains, or that they would no longer be free to traipse across the golden sand dunes of the sprawling desert floor.

Nachae drew her head down against his chest and gently stroked her long hair. Her body shook with the thoughts she so vehemently wished to deny. "I pray that I am wrong, little one. But our destiny was sealed long before you and I walked through this land."

"We'll fight," she said in a defiant voice.

He smiled wistfully and stared into the darkness. "Yes, we will fight—until none of us are left to fight—and then the white men will win anyway."

Her quaking form stiffened and she tightened her hold around his neck. "Have we any more choices left?"

He sighed. "No. I can't imagine living among the white men or the Mexicans ever again. But I will never be caged up on a reservation—never!" His voice grew so enraged that Sky Dreamer's whole body cringed fearfully in his arms.

"Our choice is final then," she said, attempting to feign a confidence she did not feel. Although she tried not to think about it, she had always known the Apache way of life would someday end. But she still prayed that somehow something would change the white man's animosity and greed, and the Indians would be left alone to live in peace and harmony on the lands they cherished, and which rightfully belonged to them. Now that Nachae had voiced his own fears, though, she knew her prayers would never be answered. Her own terror returned.

Nachae fell silent once more. She was correct—their choice was final. And his love for this woman continued to grow, though he did not think it was possible for something that seemed so perfect to keep improving. Her long hair surrounded his face and chest as she clung to him in the darkness. A longing ache began to work its way through his loins when he ran his hand over the tumbling tresses again. His eyes ascended to the shaggy branches of the juniper tree they sat beneath.

"It's not a silver pine, but will this crooked old juniper do?"

Sky Dreamer sat up and tried to make out his face in the dark shadows. Her black brows pulled together in a questioning arch as she unconsciously bit her lower lip. "Do for what?" she asked.

He did not waste time with words. Instead he rolled her back onto the ground and covered her unsuspecting body with his tall frame. Only a muffled cry flew from her mouth before his lips commanded her total surrender. He continued to kiss and tease her mouth with his darting tongue while his eager hands worked to push away the barrier of her clothing. His growing desire was more than evident as his body pressed against hers on the hard ground. Sky Dreamer responded by drawing her knees apart so that he could fit perfectly between her smooth thighs.

His lips traveled lower, nipping and taunting her tingling skin while his mouth sought out the honey-sweet nectar of her womanly realm. His mouth knew this trail of fevered flesh by heart. He had explored every secret area of her enticing form since she had become his woman and he had laid claim to each minute pore of her tender flesh. When his tongue brought her to the edge of the highest peak of enchantment, he raised himself up and allowed his throbbing saber to enter her, so that he could lift her even higher until she was soaring above the moon and beyond. Then when he, too, had flown to the utmost summit of rapture, they descended back through the wispy clouds of reality together.

Morning came too soon for Nachae, though not nearly soon enough to suit Sky Dreamer. She was plagued by dreams that caused her to bolt up from her slumber, drenched in a cold sweat and shaking violently. Yet the subject of the dreams eluded her every time she tried to recall the details. Her mind would only conjure up misty images of some indistinguishable danger, but what form it would take remained unknowable. By the time the first gray light of dawn began to drape across the land, her head was aching and she was filled with such dread that she wanted to run and hide from whatever it was that had haunted her fleeting slumber. She was sure that her nightmares must be a continuation of her uneasiness from the day before. Since she had nothing except her strange feelings of doom to go by, she decided not to mention her dreams to Nachae. His mood was so much better this morning, and she didn't want to worry him if her premonitions turned out to be nothing.

The looming shapes of the saguaro cactus were a familiar sight when they grew close to the rugged Chiricahua range. Some of the giant cactus grew as tall as fifty feet high. Clumps of greasewood surrounded their round bases. Autumn had left the stiff white spines of the prickly pear cactus barren of any blossoms, but Sky Dreamer was so inspired by the sight of the vast array of desert vegetation that she kept stopping Sparrow so that she could memorize the beauty of this land.

"Fort Bowie is only a few hours' ride from here. It is dangerous to waste time in this area," Nachae said after several long pauses for sightseeing.

Sky Dreamer's stomach twisted nervously. "Fort—you mean—" Her strange sensations of dread washed over her again. "We must hurry, there is something—I can't explain it." Her voice grew frantic, and the pallor that washed over her face made Nachae's blood run cold. He kicked Eagle in the sides and motioned for her to do the same to Sparrow as they made a hasty retreat toward the foothills of the Chiricahua Mountains, which stood off in the distance.

Late afternoon found them deep into the jagged rocks at the base of the mountains. The picturesque sights of the desert floor were just a memory as they concentrated on the treacherous trails that led to the possible locations of the new Apache rancheria. On a spear-shaped ledge, just a dozen feet above them, a spotted jaguar watched their movements with eyes that flashed with menace. Though her species would not normally attack humans, this female jaguar had recently had another encounter with mankind on the ridge opposite this hillside when she had come across a patrol of soldiers. Wedged deep in her hip was the lead from a gun, which had been fired at her earlier that day. She had escaped from the men, but the pain from the bullet was driving her to madness, and the approach of other humans into her domain was more than her tortured mind could tolerate. She crouched painfully on her haunches, making her rich coat of yellow and black spots, which resembled ebony rosettes, glisten across her powerful sleek body. Her nostrils flared slightly, catching the scent of the horses and their riders.

Eagle's high steps made Nachae nervous. The horse's head rose into the air as though he sensed an unusual scent. Nachae's first instinct was to scan the ground and the low lying rocks in search of a rattlesnake or deadly gila monster, but he could not see anything except the barren trail. Behind him, Nachae heard Sparrow's shrill whinny, but he did not have time to investigate what was causing the mare's unrest.

Sky Dreamer saw the flash of the cat's body as the large feline sprang from the ledge, but she was too surprised to warn Nachae. The jaguar's attack was so sudden, there was not time for Nachae to escape from

251

the unseen danger even if Sky Dreamer had been able to call out to him. The impact of the massive animal knocked the man to the ground as Eagle reared back, then bolted up the trail in a cloud of dust. If Sky Dreamer screamed, she was not aware of it. The instant the cat leaped onto her husband's unsuspecting body and knocked him from Eagle, she was thrown from Sparrow's arching back. The little mare retreated in the opposite direction from where Eagle had fled, leaving her rider struggling to regain her wind and senses.

Sky Dreamer's hard contact with the rocky ground knocked the air from her lungs, but she was too frantic over Nachae's predicament to worry about her trivial injuries. Her vision was blurred by the dizziness in her head, yet the sound of Nachae fighting for his life forced her spinning mind to return to alertness. The man and the cat rolled across the rocks as flailing arms, legs, and claws struggled for an upper grip. The jaguar's teeth slashed through the air when Nachae grabbed her neck in his hands in an effort to escape from her vicious jaws. Her hind legs pushed against him, drawing deep gashes into his leather leggings, which were instantly saturated with streaks of blood.

Sky Dreamer did not stop to think about her own safety when she sprang from the ground and drew her knife. Charging forward, she hesitated only long enough to be sure that the animal was within her range before she lunged into the middle of the cat and brought down her weapon. The feline screamed in surprise and swung her head around. Sky Dreamer still clung to the animal's back, and as her eyes met the golden glint in the large cat's glare, she felt her bravery ebbing from her body. She was sure she was looking into the depths of hell when she peered into those wild yellow eyes. On rubbery legs, Sky Dreamer slowly began to stand up and back away, leaving her knife jutting from the animal's hide.

The cat's glistening eyes never left the woman's face, although her razor-sharp claws still pinned Nachae beneath her heavy bulk. The distraction was long enough,

252

though for Nachae to draw his own knife. His hand shook as he began to loosen his grip on the fur and skin around the cat's neck so he could reach down to his side and latch on to his weapon.

The increased pain from her previous wound, compounded with the searing pain from the new attack on her body, made the powerful cat confused as to which of the humans posed more of a threat. Her brief moment of indecision was her downfall. Nachae pulled his knife from its sheath. The cat swung her head around just as he plunged the weapon into the side of her throat. Emitting a loud screech, followed by a hissing moan, she began to wobble back and forth above Nachae. Her blood drenched the man's face and upper body in red, making him look grotesque and demonic in her waning vision. In one last breath of ferocity, she looked down at the hideous-looking man and curled her lips back, revealing the deadly points of her slashing teeth. Nachae's trembling hand raised his knife into the air again, but the cat toppled over to the side before he was forced to inflict another wound upon her.

Nachae attempted to raise his head but was overcome by the shooting pains in his body. Sky Dreamer was sure he was dead when she saw him collapse back against the rocky ground. Rushing to his side, she fell to her knees.

"Nachae," she said in a quivering voice. His mouth opened, but he remained silent. "Don't try to move. I'll look for something to put on your wounds." He winced with pain as he tried to shake his head. Sky Dreamer rose up on her unsteady limbs, and looked around the area in desperation. She felt for the bag that hung from her hip; it contained a few herbs and a sprinkling of hoddentin—hardly enough medication to heal Nachae's deep wounds. She barely glanced at the lifeless body of the cat while she searched for a plant or some sort of roots she could use for medication. They were in a barren stretch of land where there was hardly any vegetation. All the necessary ingredients for doctoring open wounds were in the bags that hung from Sparrow's back, and the startled horse was nowhere to be seen.

A pain-racked moan from Nachae brought Sky Dreamer's attention back to the mangled body of her husband. Although his face and chest were covered with the jaguar's blood, his torn leggings and shirt were soaked with blood from his own wounds. If she didn't do something soon, he was bound to bleed to death. Determination set in, making her numb senses snap into action. Her eyes scanned the area for some sort of shelter. Several yards ahead, a lone piñon grew out of an overhanging rock and leaned its uneven boughs over the trail. Its scraggly branches did not provide much shelter from the hot sun, but at least Nachae would not be lying out in the open.

Sky Dreamer fell back down to her knees and leaned close to her husband's ear. "I'm going to try to move you out of the trail."

His lids fluttered as he nodded his head. Sky Dreamer drew in a relieved sigh that he was still able to communicate with her. She moved to his head, and slid her arms beneath his shoulders. With her hands clasped tightly together around his upper body, she began to drag him toward the stony ledge. Nachae tried to help her by pushing against the ground with his feet, but in his weakened state, he only managed to slump against his wife in agony. Using muscles she didn't know she possessed, Sky Dreamer managed to drag Nachae's limp form to the rocky ledge. The movement made his wounds bleed profusely, and the color of his skin was a ghastly shade of white as he sank back against the stone wall beneath the ledge. He still clutched his knife tightly in his hand; Sky Dreamer took the weapon from his grasp and began to cut away his shredded pants and shirt. He winced yet did not mutter a sound as she stripped away his clothes, and left him draped only in the breechcloth he wore beneath his leggings.

Sky Dreamer's hand shook as she began to wipe the blood away with the tattered pieces of his clothing. The claw marks were deep, but they weren't as severe as she had first feared. She dug into the little bag at her hip and took out a handful of moxa. Placing the herbs in her mouth, she moistened the leaves, then carefully applied them to her husband's skin. He had opened his eyelids, and as she diligently worked over him, his dark gray eyes watched her in silence. Her face was drawn by her worry and intense concentration, and her upper teeth dug relentlessly on her lower lip as she prayed that her crude medication would be helpful.

"I'm going to live," he stated, although his voice was hoarse and the reassuring smile he attempted was weak.

She exhaled heavily and gave him a halfhearted grin. "You're too stubborn to die." After patting the last of the moxa on the worst gouges, she rested back on her heels. "I have to look for something more potent to put on those wounds." She glanced around and sighed. "I'd better try to round up the horses, too."

"Eagle will come back on his own," Nachae said, then added, "And you'll probably find Sparrow not too far down the trail."

"I don't want to leave you."

Nachae reached out and touched her cheek. "I'm not going anywhere." Sky Dreamer laid her face against his strong palm as she noticed that the suffocating feeling of dread had not left her, even after the horror of the jaguar attack. She stared down at the man she loved more than life itself. It was a temptation to collapse against his strong chest and cry because she was still so scared, and because she was so relieved that he was alive. Yet she had to be brave—for herself but mostly for her injured husband.

"I won't be gone long," she said as she rose up to her feet. His head nodded slightly before his lids lowered again. Sky Dreamer forced back the panic that she felt rising in her breast. What was wrong with her? The danger was past, wasn't it? She leaned down and placed his knife beneath his limp hand, then she lightly kissed his cheek and commanded her reluctant feet to walk away from him.

Her own knife was still buried in the back of the jaguar. The huge cat was lying in a motionless heap where she had fallen after Nachae's knife had drained away the last of her life. Sky Dreamer looked in the opposite direction while she yanked her weapon from the feline's hide. In death, the cat looked as tame as a kitten. Although Sky Dreamer hated the animal for what she had done to Nachae, she also found herself feeling a tinge of remorse that such a magnificent animal had to be destroyed.

Sky Dreamer's gaze moved across the expanse of arid country that stretched out before her, and another strange sensation bolted through her. Her mind was filled with reasons why she should not leave Nachae, although they were not valid enough to stop her from going. Her body suddenly felt too tired to go in search of Sparrow, or for the medicine she would need to doctor Nachae's wounds. Her loose hair seemed too heavy and hot upon her back, and some unknown fear would not leave her alone. Yet alone was how she felt — so alone that she had to swing around and gaze at her husband's unmoving form to be sure that he was still close by. She could see his ragged breathing and the fresh blood that was drying in crusty scabs on the long claw marks across his body. Her heart ached with the love she carried for him . . . a love that expanded with each frantic beat. The hot autumn heat of the Arizona sun was unbearable, or was it just this searing feeling of doom which hovered in her shadows as Sky Dreamer turned from Nachae and began to walk away?

The hard fall from Sparrow's back had left Sky Dreamer's whole body sore and bruised. Her skirt and shirt were torn and covered with dirt, although she wasn't aware of her own miseries until she began to make her way down the rocky trail that she and Nachae had been following. The path was barely more than an open area among the rocky ledges, and the surrounding landscape had many exact replicas of the stone pathways scattered in disarray throughout the foothills. Sky Dreamer realized that if she didn't mark her trail, she could easily get lost when she tried to return to her husband. Using as little time as possible, she made little pyramids out of stones to help lead her back.

The throbbing in her bruised legs made walking on the rocky ground nearly impossible. She tried to distract her mind from her aches and pains as she searched the terrain for some sign of Sparrow, or at least for a plant whose leaves or roots she could use for medicine. It seemed as though she had been stumbling along through the jagged rocks and stepping over the clumps of sharp-spined cholla cactus for hours when she finally decided it was useless to look any further. Sparrow had obviously fled in a different direction than she was traveling and there did not appear to be one usable plant in this whole region. Every step took her farther away from Nachae, and by the position of the sun she could tell that the hour was growing late.

Lumbering back up the incline, she picked her way through the low-lying rocks while she searched out her little piles of stones. Her eyes kept blurring and a pounding in her head was threatening to drive her insane. She stopped to catch her breath for a few moments and realized that her clothes were drenched with perspiration. Confusion made her mind grow blank and for several seconds she couldn't remember where she was or what she was supposed to be doing out here in this brutal land. When her mind did finally begin to clear, she immediately thought of Nachae. How long had she been gone? When had it grown too hot to breathe?

She took a step, but her legs were too weak to hold her weight. It's just the heat, she told herself as she fought to remain standing. She tried to concentrate on getting back to Nachae. What would go through his mind if she didn't return before nightfall? Would he just lie beneath the little stone overhanging in the sparse cover of the piñon tree and wait for her until his last hope was drained away by the awesome desert heat?

Somehow, she had to find the strength to make it back to him, but the desert sun was rapidly stealing away her waning energy. She felt her knees bend and her legs crumble beneath her before she fell face-first into the unfeeling rocks and cactus. With the last of her strength, she raised her head up and looked out over the purpled hues of the declining daylight against the distant desert horizon. Silently, she asked Nachae to forgive her for leaving him alone when he needed her so badly. A movement on a far slope caught her glazed eyesight, and for a second, she thought she had imagined it. Sparrow stood in the outline of the brilliant violet sunset and watched her mistress sink back down into the fading shadows.

Chapter Twenty-one

The lieutenant's face became a mask of shock as he slowly rolled over the battered body of the young woman they had just encountered along the rocky trail. He pushed back the disheveled mass of dark hair with fingers that shook so violently he could hardly control himself. Although she was barely recognizable with her face all swollen and dirty, Randy Decker knew at once they had found Regina Atwood.

"Is she an Apache, sir?"

Lieutenant Decker did not remove his eyes from the young woman as he answered the soldier's question. "No, she's a white woman, and she's in serious need of medical attention. It looks like she was exposed to the sun for too long a time." His narrowed gaze searched her bruised face as he added, "Those damn savages!"

The private shook his head and leaned closer. "She sure looks like an Indian to me."

"This is Captain Atwood's daughter. She's been an Apache hostage for several months." The lieutenant rose to his feet and glared at the private. "Bring the buckboard to the base of the trail so that we can transport her back to the fort—immediately!"

Carefully, the lieutenant eased the girl into the cradle of his arms, cursing the heathen Apaches under his breath while he carried her down the slope and placed her in the back of the wagon. The little piles of rocks that she had stacked along the side of the rocky path

259

went unnoticed as the soldier's attention was solely directed toward the captain's daughter. As Randy Decker climbed into the buckboard and sat down beside her, he vowed to find the breed who was responsible for the degrading condition of Miss Atwood. He thought briefly of the day he had seen her running wildly through the Apache camp; he could still remember the horrified look on her face, and he grew enraged all over again. If it hadn't been for that half-breed, he could have rescued her during the attack on the village, and undoubtedly would have won her eternal admiration with his heroic deed. Now that she had been subjected to more hideous tortures at the hands of those animals, it would not be so easy to gain her trust. He glanced down at her pitiful face and shook his head. What indescribable horrors had she been forced to undergo during the past few months? he wondered with disgust surging through his veins.

The lieutenant was certain that Miss Atwood was no longer the innocent young girl she had been before her captivity. But if he could only find it in himself to put those lurid thoughts to the back of his mind, then perhaps he could continue with his original plan. He knew his uncle would be pleased to hear that his nephew had made a decent woman out of Charles Atwood's abused daughter after he had rescued her from perishing in the desert. Maybe the general would be so pleased that he would transfer the young couple back to Washington so they would be far away from this brutal place and the horrifying memories of Miss Atwood's captivity. Randy glanced at the unconscious woman and shuddered. It would be difficult for him ever to touch her intimately after she had been with those savages. He remembered the way she had looked when she had first come to Fort Bowie, and reminded himself that beneath all that grime and those uncivilized clothes was still the same beautiful young woman from Savannah, Georgia.

Eventually, Randy told himself, he might be able to overlook the fact that she was not as pure as he would like her to be.

The amulet Nachae had given to her was still hidden beneath her shirt, but Randy's gaze settled on the beaded band she wore around her slender neck. He reached out and roughly yanked the necklace away from her skin, then wadded the beaded ornament up in his hand. Had that breed given her this crude piece of rubbish? Before those savages had gotten hold of her, Regina Atwood had deserved to wear diamonds around her neck, Randy decided as he stuffed the necklace into his shirt pocket. Now, except for the fact that she was still a white woman, she was hardly better than those heathens she had been living with for the past few months. He ran his hand over the tangled mass of raven hair that hung limply around her face and shook his head. What a waste, he thought with renewed contempt for the Apaches. He planned to make every one of those animals pay for the ruination of Regina Atwood, but especially that half-breed—Nachae!

"We found her lying in the trail about halfway up Dry Gulch, sir," the lieutenant said, and flashed a proud grin when he climbed down from the buckboard. He had been able to revive her once with small sips of water, which he had administered to her parched lips, but she had lapsed into unconsciousness again before they reached the fort. "I suspect she had escaped from the savages who had taken her hostage and was attempting to walk back to the fort when she was overcome by a heat stroke."

Charles ran his hand across Regina's grimy face. Ever since Lieutenant Decker's unauthorized ambush on the Apache rancheria, the captain had been worried about her welfare. At this moment, she looked so young and

261

defenseless lying in the back of the buckboard. Charles wished he could scoop her into his arms and pretend she was still his little girl. So much had happened to her lately, however, that she had been forced to grow up much too fast. With a saddened feeling in his heart, Charles realized that she was no longer a child. He also knew she had been happy when she was living with the Apaches, so it was unlikely she was trying to escape from the Chiricahui when she fell victim to the merciless Arizona sun as Lieutenant Decker had surmised. Until she was well enough to tell him what had really happened to her, he could only draw his own conclusions. Somehow, she must have become separated from Eskinzan and the rest of the tribe when they were moving to their winter camp.

"Was she alone?" the captain asked as he motioned for her to be carried into the medical quarters.

"Yes, sir." Lieutenant Decker glanced at the captain with curiosity. How could a man sound so casual about his daughter living among a bunch of savages? The lieutenant felt a rush of resentment against his commanding officer. Soon, he told himself, he would be out of this disgusting fort, and he would never have to put up with the likes of Captain Atwood again.

"The Apaches she was traveling with must still be in the area. Do you plan to send out a unit of men to search for them?" the lieutenant asked.

Captain Atwood shrugged his shoulders as he started to follow the two men who were carrying Regina toward the fort infirmary. "No, there's no need to send anyone out. The Apaches are probably a great distance from the fort by now. I'm just grateful to know that my daughter is safe. Thank you for taking such good care of her, Lieutenant," the captain said with a quick salute as he began to walk away.

Lieutenant Decker did not bother to return the captain's salutation; he was too furious. It was beyond his comprehension that the man did not want to go after the savages who had abducted his daughter, even if there was only a remote chance he would find them. Randy Decker pulled the beaded necklace out of his pocket and stared down at the object in his hand. He crushed the colorful rope into a tight ball and clenched his teeth together furiously. This wasn't the first time Captain Atwood had turned tail and run when confronted with an important decision concerning the Apaches—but as far as Randy Decker was concerned, it was the captain's last!

While Charles walked away, he felt the lieutenant's icy stare following his every step. He was certain the younger officer would file another grievance to the head office in Washington. It had been a common occurrence during the past two years for the lieutenant to write to his uncle in Washington whenever he disagreed with the captain on an issue involving the Apaches. Since the captain and his second officer in command clashed vehemently on the subject of how to handle the Indians, Charles was amazed the lieutenant hadn't succeeded in having him overthrown from his position yet.

In the sitting area outside the medical examining room, while he waited to see Regina, Captain Atwood began to evaluate his whole life. There had been a time when he had wanted nothing more than to help Lucero's people, but he was only one man against a whole nation. He was tired of watching his own kind wipe out the proud race of Apaches with their greed. It seemed that nothing had turned out as he had planned. Fourteen years had not diminished his love for Lucero, and his attempts to protect their daughter from a life of hardship and pain had also failed. For the past few weeks Susan had been begging him to go through with their wedding plans, and then to put in for a transfer to Washington. Charles rested his aching head in his hands and tried to imagine himself leaving Arizona, Regina, and the memories of her mother behind him. He knew that he must make a decision about Susan soon; she was his responsibility since he had asked her to marry him. Perhaps it was time for him to move onward. When Regina had recuperated, he would allow her to choose the life she wanted to live, which most likely would be to return to her mother's people. Then, he would put in for a long-overdue transfer out of Fort Bowie.

"I just heard. Oh Charles, is she going to be all right?"

The captain raised his head from the cover of his hands and looked at Susan. Dressed in a flowing pink silk gown, with her blond curls done up in an elaborate coiffure, she appeared to be out of place in the rough-hewn log infirmary. Since she had been brought back to Fort Bowie after her captivity with the Apaches, she had been going overboard in her efforts to please him. What was it about Susan Wilkins that kept him from returning her attentions? Charles wondered once again.

"Regina suffered a heat stroke," he said hoarsely as he rose to his feet.

"Will she recover?"

Charles wondered if he was only imagining the slight wishful sound in his fiancée's Southern drawl. Susan had not told anyone at the fort that she knew his daughter was half Apache, yet Charles had no doubt she would use that bit of information if it suited her purposes. Being engaged to a squaw man was not a proper-bred Southern lady's ideal for a prospective husband, however, so long as Susan intended to become an officer's wife, Regina's secret was safe.

"Yes, she should fully recover in a short time," he stated in a flat voice.

"Oh—well, thank goodness!" Susan said with an exaggerated display of hands clasped against her breast. She moved to Charles's side and ignored the way he turned away from her as she wrapped her arms around his waist. "This may not be a good time to bring this up, but—"

"Let's keep quiet about Regina's Apache mother?" Charles volunteered. His face became an icy mask when he looked back down at Susan. Her cheeks grew red as she released her hold on him and moved several feet away.

"Well, it would be in everyone's best interest to keep it our own little secret, don't you agree?"

Charles gave her a complacent grin. "Of course it would, my dear."

Susan tossed her head back in a haughty fashion. She hated it when he talked to her in a fatherly tone of voice. And she hated waiting around this god-awful place while Charles debated over whether or not he planned to marry her.

"I'm fed up with this charade, Charles," she blurted out suddenly. "You brought me out to this uncivilized hole because you promised to marry me. Either we go through with our plans in the very near future or else I'll—" She paused, wondering how far she should carry her threats. The captain focused his threatening gaze on her face. At once, Susan realized that blackmail would not serve her purpose.

"Why—I'll just die of a broken heart," Susan gasped in an effort to cover up the gross mistake she had almost made.

Captain Atwood shook his head as a knowing smile curled his mouth. "All right, Susan. We'll go ahead with the wedding, if you're sure that's what you really want. And then I'll request that transfer to Washington, since I know how much you crave prestige. But you'll have to promise me something in return."

"Oh Charles, I'd do anything—just anything!"

He backed away and watched for her reactions as he said, "As long as Regina is here at the fort, you will not slander her, or her mother's memory—in any manner!"

Susan cast an insulted look in Charles's direction. "Why,

I haven't said a word to anyone!"

"You haven't had a reason to talk about it yet. But now that she's back here, I wouldn't want you to decide that it would be an easy means of getting her out of the way again. I know your feelings about the Indians and I also know how you feel about the fact that I was once married to an Apache woman."

"That's not fair," she said with a pout. "I would never do anything to hurt you or Regina. I only want all of us to be happy." She moved to Charles's side again and turned her blue eyes up toward his stern face. "And I would be happy in Washington, Charles."

Charles glanced down at her for an instant, then looked toward the closed door of the examining room. He wanted his daughter to be happy, but would that be possible—now that she was back at Fort Bowie, and subjected to the likes of Susan Wilkins and Randy Decker?

Nachae had no idea how long he had been lying beneath the piñon tree waiting for Sky Dreamer to return. He was sure he had passed out several times, and at least one night had passed since he had last seen his wife. The sun signaled that it was midday, yet she had left in late afternoon to go in search of medicine plants and her horse. Panic invaded his aching limbs as he began to inch his way out into the open area beyond the rocky ledge where she had left him. The long scratches where the jaguar had clawed him scraped against the rough terrain and broke open again as they filled with dirt and rocks. He left a bloody trail in his attempt to crawl out from the overhanging rocks and piñon tree.

A few yards away, Eagle patiently watched his master struggle to stand. Nachae had barely managed to raise himself to his knees when he spotted his faithful steed.

"*Itsa*, come here," he said in a weak voice. The horse

came to his side at once. Nachae grabbed the animal's long blond mane and began to pull his weight up to the horse's back. The claw marks had began to draw together in a natural healing process, and as Nachae stretched to mount the horse, he could feel the cuts spreading apart. The new rush of pain nearly caused him to lose consciousness again, but he willed himself to remain on Eagle's back. If he could only hang on to the stallion's mane and keep from losing his balance, he knew Eagle would take him straight into the Apache rancheria.

First, though, Nachae told himself that he had to be strong enough to look for Sky Dreamer. He dug a rope out of his buckskin bag and tied it around his wrists, then wrapped the long end of the rope around Eagle's neck. With the little strength he had left in his arms, he pulled the rope until it was so tight it was cutting into the circulation in his wrists, then he wrapped the rest of the rope around his waist and secured it into a knot. The pressure from the rope was minor when compared to the rest of his injuries, so he hardly noticed the addition of this new agony. His only hope was that he would be able to remain on Eagle's back long enough to find Sky Dreamer or at least to make it to the village to seek help.

He nudged the steed in the side, causing the horse to begin moving down the slope. Nachae fought to stay alert with every step the animal took. His head spun and blood from his wounds drenched Eagle's smooth brown-and-white coat. But he was still alert enough to notice the little piles of rocks that marked the trail. He prayed that those tiny pyramids of stone would lead him to Sky Dreamer. At the base of the rocky trail, he saw where the ground had been trampled down by the hooves of many horses and he noticed the imprints from the wheels of a wagon. His breathing seemed to grow too heavy to escape from his dry lips and the pounding in

267

his head fought to drown out his thudding heart. His last thought before he was lost to the darkness that claimed his suffering mind was that Sky Dreamer had been taken back to Fort Bowie. And if Randy Decker were to learn that she was now the wife of his most hated enemy, Nachae would never see his beautiful Sky Dreamer again.

Chapter Twenty-two

Regina sat in the shade of the small veranda and looked out past the boundaries of Fort Bowie. The autumn had stolen away the last of the sparse bit of greenery which had previously dotted the landscape, making the barren countryside appear even more uninhabitable. For this time of year, it was abnormally hot, and the unusual amount of heat seemed to coat the air with a dry, heavy feeling. Regina's hand shook as she touched the smooth skin above the neckline of her muslin dress and thought of the beaded necklace that she had cherished and would never be able to replace. She figured she had lost the piece of jewelry somewhere in the desert on the day she had fallen victim to the heat stroke. Luckily, she still had the amulet Nachae had made for her. With a dedicated vow, she swore never to remove the necklace. Even now, it was tucked down safely in the bosom of her dress.

When she saw Nachae, he would scold her for being so foolish and careless. He would remind her that she was not used to the climate in this desert region. How many times, when he had been teaching her the ways of this harsh land, had he told her always to respect the desert sun and never to take any chances of becoming too hot and thirsty when traveling in the daylight hours, no matter what time of year it was?

Once again, her gaze moved out across the bleak expanse of ground that led toward the distant Chiricahua Mountains. Her mind kept envisioning a brown-and-white horse galloping toward the front gate. On the animal's back would be her dream warrior. She could see the regal features of his dark face so clearly that it was almost frightening to think she was only imagining that he was this near—when she knew that he was so very far away. Yet it was her greatest fear that Nachae would attempt to come into the post after her. She had made a promise to her father, and as soon as she fulfilled it, she planned to return to her husband. Until then, she hoped and prayed that Nachae would stay as far away from the post as possible. With the exception of her father, there was not one soldier in the fort who was not after Nachae's hide. The warrior would meet with certain death if he tried to reach her while she was still at Fort Bowie.

A smile trembled upon her lips whenever she thought about her handsome new husband—and she had hardly thought of anything else since the soldiers had found her in the desert over a week ago. The only thing that kept her from going insane was her consistent dreams of him. Every night since she had returned to the fort, she had dreamt that Nachae had reached the Apache rancheria safely, and that Eskinzan was taking care of his wounds. In her most recent reverie, they were all together at the rancheria again—Grandfather, Waddling Woman, Juno, and Ta-O-Dee, and of course, she and Nachae were there too. She wondered if Nachae was resting against the soft furs in Eskinzan's wickiup, while Waddling Woman constantly fussed over him. Was he thinking about his wife at this exact instant when she was thinking of him?

Her dreams had also encompassed the last night they had made love in the mountain meadow, beneath the boughs of the tall silver pines. A secretive smile hovered on Regina's lips as she remembered that moonlit eve. She rested her hands across the taut flat area of her abdomen where the tiny seed had been planted. How could she think that their lives were not going to be beautiful when something so wonderful and precious was already promising them a whole new beginning? If only she could be as certain of her father's future as she was of her own right now, she would not be so reluctant to leave him again.

Regina still could not imagine her father actually married to Susan Wilkins—and the wedding was tomorrow! When she had told him that she planned to return to the Apache village, he had asked her to stay at the fort until after the wedding. For his sake, she had agreed to remain, although watching him marry that woman would be one of the most painful things she would ever be forced to do. Even worse than the impending wedding was the thought of them leaving Arizona together. The captain had already put in for a transfer from Fort Bowie and was expecting a telegram from Washington any day now. If his transfer went through, he and Susan would leave immediately. Regina tried to remind herself that she had no right to interfere in her father's life, but the idea of him falling prey to the schemes of a woman like Susan Wilkins was almost unbearable. Regina had always felt that her father's fiancée was underhanded, but in the last week she had become even more aware of Susan's conniving ways.

Ever since the day Randy Decker and his battalion of men had rescued Regina from near-death in the foothills of the Chiricahua Mountains, Susan had gone to elaborate lengths to please both her soon-to-be husband and his half-Apache daughter. She had even come to the infirmary shortly after Regina gained consciousness and begged Regina to forgive her for calling her a half-breed. In her next breath, she told Regina that it would be in her best interest not to tell anyone at the fort about her Indian mother. After all, Susan had reasoned, not everyone here would be as understanding as she was about such matters.

271

Regina clenched her hands together in anger. Susan Wilkins was far from understanding! She was calculating and sneaky. There was no doubt in Regina's mind what her future stepmother was plotting from the very first moment she had set her greedy eyes on Charles Atwood. Susan had big plans for her life as an officer's wife in Washington, and a half-breed stepdaughter would surely put a dark cloud over Susan's parade. Regina wondered how Susan would feel if she knew that the captain would have an Apache grandchild before too long? It was a tempting thought for Regina to consider telling everyone at the fort about her Apache mother and about her recent marriage to the feared warrior, Nachae—just to spite Susan. But she knew such an announcement would make her father's life more difficult too. Instead, she remained silent, and allowed everyone at the fort to believe she was just another unfortunate white woman who had been taken hostage to be tortured and abused by those loathsome savages.

"Miss Atwood?" Regina blinked as she forced her eyes to look away from the beckoning lure of the faraway mountains. In the past few months she had come to think of herself as Sky Dreamer and it sounded so strange to be called by her white name again.

"Hello, Lieutenant," she answered guardedly. She distrusted him even more than she did Susan Wilkins. Every time she glanced at him, she remembered the way he had looked when he tried to kill Nachae during the ambush on the Apache village. But now he was standing before her, presenting her with his glistening smile—the one that always seemed too forced to be sincere. Regina would never forget the demented look of hatred he had worn when he'd charged at Nachae with his long knife pointed at his heart. When she peered up at him now, it was this image that clouded her vision.

"You look beautiful today. No one would ever guess what a horrible ordeal you've recently been through, or of the close call with death you had before I found you in the desert." He took the liberty of sitting in the chair beside her without an invitation.

Regina gripped her hands together tightly. He always managed to remind her of how he was the one who had rescued her from perishing in the desert. She did not plan to thank him again, however. It was more than apparent that he had an ulterior motive for his attentiveness toward her, and Regina was certain that whatever his plan turned out to be, it would not be in her best interest.

"Has there been any word from Washington yet?" she asked, trying to change the subject.

The lieutenant's grinning expression altered slightly. "Nothing pertaining to your father's request for a transfer."

Regina wondered if it was only her imagination the way the lieutenant seemed to grow extremely cold whenever they were discussing her father. She picked up a pleated fan from the table beside her chair and began to fan herself. "Would you be in charge of Fort Bowie if my father should receive orders to report to Washington?"

Randy Decker's smile faded. "Perhaps, but only until another officer was sent to take over your father's command. By then, I would hope that every stinking savage in this whole county would be dead, and that I would no longer be needed in this dirt-infested hole either!"

His voice had changed so drastically that Regina felt a sharp-edged chill rush through the blood that pulsed through her veins. For just an instant, the lieutenant had dropped his charming facade and had allowed himself to revert to the hate-filled man that Regina had glimpsed at the Apache village on the morning of the raid. She realized what a powerful contempt this man must harbor for her mother's people, and a deep fear overcame her when she looked up at his face again. His stark white teeth were glistening from within his plastered-on smile once more, while his brown eyes stared back at her in bold observation. She drew her shaking hand across her forehead and felt a cold sweat break out upon her skin.

"Miss Atwood? Are you feeling ill?" Randy jumped up from his chair and wrapped his arm around her trembling shoulders. "Should I call the doctor?"

"No—no, I'm fine," Regina gasped. She attempted to breathe in a normal manner again. Why was she so frightened of this man? "I just need to get out of the heat."

Randy shook his head vigorously. "Of course. You shouldn't stay out in the sun too long." He slipped his arm around her waist and pulled her to her feet. Regina felt powerless to stop him as he led her into her father's quarters and helped her down onto the sofa. By the time he had released his tight hold on her, Regina was so consumed with a feeling of terror that she could barely breathe.

"Should I send for your father?" he asked. The concern in his voice was genuine. But before he could receive an answer from Regina, they were interrupted.

"Lieutenant!" Susan's shrill voice echoed from the front door. Both Randy and Regina swung around at the urgency in Susan's voice. Her blond head was tilted to the side and her hands were placed firmly on her hips. She acted as though she was not aware of Regina's presence in the room as she began to walk toward them. Her flashing blue eyes were focused on Randy Decker and the expression on her face was considerably less than friendly.

"A message just came over the telegraph for you." She leveled her enraged gaze at the lieutenant and added, "What did you tell your dear uncle this time? It must have been something especially good to deserve such an honor."

Randy Decker stumbled clumsily to his feet. "I'm sure I don't know what you're talking about, Miss Wilkins." Her name was said with a wicked drawl, while he shifted his eyes toward Regina as if to warn Susan that they were not alone. Susan barely glanced at Regina.

"Oh, you know what I'm talking about, don't you? Or would you rather that I spell it out for everyone?"

Randy never gave Susan a chance to carry out her threat. "Miss Atwood is not feeling up to listening to your rubbish." His feet moved across the floor, barely pausing long enough to grab Susan by the arm and drag her from the room.

Regina stared dumbfoundedly at the couple as they exited through the doorway. Her fear of a moment ago was replaced by a tremendous curiosity. What was going on between those two? She rose up from the sofa, ignoring the dizziness that sent her head spinning once again, and tiptoed over to the door. She could hear the murmur of their voices coming from somewhere around the corner of the building, although she could not make out what they were saying. Feeling like an eavesdropper, she decided to go back to the sofa and pretend she was not interested in their conversation. It was impossible. She just knew that whatever was being said between those two was bound to cause her father grief.

Walking quietly into the adjoining bedroom, Regina was relieved to find that the window was wide open. From here she could clearly hear Susan and Randy's voices.

"That was the most underhanded, selfish thing you've ever done. How could you do this to me?" Susan said, unaware that anyone was listening.

Randy's snide chortle echoed through the open window. "I take it my orders to report to Washington came over the telegraph today?"

Susan's voice was filled with contempt when she retorted, "You know how much Charles wanted that appointment in Washington and you took it away from him. Your uncle came through for you again."

"It wasn't the captain who wanted the transfer, was it?" he said sharply. "And if anyone deserves to go to Washington, it's me. I merely pointed that fact out to my uncle. Obviously, he agreed with me at long last."

"Well, I don't intend to let you get away with this." Angry tears joined in the sound of Susan's voice. "You deserted me once before, but I'm not going to let you ruin my only chance to make something out of my life. If you go to Washington, I'll destroy your precious family name. I'll tell everybody about our affair and how your uncle conveniently transferred you out of Georgia when I told you I was carrying your child."

"You wouldn't dare," Randy answered with another hateful laugh. "That would also destroy your chances of becoming an officer's wife and we both know you've been after that title for a long time."

"I don't intend to stay here and rot in this hellhole," Susan hissed. "Either you send a telegraph to your uncle and tell him that Charles is the man who should receive that transfer, or I will expose you for what you really are. I'll see to it that your career is ruined if it's the last thing I do."

A pause followed Susan's threat, then Randy's wicked chuckle floated into the room where Regina stood. "And," he added coldly, "it just may well be the very last thing you do."

Silence shrouded the area outside the window as Regina realized that Randy must have stalked away from Susan after his last remark. She stood rooted to the spot while her mind mulled over all the unbelievable things she had overheard. How could she allow her father to marry Susan Wilkins now? She tried to compose herself by taking several deep breaths, then forced herself to walk out of the bedroom. Susan walked into the front foyer at almost the same moment. As Regina's eyes met hers, Susan gasped with surprise. She looked past Regina, into the bedroom, while a look of realization consumed her pale features.

"You were listening, weren't you?"

Regina nodded, although she could not speak. There was nothing she wanted to say to this woman; she wished she never had to set eyes on her, or Randy Decker, again.

"Are you going to tell your father?" Susan said in hardly more than a whisper. Again, Regina's head moved up and down affirmatively.

"I'll tell everyone you're a half-breed."

Regina felt sick to her stomach and her head continued to spin. Her violet eyes became dark with fury as she stared back at Susan. At this moment she did not care about her own reputation. Her father was all that mattered. She was not going to permit Susan Wilkins to use him just to gain the social prestige she craved with a sick obsession.

"I won't tell anyone what I just overheard if you'll call off the wedding tomorrow and leave Fort Bowie immediately," Regina stated firmly. Her steady gaze never wavered from the other woman's face as she watched Susan's features fill with indecision.

Weighing her options, while trying to plan her whole future in a few seconds, Susan's face became a mask of indecision. If she did as Regina asked, she would have to return to Georgia and spend the rest of her life on her parents' plantation. Yet if Regina followed through with her threat and exposed her involvement with Randy Decker, Susan knew that her chance to become an officer's wife would be over, too. Her blue eyes became luminous as she realized that she did have one other choice. What did it matter if Charles stayed here in this god-awful place? Randy Decker was going to Washington; perhaps he would be willing to strike another bargain. Susan was sure that her ambitions matched the lieutenant's own goals. Once she pointed that out to him, they could help one another achieve them.

"All right, Regina. I'll break my engagement to your father and"—she smiled as she thought of her new plan—"I'll make arrangements to leave the fort as soon as possible."

Regina drew in a ragged sigh. She hadn't expected

Susan to concede so easily. Now she was even more leery of the other woman's motives, but she intended to see to it that Susan never caused her father another moment's heartache—no matter what she had to do to prevent it!

Chapter Twenty-three

"This is suicide, *shik'isn*. Please wait until we have had more time to gather up a larger war party."

Nachae listened silently to Juno's request, although he had no intention of changing his mind. He shifted his weight upon Eagle's back and groaned when he felt his shirt soak through with fresh blood again.

"Eskinzan was right—you are not healed enough to be doing so much riding. Come, let's return to the village until you're stronger. In the meantime, we can send for more men and plan a way to get her out of the fort, instead of going in there after her."

Nachae did not bother to answer the other man. His eyes were fixed on the forbidding outlines of Fort Bowie. There was no moon to illuminate the structures, or to fill the dark desert with a guiding light. It didn't matter to Nachae that he had torn his wounds open again, or that he had no plan to follow now that they had reached the army post. All that mattered was that Sky Dreamer was somewhere within those walls and Nachae wanted her back!

He glanced in Juno's direction and then back at the small group of warriors who had followed him to the fort. Juno was right—they could never hope to infiltrate the post with just a handful of men.

"I'm going in alone," Nachae said in a defiant tone.

"No—" Juno began, but was cut off abruptly.

"Alone!" Nachae repeated in a voice that silenced any

arguments. The pain from his wounds had driven him almost to the brink of madness. He would have fought anyone who crossed him, even his closest friend.

Juno recognized the warning in the other man's voice. "We'll wait here, but if we hear any shots being fired, we will come."

Nachae loosened his horse's reins and started toward the fort. His mind held no decisive plan. The image of Randy Decker being near his wife blinded him with uncontrollable fury. He left Eagle in a grove of trees outside the boundaries of the fort and continued on foot until he reached the stone fortress that surrounded the buildings. He paused to listen for the sounds of the guards who were always on watch at the top of the rock-and-mortar walls. Above him, he could hear the clicking of their heels as they paced back and forth. Then, after what seemed like an eternity, the sounds ceased. Nachae waited patiently, yet he grew more anxious with every breath he took. When another long period of time had passed without any more sounds from the guards, Nachae finally rose up from his crouched position against the base of the stone wall. He hoped the soldiers had left their posts for a drink or maybe had dozed off long enough for him to slip over the barricade unnoticed.

As he inched his way along the side of the wall, he felt his shirt sticking to his open wounds. He imagined how distressed Sky Dreamer would be when she saw the blood on his shirt. Several times he had found himself wondering if she'd returned to the fort of her own accord. Had she come across the battalion of soldiers while she was searching for medicine plants, and decided to return to the fort with them? Had she realized perhaps that she didn't want to continue her life as an Apache, or as his wife? A fire raged through Nachae's veins when he allowed himself to think these thoughts. He had lived far too long without love to give it up so easily now. She was his woman—his wife—and she loved him as completely as he loved her. He refused to believe she had come back to Fort Bowie willingly. Something terrible must have happened to her to prevent her from returning to him.

The walls of the fort were built in graduated heights against the rugged slopes of the hillside. At the lowest portion of the wall, Nachae shimmied over the top and dropped to the ground. At once, he fell down onto his belly and waited for any signs that someone might have spotted his arrival. After several minutes of silence, he began to crawl along the wall toward the buildings in the center of the encampment. He had no idea which buildings housed the officers' quarters so he planned to scout out each structure until he found where his wife was staying.

Every enclosure looked the same, and although the hour was late, several soldiers still dallied along the wooden planks that ran in front of the scattering of houses and offices. Nachae clutched his rifle tightly in his hand as he hid in the shadows and made his way along the backs of the buildings. He realized that his chances of getting caught were considerably higher than his hopes of finding his wife somewhere in the maze of this white man's domain. He had to take this risk though; he could not live one more day without knowing what had happened to her.

Crouching down, he moved to each building. Lights still flickered in some of the living quarters. It was easy for him to check out the occupants who were moving about in the lighted houses. It was the dark quarters that would cause him to take unnecessary chances if he was forced to sneak into them. But on this night, it appeared that fate had once again smiled upon him. As Nachae approached the third house in his quest, he heard someone walking on the front stoop. Wild rosebushes adorned the sides of the veranda where he hunkered down behind a clump of thorny vegetation as he waited to see who was pacing back and forth on the wooden stoop. As the footsteps neared the edge where he was kneeling, Nachae caught a glimpse of his wife.

His heart began to pound so rapidly he wondered if she could hear the thunderous sound roaring from behind the bushes. His love enveloped his whole being and nearly caused him to jump from the cover of the bushes to claim his bride. But he had no way of knowing if she was alone on the stoop or if someone else was nearby. She stopped and leaned on the rail—right above the rosebushes at the end of the porch. Nachae could almost touch her if he reached up his hand. It took all of his willpower to remain unmoving and silent. In the dim light that radiated through the windows of the house, he could barely make out her face, but he could tell that she was looking out into the darkness as though she could see something that only her eyes could behold. A shining reflection from the corners of her eyes made Nachae aware of the teardrops that edged her sad gaze. What thoughts filled her with such sadness? he wondered in silent agony. Her voice suddenly echoed through the darkness and almost caused him to jump out of his skin.

"Oh Nachae, I miss you so much!"

His stunned eyes flew up to her face. Disappointment rushed through him when he realized that she had not been speaking to him as he had first thought. She was still staring out toward the desert, at her invisible images, yet her thoughts were on him. His pulse leaped in a wild surge and vibrated throughout his body. She had not left him willingly—and she missed him as much as he missed her! He started to call out to her, but the sound of someone else walking up the steps of the veranda caught his attention.

"Regina? Did you hear about my appointment to the San Carlos Indian Reservation?"

She turned away from the rosebushes toward the man who had just joined her. "I just heard," she said quietly. "Are you sure it's what you want to do?"

Captain Atwood stepped closer to his daughter, until

they were both bathed in the light that shone across the porch through the front windows of the house. She was surprised to see the twinkle in his eyes as he grinned with excitement. "It's something I should have done years ago, Regina. I've already sent my resignation to Washington, and as soon as I escort Susan into Lordsburg, I'll be back to get you. After I take you back to Eskinzan, I will head up to San Carlos. As an Indian agent, maybe I'll finally be able to help the Apache people."

Regina gave her father a brave smile as she rushed into his arms. Was it possible that all their plans could really work out so perfectly? The pressure they had all been under had disintegrated into thin air when Susan informed her father that she no longer wanted to marry him. Once the ill-fated wedding had been called off, it appeared that the rest of their lives were finally falling into place. Susan was leaving in a few days, and Charles had decided to take an appointment as an Indian agent on the Apache reservation in the White Mountains. Soon Randy Decker would be gone, off to his new assignment at his uncle's side in Washington, D.C. None of those things seemed important, though, when Regina compared them with the thought of being reunited with her husband.

"I have a lot of paperwork to do before I leave. Will you be all right?"

Regina backed away from her father's embrace and gave him a wistful grin. "I'll be better when you and I are gone from this place." Charles didn't bother to answer, but merely nodded in agreement before turning to leave.

Nachae remained huddled down in the bushes. The conversation he had just overheard confirmed his hopes that his wife was truly devoted to him, and to the Apache people. Now, he just had to figure out how he was going to get her, and himself, safely away from the fort. He listened for sounds from the veranda, but it had grown quiet. Cautiously, he stood up and looked over the tops of the rosebushes. He could see her sitting in a chair—just staring off into space again. Nachae gave a low whistle, and her head jerked around. When their gazes met, it seemed as if the heavens had just exploded overhead.

Regina's mouth flew open, yet only shocked silence followed. Slowly, she rose from the chair and began to walk toward the end of the veranda. She was almost afraid to believe her eyes, yet even more fearful to know that he was really here.

"Is it really you?" Regina gasped as she reached the porch rail. "How—"

"There's no time for questions," he whispered. "I've come to take you home."

Regina had never known that it was possible to love someone as much as she loved her husband at this moment. The risk he had taken to come into the fort after her was beyond measure. He had thrown all caution to the wind to come into the fort, yet all that really mattered was that they were together again. A smile, accompanied by a mist of happy tears, lit her face with joy as she rushed down the stairs. She thought of jumping over the rail and the tops of the rosebushes in her excitement, but good sense claimed her mind in time to stop her. His arms were waiting the instant she rounded the clump of bushes and his lips immediately descended upon hers. Time—and for a moment, common sense—were left in the wings, while they became lost to the reunion of their trembling beings. Almost at the same instant, though, they both remembered that danger was near.

"Hurry!" Nachae said in a hoarse whisper. He grabbed her hand and began to pull her along behind him as he headed back to the secluded area behind the bushes.

Regina could not think, nor could she fathom that they were actually going to be able to sneak away from the post without being seen. Her father crossed through her confused thoughts—how could she go away again without telling him? "I can't leave until after I talk with my father," she said in a panicked voice, while sliding to a halt.

Nachae stopped only long enough to turn and give her an aggravated scowl. He had risked too much to get her back to argue with her. Wasting precious seconds discussing whether or not she should visit her father before they departed was not in Nachae's schedule. He tugged on her arm again and forced her dragging feet to succumb to his strength.

Between gritted teeth, she retorted, "I refuse to sneak off without telling my father where I am going." Her voice had risen slightly in her determination, and when the sound of someone calling out reached their ears, both Nachae and Regina froze in their tracks.

"Is someone there?" Randy Decker said as he peered into the dark shadows of the night.

Regina felt Nachae's grip slacken. He released her arm and retreated behind the house before she even realized that he was gone. She couldn't believe how stupid she had been to be making such a racket when her husband's life was in such danger. She swung around, hoping that she would be able to act normal enough to divert the lieutenant's attention from the direction where Nachae had just taken refuge.

"L-Lieutenant," she stuttered. Her eyes longed to glance back over her shoulder, but she forced herself to step forward instead.

"Were you talking to someone?" he said. His voice held a note of suspicion.

Regina laughed. "Oh no! I was just—" Her words were cut off by another intrusion—one she welcomed gratefully.

"Lieutenant Decker, I was just coming to see you." Susan tossed her mane of long blond curls over one shoulder as she approached the officer. She did not even acknowledge Regina. Ever since she had broken off her engagement to Charles, she had pretended as though neither the captain nor his daughter existed.

Regina was quick to notice the lieutenant's look of disgust. His feelings were apparent even in the dim light. It was then that she became aware of Susan's newest goal: If Susan Wilkins couldn't marry one officer, she would go after another one—Randy Decker.

"I have some business to attend to," the lieutenant replied curtly.

"This is important," Susan said. Her voice made it more than obvious that she did not intend to be put off by the lieutenant's dismissal. She glanced at Regina and added, "I'm sure you'll excuse us."

Since her words were more of a command than a polite suggestion, Regina eagerly excused herself. "Of course," she answered quickly. "Good night, Lieutenant." Without bothering to glance back at Susan, Regina hurried back up the front stairs and rushed into the house. She stopped and leaned against the door, praying that Susan and Randy Decker would go somewhere else to conduct their important conversation. When she reopened the door, she noticed her prayers had been answered. Slipping out again, she rushed toward the back of the house. She had to find Nachae before his presence in the fort was discovered. If he was caught, it would be all her fault!

When she skidded around the darkened corner of the house, he grabbed her roughly around her waist. Regina's shocked and terrified gasp did not deter him from dragging her behind him through the leaning shadows of the buildings. She did not offer any resistance, since she knew her foolishness could have caused a tragedy. Her only regret was that she was not going to be able to see her father before she left the fort. Nachae's anger was obvious by the forceful way he was holding on to her as they hurried toward the stone walls that surrounded the fort.

Regina was certain that she did not take a breath the

whole time they were fleeing through the darkness. Her heart felt as if it was about to pound through her rib cage when the looming tiered walls of mortar came within sight. Their escape seemed almost too easy, and when the sound of angry voices stopped their flight, Regina's numb mind was not even surprised. Nachae fell to the ground, dragging her down with him. His muscled arm held her imprisoned at his side as they listened to the couple who stood by the lowest portion of the stone wall—unaware that they were being observed once again.

"You must be crazier than I thought to suggest something so ridiculous. I would see you dead before I'd consider marrying you and taking you back to Washington with me," Randy Decker spat out hatefully.

Susan opened her mouth to throw back a deadly threat of her own, but something caught her eye. "What was that?" Startled, she jumped closer to Randy and peered into the black night air.

Moving into immediate action, the lieutenant pushed the woman to his side and drew his revolver from its holster. Years of training had conditioned him to prepare for a confrontation with the enemy at the slightest provocation.

Thinking back, Regina would never be able to piece together what actually happened in the next few seconds. She could not see the lieutenant's face, but she could see the shiny reflection of his gun as he stalked toward them. Then, she felt Nachae rise to his feet to meet the approaching soldier. Everything from that instant on was no more than a blur. Susan screamed . . . or had it been Regina's own cry that shattered the quiet night air when an orange-and-gold flash lit up the darkness and roared into the silence?

Relief flooded Regina's mind when Nachae's voice sounded through the quiet. The lieutenant's bullet obviously went wild and had not struck his target. She jumped to her feet when she heard her husband command her to climb over the wall. A frantic voice from somewhere deep inside guided her forward as she charged toward the towering stone structure. It wasn't until she was halted by the difficulty of trying to scale the wall that she realized there was no way she could jump high enough to reach the top of the barrier. Despite the nearly obscure light, she could see the summit of the wall hovering at least six feet above her head. She swung around, feeling defeated and helpless. The sight that greeted her eyes only increased her desperation.

Randy Decker's first shot had whizzed past Nachae's head. Pulling his knife from its sheath, he charged at the lieutenant. Somehow during the time he ran forward and made contact with the lieutenant, Nachae managed to shout to Regina to escape over the wall. The officer was caught off guard momentarily when the warrior rushed at him, but he was quick to regain his composure and dodge Nachae's deadly aimed weapon. The knife flew through the air, its silvery flash swallowed up by the darkness. The lieutenant pulled the trigger of his revolver for the second time.

Regina heard her horrified scream echoing through her senses, yet she could not comprehend what was happening. Randy Decker's aim had been hesitant for no more than a second, but in that brief instant — for a reason that no one would ever understand — Susan Wilkins charged between the barrel of the rifle and the tall form of the man who was on the receiving end of the bullet. Randy's pistol exploded and the repercussion seemed to mimic the deafening roar throughout the whole fort as Susan's body jerked to an abrupt stop and toppled to the ground.

Regina gasped, but the scream became lodged in her throat. Her eyes were still trying to convince her mind of what had taken place in less time than it takes for a heart to beat. In the flash which accompanied the bullet, she had seen the surprised look on Susan's face, and she knew that Susan was dead before she hit the ground. She stared in horror at the dark outline of Susan's lifeless form.

Randy Decker was attempting to sort out the deranged mishap when Nachae's attack caught him unaware. The warrior rushed forward and hit the other man on the side of the head with his fist. Lieutenant Decker staggered backward for several feet, then fell to his knees. Nachae saw that the whole fort had suddenly come to life. Lights flickered on from every building and the night was filled with shouts and sounds of chaos as the soldiers ran from their quarters to investigate the gunshots that had shattered the stillness.

Regina found her lost voice and called out a warning to her husband when she noticed the men running toward him. Nachae's head jerked around at the sound of her frantic alarm. Indecision threw his mind into a whirl when he saw the advancing soldiers—far too many of them for him to fight off alone. Yet at his feet, and at his mercy, was the man who had killed his father. For over a year, Nachae had lived for the day he would take revenge against Randy Decker. In only a matter of seconds, he could fulfill that obsession. Unfortunately, he did not have that much time. To snuff out Randy Decker's rotten existence was one thing, but to make him pay for his past crimes against the Teneh Chockonen was something Nachae needed to achieve before he could feel even a small amount of satisfaction. A glance at the waiting figure of his wife was enough to make his mind snap into action. There would be a more convenient time to conduct business with the lieutenant, Nachae surmised as he hurried toward the stone barricade.

From the top of the stone wall, Juno yelled down at Regina to grab his hand. Her startled eyes flew upward at the sound of his voice, but a sense of relief overcame her when she saw the warrior's arm reaching down to her. She paused as she glanced back to see if Nachae was coming—he had already reached her side. He grabbed her around the waist and effortlessly handed her up to his comrade, who hauled her over the top of the barrier. Gunfire and mayhem raged around her as the soldiers opened their fire. From the summit of the wall she was shoved toward the opposite side, falling clumsily to the ground. Her terrified gaze flew to the top of the wall. She could still see Juno crouched at the crest of the barrier, but it seemed like an eternity until Nachae's head appeared at the top of the wall. Regina held her breath while her husband's long legs swung over the smooth stones at the vertex of the rock wall. From the other side of the wall, shots exploded with blinding beams of light, and the night became ablaze with gunfire. Expecting Nachae, or Juno, to be hit by a flying bullet at any instant, Regina threw her hands over her eyes to block out the horror.

The thud of their feet hitting the ground sounded like an earthquake to her ears. Her stunned gaze sought out the face of each man as though she found it hard to believe that they had both made it to this side without taking a bullet. There was no time, however, to be grateful. It had been sheer luck that Juno had decided to follow Nachae to the edge of the fort. He had been waiting outside the wall ever since Nachae had first climbed over the barricade and entered the post. Once the first shot was heard, the rest of the warriors descended upon the fort and were now firing back at the soldiers who were shooting at them from the top of the wall. It would be only a matter of minutes before other soldiers would be on their mounts and headed out in pursuit.

Regina was grabbed by both men and dragged between them as they ran toward the clump of trees where Eagle and Juno's horse waited. She tried to run along with them, but her feet barely touched the ground. Her long skirt was wrapped around her legs and she was virtually helpless to do anything other than try to keep her balance as the two warriors charged forward. She did not have a chance to wonder where they were going, or how they intended to escape the hail of bullets that raged around them, until they had reached the horses and Nachae had thrown her on Eagle's back. Once he was positioned behind her and the animal galloped out from the shelter of the trees, her mind finally started to focus on the events of the past few minutes.

Susan Wilkins was dead! Regina would never forget the horrified look on Susan's face the instant after she had been hit by the bullet; it was a memory that would haunt her forever. She wished she could understand why Susan had stepped in front of Randy's gun, but they would never know what had gone through Susan's mind when she flung herself between the two men. To think that she was trying to protect Regina or Nachae did not seem possible, but still, it appeared that she had tried to shield them from danger by placing herself in the line of fire. Dying, Susan had protected the two people she had despised more than anyone.

Regina forced herself to take a deep breath. Nothing made sense anymore. Yet how could anyone ever hope to understand something so insane? Regina thought back over all the bickering and disagreements she and Susan had engaged in during the past year. She remembered how badly she had wanted that woman out of her father's life — for good. Regina was seized by a great sense of responsibility for the death of Susan Wilkins, accompanied by a deep sympathy for her father. Even though he and Susan had never been close, Regina knew that her father did harbor some feelings for his ex-fiancée. Her death would be a burden that Charles Atwood would never ease from his heart.

Regina could not lie to herself and pretend that she had ever liked Susan, nor could she deny the fact that she would not be in Nachae's arms at this moment if it had not been for Susan's attempt to help them avoid Randy Decker's bullet. She glanced up at the black sky, where not even a star dared to twinkle, and asked Usen to grant Susan a safe journey into his mysterious domain. Then, while she hoped that she still had his

291

attention, Regina thanked him for bringing her back to where she belonged—back to Nachae. She drew in a ragged sigh and leaned back against the hard sinewy body of her brave husband. Even in the wake of so much tragedy, she had never known such contentment. With every mile that took them farther away from the fort, with each minute that passed, Regina Atwood became less significant, until she was once again just a fleeting memory that was lost among the desert hollows.

Sky Dreamer felt her husband's powerful arms tighten around her waist as his torso pressed against her back. Had two bodies ever fit together so perfectly? she wondered. The autumn night grew chilly, almost as a reminder of the impending winter. Sky Dreamer was not aware of the cold, though. Nachae's nearness had lit an eternal fire within her soul, and nothing in this harsh land could douse that searing blaze.

Chapter Twenty-four

The sun was high overhead by the time the returning party finally entered the Apache rancheria. They had traveled all through the night since leaving Fort Bowie. By dawn, the warriors who had stayed behind at the fort to cover the trio's escape had caught up to them and they journeyed the rest of the way together. The braves were in good spirits, having eluded the pursuing soldatos at the base of the Chiricahua Mountains, and also because they had not lost any men during their daring foray. Once they reached the village, they would have much to brag about and to celebrate.

Sky Dreamer's shock over Susan's death had begun to recede by morning, and she concentrated on studying the terrain as they traveled. Nachae had taught her always to be aware of her surroundings when moving through strange lands. She did not ever intend to forget the rules of this rugged country again. After the attack on the village, the tribe had been very selective when they chose a site for their winter home. Hidden deep in the maze of canyons and gullies which hugged the summit of the Chiricahua Mountain range, the new rancheria was accessible only through one narrow valley. Behind the rancheria, rock cliffs guarded the village with towering stone peaks too steep to scale or descend. Anyone wishing to enter the rancheria could not do so without being observed from the tall cliffs. The tribe planned to hole up in this secluded little valley until spring, when it was rumored that a man called Geronimo was planning to rally all the outlying tribes for a fierce uprising against the white intruders.

Sky Dreamer was greeted by Grandfather and Waddling Woman with such a show of love that even the painful events of the past few hours were temporarily forgotten. With enthusiasm, she began to build a wickiup for herself and Nachae—their first home as man and wife. The structure took about four hours to build once the materials were gathered. A framework of poles and limbs formed the base of the thatched hut, over which bear grass was placed to cover the exterior. A hole was left in the top to allow smoke to escape from the fireplace, although smoke was a constant source of irritation in the confines of the small wickiups. The doorway was a low opening covered by a hanging canvas or animal hide to ensure privacy.

Sky Dreamer was overjoyed to learn that Nachae had been able to retrieve all their wedding gifts. She had feared they had been flung from the horses' backs when they had fled from the jaguar, but neither horse had lost their valuable cargo when they were rounded up. Once she had placed all their belongings inside the small hut, she was sure there had never been a more comfortable dwelling in all the world. Tired, but too excited to care, she cooked her new husband his first meal at their first home. Yet even when the tempting odors of the freshly killed venison reached Sky Dreamer's nostrils, she did not feel hungry. The anticipation of the first night she would spend with Nachae inside their own wickiup had stolen away her appetite, but left her with a greater hunger.

"You're not eating?" Nachae asked.

Sky Dreamer shook her head, marveling at the way the flames from the fire cast such tantalizing designs across the regal features of his bronzed face. While she had been busy setting up their new home, he had bathed in the small creek that carved a crooked path through the south end of the valley and then allowed Grandfather to attend to his reopened wounds. Afterward, he had rubbed mint all over his arms and legs—a distinct hint at his proposed activities for that night.

Since it was the custom that the women did all the menial chores, Sky Dreamer had not had time to care for herself yet. It was small inconveniences such as this which made her feel that the Apache ways were a bit unfair at times. They had ridden all night and half the day to reach the rancheria, but after they'd finally arrived, she had still gone immediately to work to build the wickiup and prepare her husband a feast. All the while, Nachae and the other men had been down at the creek pampering themselves and napping in the shade of huge yucca plants. That night, all the warriors planned to celebrate their cunning invasion of the army post. If it was possible for her to be upset over such an unfair custom, Sky Dreamer knew she would have a valid cause, but the sight of her virile husband sitting across from her in his clean white shirt and tan leggings made her decide to put her aggravation aside. His shiny hair hung long and full over his shoulders and the flames from the fire highlighted the bluish sheen in his ebony tresses. At times like this, Sky Dreamer felt as though he was too handsome to be real.

Nachae's worried look deepened as he observed the strange expression on his wife's face. However, she did not appear to be ill or tired. A rosy tint colored her cheeks, and her violet eyes shone like a thousand desert sunsets, making her innermost thoughts a clearly written scripture which beckoned to him with enticing promises. Nachae did not have to question her mood any longer; she had inflicted him with the same feelings of desire by nothing more than the sparkle in her beautiful gaze.

A slow grin began to work its way across his full lips as he tossed the remains of his dinner to the ground. He rose to his feet, and Sky Dreamer felt her limbs begin to quiver. Without a word, he sauntered over to her and scooped her into his strong embrace. Sky Dreamer's whole body became weak and limp although her heart began to beat out of control. He bent down and easily carried her through the low doorway of their new wickiup. The small fire that Sky Dreamer had built in the hut still blazed with short crackling flames and lit the inside of the hut with a cozy feeling that welcomed them into its hollow interior.

He carried her directly to the pile of soft furs she had spread out for their bed. As he knelt down and laid her atop the hides, his lips took possession of her waiting mouth. His lean body slid down until his legs pinned her beneath him, yet his lips never wavered. When, at long last, they finally took time to breathe, Sky Dreamer said with concern, "I don't want to cause your wounds to worsen."

The last thing on Nachae's mind was his wounds. "I'll suffer."

"And what of the celebration?"

"I'll go later."

"Not tonight," she whispered as she pushed his legs away and rolled over until she was sitting on top of his muscled abdomen. She grinned wickedly when she noticed his surprised look. All during their honeymoon he had made love to her; now, she intended to love him with the same devotion and pleasure that he had done for her. He would be lucky, she decided, if he was strong enough to walk out of the wickiup tomorrow, once she was through with him tonight.

Nachae threw his arms back against the furs and gave her total control. A woman had never made love to him before now, and he planned to enjoy each delicious second of this new experience. Sky Dreamer's grin broadened when she realized her husband had no intention of interfering in her carefully devised night of unending passion. She knew the claw marks on his chest were not healed, so she began by carefully easing his white shirt over his head and tossing it aside. Then she rose up from his unmoving form and did away with the wide sash and belt. All that remained were his kabuns and leggings. Removing his kabuns took no time at all, but she deliberately took extra time to slide his leather leggings down over his hips and past his thighs. He moaned with anticipation as she paused and began to kiss his torso and tense legs while she worked his leggings off.

The effect she was having on him had been apparent through his tight-fitting pants even before she had started to remove them. His entire body had grown rigid. She pulled the last of his leggings from his bare feet, then let her gaze rise slowly up the length of his body. She thought of the times he had looked upon her nude body in admiration, and wondered if he had felt the same sort of awe that she was feeling at this moment. His body was perfect, she decided—and it belonged to her!

When her hungry gaze met his smoldering gray eyes, she could tell that her actions were giving him as much ecstasy as his touch had always given her. Oh, how she loved having this sense of power over a man as independent and powerful as Nachae!

Gradually, she began her ascent. Her lips nipped and teased their way up his legs in slow degrees, which almost had Nachae crying out with welcoming agony. Her fingers luxuriated in the feel of his smooth tight muscles, and her nostrils were filled with the sweet scent of the mint that he had rubbed on his body after his bath. She moved with determination until her lips had covered every inch of his quivering form. Finally, she straddled his hips with her legs. His inflamed manhood pressed against her abdomen with an urgent demand, yet she paused and took the time to pull her loose-fitting dress over her head before she continued.

In naked splendor above him, Sky Dreamer could feel his desire increasing until his ravenous cravings also became her own, and soon there was no way to put off their ardent conjunction for one second longer. With a triumphant sigh, she anchored herself upon him, driving her hips downward, uniting her body with his and joining two individual mortals into one inseparable being. Again and again they lunged together, climbing higher, making each motion more dramatic than the last. And when there was no way to top the vertex of this fantastical scale, they clung to one another and allowed their soaring bodies to slide back to reality. It was moments afterward, however, before their minds were able to descend from such a tower of bliss.

"I think I should send you back to Fort Bowie more often," Nachae whispered. His voice was breathless and his face covered with a look of rapture. He pulled his very skillful wife down upon his body and wrapped his arms around her.

"For such a callous remark, I will have to punish you again." Her mouth curved with a teasing slant, but her hands were already reaching down to fulfill her threat. The instant her fingers wrapped around the center of his male domain, she felt him respond. Once again, she gloried in the power she had over this man. On the battlefield, and as an Apache brave, he was unyielding and unsurpassed. Yet here, within the comfort of the soft furs and beneath the silent ceiling of their little thatched hut, she was the victor.

Almost as though Nachae could read her deepest thoughts, he suddenly grabbed her and rolled her over, pinning her under his powerful form. He ignored her startled gasp as his dark gray eyes lit up like a flaming torch and his lips curled tauntingly with innuendo. "Do you forget, my beautiful Sky Dreamer, that I am the one who issues the punishments?" He lowered his face until their lips were almost — but not quite — touching and his breath was hot against her face. Then he added, "Or do I have to teach you a lesson?"

If his next actions were meant to be a punishment, then Sky Dreamer wished he would never cease to administer this sort of discipline—without mercy. Acting like a man who had been denied for far too long, he plummeted down into the moist niche between her silken thighs. He had sensed her domineering attitude a few moments ago, and his intention was to prove to her that, as the man, he was always in charge—regardless of the situation. But now, he realized that his show of male strength had only reinforced her authority. She wanted him to make love to her again; her jesting words had only fueled his waning control. As he loved her over and over again throughout the night, he began to wonder if she was truly a mystical shaman, or was she a witch who had cast a spell over his mind and body? A curse was the only feasible way that Nachae could explain the effect this woman had on him. Each time their sweat-drenched bodies escalated to the highest climax, it was only a matter of time before her mere presence had him aching for more.

From the center of the rancheria, the celebration rang forth with singing and the frantic beats of the drums. Then, sometime during the autumn night, the sounds died out, along with the last of the fading embers in the cooling fireplaces. Within one wickiup, however, what had once been a circle of orange-and-gold flame was now no more than a pile of gray ashes. But the heat emitting from the two enraptured lovers who occupied the little hut was equal to that of a raging forest fire!

Chapter Twenty-five

Sky Dreamer resisted the urge to open her eyes. She felt Nachae stir, then his arm fell across her midsection in a protective imprisonment. A slight smile touched her lips as she snuggled up against the warm body of her husband.

"Wake up," Waddling Woman repeated with aggravation. She gently shook the young woman's sleeping form.

Sky Dreamer finally realized that someone was actually trying to force her to wake up from her contented slumber. She lingered for just a moment longer, basking in the sweet images of her latest dream. Her musing had been filled with the laughing and high-pitched chatter of young children. She had envisioned two dark-haired toddlers running naked through the lush grass of her secret meadow. She sighed as she rubbed her eyes and blinked. She was certain that she had conceived Nachae's child on the last night that they had spent in the meadow. Could the second child in her dream belong to Juno and Ta-O-Dee?

"What is it?" she asked as she struggled to free herself from Nachae's enslaving hold.

"Bad trouble!"

Sky Dreamer immediately became alert. Waddling Woman would not come into their wickiup in the middle of the night unless something serious was happening. The woman's panicked words had also aroused Nachae.

He sat up abruptly and pushed away the fur which had been covering the lower portion of his long frame.

"Soldatos?" Sky Dreamer's eyes were wide with fright as she recalled the last ambush she had witnessed.

"Worse!" Waddling Woman began to back up toward the low doorway. "Eskinzan needs your help—now!"

Sky Dreamer sprang from her bed and grabbed for her clothes. "Is—is he ill?"

Waddling Woman shook her head and wrung her pudgy hands together. "It's Llamarada."

Nachae began to pull on his buckskin leggings.

"Llamarada?" Sky Dreamer repeated with surprise. They had not even seen her since their return to the village, and she did not particularly care to see her now.

Waddling Woman did not give either of them a chance to voice their opinion, however. Sky Dreamer and Nachae had to rush from their wickiup, half-dressed, in order to catch up to the woman.

"Has she been injured?" Sky Dreamer asked.

"She has the white man's sickness!"

Sky Dreamer's face screwed up with confusion. "What's that?"

"Smallpox is just one more way the white men have found to kill off our people," Nachae answered in an icy tone. "More than likely, it was not an accident that she came in contact with someone who was infected with smallpox. And once she was contaminated, somebody made sure she brought the disease back to her people."

A chilling tremor bolted through Sky Dreamer as she listened to her husband's cruel words. She wanted desperately to dispute him, yet she was quickly learning that everything he told her about the white men's treatment of the Apaches was the truth. "But—where has she been? I haven't seen her since we returned from Fort Bowie."

They had reached the sweat lodge, the wickiup used for tending to the sick and injured, by the time Waddling Woman replied, "She was left with the guards at the mouth of the canyon by some desperadoes who no longer wanted her around. The guards didn't realize the nature of her illness when they brought her to Eskinzan. Before that, she says she had been at the reservation at San Carlos."

Sky Dreamer's footsteps halted at the doorway. Her heart ceased to beat for a moment. She had been back at the village for over a month now. Her father undoubtedly was already working as the Indian agent at the San Carlos Reservation. Was he, at this very moment, also dying from smallpox?

"Cou—could she be mistaken?" Sky Dreamer asked in a voice filled with dread.

Waddling Woman was leading them into the hut and did not offer a reply. At once, Sky Dreamer sensed the seriousness of Llamarada's ailment. Grandfather had filled the fireplace in the center of the small sweat lodge with stones, which created an intense heat. She knew he was attempting to sweat a fever out of the woman's body. With fear seeping into every pore of her body, Sky Dreamer walked over to where Grandfather was sprinkling hoddentin over the woman while chanting in the language that was used strictly by the medicine men in the Apache tribe. He paused when the young woman walked up to him and turned his wrinkled countenance toward her. On his head, he wore the owl and hawk feather hat he used when his most powerful medicine was needed. It was the look in his dark eyes, however, that told Sky Dreamer what she dreaded most of all.

"I will fetch my medicine bag," she whispered without a glance at Llamarada. The old shaman merely nodded his gray head and returned to his chanting.

"You're not coming back," Nachae ordered as he followed his wife away from the sweat lodge.

"I must help Grandfather."

Nachae reached out and grabbed Sky Dreamer by the arm. His sudden action caused her to gasp as he swung her around. "I command you to obey me."

The sting of teardrops in the corners of her eyes made her blink with surprise. "It's not just for the woman that I must return. I have to perform my duties as a shaman of the Teneh Chockonen."

"I forbid it!"

Sky Dreamer could not speak for a moment. Her fear over the thought of a deadly disease spreading throughout the camp was replaced by anger. How could Nachae demand that she ignore the vows she had taken as a shaman of their people? She felt the tears begin to roll down her cheeks as she tried to free her arm from Nachae's tight hold.

"What you ask of me is impossible. I have taken an oath to help those who are sick and injured—no matter who they are."

"If you tend to her, you may be placing yourself in danger. Have you forgotten that you're carrying my child?"

Sky Dreamer's words of protest halted in her throat. They had never spoken of her prophesy since the night she had asked him to make love to her beneath the silver pines, yet he had not forgotten. Now he was reminding her that by helping Llamarada, she would be risking the life of their unborn child. Her confused gaze moved up to his stony expression, then back down to the ground while she contemplated one of the most important decisions of her life.

"I have to get my medicine bag," she said after a long pause. Her tone was definite, and as she walked past her husband, she could feel his cold stare following her. She almost stopped and ran back to him—to ask him to forgive her for disobeying him. But she forced her feet to continue toward their wickiup.

Every step that took her farther away from him grew heavier, until it felt as though her feet refused to move at all. When she reached their wickiup, a sudden rush of doom overcame her being. What if Nachae was right? How could she ever live with herself if something happened to their baby as a result of her decision to help Llamarada? She thought about all the trouble Llamarada had caused her and Nachae, ever since the first day she had arrived in the Apache rancheria. Nachae was right . . . nothing was as important as their child.

She swung around, expecting to see him somewhere behind her. But the whole village was empty and eerie in the coldness of the late autumn night. Even the diminishing flames in the fireplaces, which dotted the sleeping encampment with tiny circles of light, did not appear warm and welcoming.

Something stopped her from running wildly through the village to look for her husband, though at this instant, it was the only thing she wanted to do. Her gaze moved out across the quiet rancheria, and she thought of all the innocent babies who already had been born into this cruel and suffering world. How could she turn her back on any of them? The laughing, cherub faces of the little dark-eyed children that encircled her feet each time she walked through the rancheria drifted in front of her eyes. Slowly, she bent down and entered the wickiup that she had worked so hard to construct for her and Nachae's first home. In the corner was the pile of soft furs where they had lain together every night since she had first spread them out upon the ground. It was also where they made love each time their wanton bodies took control of their submissive minds. The furs were probably still warm where they had been sleeping before Waddling Woman disturbed them. Sky Dreamer wished she could crawl back into the safety and warmth of those beckoning hides and wait for Nachae to return to her.

She reluctantly tore her eyes away from the corner of the wickiup and grabbed up her fringed medicine bag. As she walked back toward the sweat lodge, she lightly rested her hand on her flat abdomen. With the exception of a slight tenderness in her breasts, there was not yet any evidence that Nachae's child grew within her womb.

But she knew of this babe's existence, and so did Nachae. She glanced around the camp when she reached the wickiup where Llamarada was lying. Nachae was still nowhere to be seen. Raising her worried gaze toward the black sky, she asked for Usen's help and guidance. She prayed that her husband would understand why she had to use the knowledge and powers which Grandfather had tediously taught to her for the past few months to help anyone who was injured or sick—even Llamarada.

Taking a deep breath, she ducked through the doorway of the sweat lodge. The steam rising from the stones hit her directly in the face and caused her face and body to break out in a flushed sweat. With hands that trembled so badly she almost could not open her medicine bag, Sky Dreamer began to join in the healing ceremony, which the old shaman was already performing. Hoddentin fell from her shaking fingers across the swollen and feverish face of the woman who had tried so vehemently to keep her and Nachae apart. Sky Dreamer forced her mind to clear away the unpleasant episodes from the past that involved this woman. Instead she drew upon all the teachings of Eskinzan and threw herself into the spiritual world of the Apache shamans.

She alternated, along with Eskinzan, between singing and chanting the secret words and songs of the medicine men, then they took turns sprinkling the sacred pollen from cattails over the sick woman. Sky Dreamer was not aware of how long they stayed in the sweat lodge. It seemed that one day began to drag into another, until she felt as though they had not left the hut for days, or even weeks. She rested while Grandfather continued to work over Llamarada. Then he slept as she repeated each of the ceremonies he had just completed. At times, other members of the tribe would join them in the hut. They would kneel down around the fireplace in the center of the lodge, swaying back and forth as they prayed to Usen to protect the rest of the village from the evil spirit that had entered Llamarada's body.

Sky Dreamer was determined to prove to herself—and especially to Nachae—that she could cure this woman. She pushed herself to the limit until there was nothing left to do except wait for the wicked illness to leave Llamarada's frail body. She refused to leave the sweat lodge, even when Eskinzan was called away to tend to another woman who had suddenly fallen ill with a raging fever. Her life was contained within the small enclosure of the lodge for nearly a week when, at long last, Llamarada's terrible fever began to subside.

Llamarada's glazed eyes fluttered back and forth for several seconds before she was able to focus her gaze. Though she was still too weak to move, her surprise at finding Nachae's wife dozing at her bedside was obvious on her pale face. Her startled gasp brought Waddling Woman's attention to her at once. She hurried over to the bedside and closely observed the ailing woman as she wiped a damp cloth over Llamarada's face.

"I think you will live," she said in a sharp voice. Llamarada's past exploits had not won her any favors with the shaman's wife. Sky Dreamer was awakened by Waddling Woman's voice, and in her abrupt ascent from the pile of furs where she had been resting, she became light-headed and dizzy. The last thing she remembered before she lost consciousness was Waddling Woman's terrified scream as the older woman rushed forward to grab her as she toppled to the ground.

She would not remember being carried back to her own wickiup by Juno. Nor would she be able to recall the way her dear friend Ta-O-Dee took care of her with loving devotion. Overexertion had taken its toll on the young medicine woman, and the only thing Sky Dreamer would be aware of when she regained consciousness was the beautiful dreams that she had experienced . . . dreams of her and Nachae—and two beautiful children running wild and free across their lush green meadow.

* * *

306

Eskinzan grinned widely as he looped his arm through the arm of his adopted granddaughter. Sky Dreamer looked around at the countryside with a renewed sense of gratitude. The smallpox epidemic had spread through the village like wildfire, but after claiming the lives of many of the weaker Teneh Chockonen, it had burned itself out as quickly as it had come. Winter had settled in, although in this part of Apacheria, the weather was still mild during the days. The nights, however, carried a chill that could eat right through the hides and furs that the Indians used to warm themselves. It was the beginning of December—Ko'baa nalk'as—which meant that it was cold even around the fire.

"Grandfather?"

"Yes, my child?"

"Do you think he will return soon?"

Eskinzan sighed. It hurt him to see his young protégée suffer, and it angered him that his grandson would be so unfeeling. Sky Dreamer had confided in him about the disagreement the young couple had had when she was called upon to help Llamarada. At first, he had been furious at Nachae for making such a selfish demand on his wife. But since learning of the child, the old man had come to understand some of his grandson's reasoning. The rebirth of their tribe was the only hope for the future of the Apache people. Each new life was too precious to place in peril, regardless of the circumstances. Yet he was also very proud of Sky Dreamer's devotion in using her inherited skills and powers to help those who needed her, even when it meant helping someone who had tried to kill her.

"Yes, he'll be back soon."

Sky Dreamer inhaled sharply and tried to contain her excitement. "When?"

"Soon," the old man repeated. "In the meantime, you must take care of yourself and my great-grandchild." His wrinkled face lit up each time he spoke of the child she was carrying.

A smile consumed Sky Dreamer's face when she thought of the impending event too. She had every intention of taking extra precautions with her health and that of her unborn child. Ever since she had overextended herself while taking care of Llamarada, Sky Dreamer had vowed to put the baby's welfare first, from now on. She could even put to rest her worries over her father's well-being, since Grandfather had sent a scout to the San Carlos Reservation to find out if Charles Atwood was in good health—and the scout had returned with word that the new agent was doing fine. Once Nachae returned, all that remained to make her life content was to ask him to forgive her for her insolence. Sometimes, she found herself wondering if she would ever be able to accept all the strange customs of her new life.

"Do you know where he went?"

The old man shrugged. "My grandson's thoughts run deep. It is not easy for him to love someone as much as he does you. He always swore that he would not allow himself to give into the predictions of my visions, yet he was not strong enough to deny them. To also be faced with the birth of a child—a child that he fears will suffer the same prejudices that he endured—is the most frightening reality he must face. Be patient, my granddaughter. He is a man worth waiting for—no matter how many times he has to run away from the feelings that frighten him so."

Sky Dreamer swallowed back the lump she felt rising in her throat. She would do anything to ease her husband's tremendous burdens, but it appeared that there was nothing she could do except wait for him.

"I keep having a dream, Grandfather."

"About the baby?" he asked with enthusiasm.

"Yes—about two babes. I think perhaps Juno and Ta-O-Dee will have another child soon, and we will raise our children together."

Eskinzan's brisk step faltered, then he came to a sudden stop. Sky Dreamer gave him a puzzled glance when she noticed the thoughtful look on his face.

"I hope you are right," he said in a worried tone. He began to lead her back toward the rancheria as he continued, "In our society the birth of twins is a bad omen. It could mean that the mother was with more than one man and that is why she conceived more than one child at a time."

"Oh Grandfather, I've never been with anyone besides my husband—not ever!"

He gave her arm a reassuring pat. "I know that, but it is one of the beliefs of the Teneh Chockonen. Let us hope that your vision of two children is what you thought. Maybe Ta-O-Dee and Juno will be blessed with another baby soon."

A new worry was added to Sky Dreamer's long list of concerns. The idea of giving birth to twins had never even entered her mind. What if Nachae believed in the ridiculous notion that twins were the result of infidelity?

"Grandfather, what will happen if my dreams mean that I am carrying twins? Will I be accused of adultery?" The horrid images of the women whose husbands found out that they were unfaithful flashed through her mind. The punishment for such a crime was usually face disfigurement. Instinctively, Sky Dreamer's hand flew to her nose. That would probably be the first thing Nachae would cut off!

Eskinzan chuckled and drew her hand down away from her face. "My grandson knows that it is only bad fortune that causes two babies to develop in the same womb."

"Bad fortune? But two babies would be twice the blessing!" Sky Dreamer said.

The old man's face grew solemn again. "When two babies are born at the same time, it is the custom that one must be destroyed. To care for one infant in these hard times is already difficult. The weaker of the two must always die so that the stronger can survive."

Sky Dreamer was not able to reply. She was too concerned with the fear that she might be carrying twins. If she was, would one of her babies be slaughtered because of some foolish custom? It was beyond her comprehension that Eskinzan could talk about the rebirth of their people in one breath, and in the next, talk of murdering an innocent baby just because it was the custom. In the past several months she had tried to learn how to live by the strange beliefs of her mother's tribe, but this was one custom she would never accept. She told herself that her dream meant what she had originally perceived: Any day now, Ta-O-Dee would tell her that she was expecting a baby too. Until then, Sky Dreamer had no intention of telling anyone else about her dreams — especially Nachae.

310

Chapter Twenty-six

Nachae had ridden the trail to his special mountain meadow a dozen times or more in the past decade. Since he had met Sky Dreamer and they had come here for their wedding trip, the meadow had become even more precious to him. As always, whenever he was troubled about something, he would come up to the top of the mountain to contemplate his life. Today he had come here because—once again—he was faced with a monumental problem which he needed to sort out in his mind.

At times, he was overwhelmed by the way everything had changed for him since Sky Dreamer had come to the Apacheria. The idea he had once harbored of killing her now seemed so unreal—almost as though it had been in another lifetime. Indeed, he did feel as if he had been reborn on the day he'd first set eyes on her beautiful young face. She had truly fulfilled nearly all of Grandfather's prophesies. Although he would always hate the white men for what they had done to his father and to the Apache people, there were days when he could not even bear the thought of leaving his wife long enough to go on a raid or into a battle against the despised whites. Lately, he just wished he could take her someplace where they could live out their lives without ever seeing another human being—although he knew that wish was just a foolish dream. His wife had been gifted with a great power that she must share with those who needed it, and she was too unselfish ever to consider not giving all of herself to everyone around her.

However, there was someone else to consider now. He had no doubt that she was carrying his child. During the past few weeks she had acquired a special glow. And her thin figure, which he knew every inch of, seemed slightly fuller beneath his exploring touch. In spite of the worries that Nachae had about fathering a child in these hard times, he could not help feeling a shiver of excitement when he thought of having a baby with his cherished Sky Dreamer. He wanted a perfect life for his wife and their child—the kind of life he had never known. Desperately, he wished that he could protect their son or daughter from the injustices and cruelties of this harsh existence. But how? Every day the Apache people lived in peril of another attack from the soldiers of the surrounding outposts. Anyone who was wise enough to look toward the future knew that there was little hope of defending the ways of their tribe for too much longer. The white men grew more powerful—in number and weapons—every day, while the Apaches only grew more and more tired of fighting.

Nachae walked the circumference of the meadow, then sat down beneath the low-hanging boughs of the same tall silver pine tree where he had made love to Sky Dreamer. The grass was not as green and velvety as it had been a couple of months ago. Winter was slowly inching its way across the land. In this part of the country, though, the seasons seemed just to drift in and out without causing too much commotion. It was always beautiful in this meadow, no matter what time of the year it happened to be. Nachae could remember riding through a blinding snowstorm in the foothills at the base of the mountain, yet once he reached his secret clearing, not a trace of the freezing weather from down below was evident in the secluded meadow. Incidents such as that one had lent to his belief that the meadow was enchanted.

Sitting in the quiet splendor of the towering trees at

this moment, he felt the magic of the meadow more than ever before. He had come here to think about the future—his and Sky Dreamer's and that of their children. For the past decade he had been certain he would never leave the Teneh Chockonen. Yet faced with the grim prospects that this life had to offer to his unborn child, he was reconsidering his options. For the first time in his life, Nachae wondered if the hardships of the Apaches were what he wanted for his own family. He thought of the way Sky Dreamer's soft hands had already grown calloused and cut from the hard work she did each day. At this very second, she was tending to a woman who carried a deadly disease—the same woman who had once challenged her into a deadly knife fight. Not a day passed when there was no new danger to face in Apacheria. His thoughts drifted to the tiny infant, Ino, and a rash of unexpected moistness coated his eyes. Was his and Sky Dreamer's child destined to meet a similar fate?

He rose to his feet and walked across the meadow once again, then turned to look back at the majestic sight of the ancient silver pine tree. Someday he wanted to bring his child up here to show him the very spot where he had been conceived. If he remained with the Teneh Chockonen, would he ever have a chance to bring any of his children to this place?

Feeling more disoriented than ever, Nachae swung onto the back of Eagle and rode away from the meadow without so much as a glance backward. He had not found the answers he'd sought, nor was he ready to return to the rancheria and admit to his wife that he had been wrong to ask her to turn her back on someone who was sick. For days he just wandered through the mountains and foothills until he found himself back in the desert region. From a distant hilltop he watched the activity down at Fort Bowie. His eyes narrowed with the hatred that he would never be able to release unless his worst enemy returned to this area. Just a short while ago there had been two goals in the warrior's life: to kill the woman from his grandfather's prophesy, and to avenge his father's death. His overpowering love for Sky Dreamer had replaced his first objective, and Randy Decker's transfer to Washington had delayed the second. But someday, Nachae was certain, his path would cross with the lieutenant's again. When that day came, Nachae would make Randy Decker suffer for every Apache life that he had destroyed, but he would take special pleasure in watching him pay for the death and mutilation of his father. When the two men finally did meet once more, Nachae would give Lieutenant Decker's soul back to the Devil, to whom it belonged.

Lately though, Nachae had found he was growing weary of feeling so much hatred and bitterness. There had to be more to life than fear and aversion. He did not want his children to grow up in an atmosphere dominated only by those venomous forces. Wandering farther into the desert, he found himself traveling over the high bluffs above Apache Pass. It had been only five moons ago when he had ridden down from these very cliffs with the intent of killing the woman from his grandfather's visions. It was startling to think of how far he had come since that hot summer day when his heart had known only emptiness.

It was not until he had crested the ridge above El Flores Rancho that he began to realize the reluctant thoughts which had been trying to present themselves into his stubborn mind for the past few days. Was it possible that he could even forgive his mother for all the years of bitterness that had been built up between the two of them? Had the time come to begin a whole new life—a life based on forgiveness and understanding rather than just contempt? His gaze traveled across the vast expanse of his mother's ranch. For as far as the eye could see, and beyond, was the sprawling acreage of the El Flores Rancho. He could see the house standing like a grand white castle of stucco and dark wood among a grove of oaks and aspens. As though time had transported him back through two decades, Nachae could imagine his mother walking through the immaculate halls of the Flores mansion. Above her flashing dark eyes, her raven hair was piled high on her head, and her taffeta skirt was rustling like dry leaves in a windstorm as her high-heeled shoes tapped briskly against the shiny wooden planks.

Antonio would watch her from a distance, usually from behind a partially closed doorway, or from behind a curtain where he would take refuge. He would hide from her, mostly because he was so terrified of facing another one of her rejections. Normally, she did not even seem to notice that he existed, and when she did, it was just to reprimand him for some minor annoyance. He could still recall how the pain would fill up his little heart each time she pretended she didn't notice him when he was trying so hard to please her. When he had left this place over ten years ago, he had sworn he would never set foot in that house again. Now, however, he was not so sure.

He nudged Eagle with his foot and started down the tree-feathered slope of the rancho. It was late afternoon and he imagined that his mother was probably just waking up from her siesta. He did not expect her to greet him with open arms and praises of love. More likely, she would order one of her vaqueros to shoot him for trespassing. But it didn't really matter how she reacted when she saw him. All that was important at this time was to settle the turmoil in his own heart and mind. He suddenly needed to tell her that he understood why she hated the man who had taken her captive and then forced her to be burdened with a son she had never wanted. Rita Flores was a beautiful woman. If it hadn't been for the shame she had endured because of her captivity, perhaps she would have fallen in love and married. After she had been with the Apaches, though, she was so consumed with hatred that there had been no room for love in her heart. When she was left with full control of El Flores Rancho, the running of the ranch became her only reason for living. Knowing that her whole objective in life was to keep El Flores Rancho all to herself had given Nachae extra pleasure whenever he raided his mother's herd.

Now, however, he was ready to put aside all the misery of the past, as he should have done a long time ago. Maybe the wall of hatred was too strong to break down and perhaps there was nothing left to rebuild a relationship upon, but Nachae had to know that he had tried. If she would permit him, he also wanted to tell her what a great and proud man his father had been. All of a sudden it was crucial to try and make her realize that Alderay was not the unfeeling savage she had always believed him to be. He wanted to ask his mother if they could start all over again—if they could learn how to accept one another for what they were, a mother and son, not just a Mexican and a half-breed.

Riding toward the main house, Nachae was overcome with such a feeling of fear that he was not sure if he could continue this mission. It was the feeling he had always had as a little boy each time he'd sought his mother's compassion. The closer he came to the house, the more he became aware of the strange quietness that shrouded the whole area. Even though it was still siesta time, there still should have been some signs of activity around the main house and the surrounding outbuildings of the large ranch. Usually Reuben could be located somewhere within the vicinity, but even he was nowhere to be found. Nachae was expecting to be confronted by at least half a dozen of his mother's hired men the instant they spotted him approaching the house. Since he had thrown all caution to the wind by riding straight into the rancho, Nachae was almost disappointed that his arrival had not drawn even one curious observer. His numerous raids on his mother's ranch had not made him a welcome visitor in these parts. It was common knowledge among her vaqueros that they were to shoot any hostile within the region, and no questions would ever be asked. If it had not been for Reuben's intercession on several occasions, Nachae was positive his mother's men would have fulfilled her desire to wipe out every Apache who trespassed on her land — particularly her half-breed son.

Nachae tied Eagle to the hitching post outside the house and carefully walked up the trio of steps to the arched veranda. At the front door he paused to knock, then decided he should just enter without taking the time to announce himself. Anyone he encountered would be overcome with terror at the sight of a hostile stalking through the house anyway. As he walked into the shiny tiled entrance of the house, he was stricken with an odd sensation of doom. He tried to shake the heavy feeling in his heart, but it only increased with every step he took. He headed toward the curved stairway, which led to the upper floor, thinking that perhaps he would find his mother still napping in her bedroom. He had taken only a couple of steps when the sound of someone calling out to him caused him to halt.

"Antonio? Is it really you?"

Nachae swung around and drew in a sigh of relief when he saw his old friend. At once, he sensed that something was drastically wrong. Reuben was dressed in a black suit, tailored in the Mexican fashion with tight-fitting trousers and a short-cropped jacket adorned with silver conchos. He should have been wearing his work clothes. And why was he here — in the main house — instead of out tending to his duties?

"What has happened?" Nachae asked.

Reuben hesitated, then glanced away for an instant. When his troubled gaze sought out the other man's eyes, his face had grown full of sorrow. "It's your mother, amigo. There was an accident a few days ago and she —"

"She's dead?" Nachae questioned with no visible sign of emotion, although inside he felt as though he was being torn apart. His tall frame remained frozen to the spot, and his face was masked in aloofness while he waited for Reuben's reply. With a slow nod of his head, Reuben confirmed Nachae's fears.

"How did it happen?"

Reuben gave his old friend a curious look. He was aware of all the hard feelings between Rita Flores and her son, yet knowing Nachae as he did, he would have expected Nachae to feel some remorse over his own mother's death. Had life among the Apaches stolen away all the humanity in his heart and left him completely cold and unfeeling?

"Her buggy overturned when she was returning from Lordsburg. She died instantly from a broken neck."

Nachae turned away from the probing stare of the other man. For as long as he lived, he would never be able to understand the way he was feeling at that moment. Coming here to make amends with his mother was the hardest thing he had ever done. It had taken all of his courage and every last ounce of his pride to walk into this house. And it had been for nothing. He would never be able to tell her that he forgave her for the way she had treated him, nor would he ever have the chance to ask for her forgiveness for all the vengeance he had sought against the El Flores Rancho throughout the years. Even worse, he could not tell her that she had misjudged the man who had taken her as his hostage so many years ago. Why had he waited so long to come here and tell his mother all these things?

He glanced back over his shoulder at Reuben and noticed that the man was still watching him uncertainly. They had been so close when they were youngsters—why did it seem now that they were as distant as strangers? Nachae swung around and motioned toward Reuben's suit. "Was the burial today?"

Reuben gave his head a slow nod. He sighed heavily, seemingly at a loss for words. Nachae remembered a time when there were not enough hours in the day for all the things they had to discuss, but then, that had been in another lifetime. Now, their worlds were as different as black and white.

"Why did you come here, amigo?"

"I came to make amends. But it looks like I was a little too late."

Nachae's admission stunned Reuben. At first, he was not even sure if he believed his old friend. It was almost too ironic that, after all this time, Antonio Flores was finally ready to put some of the bitterness out of his life. However, the expression of pain and loss in Antonio's dark gray eyes was the only proof Reuben needed. He dropped his chin down toward his chest and began to shake his head. How would Rita Flores have reciprocated her half-breed son's attempt to make amends? Until now he was positive that she would have laughed in Antonio's face and then ordered him to be shot as he left. But perhaps Rita Flores would have seen the sincerity in this man's haunted gaze, and even a heart as ruthless as hers would have softened and relented.

"El Flores Rancho could be yours, Antonio."

Nachae stared at his friend with a look of confusion. "What are you saying?"

Reuben shrugged and gestured around at the elegant Spanish-style mansion. "In Rita's will, she stated that since you carried the last of the Flores blood, then you should be eligible to inherit El Flores Rancho." He laughed slightly and added, "I think it was *her* attempt to make amends."

Nachae's shocked look turned to one of perplexity. Never in his wildest imaginings would he have thought that his mother would leave him anything—let alone all of the El Flores Rancho. Reuben's next words made him realize the deceptive reasoning behind his mother's actions, however.

"Of course, she included a few stipulations in the will: You have to claim ownership within seven days of her death, and you must also sever any relationships you have with the Apaches and—oh yes—you have to compensate for every animal you have stolen from El Flores Rancho in the past ten years." Reuben threw his hands up nonchalantly. "That is all, amigo, and then all this wonderful land and this fabulous house will be yours."

Nachae did not answer for several minutes. His mind was whirling with rejection and fury. His mother had made those demands in her will as her final revenge. It was just an accident that he had shown up only a few days after her untimely demise. Yet she knew that he would never denounce his Apache bloodline. As far as Nachae was concerned, his Apache family was the only family he had ever known. To ask him to turn his back on them completely was an impossibility. His calculating mother had wanted to be certain that he would not be able to fulfill the stipulations in her will.

Over the past decade, Nachae and his comrades had raided this ranch so often that it would take every head of cattle and every horse west of the Rio Grande to repay his debt. Rita Flores had found a definite way to make sure that her bastard son would never lay claim to any part of the El Flores Rancho. Nachae wondered if she was turning over in her freshly dug grave because he had returned. And if she could read his thoughts from the grave, then no doubt she was doing more than one turn at this precise moment.

Chapter Twenty-seven

His decision was not easy, and several times during his sojourn back to the Apache rancheria, Nachae changed his mind. Many things about his new plan worried him. But what concerned him the most was whether or not he would be able to convince Sky Dreamer to take part in his schemes.

He had already fulfilled the first clause in his mother's will by returning to El Flores Rancho within seven days of her death. He could easily gather a raiding party and rustle enough cattle and horses from Mexico to pacify his mother's attorney until he could figure out a way to dodge that portion of her will. It was the part about severing all connections with his Apache life that would be the most difficult for Nachae to carry out. And what if his wife refused to leave her newfound home with the Apaches? He knew that he must ask this of her, because there was a burning need in his soul to claim El Flores Rancho — just to spite his dead mother.

Too many days had passed since he had seen Sky Dreamer, and he had left without even telling her how much he loved her. He was terrified he would reach the village only to learn that she had been stricken by the same dread disease Llamarada had brought to their people. Nachae would never forgive himself if his wife had taken ill and he had not been with her in her time of need. He kept pushing those morbid thoughts from his mind. Instead, he told himself repeatedly how much safer their new life would be, how their children would grow up on the El Flores Rancho. He kept telling himself how he would build it into the most powerful ranch in all of New Mexico. No one then would dare to place his family in degrading categories. Yet inside, he did not feel these strong, positive emotions. His heart ached with the thought of leaving the only real family he had ever known. And his whole being cringed at the idea of turning his back on his father's people when they needed him so badly.

As he traveled along the rocky path which led to the winter camp of the Chiricahua, Nachae was relieved to notice that the dead owl markers were no longer along the trail. Such markers were used to warn travelers that an epidemic was present in the area. The heads of the owls were pointed in the direction of the infected campsite while the sickness was present, then removed when the danger had passed. He glanced up at the sky and, from the position of the sun, surmised the hour must be nearing dusk. Sky Dreamer would probably be fixing a small supper for herself, since she would not be expecting him that night. During the time he had been gone, he had almost come to hate himself for leaving the village. But then, he tried to convince himself that perhaps his trip to El Flores Rancho would turn out to be a good thing for their future and that of their children.

Skirting the village, Nachae headed straight for his own wickiup. There was only one person he wished to see right now. When he reached his home, however, his wife was nowhere to be seen. A fire had been started earlier, but it was burned almost to ashes.

Only a thin stream of smoke trailed up from the smothering embers.

"I—I did not know you had returned."

Nachae jumped at the sound of the woman's voice. His dark gray eyes narrowed with anger as he glared at Llamarada. "Where's my wife?"

Llamarada approached him with her head cast downward. Even when she spoke, she did not allow her eyes to meet his face. "I had hoped she would be here," she said timidly, then held out her hands. "I brought this for her."

Nachae remained unmoving while his eyes glanced at the small bundle of cloth in her hands. This woman did not have a right to walk honorably through the village, and as far as Nachae was concerned, she had no business coming to see his wife. He started to raise his hand into the air to dismiss this troublesome woman, but she began to speak again before he could do so.

"I heard about the baby. This is a gift for the baby—and also a peace offering. Your wife took care of me when I was very ill. She could have just let me die. I owe her twice for my life."

The anger was stolen from Nachae as he dropped his arm back down to his side. His amazement was apparent on his face as he stared at the humble form of Llamarada before him. He thought of what a precious gift his beautiful Sky Dreamer was to this land. Everyone and everything she touched became better than they had been before. Even a woman as evil and vicious as Llamarada had succumbed to Sky Dreamer's gentle, kind ways. His heart felt as though it would burst with the love he felt for his wife, and his pulse quickened as he glanced around the wickiup with expectation. At this moment, all he wanted was to see her lovely young face and to hold her against him while he told her of his overpowering love. With a slight trembling in his hands, he reached out and took the tiny woven blanket that Llamarada was still holding out to him.

"I will make sure she knows you were here."

Llamarada nodded and allowed her gaze to flicker upward for an instant. Then she swung around and departed. Nachae watched her go, feeling strange and emotional. There had been a time when he would not have accepted a gift from someone who had been shamed and outcast from the tribe. Lately though, it seemed everything was changing. The tribe was diminishing in such alarming numbers that every life had gained a new purpose—if only to help keep their race from disappearing altogether. Nachae drew the baby blanket against his pounding chest as he wondered if there would come a day when the Apache people would no longer exist on Usen's earth? He remembered Grandfather remarking once about the way the children of their race were carried in their cradleboards—always facing backward—never looking toward the future. Was there a hidden meaning in Grandfather's observation?

He began to sense another presence, which caused his breathing to halt momentarily. When he swung around, he saw her standing beside the wickiup. She was dressed in a tiered skirt of turquoise and red. Her red blouse, which was accented by the necklace he had made for her after she had saved Ino from the rattlesnake, completed her vibrantly colored outfit. A slight breeze made her waist-length hair bellow out lightly around her shoulders, and even from a distance, Nachae could see her violet eyes glowing with the love she felt for him. As their anxious eyes met, Nachae knew that he must do whatever was in his power to protect his lovely Sky Dreamer from the cruelties of the unfeeling world.

"I've missed you," she said in a quiet voice. Her gaze moved downward in a shy manner as she took another step toward him.

Nachae found that his voice was not cooperating when he tried to speak. "I—I—" He held out the blanket. "This is a gift from that woman you cared for when she was sick."

Sky Dreamer knew at once that he was speaking of Llamarada. She stepped closer and reached out to take the blanket. But when her hands touched the edge of the heavy material, it was as if her nearness had suddenly overcome all of Nachae's restraint. The blanket fell to the ground between their feet, forgotten for the moment as Nachae swept her into his arms. His hungering mouth found solace in her moist lips when they came together with a sweltering kiss.

He pulled his lips away for an instant while his embrace continued to crush her against him. "I'm sorry I left you. I'm sorry—"

Sky Dreamer placed her forefinger against his mouth to halt his words. "Never be sorry for doing what you must do. I love you because of the way you are, and when you feel the necessity to be alone, or to go away for a time, remember that I will always be waiting for you—and understanding."

Nachae wondered how he could deserve such a woman, but he was also determined to be worthy of such a treasure. There were so many things he needed to discuss with her, but they were put to the back of his mind for now. He ran his fingers through the long silken strands of her hair, which beckoned for his caress, as he held her tightly against his body. He heard her inhale sharply when he scooped her into his arms and headed into the wickiup. She grew limp within his strong embrace as she allowed herself to fall under the spell of his masculine power. His strength made her feel weak and vulnerable, yet she had never felt more secure.

A dwindling fire burned within the circular fireplace in the middle of the hut. But the lovers did not notice whether the flames existed or not. They were too enthralled with one another to care if the whole wickiup burned down around them, and by the time Nachae placed his wife down upon the soft furs, another blaze was already ignited within her whole being. He lowered his own body down until he was resting atop of her and their limbs were entangled. Sky Dreamer broke out in a fevered flush, making her breaths come in short gasps when she became aware of his inflating manhood pressing into her thigh.

Her hands moved anxiously down to caress that straining area of his buckskin leggings. When her nimble fingers ran over his bulging loins, she heard him moan softly. Her own desire increased with the realization that she did have a small amount of power over her strong, virile husband. Yet when he responded by slipping his hand beneath her skirt, causing her to lose what remained of that slight power, she realized that at moments such as these they were both completely helpless in the face of their own impulses.

Nachae felt as if he had been away from his woman forever. He quickly began to discard her clothing then, in a matter of seconds, had shoved away his own shirt and leggings. When their bodies came in contact again, their flesh was inflamed with passion. There was a core—somewhere deep inside each of them—that yearned for fulfillment. But in the ravenous instant before they meshed together and became inseparable, it felt as if they would surely die from this famished craving. Consumed with the delicious assault of one another's love, they devoured every precious second which allowed for the union of their bodies and souls. And as if they would never be satisfied, or maybe it was a deep-seated fear of never knowing if tomorrow would still permit them to hold on to one another again, they continued to make love to one another far into the night, until morning claimed the waning sky with a pale dawn light.

Sky Dreamer stirred in the warmth of her fur covering, and struggled to force her heavy eyelids apart. The coal black fringe which surrounded her eyes fluttered against the curve of her cheekbones, then finally flickered open. When her drowsy vision had cleared, she noticed the intent stare of her husband's stormy gaze.

"Were you watching me sleep?" she asked as she snuggled up against the firm, smooth feel of his bronzed body. He smelled vaguely of mint and leather—familiar odors that Sky Dreamer had come to associate with him.

"Yes," he said quietly. He wrapped his arms around her, drawing her even closer so that there was not one inch of their bodies that was not touching beneath the fur robes.

The solemn sound of his voice immediately alerted Sky Dreamer to his brooding mood. She wondered if she should ask him where he had been for the past couple of weeks, yet she preferred for him to tell her of his absence when he was ready to do so. Outside the wickiup, she could hear the noises of the daily activities, and when she glanced through the hole in the ceiling of the hut, she noticed that it was already daylight.

"I have overslept." She chuckled with a sly glance

in his direction. When she struggled to sit up and free herself from his embrace, however, she found that he would not loosen his tight hold. Sensing something was seriously wrong, her gaze flew up to his troubled face.

"What is it?" she asked, growing fearful of his strange attitude.

"My mother is dead."

He said the words so casually that it took several seconds for his statement to sink into Sky Dreamer's groggy mind. "I'm sorry," she replied in a soft voice when she finally realized what he had just said.

"Don't waste your sympathy—she wasn't worth it." Nachae's voice was flat and cold, but his insides were twisted with conflicting emotions. He wanted so badly to go on hating his mother in the same way he had for the past twenty-five harvests, but his mind was torn in two by the ironic timing of her death. He felt almost as if she had chosen this particular time to die, just so that he would not be able to ask her for some tiny amount of the motherly love he had discovered he wanted—and needed—so badly. Even from the grave she was still seeking revenge—and Nachae was determined to meet every challenge his heartless mother presented to him, despite the fact that it was tearing him apart.

"We're going to live on the El Flores Rancho," he said simply.

Sky Dreamer tilted her head back and eyed his stern face closely. "What did you say?" His words were beyond comprehension. Surely he did not mean that they were going to leave the Teneh Chockonen and go to live in the white man's world again?

"Tomorrow we are leaving the Apache rancheria and going to New Mexico to live on the El Flores Rancho."

"You—you mean leave our home with the Apaches, forever?" Her voice was shaky, and when she finished speaking, cold chills had managed to work their way into her body, causing her to quiver uncontrollably.

Nachae pressed closer to her trembling form, although it was a useless attempt to calm her, because he, too, was quaking viciously. He told himself that he should explain to her about the dangers of their lives here among the Apaches, and then he would make her realize how their children would not have to live under such a constant danger at El Flores Rancho. Yet he could not promise her that they would not face the same prejudices that he had endured in the white man's world. He knew all too well that because of their Apache bloodline, they would always confront a racial problem.

"We'll leave first thing in the morning."

Sky Dreamer could not move, nor could she dispute him. All her energy had been stolen away by his declaration and she did not have the strength to fight back. He was her husband, she loved him beyond compare, and she would do whatever he asked of her. But to do what he proposed would also mean leaving behind a part of her very soul. She had planned to live out her whole life with her mother's people, no matter what the future might bring, and she had thought Nachae had the same goal for his life. His idea of leaving his Apache family, and going to live on his mother's ranch in New Mexico, was the last thing she would have expected from him. With her head still resting against his smooth, brawny chest, she could hear the rapid pounding of his heart and the violent shivering of his whole being. She sensed that he was not telling her everything about his decision to go to El Flores Rancho, yet right now, it didn't really matter. In the morning they would leave

329

behind the life—and the people—she loved dearly. For the past few months, she had almost come to feel as though she had actually known her mother. There were even times when Sky Dreamer was certain that Lucero's spirit was with her, guiding her and helping her to accept her new life among the Teneh Chockonen. To leave her adopted family and cherished friends would be heartbreaking. To desert the kinship she felt with her mother was the most difficult of all.

Nachae's grip around her body increased. It seemed as if he was afraid of letting go for fear that she would not stay with him. Sky Dreamer drew her arms around him in a tighter embrace and responded to his desperate need with one of her own. This man was her life now, and she would follow him to hell and back—if that was his wish.

Chapter Twenty-eight

A tremendous remorse filled Sky Dreamer. To leave their family cluster behind in the mountains of Apacheria was more difficult than she had ever imagined. As she rode behind the big painted horse who carried the proud frame of her husband, Sky Dreamer tried to convince herself that he was correct in his decision to claim El Flores Rancho. In spite of everything that had happened between him and his mother, he had still been her son, and he deserved more than she had given to him when she was alive.

However, Nachae's grim attitude did little to improve her hopes for their new beginning in the white man's world. Ever since they had departed from the Apache rancheria, his mood had become increasingly distant. Sky Dreamer wanted to talk to him—no, to plead with him—not to go through with his plans to return to New Mexico, but she kept quiet. Nachae had to settle his past, once and for all, if they had any hope of ever building a strong future. To accomplish this goal, he must first come to terms with his tremendous resentments concerning El Flores Rancho and his dead mother.

"We'll be at the ranch by dusk, Sky—I mean—Regina."

Sky Dreamer jumped at the sound of Nachae's

voice. He had not spoken in the Apache tongue since they had left the rancheria, and his English words did not sound natural to her ears. Even worse was the way he forced himself to use her white name, instead of the Indian name he had chosen for her.

He did not bother to turn around when he spoke, and his next words were said in a sharp and aggravated tone. "We have been traveling on the acreage of the El Flores for most of the day. Before the sun goes down, we will be at the main house."

Sky Dreamer was afraid she would start to cry if she attempted to answer him. She looked with dismay at the tree-covered slope they were traveling along. Already, she missed the deserts of Apacheria. That night they would sleep under a white man's roof, but she did not want her husband to make love to her in a white man's bed. She thought of the little grass wickiup she had built with so much love and hope. How she would miss the home they'd left behind with the rest of their belongings. In a tearful parting, she had gifted Ta-O-Dee with all her household utensils and sparse furnishings. Nachae said it would be useless to transport the unnecessary baggage to El Flores Rancho, since they would not need any of the crude possessions once they took up residence in the grand house he would inherit from his mother's estate.

Sky Dreamer glanced up at the sky with apprehension. The sun was already hanging low in the westerly sky. Within a couple of hours they would be at their new home. A sense of panic and an overwhelming sorrow overcame her when she realized this was the last day that they would spend as Teneh Chockonen. Nachae had told her that once they reached the ranch, they would both forgo everything that was a part of their Apache life. Once again, her eyes settled on the muscled body of her strong husband. Today he was

332

wearing only his buckskin leggings and kabuns. His upper body was bare and it shone like burnished copper in the glow of the early evening sunlight. How could she ever come to think of him as Antonio Flores? He was Nachae, and nothing would ever make her think of him in any other way!

Every step her horse took seemed to come down against the hard ground with more intensity, and her vision became distorted as she fought against the tide of tears. Saying good-bye to the people she had come to love in the Apache village had taken a great deal of her stamina, and in her exhausted state, she was on the verge of crying nearly all the time. Until now, she had been able to hold the tears back and force herself to remain in control. But the realization of actually being on the El Flores Rancho, and knowing that soon they would give up their Apache way of life for good, made her so emotional that she was unable to stop the torrent of sobs which racked her tired body.

The sound of her crying brought Nachae to her side almost instantly. Yet not even his comforting embrace was enough to halt her tears. He pulled her down from Sparrow's back and cradled her in his arms. He wanted to ask her what it was that made her cry with such a deep sorrow, but he was afraid of what her answer might be, so he remained silent as he held her tightly against his bare chest.

"I — I'm all right," she managed to gasp through the choking sobs. Her eyes fought to focus clearly on her husband's face, but it was several more seconds before she managed to accomplish that minor task. "I'm so sorry. I never intended to break down like this."

"I'm the one who should be sorry," he replied in a concerned voice. He did not release his tight grip from around her quaking body as he added, "Are you feeling ill?"

She shrugged and tried unsuccessfully to stop the flow of endless tears. "Ta-O-Dee said that sometimes it is normal to feel temperamental in the early stages of pregnancy."

At once, Nachae silently scolded himself for being so unfeeling. In his vengeful quest to claim his mother's ranch, he had been pushing their endurance to the limit without a thought to his wife's delicate condition. With shame, he dropped his head down onto his chest and said, "I'm sorry I've been so rough lately."

Sky Dreamer's vast love for this man regenerated her weakened form as she reached up and wrapped her arms around his neck. He responded by pulling her against his brawny chest with another tender embrace. "We'll be at the house soon, and you will be able to rest." As he started to carefully lift her up into his arms to replace her upon Sparrow's back, she was overcome with a sense of panic.

"Wait!" she cried out in a state of alarm. He stared down at her in horror.

"What is it? Is it the child?" A strange sensation of grief washed over him. He had grossly feared the creation of this child for so long, but now that it had planted itself in her womb, he had come to realize that his reasons for living would never be complete until his love for Sky Dreamer had expanded to include a new life, a life which would carry the greatness of their love far, far into the future.

Sky Dreamer raised her lavender gaze up to his handsome face. Oh, how she loved him. The indescribable feelings which consumed her whole existence every time she looked into his eyes, or felt his powerful body close to hers, grew stronger with every fleeting second. She would live anywhere, or any way, just as long as she was with him. Yet there was one important thing she had to ask of him before she could

334

force herself to continue with his plan for their future.

"Love me beneath the Apache moon just one more time."

It took a moment for Nachae to realize what she was asking of him. He had been pushing hard to reach the ranch house by nightfall. He knew if he didn't make the transition from Nachae to Antonio Flores soon, there was a distinct possibility that he could not go through with his scheme to claim his mother's ranch. It was difficult enough to watch the heartbreak his wife was experiencing because of his drastic decision. A minute part of his mind kept telling him not to grant her this last wish to make love in the ways of a Teneh Chockonen, while the rest of him knew that he could never deny her such a simple request.

Without a word, he scooped her up into his arms and carried her over to Sparrow. Once he had placed her atop the animal, he swung his long frame onto Eagle's back and began to ride through the trees. Sky Dreamer was certain he was heading toward the ranch house without even bothering to acknowledge her request. There was not one inch of her numb body that did not feel anguish over the impending loss of the Apache way of life they were leaving behind. Each disenchanted instant that passed caused her to grow more resentful of the new life that they were heading toward.

The sun was sinking heavily into the horizon by the time Sky Dreamer became aware that Nachae was not taking her directly to his mother's house. The sounds of rushing water reached her ears, and when she glanced around, she noticed they were gradually climbing to a higher elevation through the dense trees. When they reached a clearing and were able to see the river they had only been hearing so far, Sky Dreamer gasped in wonder.

From the top of a high cliff, a frothy waterfall cascaded over the rounded edge of the bluff, and rippled down among the boulders and crevices of the rock wall. Since it was not a large waterfall, the water splashed gently into the flow of the river like a soft, early morning rain. The last of the setting sun cast silvery shadows and glistening lights that flashed like sparkling diamonds over the whole body of tumbling water. Sky Dreamer was rendered speechless by the beauty of the area as she turned and looked at Nachae. His gaze was reaching out across the expanse of the waterfall and the river, but as soon as he noticed she was watching him, his eyes became locked with hers. In the brief moment that followed, Sky Dreamer became aware of the vast pain he was suffering because of his decision to return to the white man's world. She had been afraid to tell him of her own agony, because she did not want to interfere in the resolution of his past. But now, however, she sensed he had brought her to this untamed place because he did not want to part with the way of life that bonded him to Usen's earth and to the vast heavens of the Teneh Chockonen.

Quietly, he dismounted and drew Sky Dreamer down from her horse. He carried her toward the edge of the river, gently set her feet on the ground, and took her hand. He seemed to know exactly where he was going as he inched his way along the riverbank and led her across the slippery rocks that led to the base of the waterfall. Sky Dreamer was drenched from the spray of water which splashed over the rocks. Her clothes clung to her slender form like a second skin, but she didn't notice.

She did take note, though, of the way her husband's wet buckskin pants molded to his muscled thighs and outlined every inch of his masculine body as he moved toward the waterfall. He turned to lift her over the last of the boulders which surrounded the base of the cliff at the bottom of the falls, and she allowed her eyes to sweep over his entire form. His intentions were already making themselves apparent through the straining material of his tight leggings, and the bulge of his expanding manhood caused her to grow delirious with anticipation. She permitted him to carry her over the wet stones and snuggled against his damp skin as he took her into a secluded dark cave that was hidden behind the tumbling water.

It took only a second for her eyes to adjust to the lack of light, but as soon as she could glance around at their surroundings, a sigh came from deep within her contented body. She know that her husband planned to make love to her in the quiet secrecy of this damp cave, while outside this hidden place, the water that fueled Usen's land washed over them like a cleansing tide of boundless spirit and rapture.

Nachae placed her on the floor of the little alcove, then immediately reached down and began to pull her damp clothes away from her body. The ache in her loins flared uncontrollably each time his fingers touched her skin as he discarded the rest of her garments. When he had completed this task, he stepped back and seductively appraised his woman with his dark gaze. In the darkness of the cave, her skin looked like glimmering satin, and it beckoned for his caress with an urgent call that made him powerless to ignore its bidding. He stumbled forward until she was close enough for him to bury his head into the small crevice that separated the firm roundness of her heaving bosom. His mouth laved each swollen nipple with devotion until he heard her moan softly above the roar of the waterfall.

His passionate descent upon her body had increased her yearning to such an extent that she could not corral the sweet pain which raced through her entire being. She began to tug on the leather leggings that clothed the bottom half of his lean form until they finally released their tight, wet grip from the swells of his muscled limbs. He kicked his kabuns from his feet and assisted her in her efforts to rid him of his bothersome pants, then hurriedly crushed her nude body against his own. The water that sprayed into the cave drenched them in a coating of sleek enchantment and made this union seem almost mystical.

As they slid down into the soft moss which blanketed the floor of the cave, their bare skin molded together from the moistness, making their fevered bodies almost inseparable. Nachae's lips continued their devouring caresses upon her tingling form, working their way down until he had explored every inch of her soft flesh. Then, when she returned each one of his titillating actions by moving her lips down over his taut torso, he dug his hands into the silky mass of her hip-length hair and lost himself in this ravishing glory. Finally, he could not stand a minute more of this splendrous agony, so he gently pulled her back up along his tall frame until she was stretched out upon him and the abundance of her long hair completely covered his face and upper body with its thick tresses.

She sat up, still straddling his body, and impaled herself upon his rigid member. They began to move together like a perfectly coordinated organism, plunging and then almost receding, until at last, they were forced to give in to the wild surges of passion that flooded over them like the rush of the falls that cloaked the little cave with its veil of cleansing water.

Afterward, when they were able to breathe somewhat normally, and to make their waning senses come back to reality once more, Nachae carried her out into the cool water which fell from the jagged bluffs overhead. With her slender legs wrapped tightly around his hips, he made love to her again, while standing in the mist of the purifying downpour.

"Last night we went against Apache custom," Nachae said as he traced his fingers lightly along the smooth curve of her hip.

"Again?" she asked as she molded herself against his side. Beside them, the river coursed through the ravine and disappeared into the dense trees which sheltered the hilly countryside.

He tightened his hold on her when he felt her shiver from the chill of the early morning air. Winter was rapidly clutching the land within its icy fingers. "Once it is a known fact that an Apache woman is carrying a child, it is not permissible for her husband to make love to her again until after the baby is born."

Sky Dreamer's dark brows drew together in contemplation. "I do not think I like that custom." She rolled over and placed her chin upon her husband's sinewy chest. "Besides, we are no longer living under the laws of the Teneh Chockonen, are we?"

Her voice held a strange undertone and the look upon her pretty young face was sad and distant. Nachae had realized long ago that she did not want to live at El Flores Rancho, yet she had never voiced her objections. He loved her even more for her unselfishness, but he also began to despise himself for not being able to escape from the vengeance which he felt he must gain. He did not answer her; instead, he pushed the blanket away and sat up abruptly.

"Are you ready to go?" His words were more of a command than an inquiry, and Sky Dreamer knew better than to dispute him when he was retreating into another brooding state of mind. With reluctance, she rose from their makeshift bed and wrapped the blanket around her body while she made her way to the river-bank.

Cupping her hands, she cradled the cold water from the spray of the waterfall and splashed it over her face, then quickly dressed. As she rolled up the high tops of her kabuns, she thought about the day Waddling Woman had first given her these soft moccasins. It had been over five moons ago when she had learned of her Apache bloodline—five months of learning what it meant to be a real part of Usen's great earth, and to understand the true meaning of life. In the Apache world, every rock, every tree, every thing that made up the entire universe, was alive, and each of these things contained a special power which influenced the happenings of man's daily existence. The children of the Teneh Chockonen were taught that they were the rewards of Usen's hard work—he protected them by making them invisible to their enemies and magically connected them to all of nature.

Nachae hastily tossed the bridle over Eagle's head and waited for Sky Dreamer to finish dressing. Without a word, he helped her onto her horse, then mounted Eagle, and they proceeded along the tree-feathered ridge. The fierce expression on his dark face was enough to keep Sky Dreamer quiet, too. She wondered how she would ever learn to deal with the hostility he harbored for the El Flores Rancho once they were living here every day.

"Regina," he said without warning. She nearly fell from the back of her horse at the unnatural sound of her white name rolling casually from his mouth. A worried expression caused her violet eyes to widen as she glanced up at her husband. He had stopped sud-

340

denly at the edge of the incline where they had been riding, and was staring down into the valley spread out below them. Her gaze followed his as her eyes came to rest on the impressive sight of the El Fores Rancho. The white stucco mansion loomed in the center of the wide expanse of land, surrounded by the many out-buildings and corrals. Sky Dreamer tried to focus her gaze on the place which was about to become her new home, but all she could think about was the terrible loss she had felt when Nachae had chosen to revert back to their white heritage. The sudden tears that sprang to her eyes were not intentional, yet in her tired frame of mind and body, she could not prevent the sobs which shook her body for the second time in as many days. Her hands flew up to her face as she gave in to the sorrow in her heart. She did not want to be Regina again—she was Sky Dreamer—a shaman of the Chiricahua Apaches!

Nachae stared at her display of unabashed emotion. However, he could not bring himself to give her any sort of comfort. He was consumed with the same sort of pain she was experiencing at this time, and he felt the identical sense of unnaturalness in the sound of his own voice calling out her white title. For how long he sat there—atop the hillside that overlooked El Flores Rancho—he did not know. Time had no mean-ing when his whole existence—and that of his family—teetered on the crest of this ridge. However, the decision which came to rest in his complex mind was one that he would live with for the rest of his life.

"I want the safety of my wife and my child to be guaranteed," he said with a forceful tone after a si-lence that seemed to go on forever.

Sky Dreamer wiped away the blanket of tears that coated her face and gave her waist-length hair a brisk toss over her shoulder. "Nothing in life carries a guarantee, my husband." Her voice grew angry, in spite of her recent bout of tears. She wondered what madness had taken possession of his senses. Nachae intentionally avoided looking in her direction. It was not easy for him to admit that he could be wrong, so he chose to deny that he might have made a mistake in coming back to the El Fores Rancho.

"Wealth and power in the white man's world is a far greater guarantee than starvation and fear in the Apache life." Even as the words sprang from Nachae's mouth, he realized how foolish he must sound to his wife. He wanted to explain to her about the compulsion he felt to hurt his mother as deeply as she had hurt the little boy called Antonio Flores. It didn't matter that Rita Flores was dead—Nachae had convinced himself that she would never be able to rest in peace if he were to claim the El Flores Rancho. His mouth opened with the intent of telling his wife about his devouring need for revenge against his mother, but then he was struck with a new irony: Once he rode down the slope of this tree-infested hillside, his mother would be the victor at long last. To turn his back on his Apache bloodline would be the death of the warrior, Nachae, and he sensed that it would also destroy the rare and gentle spirit of his beautiful Sky Dreamer.

Nachae's stormy gaze traveled over the extensive grounds of the El Flores Rancho. In distorted flashes from the distant past, he envisioned the wicked smile his mother would wear upon her face for all eternity if she won this final battle in the long embittered war she had waged with her half-breed son. Her haunting visage increased Nachae's determination to best his mother in her own game. With a sideways glance, he studied the brave young woman who rode beside him. Her tears had dissolved with her angry declaration a moment ago, and now she sat rigidly atop her horse with a look of defiant resignation on her tearstained face. Nachae found himself drawing from the strength he could see etched in her expression and echoing throughout her violet gaze as he felt his love and devotion expanding with every beat of his pain-filled heart. He had just fought the most difficult battle of his life. . . and it was entirely within himself. He straightened his tall form on Eagle's back and returned his raking observation toward the sprawling ranch below them.

The distant form of a man walked out from one of the buildings down below, and paused to gaze up at the hillside where the couple was halted. He raised his hand in a gesture of recognition and received a reply when Nachae's arm waved back. Reuben Gonzales waited in the center of the vast courtyard of the El Flores Rancho for what seemed like hours for his friend to ride the rest of the way into the ranch. He was anxious to meet the young woman Antonio told him had recently became his wife, and he was looking forward to helping Rita's son seek his just reward after all these years.

But as Reuben stared up at the hillside, he became aware for the empty spot that now existed where the pair of riders had just stood. He blinked and rubbed at his eyes, then concentrated on the area again. Had he only imagined the image of his friend and the woman atop of the hill? He waited for a long time, hoping to get a glimpse of them somewhere along the ridge, but the slope remained barren and silent. The man scratched his head absentmindedly, while wondering if he was having hallucinations. He could have sworn he had seen the couple, yet it was obvious they were nowhere in sight. With a defeated sigh, Reuben told himself that he had not actually seen his old friend, nor the beautiful raven-haired girl who rode at his side. Shaking his head with disbelief, he forced himself to stop his intent study of the distant horizon. Maybe Antonio and his bride would arrive tomorrow, Reuben decided as he turned away and went back to the chores he had to do on this hazy winter morning.

Chapter Twenty-nine

NII' CHEHE, (June) 1876

The council of war chiefs sat in a silent circle around the circumference of the large wickiup. The desert sun drenched the land with a heat that made the air feel as if it were trying to snuff out the inhabitants of this scorching land each time they took a breath. Each man wore almost identical ominous expressions on their faces. Their thoughts were engrossed in the many reasons why they had assembled here on this smoldering summer day. The past winter had not gone well for the people of their tribe. The soldiers of the white man's army had been relentless in their quest to gather up the last of the Chiricahua who still resisted the reservations since Cochise's death two years ago. Twice during the long cold months, the Indians had been forced to relocate their village in a never-ending effort to elude the advancing soldiers and to protect their families from another raid.

The new breed of warriors who were rising up to meet the challenge of avoiding the white man's domination were beyond any sort of reasoning concerning life on the desolate reservations. For their leader, they had chosen a man called Geronimo—a name he had earned during his daring raids in Mexico. At this time, he was still an unknown figure compared to the notoriety he would achieve in the decade yet to come.

Eskinzan escorted his young protégée into the wickiup and eased her down onto a pile of soft furs among the throng of men who had been invited to join in this important parley. He heard her exhale softly as she attempted to find a small amount of comfort in the cross-legged position she was forced to assume while in the presence of the council. The weight of her unborn child bulged out in an awkward manner before her and rested heavily upon her lap. The old shaman cound not help feeling sympathy for her now that her time was growing near. The days were not easy for the young woman, with the heat of the merciless summer sun and the excessive burden of the large babe she carried within her slight body. The old medicine man worried about the impending birth of his great-grandchild, and constantly asked Usen to grant his adopted granddaughter a safe delivery.

"What do you envision, wise one?" the man sitting at the far end of the wickiup asked the old man when they were all seated. He pushed his heavy mass of bluntly cut black hair back over his shoulder and leaned his massively built body forward while he waited for a reply. The features of his face were cut sharply and accented the ebony eyes which were set deep beneath overhung brows. His nose curved in a beaklike shape in the center of his chiseled features, making his appearance all the more frightening. Beside him, a younger man sat silently watching the old man and the woman who had just entered. The look of love which filtered into his dark gray eyes when he gazed at his wife from across the circle of fierce-looking men was a brief exchange that did not go unnoticed by the elderly shaman.

Eskinzan shifted his gaze from the face of his

346

grandson and concentrated on the forbidding face of the man who had just spoken to him. Geronimo did not back down from the old man's scrutiny. The shaman had seen this man many times through the years, but most recently in his visions of the future. Now those images of the bloody and unremitting battles that would take place in the course of this man's fight for freedom flashed through the medicine man's mind with distinct clarity. Eskinzan's silver head began to move up and down slowly as he mulled over the vast responsibility of the decision he would make today.

"I went to the top of the mountain last night," the shaman said with a wide sweep of his gnarled hand. His gaze became misted with the images that only his eyes could see from within their knowing pools of knowledge. "From this high position, I looked down at all of Apacheria, and saw the land as it will be in the years to come for the children of our tribe who have grown hungry and cold from lack of food and shelter during the past few months." His dark eyes glanced at the swell of Sky Dreamer's large abdomen as he added, "I also saw the future of the ones who are not yet born unto this doomed society." A hushed silence filled the interior of the hut as all who were present waited for the old man's dire predictions.

"The white men will not stop in their destruction of our lands and our people until they have gained control over everything and everyone."

A low murmuring began to circulate throughout the council with the grim speculation of the elder medicine man's words. Geronimo's dark look remained undaunted as he turned his attentions toward the young woman who sat at Eskinzan's side. "And what of your nadzeels? Tell this council about your dreams of our people's fate."

Sky Dreamer's eyes leveled with the man's narrowed

gaze. He emitted an aura of death with nothing more than his presence, yet she felt no fear when she met his unwavering stare. She forced herself not to look at her husband when she began to speak, although she did not need to see his face to know how he would feel when he heard the words she was about to say. Since the day they had ridden away from El Flores Rancho and returned to the village, hardly a day had passed that Nachae did not voice his deep concern for the safety of his family.

"Before the moon of the Nii' Chehe has passed, in a land that is far to the north of Apacheria, the white man's army will clash with a powerful force of men whose skin is the same color of ours. The Indians will slaughter the whites with such brutality that the whole country will talk of the battle for many, many harvests to come." A round of gasps echoed throughout the wickiup at the vision her words had created within the men's minds. She paused and took a deep breath. The pressure from the weight of her unborn child was pressing against her ribs and causing her to become short of breath, yet she forced herself to continue.

"After the shock of the Indians' victory has worn off, the white man's army will regroup its forces and then focus its unrelenting rage against every red man who walks the floor of Usen's earth." She glanced at Eskinzan and noticed that he wore a look of dread upon his aging face. She knew she should have told him about her latest dream, but she had not felt up to deciphering its deadly meaning until absolutely necessary. With a nervous tilt of her head, she chanced a quick glance at her husband. His expression of horror caused her entire being to become filled with such an engulfing fear that it almost threatened to steal away the control of her senses.

The men in the circle began to talk rapidly among

one another as they mulled over the young shaman's words of doom. Talk of retreat to the reservations, intermingled with brave words of strong uprisings against the despised soldatos, filled the crowded wickiup. After a few minutes of loud commotion, Geronimo raised his hand and drew the group into complete silence. His black eyes settled on the young woman once again in a narrowed stare. Admiration moved through his normally unfeeling heart when he noticed the way she returned his watchful eye with her straightforward gaze.

"I believe that the old wise one would not allow this young medicine woman to attend our council meeting unless he believed her to have great powers." He glanced at Eskinzan as the old man gave his head a slow nod of agreement. "It is upon her words that I will base my decision," Geronimo continued. "I say that we should take our women, children, and old ones into the land of Sonora where they will be made invisible to our enemies. And then, the strong ones such as ourselves"—he hit against his chest with his doubled-up fist, then motioned toward Nachae to emphasize his meaning—"will come back to Apacheria and wage a war that will not end until we have reclaimed our lands and made the ground beneath our feet run red with the blood of the hated White-Eyes!" He shook his fist in the air viciously as the rest of the men cheered and howled with false thoughts of victory running rampant through their heads.

Sky Dreamer's worried gaze moved toward Eskinzan. His expression matched the one she wore upon her pale, drawn face. In their wisdom, they each understood the vast meanings of her dreams and the hidden conclusions which were contained in each of her visions. The only battle the Teneh Chockonen could win would be the one they would have to fight within themselves once they were forced to give in to the white man's iron rule over their beloved Apacheria. Unknown to those who sat in the wickiup today, there would still be ten bloody harvests of fighting and sorrow before that final, tragic moment would arrive, and nearly every last one of the proud Apaches would be herded into the enslaving confines of the hated reservations. But it would be only two sunsets until Sky Dreamer's most recent dream of death and mayhem would write itself down in the journals of this country's brutal history.

Word of Custer's defeat at the Little Big Horn reached the Apache village in late June. When it was realized that the battle corresponded to what Sky Dreamer had seen in her dreams, her worth as a shaman increased. Even Eskinzan was awed by her powers and did not hesitate to brag to everyone in the rancheria that it was his teachings that had summoned forth her powerful medicine.

Along with the message of the Sioux's great triumph also came word of a tough regiment of soldiers who had been sent to Fort Bowie to reinforce the orders to bring all the remaining Apaches onto the reservation at San Carlos. It was rumored that a special force had been organized for the dangerous task, and they were being led by a newly appointed captain who had just arrived in Arizona from his post in Washington, D.C.

Within days of the announcement about the approaching troops, the Chiricahua had made the decision to follow through with Geronimo's plan. Moving the village in the deathly heat of the Arizona summer was not an easy task, however. Those of the tribe who were less than fit found the perilous journey to be almost too much for their waning endurance. Several of the oldest members of the clan fell victim to the merciless heat, and one infant died during the night from a cause that was unknown to the shaman who had attended the baby girl when she had stopped breathing.

The bodies of the dead were quickly interred. It was a bad omen for those who were still alive to be in the presence of someone who was dead for any length of time. Everything the person had owned when he died was always buried with him. If the burial was postponed for too long, "Ghost Sickness" could destroy the relatives of the deceased by bringing the ghost of the dead person back to claim his belongings, and possibly to cause the death of his loved ones. It was also an Apache belief that illness from some mysterious disease would befall anyone who indulged in the simple gesture of purposely staring at a corpse.

So it was with the heavy blanket of death hanging over them that the Chiricahua tribe trudged through the harsh deserts of Arizona and moved across the even crueler lands of Sonora. Strong feelings of salvation pushed them onward to their new destination. The leaders knew of a lush oasis in the neighboring Mexican lands where there was plenty of water for drinking and deep grasses for the horses. But most importantly to the spiritual Teneh Chockonen was the belief that they would be invisible when they reached their journey's end, and therefore, safe from another ambush.

Chapter Thirty

Nachae walked beside Eagle with his head held high. Not even Juno dared to jeer him about taking his woman's place and allowing his wife to ride on the horse's back. The entire population of the village was aware that Sky Dreamer was about to give birth any day, and that this journey was a difficult one for the young shaman. Her kindness toward everyone she had ever come in contact with since her entry into the tribe had gained her great respect, and not one person lacked sympathy for her as they moved through the hot desert sand.

It was the beginning of July—Itsi'dildzig—the month when meat spoils. The heat seemed to seep up from the ground, and even the leather soles of the Indians' high kabuns did not keep the devouring steam from scorching the bottoms of the travelers' tender feet. For nearly five days the group moved southward across the arid desert, stopping when necessary but only for brief periods of time. They traveled late into the night, when it was cooler, and slept for short times before moving on again.

On the fifth day, Nachae told Sky Dreamer that they would reach their destination by late afternoon. It was on this day when she felt the first pangs of labor. She tried to ignore the little twinges, hoping they would go away even though she knew they wouldn't. When the group stopped for a short siesta in the shade of a clump of piñon trees, Sky Dreamer waited until Nachae helped her down from Sparrow's back before she confided in him about the minor pains that had been plaguing her since midmorning.

"How much longer until we reach the new location," she asked as her husband lowered her to the ground. Her stomach felt heavy and low, and her legs were almost too shaky to support her unbalanced weight.

Nachae grabbed her as she slumped against him. "Has it started?" The worry in his voice made Sky Dreamer's love for him spread like wildfire. She wondered how she had ever been so lucky to find such a wonderful man for her husband.

"I love you," she said impulsively.

His face became a frown as he gently eased her down to the ground in a sitting position against the trunk of a piñon tree. "I love you too," he answered in a stern tone. His scowl deepened as he handed her a water flask. "How long?"

"Not too long," she replied with an exhausted sigh as she rested her aching back against the hard tree trunk. "The pains are far apart and not too strong yet."

Nachae sat down next to her and gave her distended abdomen a worried glance. Around her expanded waistline, she wore the maternity belt which Eskinzan had placed over her midsection several days earlier. The belt was made from skins of both a white-tailed and a black-tailed deer, a mountain lion, and an antelope. These animals were believed to have easy births, so the belt was constructed from their hides, then blessed by the shaman before it was placed upon the expectant mother. "We'll be at the new sight by the evening meal. But I don't think you should travel any farther."

A nagging twinge of pain tugged at the base of Sky Dreamer's rounded stomach, but she pretended to ignore it. "I want the baby to be born at the rancheria. I know I'll be all right until we reach the new location."

Nachae's long hair fell over his bare shoulders as he dropped his head down against his chest. She was too stubborn to argue with, even though he knew she should not ride on the horse if she was about to give birth. Yet he also understood why she would want to have their child born at their new camp, instead of out here in the middle of the desert.

"We'll try to make it," he said, forcing his tone to remain gruff. "But if I feel that we should stop, you must agree."

Sky Dreamer nodded and smiled to herself. His protectiveness toward her and their child was overwhelming at times, and she cherished him all the more for it. If she had not been so exhausted, she might have cried from the excitement and happiness she felt at the prospect of their baby's rapidly approaching birth. And although she had no intention of telling Nachae how tired she really was, she knew she would have to rest if there was any hope that she would be able to complete their journey before she was forced to give in to the increasing pains.

Sky Dreamer was anxious for the siesta to be over so they could get on their way again. It seemed as though the rest of the tribe slept for hours, or maybe it was just that she was growing more nervous with every twinge and ache, which signaled the advance of her labor.

Nachae did not close his eyes—even for an instant. He watched every movement his wife made until she wanted to club him over the head so he would let her suffer in privacy. By the time the rest of the tribe was ready to move on again, Sky Dreamer and Nachae were staring at one another with intense observation. Since she was determined to prove to her husband that she was capable of making it to the new camp, she was not about to give him the satisfaction of knowing whenever she was struck with another pain. Her attempts to hide her misery from him, however, only fueled Nachae's irritation and worry.

Once he had helped her onto Sparrow and fell into the back of the long cavalcade, his mood was less than cheerful. He allowed the rest of the horses, along with the women and children, who traveled on foot, to gain a great deal of distance in front of them. This action immediately drew everyone's attention back to the lagging pair at the end of the line. Eskinzan, Waddling Woman, Ta-O-Dee, and Juno stopped their trek and waited for them to catch up, then surrounded the couple with concerned expressions upon their faces.

"The baby is coming," Nachae said fiercely, although everyone took note of the trembling in his voice when he spoke. He gave Sky Dreamer a dark scowl, and she retaliated by smiling sheepishly. "She is too stubborn to stop until we reach the new campsite," he added in defense of his foul mood.

"She is right," Eskinzan retorted. "It will be better if the baby is born in the new rancheria." He climbed down from his horse and walked over to Sparrow. With his gnarled old hands, he gently touched Sky Dreamer's rounded stomach and shook his gray head in a knowing fashion. He leaned back, grinned up at the young woman, and continued, "There is plenty of time. We will ride ahead and prepare a wickiup for the birth." He directed a stern gaze at his grandson. "You be kind to her and quit trying to act so mean."

Nachae opened his mouth to defend his behavior,

but thought better of it—Grandfather knew him too well. Trying to pretend he could remain detached from his feelings was a useless effort whenever his wife was concerned. No matter how hard he tried to hide his boundless devotion toward her, everyone—including Sky Dreamer—could see right through him. He hung his head down and sighed, then looked up at his young wife. A trace of a smile hovered on his lips, which caused her tired expression to turn into a look of relief.

"I think we should be on our way," she said quietly as their eyes met. Almost as though he could not control himself, Nachae suddenly reached up and drew her head down with his hands. His lips brushed up against her unsuspecting mouth as he kissed her with an urgency that stole her breath away. As he released his grip on her and pulled away, a pain cut through her abdomen that caused her to gasp with surprise.

"I'm sorry," Nachae said in alarm, thinking that he had somehow harmed her with his impulsive show of emotion. His expression turned into another frown when his wife began to chuckle.

"It's not you," she said with a loving grin. "I think your baby is just reminding us that we have other business to attend to before we can do that again." Her dark brows raised up in a suggestive arch. A glowering frown consumed his face when he realized his wife's speculation. Without replying, he grabbed Eagle's reins and started to lead him through the trees that had began to speckle the barren land. Already the rest of the group had disappeared from view, making Nachae's nervousness return with great intensity.

He tried to concentrate on the trail, but his eyes kept wandering back to check on Sky Dreamer's condition. He could tell by the perspiration which cloaked her face that her labor was growing stronger. His admiration for her bravery also expanded. She did not complain once as they continued toward the new camp, even though he could see the agony she was going through.

Not wanting to tell Nachae that she was afraid she could not go on much longer, Sky Dreamer hid the pains from her husband by digging her teeth into her lower lip to keep from crying out. The pressure from straddling the wide back of the horse had caused her whole body to become inflamed with pain, and when she felt a gush of hot liquid rush from within her when her bag of water broke, coating Sparrow's back and running down her legs, she was sure she could not go any farther.

"Stop!" she gasped as she slumped to the side of the animal's back. Nachae was at her side before she had a chance to tumble to the ground. "I can't go on," she said in breathless gasps.

Nachae pulled her from the horse as they both slid to the ground. Terror rendered him speechless for a moment. "We're almost there," he said in a panic when he found his voice again. His shaking hand pointed toward a narrow opening in the dense trees. "The camp is just on the other side of those trees."

Sky Dreamer swallowed hard and glanced in the direction he was pointing. She knew she had to get back on her horse and go the rest of the way to the camp, although her body throbbed with renewed misery at just the thought of having to stretch her legs over the horse's back again.

Nachae did not wait for her to answer. He was too consumed with fear at the idea of her having the baby without the aid of anyone other than himself. "I'll hold you," he said as he carefully placed her sideways on Eagle, then swung himself up behind her, holding Sparrow's reins so the little mare would follow. His strong embrace held her tightly against his chest as he kicked Eagle in the sides and resumed their slow pace.

The jarring of the animal's steps was almost too much for Sky Dreamer to tolerate. She forced herself to lean against her husband while she tried to block out the sharp pains, which were cutting through her whole body almost nonstop. She was not even aware of the beautiful oasis of tall oaks and deep green grasses they had entered when they reached the new campsite until she felt herself being lifted from the horse.

"The wickiup is not ready yet," Ta-O-Dee said with a worried glance at Sky Dreamer. She rushed to Nachae's side when he placed Sky Dreamer down beneath a nearby oak. "I'll stay with her while you help the others build the hut."

He hesitated, not wanting to leave his wife lying upon the hard ground, but he knew the sooner the wickiup was built, the quicker she would be able to rest within its shelter. He joined the group who was working to erect the grass hut, although he was too nervous to be of any help. His eyes could not stay away from the writhing figure of his laboring wife, and each time he saw her suffer another pain, he blamed himself for her agony.

With the help of so many, the wickiup was finished in no time. Waddling Woman began to spread furs along one side of the hut while she ordered Nachae to carry Sky Dreamer into the lodge. He rushed to his wife's side and gathered her in his arms. He was certain the baby would arrive before they had everything prepared, yet even after he had placed her upon the soft furs and followed Waddling Woman's command to pound a stake in the center of the wickiup, Sky Dreamer was still not delivered of the child.

He fell on his knees at her side and ran his trembling hand over her large stomach. He hated this child for the pain it was causing her to endure—and he hated himself even more. He remembered all the years when he had determinedly told himself he would never father a child. Yet his love for Sky Dreamer had wiped away all of his reserve and enveloped him in such a raging passion that it was not in his power to avoid such an affliction. Now, he prayed to Usen to see to it that his wife would not have to suffer unmercifully because of his strong love for her.

Ta-O-Dee had helped Sky Dreamer remove her clothes and the maternity belt, then had given her a long strip of leather to bite down on with each contraction. When the latest spasm passed, Sky Dreamer glanced over at her husband and noticed that his head was down and his hands were clasped tightly together. She pulled the leather band from her mouth and smiled weakly at him.

"I'm going to be fine, and so is the baby." She reached up and touched his perspiring cheek lightly. "Please don't worry, and I'll understand if you don't want to stay here with me."

Nachae could not manage to return her smile, and he could not believe that she actually thought she was going to be all right. How could one woman suffer this much pain and still be fine? He thought about her suggestion that he should leave. Outside the wickiup, he could hear Grandfather chanting and singing the songs which accompanied an impending birth. His mind did not want to function as he tried to debate on whether or not he should remain with his wife. If something happened to her and he was not here, he would never forgive himself. But still, he was not sure if he could stand to suffer through another minute of her pain.

He did not have time to consider a decision because

Sky Dreamer was overcome with a pain so intense her whole body arched upward. Nachae's frightened gaze flew to Waddling Woman. She was busy spreading clean rags around the base of the stake that Nachae had pounded into the ground.

"Help her!" he yelled in a horror-filled tone of voice. Waddling Woman gave him an aggravated glare and continued to work around the pole.

A startled gasp flew from him when Ta-O-Dee gently touched his shoulder. He looked at the other woman with a pleading expression. "What's happening?"

"She's having your baby—that's all." Ta-O-Dee's hand reached out and rested on her friend's contracting stomach. She gave Sky Dreamer a reasurring smile and began to wipe the sweat from her forehead with a damp rag. In a whisper, Ta-O-Dee leaned toward Nachae and added, "It won't be long, but perhaps you should leave. You will frighten her with the way you are acting."

Nachae grew indignant at Ta-O-Dee's statement. The way he was acting? How could everyone remain so calm when his wife was dying? He would not allow them to chase him away from Sky Dreamer when it was obvious how much she needed him. With a huff, he pushed Ta-O-Dee aside and grabbed the wet cloth from her hand. He missed the grin that came to rest on Ta-O-Dee's face when he claimed her job and began wiping down Sky Dreamer's perspiring face.

Sky Dreamer, though, no longer seemed aware of his presence as she concentrated on the pains, which were constant now. She was not frightened of the birthing process because of her teachings as a shaman, but she had never imagined anything could hurt so much. She bit down on the strip of leather that Ta-O-Dee had given to her until she tasted her own blood in her mouth and felt it running down her throat. She barely had time to catch her breath before another pain would consume her with such an engulfing tide that she couldn't help wondering if it would ever end.

"It is time to take her over to the stake," Waddling Woman said as she kneeled down and examined Sky Dreamer's pelvic area. "The baby is moving down and will be ready to enter this world soon."

Nachae felt numb as he and Ta-O-Dee helped Sky Dreamer move to the middle of the wickiup. He had no idea why they were taking her to the pole, nor did he care. He only wanted this ordeal to be over with, and to know that his wife would still be alive when it was finished. Sky Dreamer, however, seemed to know exactly what she was supposed to do once they reached the stake. She knelt down on her knees and dropped the leather strip, then clasped her hands tightly around the pole. When another contraction gripped her body with an indescribable surge of pain, she used the wooden stake to brace herself as she bore down with the natural urge to push the child from her body.

Nachae knelt behind her and supported her straining body as each wave of pain cut through her. How long they knelt at the pole, he did not know. But it seemed to Nachae that they had been there forever. Waddling Woman was also on her knees in front of Sky Dreamer, coaxing her to push harder with each new contraction. Still, it appeared Sky Dreamer's efforts were in vain. Her legs and the layers of cloth which Waddling Woman had spread around the pole were drenched with blood, and even Ta-O-Dee's voice had acquired a vague note of panic as she joined Waddling Woman in repeating the gentle commands for Sky Dreamer to bear down when the pains came.

Nachae was too scared to think coherently. His eyes

were glued to the blood which continued to soak the once-clean rags. He was certain Sky Dreamer was bleeding to death while she was trying to deliver their child, and he felt helpless to save her. He wanted to rip the creature from her body before it could harm her any further. But he could not move because of the tremendous fear he felt every time another spasm of pain overcame his wife's weakening form. If Sky Dreamer died, he decided, he would not take another breath either.

"One more push," Waddling Woman cried out. Ta-O-Dee's excited pleas filled the wickiup and snapped Nachae's attention to the dark wet head which was emerging from between Sky Dreamer's thighs. He helped her lean forward as she bore down once again. She then collapsed back against him in an exhausted slump. His thoughts of destroying the wicked thing that was causing his beloved Sky Dreamer so much pain disintegrated the instant his eyes came to rest on the tiny infant who had just slipped into Waddling Woman's waiting hands. His eyes misted with awe at the sight of the baby as it opened its tiny mouth and issued forth a robust cry.

Waddling Woman raised her moist gaze to Nachae and smiled. "A *shitsi'*," she exclaimed. Producing a sharp knife, she quickly cut the umbilical cord and tied the end that protruded from the child's stomach with a piece of twine.

"A daughter?" Sky Dreamer whispered, and tilted her head back to gaze up at her husband. She opened her mouth to speak again, but her face suddenly contorted with pain once again. She grabbed for the stake as a startled cry escaped from her mouth.

Nachae watched in horror as Waddling Woman thrust the infant into his unsuspecting hands and positioned herself in front of Sky Dreamer once more. He felt as though he were watching a repeat of everything that had just happened when Waddling Woman and Ta-O-Dee resumed their orders for his wife to push, while Sky Dreamer's body arched toward the pole to rid itself of this second creation. His mind seemed to move into a daze when he heard Waddling Woman's frantic voice calling to Eskinzan for assistance.

The small interior of the wickiup became a chaotic mass of people when Eskinzan was issued in and began to sprinkle the hoddentin over the writhing body of Sky Dreamer. She was no longer leaning against the pole because she had grown too weak to remain upright. Now, she was lying back upon the soft furs with her knees drawn up as Nachae stared dumbfoundedly at the tiny foot that was emerging through a waterfall of blood from within her body. Waddling Woman's bulk abruptly blocked his view as she huddled between Sky Dreamer's knees.

Eskinzan's chanting had drowned out the rest of the sounds in the crowded enclosure and Nachae felt as if he were removed from his body while he watched the activity around him in a blank stupor. He was not even aware of the crying newborn he still cradled in his large hands. It was not until Ta-O-Dee pried the infant from his arms that his mind was able to focus on the events which had just taken place.

"She's dead," he said flatly as his tear-filled eyes searched Ta-O-Dee's face.

Ta-O-Dee drew in a deep sigh and glanced down at the two tiny girls she held in her arms. "No, but she's lost a lot of blood."

Nachae moved past her, unaware of the tears that filled the corners of his gray gaze. Waddling Woman was gathering up the cloths which contained the *bil goleehii*—the afterbirth—but she quickly hurried out of Nachae's way when he approached. While Grandfather knelt over Sky Dreamer, he sang in a quiet tone and sprinkled hoddentin over her face and unmoving body. Her eyes were closed and her pale face looked pinched and drawn. Eskinzan's aging face turned upward and his worried eyes rested on the tall frame of his grandson.

"She has had a difficult time, but she will not die," the old shaman stated with assurance. "In my visions of the future she always walks in good health and happiness."

Relief washed over Nachae instantly. There had been a time when he had doubted the strength of the shaman's predictions, but since Sky Dreamer's arrival, he had grown to trust his grandfather's visions more with each passing day. He fell down beside the still form of his wife, dropped his head into his hands, and allowed his waning emotions to overcome his strong exterior. If his beautiful Sky Dreamer was going to be all right, then nothing else mattered. All of a sudden a horrifying thought intruded into his thoughts of gratitude and joy. Dread seeped into his body as he lifted his face from his shaking hands and glanced back at the ancient face of his grandfather.

When twins were born to an Apache, it was the custom for one of the children to be destroyed. To feed one infant at a time was a heavy burden for a family; to feed two babies at the same time was an impossibility. Nachae became aware of the strange atmosphere in the wickiup as he realized that everyone was watching him.

Her face was shaded with pain as Waddling Woman took one of the infants from Ta-O-Dee and slowly approached Nachae. She laid the child beside him and backed away. The other infant's cries filled the wickiup like a deafening roar. Eskinzan began to speak in a voice that was loud enough to overcome the crying, through Nachae vainly tried to block out the meaning in the shaman's words.

"This female child was born last. She entered this world backward because she has no future." The old man leaned closer to the child and pointed at her miniature face. "See, she does not cry to make us aware that she even exists. She knows she was not meant to survive the delivery. I think Usen must be surprised that she began to breathe." The baby Ta-O-Dee held suddenly became quiet, and her silence was even more shattering. Eskinzan reached out and touched his grandson on the arm in an affectionate gesture. "Take her away before her sister senses her presence."

Nachae stared at the tiny child who was lying at his side. She did not have a healthy color to her skin like the little girl Ta-O-Dee held in her arms, nor did she cry robustly and try to focus her dark eyes on this wondrous new world that she had just entered. Her misted eyes seemed distant, and seemed to hold a sadness within their miniature depths. It was almost as if she understood that since she was the weaker of the two, she would not be permitted to remain. For the first time since he had taken the Netdahe oath, Nachae questioned the wisdom of the Apache religion. He looked away from the child and gazed back down at her mother. Sky Dreamer's face no longer looked ashen and deathly. It appeared now that she was sleeping peacefully, in spite of the terrible ordeal she had just gone through. Had Grandfather asked Usen to whisk her away to the land of her peaceful musing so that she would not be aware of the demonic deed that was about to take place?

Nachae scooped the little bundle into his arms and stood up. His body was shaking in visible spasms, and for a moment he felt as though he was about to lose his grip on reality. Waddling Woman appeared at his side and draped a tiny woven blanket over the baby, then silently backed away. He stared at the blanket—and at the child beneath it. Everyone expected him to follow the barbaric customs that no longer seemed to hold any meaning to him, yet it appeared he had no other choice. His heavy footsteps moved through the wickiup and out into the soft glow of the dusk that had overcome the green field of oak trees. His gray gaze traveled upward, past the bushy tree tops toward the fading azure sky. He asked for forgiveness of what he was about to do, and he prayed for the courage to live with his decision.

Chapter Thirty-one

Each breeze that swished through the dense trees sounded like a banshee wailing, and the forest appeared haunted and forbidding as the shadows of the night wore on and then began to mingle with the gray dawn. Nachae walked in an endless circle all through the night. At times, he was not even aware of his surroundings. His mind was spinning with turmoil and pain, and his heart felt as if it had become disengaged from his body.

The child he still held within his arms had long ago grown quiet. For a short while during the torturous night, she had whimpered and moved slightly inside the tight roll of the blanket in which she was wrapped. Her tiny heart-shaped mouth had instinctively opened and closed in a frantic search for nourishment, but once she had discovered that her efforts were in vain, she had given up her pathetic quest. On several occasions Nachae was certain she had also given up her brave attempt to survive. Yet each time he was convinced she had stopped breathing, he would raise her miniature form up to his face and feel the gentle spray of soft breath.

Once, he placed her beneath the upturned roots of an old oak tree, intending to leave her in the deep dark hole to perish. But his steps halted only inches from the spot as he rushed back and rescued her from the clutches of the dead tree. Throughout his life, he had always thought he had known the greatest forms of suffering, but nothing in his past could compare to the grief he was experiencing now. This little girl was a part of him — and a part of his beautiful Sky Dreamer. It had been such a short time ago when she had nearly died while trying to give birth to this child. Yet because of some cruel custom, he was expected to kill this innocent child as if she were a troublesome animal whose life could easily be snuffed out. How could anything be so unjust?

Through the darkness of night, he stumbled in and out of the looming black shapes of the forest — senselessly lost to his overwhelming pain at the idea of having to murder his own daughter. He had chosen to live as a true Teneh Chockonen, but he could not accept the inhuman custom that he was faced with at this time. The birth of a child was supposed to be filled with joy and new beginnings. But the excitement and anticipation he had previously harbored before the births of his twin daughters had turned into a tragedy of unspeakable measures. As the dawn began to creep slowly above the jagged tops of the trees, Nachae sat in the shadow of an ancient oak and stared at the tiny form lying in his arms. It seemed so ironic that she had been created only to be destroyed after such a brief stay in this world. He glanced up at the tall old tree, which hovered overhead and cast its heavy shadow upon him and the tiny girl as the sun started to inch its way over the towering forest. He thought about another Apache custom, one of great meaning and beauty. This custom was to drape the afterbirth through the branches of a strong, healthy tree which was standing somewhere close to the spot where the birth had occurred. Then each spring, as the tree renewed itself with new leaves to fill its barren branches, the child whose afterbirth it had once contained would also grow stronger and healthier.

The baby made a pitiful attempt to cry again, and the weak sound seemed to echo throughout Nachae's whirling mind for what seemed like an eternity. Echo—his mind began to repeat over and over again—he would call this female child Echo, he decided with a swelling of love in his breast. Now that she had a name, he knew he would never be able to murder or desert her. And if by going against the Apache customs and sparing the life of this infant meant he would be outcast from the village, then he would bravely face his punishment.

He rose to his feet abruptly, realizing the urgency of his new plight. Echo had been born almost half a sunset ago, and if there was any hope for her survival, he knew he had to hurry. He ran through the dense trees like a man possessed. The July sun was already shedding a warm glow upon the highest peaks of the tall trees, and soon, the whole valley would be graced with its heat and light. But the floor of the forest was still filled with dark hollows and lingering mists of the recent night.

In the rancheria, several women were lighting their fires and getting ready to prepare the meager morning meal. Nachae was oblivious to anything around him as he rushed toward the wickiup where he knew he would find his wife. He was breathless as he ducked through the low doorway of the hut, and once inside, he had to pause to catch his breath. Waddling Woman jumped up to her feet in a startled daze at the rude interruption. Her eyes immediately came to rest upon the blanket he was still carrying in his embrace.

"I will not kill this child," he blurted out with a defiant rise of his chin. His gray eyes narrowed as he

369

waited for the woman to rebuke him. However, she only shrugged and lowered her head. In silence, she moved past his towering frame and exited the wickiup, leaving him alone with his sleeping wife and the other child who slept beside her. Nachae approached them with slow steps, then lowered himself down upon the furs that blanketed the floor. His actions awoke Sky Dreamer with a start, and her eyes focused their weary sights on his face. She drew in a deep breath, then exhaled it with a trembling sigh.

"I—I was worried about you," she said in a voice that contained the same sadness which filled her violet gaze.

A tired smile fell across the warrior's face as he rested his eyes upon his wife. He opened his mouth to speak, but suddenly he could not find the right words to convey the deep emotions he was feeling at this moment. His hand reached down and pushed back the cover of the woven blanket. A tiny sigh escaped from Echo when the fresh air hit her cherub face. Sky Dreamer gasped and threw her hand over her mouth to keep from crying out. Her eyes filled with a sheet of tears as she sought out the source of the minute sound. When her stunned gaze met with that of her husband's, his eyes were consumed with a dampness that matched her own.

"I have named her Echo," he said quietly.

Sky Dreamer could not speak because of the tremendous joy and love that flooded her. Earlier, she had cried for the agony she knew her husband must be suffering because of his grim task, then she had cried for the loss of this baby, and now she released another river of tears because of her daughter's return. She was aware of Nachae's strong desire to live within the realm of the Apache customs and beliefs, so she understood the tumult he must have gone through. As she reached out her arms to take the little girl from her husband, she vowed to help him to bear this burden. Somehow she, too, would shoulder a part of the responsibility for his decision to go against the laws of the Teneh Chockonen.

Her hands shook as she gently eased the child to her bosom. Panic raced through Sky Dreamer's heart when she felt the chill upon the baby's soft skin, and as she became aware of how little strength the infant had left in her tiny form. Determination set into the new mother's being, and added to her growing will to make this child as strong and healthy as her twin sister. The tiny girl was almost too weak to open her mouth, but Sky Dreamer prodded her with patient urging until the miniature lips pried apart and was finally able to latch on to her mother's breast. For several more minutes, the baby's mouth just hung open in a limp gape, but then she began to move her lips slowly until her natural impulses began to take control of her small body.

In unison, Sky Dreamer and Nachae exhaled with relief. Their gazes locked for an instant as Nachae reached out and caressed the downy black hair that covered the baby's head in thick abundance. His eyes moved downward and settled on the other infant. "Have you chosen a name for this one?"

"I was waiting for you to return, so that we could choose one together," she replied in a voice that still contained almost too much emotion to speak without cracking.

Nachae leaned down and gently scooped his nameless daughter up into his large hands. Since he knew that most Apache babies were referred to by a nickname for the first couple of years, he did not feel the need to decide on a name immediately. With an intent study of her tiny round face, though, he decided that

371

she should have a name that would give her a true identity. By the order in which she had been born, she had made it apparent that she was born to be a leader. Nachae also sensed she would always be the stronger of the two girls, so she deserved a name that would grant her the wisdom to use her strength with kindness and understanding.

"Morning Star," he said simply, without explanation.

A peaceful feeling overcame Sky Dreamer, making her more aware of her mother's presence than ever before. She was consumed with so much happiness that she wondered if she was really awake, or was this just another beautiful dream that had somehow become entangled with reality?

Nachae heard the sound of the high-pitched music first, but when his eyes flew to his wife's face, he knew she had heard it too. He was too stunned to move for an instant as panic, then rage, engulfed his entire essense. His head flung back as an angry cry emitted from deep in his throat.

"No! No!" he said from between gritted teeth as he hit his fist viciously against his thigh. His mind could not conceive this vast punishment. In his confusion, he wondered if Usen had brought the soldiers to this hidden oasis because of his decision to go against the ancient laws of his people by allowing both of his daughters to live. There was not time, however, to ponder over Usen's reasoning. Outside the wickiup, he could already hear the shouts and cries of his people as they became aware of the soldiers' approach.

Shock rendered Sky Dreamer senseless. She tried to make her mind comprehend what was about to take place, but fear had stolen away the last of her senses. Had everything they'd gone through in the past few weeks to reach this place been for nothing? They were supposed to be safe now . . . they were even supposed to be invisible to their enemies here. She was only vaguely aware of her husband thrusting their other daughter into her arms, but when she looked down at the two infants at her bosom, Sky Dreamer became as outraged as her husband. How could life be so unfair? In her arms she held the promises of the future, yet outside the sparse shelter of this grass hut, destruction and death were waiting to crush every last hope and dream of an entire race of people.

She cried out in pain and alarm when Nachae scooped her up into his arms. He did not grant her an explanation as he pressed her and the two infants against his body and rushed from the wickiup. Both babies began to cry in fear as they were jostled roughly in the tight space between their parents' bodies. But their cries were not heard above the sounds of the ambush, which had gripped the rancheria within its hellish clutches.

The air was thick with gray dust that hung over the entire village like a blanket of floating doom. Several children ran blindly through the choking fog in a frantic search for their parents, and an older woman nearly crashed into Nachae as she looked wildly for her loved ones, who had already become lost amid the pandemonium. Every so often the high-pitched notes of a bugle would drift through the maze of screams and gunshots. The musical sounds, as always, seemed ridiculously out of place to those who happened to hear them.

The frames of the newly built wickiups had not even had time to settle into the ground, yet their blackened ruins would now scar the earth for a long time to come. Torches had been lit before the soldiers had even ridden into the rancheria and were thrown on the grass roofs as the men charged into the cluster of little huts. Smoke filled the air with a suffocating fog that impaired all those who ran blindly through it. Even the soldiers were temporarily lost in the thick haze. They charged into one another's horses, and shot at fleeting flashes without any awareness of their aim. Indians and soldiers alike fell victim to the mass confusion which seized the day.

Nachae had only one thought in his mind as he pushed himself through the dense smoke. His eyes were unseeing to all that happened around him, though it was not because of the smoke and dust. He also willed his ears to close out the sounds of agony and death which filled the air. Charging to the edge of the village, he ran through the trees in the same direction from which he had just returned from his long night's vigil. His destination was clearly printed in his mind, so his feet moved through the smoke-filled encampment as if they had wings attached to the soles of his moccasins, while he rushed his family toward the safety he hoped to find waiting in the forest. His frantic plight went unnoticed amid the chaos and the veil of heavy smoke. He did not have far to go to reach the giant overturned oak—the same dead tree where he had tried to leave Echo to perish.

As he shoved Sky Dreamer and his newborn daughters into the black hole beneath the gnarled old roots, he afforded himself only an instant to gaze at his wife's face. Every breath he had taken during the past decade had been filled with her presence, and for the past year, her beautiful existence had given him more happiness than he had ever thought possible. If this was his last chance to look upon her in this lifetime, then he realized that this moment would be his greatest victory. To see the love which was expressed in her violet eyes when she returned his gaze could conquer a thousand armies and more. He tore his eyes from her face and abruptly turned away. He wanted to carry with him into battle the memory of her undying love, not the sorrow and fear which he could already see overpowering her tender expression.

Sky Dreamer watched her husband moving back through the forest as he disappeared out of view. She continued to stare at the empty spot where he had just been only seconds before, until her vision became distorted and blurred with her intent gaze. The crying babies in her arms partially snapped her mind from its numb trance. Instinctively, she began to croon to the infants until they became silent, although her ears did not hear when their startled cries had finally ceased. A deep shock had invaded her body from the moment she'd realized that the rancheria was once again under attack, and it had finally taken complete control of her staggering senses. She burrowed farther into the musty black hole and curled her body around the two tiny infants. Holding her hands over her ears and squeezing her eyelids tightly together, she forced herself to retreat from the horrifying sights and sounds that filtered through the branches of the tall trees. She told herself that if Nachae did not return to her, then she would never leave this living tomb. With this thought planted deep within her consciousness, she retreated into a world of darkness where not even dreams dared to enter.

Randy Decker charged his horse back and forth at a gallop. His spotlessly clean white hat was tossed from his head in his wild escapade through the rash of burning wickiups as he cursed his men's stupidity. They had not been ordered to set fire to the village as soon as they had entered, and now, there was absolutely no way to see through the blackening smoke. For two weeks, he had been planning this raid while they had followed the band of Chiricahua into this entrapment—two long weeks of anxiously plotting the death of that worthless half-breed and his good-for-nothing white squaw!

The past winter he had spent in Washington had only fueled his sadistic urges to kill Nachae. His urge to kill Regina Atwood had grown stronger too. He knew she was still with that savage, because he had caught a glimpse of her several days ago. Her condition was apparent, and the idea that he would also wipe out the little bastard who belonged to that half-breed would make his victory all the more sweet. He had recently been promoted to a captain's rank, but Randy was certain that after today, he would be in line for another promotion. His enthusiasm to return to Arizona to lead the chase to the hostiles had already earned him extra points with his uncle.

The grave mistake his command had made, however, might make his triumph today less than satisfactory. Fury masked his face as he raced back and forth in the dense fog and continued his verbal assault upon his men. In his crazed state of mind, he was not aware of the man who suddenly appeared out of the deep smoke—that is, not until the warrior issued forth a cry that reached down into the captain's very soul. Randy Decker pulled on his reins, causing his horse to skid forward. With the erratic movement of the animal, the captain was thrown from its back and landed roughly at the feet of the very savage he had been stalking.

Neither man was able to move for a moment as they stared at one another in disbelief. They had both been waiting for this day for so long, and now that it had finally arrived, their confrontation seemed almost too simple. Before Decker had risen to his feet, he had his long sword drawn from its sheath. A wicked smirk curled his lips when he noticed that the only weapon the breed possessed was a hunting knife. With a scream that hinted at the captain's demented frame of mind, he charged at the warrior with his sword.

Nachae dodged the officer's lunge and fell to the ground. His arm reached out in one swift motion, catching the captain around the ankles of his shiny black boots and knocking him off balance. As Randy crashed back down to the ground, Nachae used this moment to gain the upper position. His weight came down on the captain's sprawling form, and for one quick instant, Nachae thought the battle was about to conclude. But the sword still remained in the officer's hand, and before Nachae could bring his knife up to the other man's throat, Randy brought his saber up and pushed it into the Indian's side.

A look of shock filtered into Nachae's dark face when he felt the blade scrape against his rib cage. He was left temporarily incapacitated as the pain of the brutal contact raced through his body. Yet his will to be the victor in this long-running war overcame his pain. He brought down the knife and pushed the blade into the skin beneath the other man's neck. Their eyes met for one last glance as Nachae started to push the knife deeper into the skin. He heard the saber drop from the captain's hand and land against the hard ground. Feeling the violent tremors that shook the captain's body, he saw the fear of dying written in Randy Decker's bulging gaze. He recalled the image of his father's withered body hanging on a stake that had been torched by this man's hand, and he thought of the many other Apaches who had also been in this man's path of death for the past few years. Slicing Randy Decker's throat was much too kind.

Nachae released his hold on the officer and staggered up to his feet. Blood oozed from the gaping wound in his side and coated his leather leggings in a shower of gruesome red. His dark eyes never left the captain's face, and he glorified in the look of horror which entered the other man's expression when Randy Decker sensed the warrior's intent. In a wild attempt to escape, the captain sprang to his feet and tried to flee into the thick layer of smoke. But Nachae reached out and effortlessly grabbed him by the back of his shirt, pulling him up against his own body. With his knife positioned against the officer's throat again, Nachae pulled the man's arm roughly behind his back, then began to push him through the burning village.

They encountered a pair of soldiers who still sat atop their mounts, one of which was the bugle player. Their attention was immediately drawn to their commanding officer's precarious situation.

"Tell them to sound the retreat," Nachae commanded into the captain's ear with his teeth clenched tightly together. When the officer remained silent, Nachae pushed his knife into the other man's throat until he heard the man scream for mercy. "Tell them," he repeated.

"You—you're going to kill me anyway," Captain Decker retorted.

"Yes, but the methods I will use will not be nearly as painful if you do as I ask." Nachae felt the captain's body go limp against his own as the soldier mulled over his threat. He could almost imagine the thoughts which were consuming Decker's mind at this moment—recollections of the many ways the officer had tortured and murdered Apaches while serving in this territory. "Do it!" Nachae shouted with impatience. He twisted the tip of the knife into the flesh of the captain's neck. Blood spurted forward like a miniature fountain from the captain's throat and drenched the warrior's hand with its sticky substance.

"Re — retreat," Randy Decker screamed out in a breathless gasp. The two young soldiers only continued to stare at him in confusion. "Sound retreat!" he shouted again. There was a very small voice somewhere in the captain's subconciousness which kept telling him that he still had a chance to turn the tables on the half-breed, and it was this bit of confidence that urged him to comply with the demand's of the savage.

The private who held the bugle slowly began to raise the instrument to his lips, he hesitated for a second, and Nachae moved the knife a hair deeper into the captain's throat. The look of agony that covered the commander's face threw the young soldier into a panic and he quickly played a frantic succession of notes. The two soldiers continued to stare at their leader until the captain finally shouted for them to leave the vicinity. Their hesitation made a horrified cry erupt from the officer's throat when his captor forced the knife to move farther down the line of his straining neck. In fear, the soldiers swung around and charged into the heavy curtain of smoke.

In the time that followed the retreat, Nachae stood his ground with the officer until the terror of the attack began to fade, leaving behind only the crackling of the burning terrain and what was left of the clump of thatched huts. The smoke began to dissolve into ghostly spirals, revealing the devastation that the brief attack had left upon the waning inhabitants of the Apache rancheria. Silence surrounded the warrior as he began to lead his prisoner toward the center of the encampment.

Bodies of the dead and dying were scattered among the skeletal ruins of the village. Those who were still able to walk or crawl along the smoldering landscape made their way toward the edge of the camp where, luckily, the fires had burned themselves out before they had reached the tall trees. Had this ambush occurred anywhere but in this oasis of lush vegetation where the ground was left moist from several underground springs, the whole countryside would have gone up in flames. When the last of the smoke had died away, the survivors stood in awe of their good fortune, in spite of the deadly attack.

The fire had raged out of control to the very edge of the dense forest, then had stopped as abruptly as if it had been commanded to do so. Yet even in the wake of this unbelievable occurrence, the tribe felt an overpowering urge to depart from this land as soon as they could bury their dead. This valley would never again be inhabited by the Chiricahua because of the spirits who would walk its charred ground for all eternity.

Epilogue

Sky Dreamer stopped her horse at the edge of the thick forest and fought against the urge to glance back one last time. She had not even had the chance to see what this secluded place had looked like before it had been destroyed by the soldier's torches. Nachae had intentionally avoided taking her through the center of the village, and it was a morbid sense of curiosity that drew her eyes toward that area now.

She swallowed hard and swung around on her horse's back. A tremendous sense of loss filled her with renewed pain. She had not needed to see the beauty that had once filled this clearing with lush greenery and serenity to know how much had been destroyed by the soldatos' brutal ambush once again. But she would always carry with her the sight of death and emptiness that shrouded this land today.

In the mist of the smoldering rancheria stood a lone monument to serve as a deadly reminder of mankind's greed and intense prejudices. There was no need for Sky Dreamer to ask anyone who it was that hung upside down from the crude stake in the center of the blackened village. His nude body was lacking both its arms, and his male organs had been removed in a brutal manner. His stiff, upside-down form reminded Sky Dreamer of a broken, discarded wooden doll that some bored child had grown tired of playing with, then had decided to disassemble for a lack of anything better to do. The man's face was beyond recognition because of the violent manner in which he had died, yet it was a fitting death for a man who had lived with so much hatred in his heart. It was, in fact, the man's heart which was impaled on the top of the pole from where his rigid form was hung. The remains of that vital organ were beginning to shrivel up into a twisted ball and its vibrant pink color was starting to blacken from the heat of the summer sun. Sky Dreamer could not tear her eyes away from the jagged hole in the mutilated chest. It seemed so appropriate for the man's spirit to be void of his heart for all eternity, since Randy Decker had not possessed the ability to use that valuable commodity in life. It was equally fitting for his mortal remains to be left to decorate the decaying land as a grim reminder of his murderous reign of terror against the Teneh Chockonen.

"Never look back, always face the future. That will be our new custom."

Sky Dreamer managed a brave smile as the old shaman rode up beside her and offered his words of wisdom to her. She glanced down at the two roughly made cradleboards that hung on either side of her horse's back and thought about Grandfather's statement again. Nachae had purposely hung Morning Star's and Echo's carriers so that they faced forward, rather than the usual direction of toward the back. Did his actions contain a hidden meaning? she wondered.

"Are you ready to go?" Nachae asked softly as he

rode up to where the old man and his wife were waiting. He winced slightly as he reached out his hand and gently stroked the soft downy head of the nearest infant who slept peacefully in her cradleboard. With a sigh of annoyance, he dismissed the pain in his bandaged side as he concentrated on more pleasant thoughts.

When they returned to their home in the Chiricahua Mountains, he intended to build both of his daughters much better carriers than the ones he had thrown together today for their journey back to the true lands of Apacheria. He would decorate them with amulets of pollen which had been blessed by Grandfather. Already he had devised the designs he would create from turquoise beads that would adorn both cradleboards. Echo's carrier would be designed with the peaceful image of the setting sun, and Morning Star would ride in a cradleboard that depicted the dawn of a new day. From a tree that had been struck by lightning, Nachae planned to obtain chips of bark, then he would tie the pieces of wood to the canopies of the cradleboards as symbols of good luck. When his daughters were older, he would take them to the top of the White Mountain Range and show them the towering silver pine tree that guarded the spot where they had been conceived. His gray eyes ascended and met with the soft glow of his wife's lavender's gaze as a smile curved his full mouth with tenderness.

"Yes, we're ready to go back home," she replied in a quiet tone. Without so much as another glance back at the past, Sky Dreamer urged her horse to move forward. There would always be another battle to fight, and another victory to claim. But her dreams of the future showed two little girls who would grow up to be strong and brave as they faced whatever adversities their lives had to offer. And in her beautiful reverie, she still envisioned herself walking hand in hand with the dream warrior who stalked the deepest recesses of her mind's secret passages.